Kat Cantrell read her first Mills & Boon novel in third grade and has been scribbling in notebooks since she learned to spell. What else would she write but romance? She majored in literature, officially with the intent to teach, but somehow ended up buried in middle management in corporate America, until she became a stay-at-home mum and full-time writer.

Kat, her husband and their two boys live in north Texas. When she's not writing about characters on the journey to happily-ever-after, she can be found at a football game, watching the TV show *Friends* or listening to '80s music.

Kat was the 2011 Harlequin So You Think You Can Write winner and a 2012 RWA Golden Heart finalist for best unpublished series contemporary manuscript.

MATCHED TO A BILLIONAIRE

BY
KAT CANTRELL

To Jennifer Hayward,
because you're always there for me.
And because you liked Leo from the beginning.

One

Leo Reynolds wished he could marry his admin. It would make life so much simpler.

Unfortunately, she was already married and nearly twice his age. Plus, women didn't stick around once they figured out he worked a hundred hours a week on a consistent basis. Loneliness was the price of catapulting Reynolds Capital Management into the big leagues of the venture capital game.

"You're a life saver, Mrs. Gordon." Leo shot her a grateful smile and leaned back in his chair.

His laptop was refusing to speak to the printer and a critical document had gotten caught in the middle of the dispute. The signed hard copy now in his hand was due to Garrett Engineering on the other side of Dallas in less than an hour.

"I'd hardly call printing a proposal saving your life." Mrs. Gordon glanced at her watch in a deliberate gesture designed to point out the time. "It's late and it's Friday. Take Jenna to that new restaurant in Victory Park and let me handle the proposal. Relax for once. It'll be good for you."

Leo grimaced as a ping of remorse bloomed and faded. "Jenna and I split up. She's already seeing someone else."

Hopefully, the new relationship would make her happy. She deserved a man who could shower her with attention and affection. He regretted not being able to give her what she wanted, but it would be patently unfair to let Jenna keep hoping he'd ever become a man capable of focusing on a re-lationship. As a result, he'd lost a comfortable companion.

"Of course she is. It's not like she ever saw *you*." Mrs. Gordon crossed her arms and looked down her nose at Leo with a tsk. "Now who are you going to take to the museum dedication?"

Leo groaned. He'd conveniently forgotten about that, but it wasn't as if he could skip the dedication. The new children's museum in the Dallas Arts District bore his name, after all, since he'd donated the money to build it. "You're free next Saturday, aren't you?"

Mrs. Gordon cackled as though Leo had been joking. "One of these days, I'm going to say yes when you ask me out and really mess with you. If Jenna's not in the picture, find another woman. They seem to be pretty thick on the ground."

Yeah, he tripped over women on a regular basis who would like to go out with him. Or at least they thought they did, right up until they realized they wouldn't be satisfied with what little time and attention he could give. It never took very long to reach that point.

A vague hollow feeling invaded his gut, one he'd experienced more and more lately. He'd written it off as an increased urgency to hit that elusive, unachieved mark of success. But now that it had happened during a discussion about his personal life, he wasn't so convinced.

"I hate dating." *And small talk.* That getting-to-know-you period took time and energy he didn't care to expend. Reynolds Capital Management came first. Always.

"That's because you don't do it often enough."

Here they went, off on her favorite subject. She never got tired of scolding him about the lack of a permanent female in his life.

"Have you been talking to my mother again?"

"We went to lunch Tuesday, as a matter of fact. She says hi." Mrs. Gordon raised her eyebrows and planted guilt simultaneously, as Leo was sure she intended. He got it. He should call his mother. And date eligible women.

Problem was, he not only hated dating, he also hated constantly standing up dates and disappointing women who deserved better. But he liked companionship and, well, he *was* a guy—sex was nice, too. Why couldn't the perfect woman fall in his lap so he could focus on work?

"It is late," Leo said in what was no doubt a transparent attempt to change the subject. "Why don't *you* go home and I'll take the proposal to Garrett?"

He had until five o'clock to get it to Garrett Engineering, formally expressing his interest in doing business with them.

What Steve Jobs was to cell phones, Tommy Garrett was to internal combustion engines. Or would be, as soon as funding was in place. Garrett had invented a revolutionary modification to increase the gas mileage of a standard car engine and Leo intended to be Garrett's venture capital firm of choice. The partnership would net a sizable, long-term profit for both men, and Leo could do what he did best— pull strings behind the scenes.

If Leo won the deal.

No, not *if. When.*

Leo would never rest until his company hit that sweet spot of security, where longevity was a given, not a question mark. His first million hadn't done it. Neither had the first eight figures, because his profits went straight back into leveraged investments that wouldn't pay off until some point in the future. So he didn't rest.

"Since you've scared off yet another female with your dogged determination to work yourself into an early grave, be my guest." Mrs. Gordon waved her approval for Leo to deliver the proposal. "I filled up your car with gas this morning. It wouldn't kill you to glance at the gauge once in a while."

"Thanks. You're too good to me. By the way," Leo threw in as Mrs. Gordon pulled her handbag from a desk drawer,

"I was thinking of having a gathering at my house to wine and dine Tommy Garrett. If I ask very nicely, would you plan it?"

"It's not my job to be your stand-in wife." Mrs. Gordon firmed her mouth, which meant she had a lot more to say but didn't know how to do so tactfully. In the eight years she'd been keeping him sane, he'd seen that look a lot.

With a half laugh, Leo said, "Of course not. That's not part of your job description."

Except it had the ring of uncomfortable truth. When his hair grew too long, Mrs. Gordon scheduled a haircut. His mother's birthday—Mrs. Gordon picked out the gift. The wine-and-dine request had been a bit of a blurred line, but based on the set of Mrs. Gordon's mouth, he'd pretty well turned the line into a trapezoid.

Mrs. Gordon shut down her computer for the night. "Well, it should be part of someone's job description."

"What, like a party planner?" Maybe he should hire a professional in some capacity, which wouldn't cover all his social obligations. But it was better than nothing.

"Like a girlfriend. Or someone who might actually still be around in six weeks. Hire a wife," she said with a nod. "You need a good woman to take care of you outside of the office. Ask *her* to glance at your gas gauge. She can schmooze Garrett and make sure your life is running smoothly. Keep you warm at night."

Her eyebrows waggled but Leo barely noticed.

Hire a wife.

Could you even do such a thing? It seemed too perfect a solution.

He had no time—or the desire—to sift through women until he found one he liked but who also wouldn't expect him to be available. Reynolds Capital Management did not manage itself. His employees and partners depended on him.

A wife couldn't leave him with no notice. It was the ultimate security.

Leo would have a permanent companion to help fill that occasional hollow feeling, one with no hidden agenda involving his assets and connections. They'd both know from the get-go what to expect—stability. There'd be no hard feelings when she realized he hadn't been kidding about giving 100 percent to his company, leaving nothing left over for her.

All or nothing. Commitment was Leo's kryptonite. Once he latched on to something, he gave it everything and then some. Early on, he'd realized that trait was inherited and tried not to make the same mistakes as his father.

Then he'd met Carmen, who taught him the true depths of his weaknesses, and how easily one obsession could become the center of his existence. He practiced putting everything but the goal aside until it was second nature.

Love or success. His personality didn't allow for both and after clawing his way out of the ghetto, he refused to gamble his future.

If he had an understanding wife, work and his personal life would remain completely separate. And best of all, Leo would never have to engage in small talk with a new woman or experience that sharp pang of guilt over canceling on one ever again.

Leo tugged on his suit jacket and hand delivered the proposal to Garrett's people in their tiny downtown office. It wouldn't be tiny for long. Investors far and wide were clamoring to get in on the ground floor with Garrett's technology. Once the company went public, its worth would shoot to legendary status.

Leo had to land the deal with Tommy Garrett, and the wine-and-dine thing would be a fantastic opportunity to solidify his chances. A wife could handle the logistics, leaving Leo to engage in uninterrupted dialogue with Garrett about what Reynolds Capital could do for him that no one else could. His offer to Garrett didn't expire for several weeks. He had plenty of time to get a wife in place.

When Leo returned to his darkened office, he sat at his

laptop. Within fifteen minutes, Google provided a potential answer to the question of how to hire a wife. He'd had to wade through all the cleaning services and concierge services, then a few distasteful escort services, to find the definitive solution.

A matchmaking service.

Yes. Of course. It was not what he'd had in mind when he started the quest. Actually, he hadn't been sure *what* he'd intended to find. But this was an intriguing answer. Leo had always thought he'd get married one day, when he could afford to transfer his energy to a relationship. Yet here he was on the downside of thirty-five and Reynolds Capital Management still took all of his focus. All of his time.

He stared at the logo for EA International. The website was professional and tasteful, with earth tones and a classic font. Most importantly, this particular matchmaker catered to exclusive clients, promising discretion and a money-back guarantee. Guarantees warmed Leo's heart.

The tagline said it all—*Let us help you find "the one."*

Presumably, "the one" for Leo would fit all his qualifications. EA International would do the screening, the interviewing, the background checks, and ultimately filter out candidates who were looking for some mystical connection. Love didn't pay the bills, and Leo would never allow the power to be turned off on his family, the way his own father had.

It was brilliant. The matchmaker would do everything required to find Leo a wife. One he could never disappoint. All he had to do was make a phone call.

Then, with that settled, he could get back to work.

Daniella White had dreamed of her wedding since the first time she'd created crayon invitations to a ceremony starring Mr. Fourpaws as the tattered velveteen groom and herself as the fairy-tale bride wrapped in dingy sheets. Someday she'd wear a beautiful dress of delicate lace and silver heels. The guests would receive heavy card-stock invitations with a vellum overlay and eat a three-tiered French vanilla cake with fondant flowers.

Best of all, a handsome husband-to-be would wait for her at the end of a church aisle, wearing a tender smile. Later that night, the love of her life would sweep her away to a romantic honeymoon somewhere exotic and breathtaking. Theirs would be a marriage of grand passion and enduring love.

When her real wedding day finally arrived, Dannie could never have envisioned it would involve a groom she'd never met in person. Or that in a few minutes, she'd be marrying Leo Reynolds in the living room of a matchmaker's house in North Dallas, with only a handful of guests in attendance.

"What do you think, Mom?" Dannie beamed at her mother in the cheval mirror and straightened a three-quarter-length sleeve. A dress of any sort usually appealed to Dannie, but this unadorned ecru one would be her wedding dress and she wanted to love it. She didn't. But she'd make the best of it, like always.

EA International's sophisticated computer program had matched her with businessman Leo Reynolds and he expected a wife with a certain refinement—one who dressed the part, acted the part, lived the part. Dannie had spent the past month under the matchmaker's intensive tutelage to become exactly right for that part.

Dannie's mother coughed profusely, hand to her chest as if she'd clear the scar tissue from her lungs through sheer will alone. "You're beautiful, baby," she said when she'd recovered. "Every bit a proper wife. I'm so proud of what you've accomplished."

Yeah, it was really hard to put my name in a database. Dannie bit back the comment. She wasn't a smart aleck anymore. No one ever got her jokes anyway.

Two sharp raps at the door shoved Dannie's heart into her throat. Elise Arundel, Dannie's fairy godmother–slash–

matchmaker, popped into the room, her sleek, dark pageboy swinging. "Oh, Dannie. You look lovely."

Dannie smiled demurely. She needed a lot of practice at being demure.

"Thanks to you."

"I didn't pick out that dress." Elise nodded once. "You did. It's perfect for your willowy frame. I've never had anyone who glommed on to cut and style with such natural talent."

"I made up for it by being hopeless with cosmetics." Dannie frowned. Did that seem too outspoken? Ungrateful? That was the problem with changing your personality to become a society wife—nothing came naturally.

Elise's critical eye swept over Dannie's face and she dismissed the comment with a flick of her manicured hand. "You're flawless. Leo's socks will be knocked off."

And there went her pulse again.

The figure in the mirror stared back at her, almost a stranger, but with her dark brown hair and almond-colored eyes. Would Leo be happy with her sophisticated chignon? The erect posture? The scared-to-death woman in the ecru dress? What if he didn't like brunettes?

She was being silly. He'd seen her picture, of course, as she'd seen his. They'd spoken on the phone twice. Their conversations had been pleasant and they'd worked through several important marital issues: they'd allow the intimate side of their relationship to evolve over time, a clarification that had clinched it since he didn't believe he was buying an "exchange of services," and he was open to eventually having children.

Neither of them had any illusions about the purpose of this marriage—a permanent means to an end.

Why was she so nervous about what was essentially an arranged marriage?

Her mother smoothed a hand over Dannie's hair. "Soon you'll be Mrs. Leo Reynolds and all your dreams will come true. For the rest of your life, you'll have the security and companionship I never had." Racking coughs punctuated the sentiment and the ticking clock in Dannie's mind sped up. Pulmonary fibrosis was killing her mother.

Dannie was marrying Leo to save her.

And she'd never forget what she owed him. What she owed Elise.

Her mom was right. Dannie had always dreamed of being a wife and mother and now she was getting that chance. Marriage based on compatibility would provide security for her and her mom. She had no business being sad that security couldn't be based on love.

Maybe love could grow over time, along with intimacy. She'd hang on to that hope.

With a misty smile, Elise opened the door wider. "Leo's waiting for you in front of the fireplace. Here's your bouquet. Simple and tasteful, with orchids and roses, like you requested."

The clutch of flowers nearly wrenched the tears loose from Dannie's eyes. "It's beautiful. Everything is beautiful. I can't thank you enough."

She still couldn't believe Elise had selected *her* for the EA International matchmaking program. When she'd applied, it had all seemed like such a long shot, but what choice did she have? Her mother needed expensive long-term care, which neither of them could afford, so Dannie gladly did whatever her mother needed—doctor's appointments, cooking, cleaning. Her father had left before she'd been born, so it had been the two of them against the world since the beginning.

Unfortunately, employers rarely forgave the amount of time off Dannie required. After being fired from the third job in a row, her situation felt pretty dire. She'd searched in vain for a work-from-home job or one with a flexible schedule. After hours at the library's computer, she'd been about to give up when the ad for EA International caught her eye.

Have you ever dreamed of a different sort of career? Coupled with a picture of a bride, how could she not click on it?

EA International invited women with superior administrative skills, a desire to better themselves and the drive to become "the woman behind the man" to apply for a bold, innovative training program.

Who had better admin skills than someone managing the care of a perpetually ill mother? Without much to lose, Dannie sent her information into the ether and shock of all shocks, got the call.

It was fate that EA International was based in Dallas, where Dannie lived.

Elise polished Dannie until she shone and then matched her with a man who needed an elegant society wife. In exchange for organizing Leo's household and hosting parties, Dannie could take care of her mother without any more financial worries.

A marriage that was little more than a contract seemed a small price to pay.

"You're one of my most successful graduates." Elise handed Dannie the bouquet and shifted a couple of flowers to face the outside. "I predict you'll be one of my most successful matches, as well. You and Leo couldn't be better suited."

Dannie's stomach lurched. She wanted to like him. To enjoy being married. Would she be attracted to him? What if she wasn't? Would the intimate side of their marriage never happen? Maybe she should have insisted they meet first in spite of their mutual agreement not to.

It hardly mattered. Attraction wasn't a factor here, but surely they'd eventually hold a great deal of affection for each other, regardless of what he looked like.

Nose to the bouquet, Dannie inhaled the sweet scent of her wedding flowers. "We have similar goals and both recognize the practicality of this union. I expect we'll be very happy together."

Leo had gobs of money. She'd have been happy with half a gob. That level of wealth intimidated her, but Elise insisted she could handle it. After all, Dannie would have a valued place in his life and she might eventually be the mother of his children. Her training had made it very clear the woman behind the man worked as hard as women in other careers.

"Happy is exactly what you'll be." Elise pinched the clasp of Dannie's necklace, dragging it to the nape of her neck. The open-heart lavaliere hanging from the chain had been a gift from the matchmaker when Dannie agreed to marry Leo. "My computer program is never wrong."

Dannie's mother chimed in. "This is the best kind of match, one that will last forever, because it's based on compatibility, not feelings. It's everything Dannie wants in a marriage."

Dannie forced a nod, though she wished she could disagree, and spared only a passing thought to Rob. She'd been so gaga over him.

Look where that had gotten her—brokenhearted and determined to make over her temperament so no man could call her opinionated and blunt again. She'd screwed up that relationship but good.

She wasn't going to screw up this one. Her mother couldn't afford it.

"Yes," she agreed. "Security and companionship. What else could I possibly ask for?"

Fairy tales were stories about magical solutions to problems and full of people who fell in love, but whose relationships couldn't possibly stand the test of time. In real life, women had to make sacrifices and Dannie was making hers.

Without any further melancholy and ridiculousness, she marched out the door of the room she'd stayed in during her transformation and went to meet her fate on a prayer that she and Leo would at least grow to care for each other. If there was more, great. She'd consider it a bonus.

Her mother and Elise followed. Dannie paused at the top of the sweeping staircase and took in the scene below.

With cheerful optimism, Elise had placed flower arrangements on the mantel and on each side of the fireplace. Dannie's heart fluttered at the thoughtfulness of the woman who had become her friend. A photographer stood at the back of the room, poised to snap memories at a moment's notice, and the gray-haired minister Elise had recommended waited in front of the fireplace.

To his right was Leo Reynolds. Her husband-to-be.

He looked up and met her gaze.

A shock of…something zapped across her shoulders. He looked exactly like his picture, but in person—*hello*. Dark, straight hair brushed his collar and an expensive, well-designed suit encased a masculine body Leo clearly kept in great shape. Classic, smooth features formed a face handsome enough to sell out an entire print run of *GQ* magazine. More Ashley than Rhett, which was appropriate since she'd banished her inner Scarlett O'Hara to a place where the sun didn't shine.

Leo also looked kind, as though he wouldn't hesitate to carry an elderly lady's groceries to the car. Dannie almost snorted. If Leo Reynolds had ever seen the inside of a grocery store, she'd eat her bouquet. He was a busy man and it was a good thing for her that he was, or he wouldn't need a wife.

Not for the first time, she wondered why he'd resorted to a matchmaker. He was good-looking, rich and well-spoken. By all rights, the eligible-woman line should be wrapped around the block.

Eyes on Leo, she descended the stairs with practiced ease—she'd done it in four-inch heels dozens of times and didn't falter today despite the severity of the occasion. In far too few steps, she reached Leo. In her bone-colored pumps, she and Leo were nearly the same height.

She searched his expression as he did the same to her. What did you say to a man you were about to marry but whom you were seeing for the first time in the flesh? *Hey, fancy meeting you here.*

A hysterical giggle nearly slipped out. Not an auspicious start.

"Hello." Well, that should be reasonably safe.

"Hello," Leo returned and smiled, setting off a nice, warm flutter in her chest.

Up close, he was solid and powerful, capable of carrying a baby in one arm and taking out a carjacker with the other. The flutter that thought set off was a little warmer and little more south than the first one. In theory, she'd known Leo equated to safety. But reality was far more... real. And affecting.

They faced front. Nerves locked Dannie's knees and she tried to loosen them without drawing attention. If she pitched over in the middle of her wedding ceremony, Elise would never forgive her.

"Let's begin." The minister raised a Bible in his wrinkled hands and began reciting the vows Leo had insisted Dannie select.

The words flowed from the minister's mouth, sounding completely different aloud than she would have imagined. For better or worse, richer or poorer. None of that really applied, not in the way it did for most couples. Those vows were a call to remember the reasons you fell in love in the first place when marriage got tough.

From her peripheral vision, she tried to catch a glimpse of Leo to see how all this was registering. Suddenly she wished they'd had a few more conversations so she'd know better what he might be thinking.

It had just seemed so unnecessary. Elise wouldn't have allowed her to marry someone awful. Her screening process was diligent and faultless, matching her with Leo on all forty-seven points of the personality profile. So long as he wasn't a criminal or a wife beater, what did it matter if he had a good sense of humor or liked sweeping historical dramas?

"Do you take Leo as your lawfully wedded husband?" the minister intoned.

Dannie cleared her throat. "I do."

With a trembling hand, she slipped a plain platinum band on Leo's finger. Or tried to. She couldn't get it over the knuckle and when he covered her hand with his to assist, she glanced up to meet his blue eyes.

That same odd shock she'd experienced on the stairs rocked her shoulders. It wasn't awareness, but deeper, as if she'd just seen someone she knew but couldn't place.

She shook it off. Nerves. That's all.

Leo repeated, "I do," his voice even and strong. Because he wasn't nervous. Why would he be, with all that masculine confidence?

The platinum band he slid on her finger matched his and winked in the living room's overhead lighting. She stared at it, transfixed by the sheer weight such a simple band added to her hand.

Divorce wasn't an option.

Both she and Leo had indicated a strong belief in honoring commitments in their profiles and it had been the first thing addressed in their phone conversation. Leo had been far too generous in the original prenuptial agreement and she'd refused to marry him without serious alterations, namely that any future children would be provided for but she'd get nothing. In her mind, that was the best way to demonstrate the seriousness of her word.

Leo represented security, not free money. And in exchange for that security, she'd be the wife he needed.

This marriage was a permanent solution to their problems, not a love match. Which was fine by her. Leo would never leave her the way her father had and she'd never have to worry about whether he'd stop loving her if she screwed up.

The minister signaled the end of the short ceremony with the traditional, "You may kiss the bride."

Oh, why had she asked for that part? It was going to be so weird. But it was her *wedding*. Shouldn't she get a kiss from her husband? A kiss to seal their bargain.

Leo turned to her, his expression unreadable. As his lips descended, she closed her eyes. Their mouths touched.

And held for a shimmering moment, launching a typhoon of flutters in her abdomen. Maybe the possibility of having a whole lot more than just affection between them wasn't as remote as she'd thought.

Then he recoiled as if he'd licked a lemon wedge and stepped away.

Their first kiss. How…disappointingly brief, with a hint of possible sparks she'd had no time to enjoy. Hadn't he felt it? Obviously not.

Her mother and Elise clapped, gathering around her and Leo to gush with congratulations.

Dannie swallowed. What had she expected—Leo would magically transform from a venture capitalist into Prince Charming? Elise's computer program had matched her with the perfect husband, one who would take care of her and her mother and treat Dannie well. She should be happy they'd have a fulfilling partnership.

She should *not* be thinking about how Leo might kiss her if they'd met under different circumstances. If they were getting married because they'd fallen in love, and during the ceremony he'd slid her a sizzling glance that said he couldn't wait for the honeymoon.

She shouldn't be dwelling on it, but the thought wouldn't fade—what would his calm blue eyes look like when they were hot with passion?

Two

Daniella stood by the door with her hands clasped and chin down. Leo's new wife was refined and unassuming, exactly as he had specified. What he had not expected was to find her picture had lied. And it was a monstrous lie of epic proportions.

She wasn't girl-next-door attractive, as he'd believed. This woman he'd married radiated sensuous energy, as if her spirit was leashed behind a barrier of skin that could barely contain it. If that leash ever broke—look out.

She wasn't merely gorgeous; in person, Daniella defied description.

The stuff of poetry and Michael Bublé songs. If one was inclined toward that sort of thing.

Even her name was exotic and unusual. He couldn't stop looking at her. He couldn't stop thinking about the way-too-short kiss he'd broken off because it felt like the beginning of something that would take a very long time to finish. His entire body buzzed in response to that concentrated energy it badly wanted to explore.

What was he going to do with a woman like *that*?

"I'm ready to leave whenever you are, Leo." Her voice, soft but self-assured, carried across the foyer of Ms. Arundel's house.

He was going to take her home. Regardless of having *distraction* written all over her, they were married.

His recon skills clearly needed help. Why hadn't he met

her first? Because he'd dotted as many *i*'s and crossed as many *t*'s as possible before fully committing to this idea. Or so he'd thought. Leo had spoken with other satisfied clients of EA International and then personally met with Elise Arundel several times. He had confidence in her ability to find the right match, and the thorough background check Ms. Arundel had supplied confirmed her choice.

Daniella White was the perfect woman to be his wife.

Their phone calls had sealed the deal. He'd recognized her suitability immediately and everything fell into place. Why wait to marry when they were like-minded and neither cared if there was any attraction between them? It was better to get on with it.

If he had it to do over, he'd add one more criteria— *doesn't make the roof of my mouth tingle.* It was Carmen all over again, but worse, because he was no longer a lovesick seventeen-year-old and Daniella was his wife. No woman could be allowed to set him on the same catastrophic path as his father, not when Leo knew how hard it was to repurpose himself. What painful test of his inherent all-in personality had he inadvertently set himself up for now?

His marriage was supposed to be about compatibility and convenience, not a headlong sprint into the depths of craziness. It was important to start it off on the right foot.

"Did my driver get all of your belongings?" he asked her and winced.

That wasn't the right foot. *My driver.* As if he regularly employed servants to do his bidding. Was he *really* going to act that pretentious around his new bride? He usually drove himself, for crying out loud. He'd only hired a car because he thought Daniella might enjoy it.

She nodded, taking it in stride. "Yes, thank you."

"Have you said your goodbyes to everyone?"

"Yes. I'm ready."

The conversation was almost painful. This was why he'd rather have a root canal than take a woman to dinner, why he'd opted to skip dating entirely. They were married, well matched and should be able to shoot right past small talk.

Leo waited until they were seated in the town car before speaking again. She crossed her long legs, arranging them gracefully, skin sliding against skin, heels to one side. And he was openly watching her as if it was his own private movie.

Before he started drooling, he peeled his gaze from the smooth expanse of leg below her skirt. "If you don't mind, I'd like to invite my parents over tonight to meet you."

"I would be very happy to meet your parents." She clasped her hands together, resting them in her lap serenely. "You could have invited them to the ceremony. I recall from your profile how important family is to you."

He shrugged, mystified why it pleased him so much that she remembered. "They're less than thrilled about this marriage. My mother would have preferred I marry someone I was in love with."

"I'm sorry." Her hand rested on his sleeve for a brief, reassuring moment, then was gone. "You have to live your life according to what makes sense for you, not your mother."

Everything about her was gracious. Her speech, her mannerisms. Class and style delineated her from the masses and it was hard to believe she'd come from the same type of downtrodden, poverty-stricken neighborhood as he had. She had strength and compassion to spare, and he admired her pledge to care for her mother.

So she possessed a compelling sensuality and he couldn't take his eyes off of her. This was all new. By tomorrow, the edge would surely have worn off.

He relaxed. Slightly.

This marriage was going to work, allowing him to focus on his company guilt-free, while his wife handled wifely things and required none of his attention. He'd paid Ms. Arundel a sizable chunk of change to ensure it.

"Daniella, I realize we barely know each other, but I'd

like to change that. First and foremost, you can always talk to me. Tell me if you need something or have problems. Any problem at all."

"Thank you. That's very kind."

Gratitude beamed from her expression and it made him vaguely uncomfortable, as if he was the lord of the manor, bestowing favors upon the adoring masses. They were equals in this marriage. "As I told you on the phone, I have a lot of social obligations. I'll depend on you to handle them, but you can come to me if you need help or have questions."

"Yes, I understand." She started to say something else and appeared to change her mind, as if afraid to say too much. Probably nervous and unsure.

"Daniella." Leo paused, weighing the best approach to ease the tautness between them. She gazed at him expectantly, her almond-colored eyes bright, with a hint of vulnerability. That nearly undid him. "We're married. I want you to trust me, to feel relaxed around me."

A building was only as good as its foundation.

"I do." She nodded, her expression so serious, he almost told her a joke to see if she'd smile. "You're everything I expected. I'm very happy with Elise's choice."

She was clutching her hands together so tightly, her knuckles had gone white. The art of small talk was not his forte, but surely he could do better than this.

"I'm pleased, as well." Pleased, not happy. This marriage had never been about being happy, but being sensible. "But now we have to live together and it should be comfortable for us both. You can talk to me about anything. Finances. Religion. Politics."

Sex.

His mind had *not* jumped straight to that…but it had, and unashamedly so, with vivid mental images of what her legs looked like under that prim skirt. She glanced at him, held his gaze. A spark flared between them and again, he sensed her energy, coiled and ready to whip out—and his body strained to catch it.

Stop, he commanded his active imagination. He and Daniella had an agreement. A civilized, rational agreement, which did not include sliding a hand over her thigh. His fingers curled and he shoved them under his leg.

She looked down and shifted, angling slightly away. One finger drummed nervously against her skirt. "Thank you. I appreciate that."

His very carnal reaction to a mere glance had obviously upset her.

He cleared his throat. "Are you still okay with letting the intimate side of our relationship unfold naturally?"

Her eyes widened and he almost groaned.

What a fantastic way to set her at ease. He needed to dunk his head in a bucket of cold water or something before he scared her into complete silence. Though that might be better than her constantly starting sentences with *yes,* as if she thought he expected a trained parrot.

"Yes." She met his gaze squarely and earned a couple of points for courage. "Why wouldn't I be?"

Because you feel this draw between us and it's making your palms sweat, too.

Chemistry had been far down the priority list, for both of them.

He just hadn't anticipated having so much of it right out of the gate. Or that it would pose a very real danger of becoming such a distraction, the exact opposite of his intent in hiring a matchmaker.

His focus should be on work. Not on getting his wife naked. Indulgent pleasures weren't on the menu, particularly not for someone with his inability to stop indulging.

"I want to be sure we're on the same page," he said.

"We are. Our marriage will be companionable with a progression toward intimacy when it seems appropriate." Her tone wavered, just a touch, and was coupled with a glint in her eyes he couldn't interpret. "Like we discussed."

His exact words. And suddenly he wished he could take it all back. Wished he could put a glint of happiness in her eyes instead of the look currently drilling a hole through his chest. The unsettling feeling bothered him more than the chemistry, because he had no clue what to do with it.

"We'll have separate bedrooms, for now." That had been his intent from the beginning and seemed even more necessary given her nervousness. It should solve everything. The back of his throat burned with inexplicable disappointment. "Take things slowly."

Separate bedrooms would serve to put some distance between them. Ease the tension, give them both time to acclimate. Give the chemistry time to cool. And definitely allow him to refocus.

Then they'd settle into what he'd envisioned: a marriage where they had fulfilling lives outside of each other and enjoyed a pleasant relationship both in the bedroom and out. No one with his intense personality could have any other kind of marriage.

His phone beeped and he glanced at it. He'd taken a half day to attend his wedding and given his employees the rest of the day off as well, but he was never "out of the office."

The email was a brief courtesy notice from Tommy Garrett's people to let him know Garrett Engineering had narrowed the field to Leo and another firm, Moreno Partners. Excellent. The timing couldn't be better. His new wife could organize the wine and dine for Garrett as soon as she was settled.

"Do you need to make a call?" Daniella asked politely. "I don't mind. Pretend I'm not here."

That wasn't even possible. "Thanks, but it was an email. No response needed."

A different strategy was in order. In light of the wife he'd ended up with, thinking of her as an employee might work best to stave off the urge to spend the weekend in bed, making his wife laugh and then making her gasp with pleasure. And then hitting *repeat* a hundred times.

If he fit Daniella into a predefined box, she'd slide into his life with little disruption and that was exactly what he wanted. What he needed.

Success guaranteed security. It was the only thing that could and no price was too high to ensure he kept his focus on Reynolds Capital Management—even continued solitude.

Dannie kept her mouth shut for the rest of the ride to her new life.

Where she would not share a bedroom with her husband.

She was alternately very glad for the space and very confused. The flash of awareness between them must be one-sided. Or she'd imagined it. Leo could not have been more clear about his lack of interest in her.

Maybe he'd seen right through Elise's makeover.

And now her fantasy about the way he'd kiss if he really meant it had shattered. Such a shame. Her husband was attractive in that unattainable way of movie stars, but in her imagination, he kissed like a pirate on shore leave, and no one could take that away.

She stole a peek at this hard-to-read man she'd married for life.

Her lungs froze. What if Leo decided he didn't like her after all? Just because he claimed to have a strong sense of commitment didn't mean he'd tolerate screwups. And screwups were her specialty.

Her mother was counting on her. She was counting on herself, too. If Leo divorced her, she'd have nothing. One of his first acts upon learning she'd accepted his proposal was to hire a full-time caregiver for her mother who specialized in pulmonary rehabilitation. The nurse was slated to start today.

Without Leo, her mother would surely die a very slow and painful death. And Dannie would be forced to watch helplessly.

Her nails bit into her palm and she nearly yelped. Long nails. Yet another thing she had to get used to, along with all the other things Elise had done to make her over into Leo's perfect wife. Organization and conversation skills came naturally, but the polish—that had taken a while to achieve.

She had to remember her job here was to become the behind-the-scenes support for a successful man. Not to be swept away in a haze of passion for her new husband.

"We're here," Leo said in his smooth voice.

Dannie glanced out the window and tried not to gape. Leo's house practically needed its own zip code.

They'd discussed her comfort level with managing a large house. During the conversation, she'd pictured a two-story, four-bedroom house with a big backyard, located in a quiet suburban neighborhood. That would have been her idea of large after the small two-bedroom apartment she'd shared with her mother.

She'd known the house was in Preston Hollow, one of the most elite neighborhoods of Dallas. But *this* she could never have anticipated.

Wrought-iron gates caught between two large brick-and-stone posts swung open as if by magic and the driver turned the car onto the cobblestone drive leading up to the house. Colossal trees lined the drive, partially blocking the sun and lending a hushed, otherworldly feel to the grounds. And *grounds* was the only fitting term. Neatly manicured grass stretched away on both sides of the car all the way to the high stone wall surrounding Leo's house.

Her house. *Their* house.

The car halted in a semicircular crushed-stone driveway, and the hulking residence immediately cast it in shadow. The manor sprawled across the property, pointy rooflines dominating the brick-and-stone structure. Four—no, five—chimneys stabbed toward the sky.

She should have asked for a picture before agreeing to handle a property this size. What was she *doing* here?

"What do you think?" Leo asked, but it was hardly a question she could answer honestly.

"It's very..." *Gothic.* "Nice."

She bit the inside of her lip. All of Elise's hard work would go up in smoke if Dannie couldn't keep her smart-aleck gene under control. The thought of Elise calmed her. They'd done exhaustive work together to prep Dannie for this, with endless days of learning to set a table, to make proper tea. Practicing how to sit, how to walk, how to introduce people. In between, Elise had transformed Dannie's appearance into something worthy of a magazine cover.

This was it—the test of whether the makeover would stick or Dannie would fail.

With a deep breath, Dannie smiled. "It's beautiful, Leo. I'm very eager to learn my way around."

"Let me show you." He placed a hand at the small of her back as she exited the car and kept it there, guiding and supporting, as they ascended the stone steps to the front door. "Please think of this as your home. Anything you want to change is open for discussion."

Anything. Except the arranged-marriage part.

It was ridiculous to even think that. But her wedding day felt so anticlimactic. And disappointing. She shouldn't be wishing Leo would sweep her up in his arms and carry her over the threshold, Rhett-style. Or wishing they had a timeless romance.

The palm at her back signaled security. Not passion. A partnership based on mutual affection was enough. Dannie was Leo's wife, not the love of his life, and she didn't have the luxury of entertaining daydreams of eventually being both.

Leo led her into the foyer. The interior of the house

opened before her, with soaring ceilings, twenty-foot windows and grand arches leading to long hallways. It reminded her of a cathedral, beautiful and opulent.

The tour of her new home took close to thirty minutes. By the time Leo concluded it in the kitchen, she was out of breath and ready to get started on the first thing she wanted to change—her shoes. The house had *four* flights of stairs.

Leo leaned a hip against the granite island in the center of the kitchen and picked up a cell phone from the counter. "For you. The number is written here, along with the alarm system security codes and the code for wireless internet access."

She took the phone with numb fingers and stared at the glossy screen. Her current cell phone was of the make-a-call-only variety. It would take hours to figure out how this one worked. "Thank you. Is your phone number written down, too?"

"I programmed it into your phone. Here's the user manual." He slid it across the counter and stuck a hand in his pocket, casually, as though they were a normal married couple chatting in the kitchen. "This model has great planning features. Feel free to add things to my schedule as needed. My admin's phone number is programmed in, as well. Mrs. Gordon. She's eager to meet you."

He had an admin, one who knew him far better than Dannie did, like how to make his coffee and whether he paced while on the phone or sat at his desk.

Suddenly, she felt completely out of her depth. "Oh. All right. I'll contact her right away."

"The car and driver will be on call for as long as you like," he continued, and his mellow voice soothed her nerves as he ticked off the items on his mental list. His confidence and self-assurance were potent. "But please, take some time to visit a dealership and buy yourself a car. Whatever kind you like. You'll want the independence."

A *car*. Any car she wanted. She'd been hopping public

transportation for so long, she nearly swooned at the idea. Was there anything he hadn't thought of? "That's very nice. Thank you."

But he wasn't finished waving his benevolence around. "I opened a bank account for you. It will be replenished regularly, but if you find yourself low, let me know. Spend it like it's your money, not mine." From his pocket, he produced a shiny black credit card and handed it to her. "No limit."

"Leo." He'd spun her around so many times now, she could hardly keep her balance. The phone and credit card in her hands blurred as she blinked back overwhelmed, appreciative tears. "This is all very generous. I'm sorry if this is too forward, but I have to ask. Why would you do all this and expect nothing in return?"

His dark eyebrows drew together in confusion. "I expect quite a bit in return, actually."

"I meant in the bedroom."

Leo went still.

Yeah, far too forward. But jeez, really? A no-limit credit card and he didn't even want one conjugal visit a month? There was a punch line here she didn't get and she'd prefer not to have it smack her in the face later.

"Daniella..." Leo swallowed and she realized he was at a loss for words.

Why couldn't she keep her big mouth closed? She should have stuck to *yes* and *thank you*.

"I'm sorry," she said in a rush. "Forgive me. You've been nothing but kind and I have no right to question your motives."

The lines of his handsome face smoothed out and he held up a hand. "No apology needed. I want to have a good relationship, where you feel like we're equals. The best way to achieve that is to give you your own money and the power to do as you like with it."

She stared at him. *Power*. He'd been granting her power with these gestures. The man she'd married was thoughtful, generous and very insightful. This whole experience could have gone very differently. Gratitude welled in her chest. "I don't know what to say."

"You don't have to say anything." He smiled and it was as powerful as it was comforting. "Remember, I'm going to be at the office a lot. You should find a hobby or volunteer work to keep you busy. A car will come in handy."

Implausibly, he was giving her the ability to entertain herself, when her sole focus should be on him and his needs. "Won't I be busy with all your social obligations?"

He waved it off. "That won't take one hundred percent of your time. You're building a life here and when our paths cross, we should enjoy each other's company. You can regale me with stories of the things you're involved in."

Elise had coached her on this extensively. It was part of her role to provide stimulating conversation for Leo's business associates. Who better to practice with than her husband? After all, they *were* a married couple having a chat in the kitchen. "That makes sense."

"Good." His eyes warmed, transforming him from movie-star handsome into something else entirely. Her breath caught.

If that's what happened to his eyes when he was pleased, she *really* wanted to see them stormy with desire.

She shook her head. They were talking about *hobbies*.

Leo took her hand, casually, as if he'd done it a thousand times. "I don't want you to be disappointed by our marriage. In the past, it's been a struggle to balance work and a relationship because the expectations weren't clear from the beginning. Women in my circles tend to demand attention I can't give them and I'm grateful we won't have that issue."

The feel of her hand in his sparked all the way up her arm, unsettling her. It was the only plausible excuse for why she blurted out, "You couldn't find one woman besides me who was willing to forgive your absence in exchange for a life of luxury?"

Her mother would have a coronary if she could hear Dannie being so outspoken. But he'd said in the car they could discuss anything. She hoped he meant it.

"Sure. But I wanted the right woman."

All at once, the reason he'd gone to a matchmaker seemed painfully obvious. He'd tried to buy his way out of putting any effort into a relationship and his previous girlfriends had told him to take a hike. So to avoid a repetition, he bought a wife.

Her.

No wonder he'd been so adamant about honoring commitments. He didn't want her to bail when she figured out she'd be all alone in this big house from now on.

Gothic indeed.

"I see."

"Daniella." His gaze bored into hers, pleading with her to believe…something. But what? "Neither of us have any illusions about this marriage, and that's why it will work. I understand the drive for security. I'm happy to provide it for you because it's a drive we share."

She nodded and excused herself to unpack—and get some breathing room. Security *was* important and she'd married a good, solid man who'd never leave her like her father had. She just hadn't expected gratefulness for that security to blossom into unexpected warmth toward the husband who'd provided it. And who promised to never be around.

As she climbed the stairs to her room, she realized what his unspoken plea had been meant to communicate.

He needed her as much as she needed him.

Three

The scraps of silk had definitely not been in Dannie's suitcase when she packed it.

She fingered the baby-doll lingerie set and noticed the note: "For a red-hot wedding night. —Elise."

Dannie held up the top. Such as it was. Black lace cups overlaid red silk triangles, which tied around the neck halterstyle. Red silk draped from the bust, allowing a flirty peek at the tiny G-string panties beneath. Or it would if she was insane enough to actually wear something so blatantly sexy for her husband.

This lingerie was definitely the ticket to a red-hot wedding night. For some other woman, not Daniella Reynolds. Dannie had married a workaholic. With her eyes wide-open.

She tucked the sexy lingerie into the very back of the drawer she'd designated for sleepwear. Ha. There'd be no sleeping going on if she wore *that* outfit. She sighed. Well, it would be the case if her husband pried his eyes off his bottom line. And was attracted to her. And they shared a bedroom.

And what exactly had she expected? That Leo would take one look at his new wife and fall madly in love? She needed to get over herself and stop acting as though Leo had taken away something that she'd never planned on having in the first place.

Elise, the eternal optimist despite being perfectly aware Dannie and Leo had only met that same day, couldn't have known how things would shake out. It was still depressing to be so soundly rejected. How would there be a possibility of children if they didn't share a bedroom?

Dannie slammed the drawer a little harder than an adult probably should have and stomped to the bed to finish unpacking her meager wardrobe.

If she was going to be alone, this was certainly the place to do it. Her bedroom rivaled the finest luxury suite she'd ever seen featured in a movie. She didn't have to leave. Ever. There was a minibar with a small refrigerator, fully stocked. An electronic tablet lay on the bedside table and she suspected Leo had already downloaded hundreds of books since her profile had said she liked to read.

The entertainment center came equipped with a fifty-inch flat-screen TV, cable, a DVD player, a sound system worthy of a nightclub and a fancy touch-screen remote. The owners' manuals lay on the raw silk comforter. Of course. Leo never missed a trick.

She wondered where he kept the owner's manual for Leo Reynolds. That was something she'd gladly read from cover to cover. A forty-seven-point profile only went so far into understanding the man.

There had to be more to Leo than met the eye, because no one voluntarily cut themselves off from people without a reason.

By the time she folded the last pair of socks, the hour had grown late. Leo's parents were due in thirty minutes. She called her mother to see how she was getting along with the nurse and smiled at the effusive recounting of how her mother's new caregiver played a serious game of gin rummy. Her mother sounded happy.

Relieved, Dannie went into the bathroom, where she had left half a cosmetic counter's inventory strewn across the marble vanity. She took a few minutes to organize it in the drawers, which had built-in compartments of different sizes. The bathroom alone was bigger than her entire apartment.

Dannie agonized over what to wear and finally selected a simple pale lavender skirt and dove-gray button-up shirt. Her small wardrobe of coordinated pieces had been another gift from Elise. She was between sizes so everything had to be altered, adding yet more cost to the already expensive clothes. Shoes, however, posed no problems whatsoever. She stepped into a pair of calfskin sling backs that fit as if they'd been custom-made for her foot, then redid her chignon and makeup.

Who *was* that woman in the mirror?

"Daniella Reynolds," she whispered to her reflection, then said it louder to get used to the sound of it. Only telemarketers and her grandmother called her Daniella. She liked the way Leo said it, though.

Since it was far past time to assume her duties as hostess to Leo's parents, she navigated downstairs with only one wrong turn.

Leo was not in the lavishly appointed living room. Or the kitchen, or any of the other maze of rooms on the first floor. Finally she spied his dark head bent over the desk in his study, where he was clearly engrossed in the dollar signs marching across his laptop screen.

Leo was working. Gee. What a shock. Why hadn't she thought to check his study first? Wishful thinking?

For a moment, she watched him, curious to see her husband unguarded. Towering bookshelves lined the room and should have dwarfed the man in it. They didn't. Leo's persona dominated the room. He'd shed his suit jacket and rolled up his shirtsleeves to midforearm. With his hair slightly rumpled, he was kind of adorable.

He glanced up with a distracted, lopsided half smile and her stomach flipped with a long, feminine pull. Okay, he was more than adorable. He was quite delicious and thoroughly untouchable, a combination she suddenly found irresistible. Her inner Scarlett conjured up a naughty mental scenario involving that red-hot lingerie and Leo's desk. *Hey, here's a bottom line you can check out.*

"Busy?" she croaked and cleared her throat. Duh. Of course he was.

"I'm, uh, just finishing up." He shot a furtive glance at his laptop as if the screen contained something shamefully un-work-related.

"What are you doing? Watching YouTube videos?" *Shut up, Scarlett.* It was none of her business whether he was monitoring stock prices or carousing in a role-playing-game forum. "I mean..."

Well, there was really no recovery for that slip.

"No." He shut the lid and she thought that would be the end of it. But then his mouth twitched. "I mentor college students online. I was walking through a business plan with one. Via chat."

"That's wonderful." What in the world was shameful about that? "They must really pay close attention when they see your name pop up. That's like winning the mentor lottery."

Her new husband was so generous and kind. Of course he was. Elise wouldn't have matched her with this man otherwise.

"I mentor anonymously."

"Oh. Why?"

"The business world is—" Flustered, he threaded fingers through his already slightly rumpled hair and she itched to smooth it back for him. "Let's just say my competitors won't hesitate to pounce on weakness. I don't present them with any."

Mentoring the next generation of businessmen could be perceived as a weakness? "Richard Branson mentors young kids. I don't see why he can do it, but you can't."

"He's considered successful." The unspoken *I'm not* hung in the air, but Leo stood and rolled his sleeves down, then rounded the desk, clearly signaling the end of the conversation. "Shall we?"

Her mouth fell open and she clamped it closed, swallowing the dozens of questions that sprang to her lips. His expression had closed off and even she could read the tread-with-caution sign. "Of course."

The doorbell rang and she trailed Leo to the foyer to meet Mr. and Mrs. Reynolds. Leo introduced his parents and Dannie shook hands with smiling, silver-haired Mr. Reynolds.

The spritely woman with Leo's dark hair bounded into the house and swept Dannie up in a fierce hug. "I'm so happy to meet you!"

"I'm happy to meet you, too, Mrs. Reynolds." Dannie breathed in her new mother-in-law's perfume, which reminded her of vanilla cookies.

"Oh, please. I'm Susan."

"I'm sorry, but I was expecting someone…" *Cold. Unforgiving. Judgmental.* "…older."

Susan laughed. "Aren't you sweet? Come with me to the kitchen and let Leo talk to his father while we fetch drinks."

After a glance at Leo to gauge the appropriateness, Dannie followed Susan into the kitchen and proceeded to watch while Leo's mother bustled around gathering glasses and chattering as if they were old friends. Obviously Susan felt comfortable in her son's house. Unlike her son's wife. Dannie wouldn't have known which cabinet contained glasses.

"I apologize for missing the ceremony, Daniella." Susan handed her a glass of tea and touched her shoulder. "It was a stupid, useless protest. But I'm mad at Leo, not you."

"Oh." She had to find a new response. That one was wearing thin. But it had been so appropriate. All day.

"He's just so…*Leo*. You know?" Susan sighed dramatically and Dannie nodded, though she didn't know. But she'd like to. "Too focused. Too intense. Too everything but what matters."

No way was she letting that pass. "What matters?"

"Life. Love. Grandchildren." With narrow eyes, Susan peered at Dannie. "Did he tell you that he draws?"

The tea she'd just sipped almost went down the wrong pipe. "Draws what?"

Susan snorted. "That's what I thought. Leo would rather die than let anyone know he does something frivolous. He can draw anything. Animals. Landscapes. Bridges and buildings. He's very talented. Like his namesake."

"Leo was named after someone who draws?" She envisioned a stooped grandfather doodling cartoon characters on the back of a grocery list.

"Leonardo da Vinci."

Dannie nearly dropped her tea. Leo's full name was Leonardo? Not Leonard? She'd noticed the little extra squiggle at the end of his name on the marriage license but had been so fixated on signing her own name she hadn't thought anything of it.

It shouldn't matter. But it did.

She'd married a man with a romantic name who created art from nothing more than pen and paper. She wanted to see something he'd drawn. Better yet, she wanted him to voluntarily show it to her. To share a deep-seated piece of himself. To connect with his wife.

Leo's mother had torn open a tiny corner of her son's personality and it whipped up a fervor to tear away more. They'd been *matched* and Dannie hungered to learn what they might share beyond a love of books, family and commitment.

"Daniella." Susan crooked her finger and Dannie leaned in. "I get that your marriage to my son is some kind of arrangement and presumably, that's all right with you. I won't pry. But Leo needs someone to love him, someone he can love in return, and neither will come easy. If it's not going to be you, please step aside."

Her pulse hammered in her throat. This marriage was

nothing more than a means to an end. An arrangement between two people based on compatibility, not love—exactly what she'd signed up for. But nothing close to what she wanted, what she dreamed could be possible.

Leo had asked for a wife to run his household, organize his parties and charm his business associates. Most important, his wife should give him what he needed, which wasn't necessarily the same as what he *professed* to need.

The woman behind the man had to be smart about how best to do her job.

Her inner Scarlett snickered and said *new plan*.

"What if it *is* going to be me?"

Leo had such a generous heart, but he cut himself off from people. He needed Dannie's help to understand why. If she could figure him out, it could lead to so much more than an arrangement. It could lead to the enduring love story she'd dreamed of.

Susan's smile could have powered every light in Paris. "Then I say welcome to the family."

Leo shut the door behind his parents and paused a moment before turning. For fortification. It did nothing to ease the screaming awareness of his vibrant wife. Sure enough, when he spun, there she was. Watching him with those keen eyes, chest rising and falling slightly, straining against her soft gray shirt.

He was noticing the way she *breathed*.

Clearly, he needed to go bury himself in a spreadsheet for a couple of hours.

His parents had liked Daniella, fortunately, because their lively discussion covered the fact that Leo hadn't contributed much. He'd been too busy pretending not to be preoccupied by his wife. But she'd been so amazing. A good conversationalist. A good hostess. Warm, friendly. Sexy.

It was just the two of them now. Talking was unavoidable.

"Thank you for entertaining my parents."

She shot him a perplexed look. "You're welcome. That's what I'm here for. Right?"

Since she was gazing at him expectantly, he answered her, though the question should have been rhetorical. "Yes, and I appreciate it."

"I enjoyed meeting your parents. Your mother is very interesting."

That sounded like a lead-up if he'd ever heard one. "What did she say to you in the kitchen?"

"Nothing of consequence." The smile on his wife's face was gracious and innocent. Too much so.

"Don't listen to anything my mother says, Daniella. She suffers from a terrible affliction with no cure—overt romanticism."

"Dannie."

"What?"

She'd inched forward until they were breathing the same air. And her chest nearly touched his with each small inhalation. "Daniella is too formal and stuck-up, don't you think? Call me Dannie."

He shook his head. The more formality the better for his peace of mind. "There's nothing wrong with the name *Daniella*. It's unusual. Beautiful. It suits you."

Her eyes lit up and suddenly, she was the only one breathing because all the organs in his chest stopped functioning. Nothing to the south suffered from the same problem. Everything there hummed on high alert.

"You think I'm beautiful?"

Had he said that? His brain was not refreshing fast enough. "Your name. I said your name is beautiful." Her expression fell and he cursed. If only he could converse with his wife exclusively by email, then maybe he could avoid hurting her feelings. "Of course you are, too. Very lovely."

Nice save, he thought sarcastically. *Lovely.* That described a winter snowscape. From the perspective of an eighty-year-old woman. This was the point where he usually escaped to go do something where he possessed proficiency—work.

Without looking at her again, he muttered, "Good night."

"Leo." A firm hand on his arm stopped him before he'd taken two steps past her. "I asked you to call me Dannie because that's what my friends call me. We're friends, aren't we?"

The warmth in her voice washed over him, settling inside with a slow burn. He didn't turn, didn't dare face her.

Something fundamental had changed in her demeanor—the leash she'd kept on her energy had snapped and yeah, he needed to look out. It leached into the air, electrifying it. She certainly wasn't afraid to speak to him any longer. "I... Yes. Of course."

She brushed against his arm as she rounded it, apparently not content to talk to his back. Her shirt gaped slightly, revealing a tantalizing peek at her cleavage. The slow burn blazed faster. They were talking about being friends, not lovers. What was wrong with him?

Dannie. No, too intimate. *Daniella* was too intriguing. What was he supposed to call her, *hey, you*?

He couldn't compartmentalize his wife. That was bad.

"Friends," he rasped because he had to say something.

Okay, good. Daniella could go into the friends box. It could work. He'd envisioned having a companion to fill a hole in his life. Now he had one.

"Friends." Without breaking eye contact, she reached up and loosened his tie, leaning into it, fingers lingering far too long for the simple task. "Who help each other relax."

Relax? Every nerve in his body skated along a razor's edge, desperately seeking release from the power of his wife's touch. The faint scent of strawberries wafted from her glossy lips and he wanted to taste it. "What makes you think I need to relax?"

"I can feel the tension from here, Leo."

Was that what they were calling it these days? Felt like a good, old-fashioned hard-on to him.

As if pulled by imperceptible threads, his body circled closer to hers and the promise of heat turned into a reality as their lower halves brushed once, twice. His hand flew to the small of her back to clamp her tight against him.

Fingers still tangled in his loosened tie, she tugged slightly. Her face tipped up, lips primed to be taken in another kiss, but this time nothing prevented him from finishing it. From dragging his lips down the length of his wife's torso, straight to...

He cursed—they'd agreed to be platonic only a few hours ago and they were in the middle of an innocuous conversation about being *friends*. Yet he was salivating at the thought of kissing her, of laughing together over a joke, of being so much more than a convenience to each other.

He took a deliberate step backward and her hand dropped from his tie.

If she had this strong an effect on him, he was in hotter water than he'd realized. He did *not* want to be so obsessed with his wife.

"I'm tense because I have a lot of work to do." He willed his body and his bothersome loneliness back into submission. Or tried to. Seemed as though it was destined to be a losing battle. Since she was clearly no longer too scared to talk, he'd have to put space between them another way. "We'll spend time together, but this will not be a conventional relationship. If that's not going to work for you, we should get an annulment."

A hint of hurt crept into her expression. His chest panged. She'd just asked to be friends and loosened his tie. Why was he turning it into a cardinal offense? Wasn't this part of letting their relationship grow more intimate naturally?

"What happened to make you so jaded?" she asked quietly, not the slightest bit cowed by his speech. He liked it better when she said nothing more than *yes* and *thank you*.

"I'm not jaded. I don't have anything against relationships or love in general. Without it, I wouldn't be here. My parents still make googly eyes at each other across the table. Didn't you notice?"

"Of course. They're a very happy couple. Why don't you want the same?"

There was the reason he'd nipped the tie loosening in the bud. They were married and might even become friends, but they were never going to be anything more, and it was a disservice to Daniella to let her have the smallest hope otherwise.

He was already doing himself a disservice by even contemplating "otherwise."

"Oh, they're happy, all right." He rolled his eyes. "At the expense of everything else. My parents have no money. No savings."

And they refused to accept what they called handouts from Leo. He'd like nothing more than to take care of them, had offered a house, cars, even vacations, to no avail. Apparently, they enjoyed the gangs and graffiti spray-painted on the front sidewalk. Their memories appeared to be short, but Leo could never forget the gun-wielding thief who'd broken into their house when he was six. The terror had fueled his drive to escape and kept him on the straight and narrow.

"You fault your parents for being happy over making money?"

"No, I don't blame my father for working a low-paying job so he could be home with my mom and me. I choose to live my life differently. I'll never force my child to be grateful for one gift under the Christmas tree. To stay home from school on the days when the rest of the class goes on field trips to the zoo because I can't afford for my kid to go."

"Oh, Leo."

The compassion shining in her eyes unearthed something poignant inside. That had to go. This wasn't about feeling sorry for poor, little Leo Reynolds from the section of east

Dallas where even the churches had bars on the windows. It was about making a point.

"See all this?" He cut a hand through the air to indicate the house at large. "I worked for every dime. I held three jobs in college so I could graduate with no debt and then put my nose to the grindstone for years to get ahead. I'm still not there. If I take my eye off the prize for even a moment, poof. It all vanishes."

His wife gazed at him without speaking, lips pursed in a plump bow. Firm breasts strained against her blouse, inviting him to spread the fabric wide and—maybe he needed to internalize which prize he wasn't supposed to take his eyes off of.

Other venture capital companies were unearthing the next Google or staking start-ups that sold to competitors for billions of dollars. Reynolds Capital would be there soon if he kept on course. All he had to do was resist temptation. He'd married a woman who would help him avoid the dangers of giving in.

If she'd just stay in her box, that is.

He breathed in the scent of strawberries and the sizzling energy of his wife. "I work, Daniella. All the time. I can't invest in a relationship. It wouldn't be fair if I let you believe in that possibility."

He couldn't let himself dwell on the possibilities, either. No weakness. Indulgence led to immersion and immersion led to ruin. Carmen had proved that, nearly derailing his entire senior year and subsequently, his life. It was easier to never start down that path and the last thing he wanted was to hurt Daniella.

Four

Dannie slept poorly that night. The bed was comfortable, but she wasn't. Leo had her tied up in knots.

Now that she knew how truly earthshaking his eyes looked when they were hot with passion, she didn't know if she'd ever be comfortable again. The spike of awareness inside—deep, *deep* inside—had peaked the second he touched her and then died a miserable death during the "I'm a workaholic, deal with it" conversation.

He was definitely attracted to her. And perfectly willing to ignore it in favor of his bottom line. How exactly did he envision them moving past being polite strangers?

Her new plan might need some refining. Just because she and Leo's mother thought he might benefit from a woman's tender affections didn't mean Leo thought that. And if Dannie irritated him any further with unwanted advances, he might seek that annulment on his own. At which point she'd get nothing and she'd let her mother and Elise down. Plus herself.

But as far she was concerned, they were married for life, and she wanted to eventually be friends *and* lovers. Despite Leo's impassioned speech, she really didn't understand why he didn't want that, too.

Hence the sleepless night.

She woke in the morning, groggy but determined to be a better wife to Leo Reynolds than he could ever dream. Rob had wanted a fade-into-the-background woman and she'd messed up. Elise's training had taught her how to beat back that strong-willed inner Scarlett.

Leo was going to get what he'd asked for.

If she addressed his needs—especially the unrealized ones—maybe *that* would lead them into a deeper relationship.

After she dressed and arrived downstairs, one of the maids informed her Leo had already left for the day. Instead of wallowing in disappointment she had no business feeling, she familiarized herself with the kitchen as she toasted bread and scrambled eggs. Tomorrow morning, she'd set an alarm and be up early to make Leo coffee or breakfast or whatever he preferred, which she needed to learn pronto if she hoped to see him in the morning.

Dannie spent the rest of the morning in an endless parade of tasks: learning the ins and outs of a difficult phone that she refused to believe was smarter than she was, memorizing the brands of Leo's clothes, determining how he preferred his closet to be organized, researching the recommended care of all the fabrics. As mistress of the household, it was her responsibility to ensure the servants did their jobs well and correct poor performance as necessary. By lunch, her brain hurt.

And she hadn't even started on Leo's social calendar.

Once she tapped into the wealth of information named Mrs. Gordon, Dannie breathed a little easier. Leo's admin talked for a solid hour and then sent a dozen emails full of links and instructions about the care and feeding of a venture capitalist.

Dannie read everything twice as she absently shoved a sandwich in her mouth.

Mrs. Gordon wrapped up the exchange with a tip about an invitation to an alumni event from Leo's college, which was that very night. She kindly agreed to delete the reminder entry she'd already set up so Dannie could practice scheduling.

Perfect. Dannie plunked the stupid phone into her palm and eyed it. "I'm the boss. You better cooperate," she told it, and proceeded to manhandle the appointment onto Leo's calendar.

When his acceptance appeared, she nearly broke into an impromptu dance. Until she noticed she'd scheduled it for tomorrow night. Grimly, she rescheduled and got it right the second time. Leo was probably sitting in his office shaking his head as he accepted the updated request.

Enough of that job. Dannie went to agonize over her meager wardrobe in anticipation of her first social appearance as Mrs. Leo Reynolds. This she'd have to get right on the first shot. She couldn't carry a second outfit in her clutch in case of dress remorse.

Leo walked through the door at precisely six o'clock. Dannie was ready and waiting for him in the kitchen, the closest room to the detached garage. The salmon-colored dress she wore accentuated her figure but had tasteful, elegant lines. Elise had taught her to pick flattering clothes and it looked fantastic on her, especially coupled with strappy Jimmy Choos heels. Would Leo notice?

"How was your day?" she asked politely while taking in the stress lines and shadows around his eyes that said he'd slept poorly, as well.

Something unfolded in her chest, urging her to smooth back the dark hair from his forehead and lightly massage his temples. Or whatever would soothe him. She wanted to know what to do for him, what he'd appreciate.

He set a brown leather messenger bag on the island in the kitchen. "Fine. And yours?"

"Wonderful." Except for the part where he hadn't kissed her goodbye. Or hello. *Shut up, Scarlett.* "The alumni gala is at the Renaissance Hotel. My driver will take us as soon as we're ready."

He hadn't said a word about her dress. Perhaps she'd take that as a sign he wouldn't be ashamed to be seen with her and not dwell on whether it got a response or not. Compliments weren't the reason she'd married Leo.

"That's fine. Let me change and we'll go." Leo set off for the stairs, fingers already working on his tie, which she'd have gladly taken off for him, if he'd let her. "They're giving an award to a friend of mine, and we should take him to dinner afterward."

Reservations. Where? For how many? But Leo was gone before she could ask.

Totally winging it, she called the most expensive restaurant she'd heard of and booked a table for four in Leo's name. If nothing else, the restaurant might be willing to add a few more to the party for a distinguished guest like Leo Reynolds.

Leo returned to the kitchen a short time later and she forgot all about a little thing like reservations. In black tie, Leo simply stole her breath.

"Ready?" he asked with raised eyebrows, likely because her fish-mouth impersonation amused him.

He was so delicious with his dark hair and dark suit, all crisp and masculine with a slight sensuous edge that set off something sharp and hot inside her. Last night, she'd felt just enough of the body he carried under that suit and the memory reintroduced itself as she let her eyes travel the entire length of her husband.

He cleared his throat and her gaze snapped to his. He was still waiting on her response.

"Ready," she squeaked and grabbed her clutch.

Leo kept up the conversation as they rode to the hotel with his confident, steady presence. She suspected—and appreciated—it was a ploy to dispel her nervousness, but it didn't work.

Leo escorted her through the lobby of the hotel with a hand at the small of her back. She liked the way his hand fit there. It served a dual purpose of providing support and showing everyone they were together.

And boy, did people notice. Heads swiveled as they entered the crush in the Renaissance ballroom. A string quartet played Strauss on a small platform in the corner, but the music couldn't cover the rush of whispers that surely were about the woman with Leo.

One flawless society wife in progress. Who hadn't gone to college but was going to be brilliant or die trying. Dannie squared her shoulders.

The neckline of her dress slipped, revealing a healthy slice of breast. Surreptitiously, she fingered it back into place. The deep vee over her cleavage wasn't terribly daring, but it was low-cut and the spaghetti straps were too long for her torso. Since the svelte salmon-colored dress had cost Elise seven hundred dollars, paying to have it altered felt like a sin.

It slipped down again as Leo steered her toward the far corner. As she walked, she lowered one shoulder, Quasimodo-style, hoping to nudge the neckline back where it belonged through a combination of shifting her balance and sheer will.

"Are you okay?" Leo whispered.

She should have worn the dress all day and practiced walking in it. Hindsight. Double-sided tape could have fixed the problem in a jiffy.

"Of course." She pasted on a serene smile as they halted before a group of men and women Leo clearly knew. Nodding, she greeted people and used all her tricks to remember names. Constantly being fired from a variety of jobs had an upside—few situations or people intimidated her.

"And this is Jenna Crisp," Leo concluded, indicating a gorgeous redhead on the arm of Leo's friend Dax Wakefield, who was receiving the alumni award that evening. "Jenna, this is my wife, Daniella Reynolds."

Dannie shook the woman's hand but Jenna wasn't looking at her. The redhead's attention was on Leo. Hmm. Dannie glanced at him. He didn't notice Jenna's scrutiny. Too busy discussing a patent infringement case with Dax. "I'm happy to meet you, Jenna. Have you known Leo long?"

Jenna focused on Dannie, and her expression noticeably cooled. "Long enough. How did you two meet, again?"

The redhead's tone oozed with challenge, as if there might be something tawdry to the story.

That was one area they'd definitely not covered. Did his friends know he'd gone to a matchmaker? She'd have to settle for a half-truth lest she embarrass Leo. "A mutual acquaintance introduced us."

"Interesting." The other woman nodded, sweeping long locks over her bare shoulders. She curled her lips in a semblance of a smile, which didn't fool Dannie for a second. Jenna did not like her.

"That's how Dax and I met, too. Leo introduced us."

"Oh?" Leo—a matchmaker himself? That *was* interesting. "I'm sure he was happy to help his friends find each other."

"You think so? Considering the fact that Leo and I were dating at the time, I wasn't sure what to make of it."

Oh, dear. No wonder the daggers in Jenna's eyes were so sharp. Dannie groaned inwardly. The dinner reservations had just gotten a whole lot more complicated than whether the table would be big enough.

"I'm sorry. I can't speak for Leo. If you're curious about his motives, you'd best ask him. Champagne?" she offered brightly, intending to put some distance between herself and Leo's ex-girlfriend. At least until she figured out how to navigate the bloody water full of sharks her husband had dropped her into.

"That would be lovely," Jenna said just as brightly and took Leo's arm to join in his conversation with Dax, physically blocking Dannie from the group.

In historical novels, they called that the cut direct. In real life, Dannie called it something else entirely, and if she said that many four-letter words out loud, Leo would have a heart attack.

Instead, she went to get Jenna and Leo a glass of champagne.

Really, she understood Jenna's animosity. She'd be confused, too, if Leo had shuffled her off on a friend and then promptly married someone else. Dannie also had the superior position between them, a point Jenna likely hadn't missed. At the end of the day, Dannie's last name was Reynolds and Jenna's wasn't.

Now she wondered what had really happened between Jenna and Leo. It was a little uncivilized of Leo not to have warned her. Men. Didn't he realize what he'd dragged Dannie into?

In reality, he probably hadn't considered it a problem. And it wasn't. Their marriage was an arrangement and her emotions weren't Leo's primary concern. That put a little steel in her spine. She had a job to do.

When she rejoined the group, Leo shot her a sidelong smile in gratitude for the glass of champagne. The flutters his very private grin set off were enough to forgive him. Almost.

A good wife might choose to forget the whole conversation. She bit her lip.

Then again, a good wife who paid attention to unspoken nuances might also ensure she didn't mistakenly cause her husband embarrassment. Forewarned was forearmed, and if Leo expected her to chat up his associates, she should know exactly what that association was. Right?

"You used to date Jenna?" she murmured in his ear as Dax engaged his date in their own conversation.

"Briefly." Leo's gaze sought out the woman in question, his eyes narrowing and growing a tad frigid. "She told you? I'm surprised she'd be so tactless. And I apologize if I put you in an uncomfortable position."

He'd leaned in, breath teasing along her cheek as he

spoke, and she caught a whiff of something fresh and maybe a little wintry but definitely all male. His hip brushed hers. Heat pooled at the contact and spread, giving a whole new meaning to an uncomfortable position.

She waved off his apology. "Nothing I can't handle. I'm sure you didn't do it on purpose."

He'd apologized instead of calling her out for sticking her nose in his business. That was a relief. Walking that line between being a complement to Leo and fading into the background was harder than she'd anticipated. Regardless, she was going to be a star wife. No compromise.

Leo frowned. "We only went out for a little while and obviously it didn't work out, or I wouldn't have introduced her to a friend. Jenna wanted more than I could give and Dax pays attention to her. It seemed perfect."

Oh. Of course. Jenna was the reason Leo needed a wife who wouldn't expect him to be around—she'd presumed to spend time with a man she liked and grew weary of the "I'm a workaholic, deal with it" speech.

The longing glances Jenna kept throwing Leo's way made a heck of a lot more sense now. Despite most likely being told in no uncertain terms not to get emotionally involved, Jenna had done it anyway. Only to be cast aside.

It was a sobering reminder. Dannie had a lot to lose if she made the same mistake.

Sobering. But ineffective.

As her husband's hand came to rest against the small of her back, she couldn't help but be tremendously encouraged that Leo had cared enough about Jenna to help her find happiness with someone better suited for her. In the kitchen yesterday, he'd expressed genuine interest in ensuring Dannie wasn't disappointed with their marriage.

Small gestures, but in Dannie's mind, they added up to something much larger. He had a good heart underneath all that business acumen. And despite his determination to keep her at arm's length, he needed her to break through the shell he kept around himself.

But how?

The champagne left a bitter taste in Leo's mouth.

If he'd known Jenna would deliberately upset Daniella, he'd never have brought his wife within a mile of her.

He should be having a conversation with Miles Bennett, who was about to launch a software product with some good buzz around it. John Hu was on his radar to speak to as well, and there John was by the bar, talking to Gene Ross's ancient wife. That conversation couldn't be about anything other than Mrs. Ross's show poodle or Miami this time of year, and Leo had no qualms about interrupting either.

Several recent investments hadn't panned out the way he'd hoped. He needed new blood now. Yesterday would have been better.

Instead of the dozen other things he should be doing, he was watching his wife. Out of the corner of his eye, no less, while he pretended to talk to Dax, who pretended he didn't notice Leo's fixation.

Daniella dazzled everyone, despite Jenna's mean-spirited disclosure.

The mechanics of marriage were still new and he hadn't fully considered the potential ramifications of introducing the two women. A wife was supposed to be *less* complicated than regular females, not more. Was Daniella uncomfortable being in the same room with Jenna? Or was she taking it in stride like everything else?

Daniella didn't *look* upset. She looked like a gift-wrapped present he'd put on his list a month ago and Christmas was still a week away.

That dress. It dipped against her breasts, revealing just enough to be interesting but not enough to be labeled indecent. The zipper in the back called his name. One tug and the wrapping would peel away, revealing a very nice gift indeed. The delicate shoes she wore emphasized her shapely legs and he liked that far more than he wanted to.

Daniella was the most gorgeous woman in the room. And the most interesting, the most poised and the most vivacious. Bar none. And he wasn't the only one who thought so, instilling in him a quiet sense of pride with every appreciative glance she earned.

In case she was more upset about Jenna than she let on, he kept a close eye on her as she talked to a couple of Reynolds Capital's partners. No hardship on his part to watch her graceful hands gesture and her pink-stained lips form words. Then she laughed and the dress slipped a tantalizing inch farther down her breasts. And then another inch.

A flash of heat tensed his entire body and tightened his pants uncomfortably.

He swore and Dax stared at him as if he'd lost his mind. Which didn't appear to be as far out of the realm of possibility as it should.

"I need a refill," Leo explained and waved his empty champagne flute at a passing waiter.

When the waiter returned, he downed the glass in two gulps. It didn't cool him down. Something needed to change, very quickly.

He glanced at Daniella. She didn't turn her head, but her eyes swiveled and she met his gaze with a secret smile, as if to say, *later*.

Or maybe that was his lower half projecting her meaning. The upper half refused to entertain even one little fantasy about later. Intimacy was supposed to be a progression, and abandoning that idea on day two didn't bode well for Leo's state of mind.

They hadn't developed a *friendship* yet and he was fantasizing about skipping right over that.

The music swelled, signaling the start of the awards ceremony. Daniella moved toward him at the same moment he stepped forward to grasp her arm. They bumped hips and somehow, the button on his jacket caught her dress.

One of Daniella's nipples popped free of the fabric, searing his vision and sending a surge straight to his groin. She gasped with a feminine squeal of humiliation, hands flying to her chest.

Instantly, Leo whirled her into a snug embrace, hiding her from view. And oh, dear God. His wife's body aligned with his like flowing honey, clinging sweetly to every groove.

"No one saw," he murmured into her hair and prayed she wouldn't take offense to the obvious erection pushing into her abdomen. It wasn't as though he could step away and compose himself.

The sight of that bare, rosy nipple was emblazoned on his brain and worse, both of her nipples pressed against his chest, raising the temperature in the stuffy ballroom about a hundred degrees.

"Are you all…arranged?" he asked hoarsely.

She was shaking. Or was that him?

"I can't," she whispered and her hand worked between their bodies, brushing his erection an ungodly number of times. "The button won't come loose."

He nearly groaned. "We'll have to get to the hall. Somehow. Can you turn?"

"Yes. If you keep your arm around me."

They did a fair impression of Siamese twins, shuffling as one toward the back of the ballroom, Daniella clutching Leo with one hand and her dress with the other. Which meant her hands were nowhere near his erection—and that was good. One more brush of those manicured nails against him would have produced fireworks better left unlit in public.

Miraculously, the crowd had thinned. The awards presenter droned from the next room. Leo was missing the ceremony but Dax would have to understand.

An eternity later, they reached the hall and Leo hustled

Daniella into a deep alcove housing a giant sculpture of a mermaid.

"We're totally hidden from view. It's okay," he said.

She took a half step backward, as far as their tangled clothes would allow.

"My definition of okay and yours must be different." Head bent, she studiously fingered the threads holding his button hostage until they finally came apart. "I'm sorry, Leo. You must be mortified."

Her head was still down, as if she didn't want to look at him.

"Me?" He tipped her chin up with a loosely fisted hand. Her cheeks were on fire. "You're the one who has a reason to be mortified. I can't imagine how you must feel. First I force you to make nice to Jenna and then almost rip off your dress. I'm the one who's sorry."

"It's not *your* fault," she countered fiercely. "This dress doesn't fit quite right. I shouldn't have worn it."

Five minutes ago, he'd have agreed. If she'd dressed a little more matronly, he might be having that conversation with John Hu right now. Except the alternative—being wedged into a secluded alcove with his wife—suddenly didn't seem so terrible. "That dress fits you perfectly."

She shook her head as she twisted the waistline back into place. "All my clothes have to be altered. I know that. But I didn't have this one done. Stupid. I should have thought about the consequences. My job is to make you look good, not embarrass you in public. I'm sorry. I'm not making a very good first impression."

That's what she was worried about? That she'd messed up and displeased him? A weight settled onto his chest. Did she think he was that concerned about their agreement?

Obviously so.

"On the contrary, you've made a great impression. Exactly as I expected. I watched you with my business associates. They liked you." She'd charmed them easily and he could already envision her doing the same at future events. Daniella was amazing, through and through.

"Really?" The disbelief in her voice settled that weight a little deeper. She seemed so disheartened by what was such a small blip in the evening.

Daniella was his wife, not a casual date he might or might not see again. The very act of making her his wife changed everything. He wanted her to be happy, which he hadn't planned, could never have predicted. Not only did he want her to be happy, he'd discovered a healthy drive to care for her and ensure her security. He wanted her to know she could depend on him, always.

Problem being, of course, that his experience with serious relationships started and ended with the woman in front of him.

He nodded, scouting for a way to put a smile back on her face. "If nothing else, you can take solace in the fact that your wardrobe malfunction didn't take place on national TV."

She laughed, as he'd intended. The resurrection of his hard-on, he hadn't. But who could blame him? Her laugh curled through him like fine wine and came coupled with the distinct memory of her beautiful breast.

The secluded alcove grew close and heavy with awareness as she locked on to his gaze. Her irises warmed. "Thank you for rescuing me. It was very chivalrous."

The back of his neck heated at the adoration in her eyes. He felt like a fake. There wasn't a romantic bone in his body. "I wouldn't have abandoned you."

"Your button." Without breaking eye contact, she touched it with her fingertips. "It's loose."

"No problem." He swallowed and his throat was on fire. Everything was on fire. "I have another one."

Slim eyebrows arched as she cocked her head. Loose tendrils of dark brown hair fell against her cheeks and he barely resisted an urge to tuck them back for her. And as a treat for himself. The shiny, slightly wavy locks would be soft against his fingers.

"Should we rejoin the party?" she asked in an incredible show of courage. Not many people would walk back into a room where they'd performed a free peep show. His admiration for her swelled. "As long as I don't move around too much, I should stay tucked away."

His gaze dropped to her cleavage automatically. She was quite tucked away, but the promise of what he knew lay beneath the fabric teased him. How easily he could thumb down that dress and run the pads across those taut nipples. No effort required at all. No one could see them back here behind the sculpture.

He sucked in a hot breath.

"Leo," she murmured and slid lithe fingers along his lapels, straightening them as she traveled south.

"Hmm?" She was so close he could see golden flecks in her eyes. Raw energy radiated from her, wrapping around him in a heated veil.

"The party?" Her lips met on the last syllable and he recalled how they'd sparked against his when he'd kissed her at their wedding ceremony.

This was like a first date, wasn't it? He'd kissed women on dates, lots of times. It might even be considered expected. A major disappointment if he didn't do it.

Would kissing her be as hot the second time? Hotter?

His curiosity would only be satisfied one way.

"We should go back. Shouldn't we?" she asked. But she stood there, frozen, peeking up from beneath her lashes coyly, as if she could read the intent in his eyes.

Yes. They should go back. His body strained toward her, desperate to be closer.

The scent of strawberries wafted to him on a sensuous cloud as she swayed into his space. Or maybe he was the one who moved.

Like honey, he thought as their bodies met. Their lips

touched hesitantly, then firmly, deliberately, and his mind pushed out everything except the sizzle of flesh on flesh.

His wife's mouth opened under his and he swept her deep into his embrace as he kissed her. His back hit the wall but he scarcely noticed as Daniella came alive, hands in his hair, her mouth strong and ferocious against his.

Hunger thundered through his veins. His hips circled against hers involuntarily, uncontrollably as he sought to ease the ache she'd inflamed. With one hand, he enveloped her neck and pushed, tipping her head back so he could open her wider, then tentatively stroked her tongue with his.

She stroked him back, deeper, harder. Leo groaned against her mouth. She kissed like a horny teenager's fantasy. Deep. Wet. Carnal.

Those perfect breasts haunted him. *Touch them,* his libido begged. The temptation was almost too much to bear, but he feared if he gave in to it, he might never surface.

Home. They could go home. Right now. They lived together, after all.

If he took her home, he could strip that dress away to taste every peak and valley of his wife's body. Especially the parts he hadn't yet seen but could feel easily through the silky drape of cloth over her luscious skin.

The kiss deepened, heating further, enflaming his skin. Desire screamed through his body. He'd never kissed a woman on a date quite like this. Hell, he'd never kissed a woman like this *ever,* not even in bed.

She was luring him into a dark pit of need and surfacing suddenly wasn't so appealing.

He trailed openmouthed kisses along her throat and palmed her sexy rear again. Unbelievably, this incredible, stimulating woman was *his.* She moaned under his touch and her head fell back.

"Leo," she murmured as he slipped a pin from her fancy done-up hair. "Don't you need to go back?"

As if she'd thrown a bucket of water over him, his lust-hazed bubble burst. They were in the hallway of a hotel and his wife was reminding *him* of the importance of circulating at the alumni ceremony.

He pulled back to breathe the cool air of sanity. "I do."

Her face remained composed, but a storm of desire brewed in her gaze, one he suspected would easily explode again with his touch. She'd been just as turned on as he had.

"Till later, then?" she asked.

Oh, no. That wouldn't do at all. *Focus, Reynolds.*

At least four people he must speak with mingled in the ballroom less than a hundred yards away and his wife's mussed hair and plump, kiss-stung lips alone threatened to steal his composure. If he had to suffer through the rest of the night while anticipating *later,* nothing of consequence would be accomplished.

You're weak, the nasty voice of his conscience whispered. And that was the real reason he couldn't lose his single-mindedness.

If he let himself indulge—in drawing, in a woman, in *anything* other than the goal—he'd be lost. Look what had just happened with a simple kiss.

He released her and his body cooled a degree or two. It wasn't enough to erase the imprint of her in his senses. "I apologize. That was inappropriate. Please, take a few moments in the ladies' room and meet me back in the ballroom. We'll act as if that never happened."

Disappointment replaced the desire in her expression and made him feel like a world-class jerk.

"If that's what you want."

It was absolutely not what he wanted. But distance was what he needed in order to get a measure of control.

This marriage should be the perfect blend of necessity and convenience. *Should be.* But the possibility of being friends was already out the window due to the curse of his weaknesses, and it would only get worse the further under his skin she dug.

"This is a business event and I haven't been treating it like one."

"Of course." Her tone had become professional, as it should. Even in this, she remained poised, doing her duty as expected, because *she* wasn't weak. She was thoroughly brilliant.

He hated putting up a barrier, but she'd become exactly what he'd suspected she would—a disturbance he couldn't afford.

But she was also proving to be exactly what he'd hoped. The perfect complement of a wife. She deserved happiness and he'd provide no assurance of security—for either of them—if he took his eye off the success of Reynolds Capital Management for even a moment. His wife would not be forced into the poorhouse because of him, like his father had done to Leo's mother.

No more digressions. It was too dangerous to kiss her. Or think about her as a friend.

Daniella was back in the employee box. She had to stay there.

How in the world was he going to forget what those strawberry-scented lips could do?

Five

Leo was already gone by the time Dannie emerged from her bedroom the next morning. Even though she'd set an alarm, he still beat her.

She'd screwed up at the alumni gala. Leo had been kissing her—*oh, my God,* had he been kissing her—and then he hit the brakes. Of course work came first, and the woman behind the man should never forget that. But to pretend *that kiss* hadn't happened? It was impossible. She wasn't naive enough to believe she'd break through his shell in one evening, but she thought she'd lifted it a little at least.

At home, his obsession with work shouldn't be a factor, especially before he left for the office. Tomorrow morning, she'd shove the alarm back thirty minutes. If she beat him to the kitchen, they'd have a chance to talk and maybe share a laugh. Then think about each other fondly over the course of the day.

All good elements of both friendship and marriage.

The next morning she missed him again, and continued to miss him for a week.

Four declined event appointments should have clued her in, but it wasn't until she caught the startled look on his face when he came out of his bedroom one morning that she realized he'd been avoiding her.

"Good morning." She smiled despite his wary expression and the fact that she'd been awake since five hoping to catch him.

"Morning." He nodded and brushed past without another word.

Stung, she watched him retreat down the stairs and vowed not to think about Leo Reynolds the rest of the day. She had a job to do here.

Dannie spent an hour with the staff going over weekly household accounts, then interviewed a prospective maid to replace one who had given notice. She enjoyed organizing Leo's life. At the alumni gala, she'd navigated Leo's social circles, recovered from a humiliating dress fail and smiled through dinner with her husband's ex-girlfriend.

What more could Leo possibly want in a wife?

At four o'clock, Leo texted her with a short message she'd come to expect: I'll be home late. Make dinner plans on your own.

As she'd been doing for a week. Leo clearly planned to keep her at arm's length, despite *that kiss*.

Fuming, she called her mother and invited her over for dinner. Might as well take advantage of the cook Leo kept on staff. She and her mother ate prime rib and lobster bisque, both wonderfully prepared, but neither could keep her attention. Her mother raved about the food, about Dannie's marriage, about how much she liked her new nurse. Dannie smiled but nothing penetrated the cloud of frustration cloaking what should have been a nice evening with her mom.

As far back as Dannie could remember, her mother had constantly passed on relationship advice: *Men don't stick around. Don't listen to their pretty words and promises.* And variations aplenty espousing the evils of falling in love. The whole point of this arranged marriage was so Dannie wouldn't end up alone and miserable like her mother. And despite her mother's best attempts to squash Dannie's romanticism, it was still there, buried underneath reality.

All men couldn't be like her father. Leo didn't flatter her with slick charm, and he'd been nothing but honest with her. Furthermore, her husband had kissed her passionately, madly, more completely than Dannie had ever been kissed in her life. She couldn't pretend it hadn't happened or that she didn't want more than an occasional text message out of her marriage.

They'd never get past being virtual strangers at this rate. Maybe it was for the best, if Jenna's fate bore any credence to what might become Dannie's story. But she couldn't accept that she and Leo would *never* see each other. Surely they could spend a little time together. An hour. Thirty minutes.

How was she supposed to handle his social commitments and take care of his every need if he kept avoiding her?

After she saw her mother off in the chauffeured car that Dannie couldn't quite give up yet, she parked on the couch nearest the stairs, determined to wait for Leo until the cows came home, if necessary. They needed to talk.

An hour later, Dannie started to wonder if Leo intended to sleep at the office. He wouldn't. Would he? Had she screwed up so badly that he couldn't even stand to be in the same house with her?

She flung her head back on a cushion and stared at the ceiling. He certainly hadn't lied to her. He did work all the time and she had done nothing to find her own amusements. Because she didn't want to. She wanted to be Leo's wife in every sense of the word, or at least she thought she did, despite being given little opportunity to find out.

Another hour passed. This was ridiculous. Not only was he hindering her ability to take care of him, but he'd agreed they could be friends. How did he think friendship developed?

New tactics were in order. Before she could remind herself of all the reasons she shouldn't, she sent Leo a text message: I heard a noise. I think someone is in the house. Can you come home?

Immediately, he responded: Call the police and hit the intruder alarm.

She rolled her eyes and texted him back: I'm scared. I'd like you to come home.

Leo: Be there as soon as I can.

Bingo. She huffed out a relieved breath. It had been a gamble, but only a small one. Leo had a good heart, which wouldn't have allowed him to do anything else but come home to his wife.

Twenty minutes later, Leo pulled into the drive at the front of the house. Dannie flicked on the enormous carriage lights flanking the entrance arch, illuminating the wide porch, and met him on the steps.

"Are you okay?" he asked, his hard gaze sweeping the shadows behind her.

His frame bristled with tension, saying in no uncertain terms he'd protect her from any threat imaginable, and it pulled a long, liquid flash from her core that sizzled. An intruder wouldn't stand a chance against so much coiled intensity.

"I'm fine." In a manner of speaking.

Leo's dark suit looked as superb on him as a tuxedo did. More so, because he was at full alert inside it, his body all hard and masculine. Warrior Leo made her mouth water. She might have to fan herself.

"Did you call the police?" He ushered her inside quickly, one hand steady at her back.

"No. I didn't hear the noise again and I didn't want to waste anyone's time." Especially since the noise was entirely fictional. Hopefully, once she hashed things out with Leo, an excuse wouldn't be necessary to get his attention.

He shot off a series of questions and she answered until he was satisfied there was no imminent danger. "Next time, push the panic button. That's what the security alarm is for."

"Did I interrupt something important at work?"

Lines deepened around his eyes as his carriage relaxed and he smiled. "It's all important. But it's okay. It'll still be there in the morning."

Relaxed Leo was nice, too. So much more approachable. She returned his smile and tugged on his arm. "Then sit down for a minute. Tell me about your day."

He didn't budge from his statue impression in the foyer. "Not much to tell. Why don't you go on up to bed? I'll hang out downstairs and make sure there's really nothing to worry about."

Oh, no, you don't. "I'm not tired. You're here. I'm here. Come talk to me for a minute."

He hefted the messenger bag in his hand a little higher in emphasis with an apologetic shrug. "I have some work to finish up."

"That'll be there in the morning, too." Gently, she took the bag from him and laid it on the Hepplewhite table against the wall, a little surprised he'd let her. "We haven't talked since the alumni gala."

The mere mention of it laced the atmosphere with a heaviness that prickled her skin. Leo's gaze fell on hers and silence stretched between them. Was he remembering the kiss? Or was he still determined to forget about it? If so, she'd like to learn that trick.

"There's a reason for that," he finally said.

Her stomach tumbled at his frank admission that he'd been avoiding her. She nodded. "I suspected as much. That's why I want to talk."

His gaze swept over her face. "I thought you wanted me to tell you about my day."

"I do." She started to reach out but stopped as she took in the firm line of his mouth. "But we need to talk regardless. I was hoping to be a little more civil about it, though."

"Maybe we can catch up tomorrow." He picked up the messenger bag from the table, but before he could stride from the foyer, she stepped in front of him, blocking his path.

Arms crossed, she stared him down. "Be straight with

me. I can handle it. Are you regretting your choice in wives? Maybe you're wishing you'd picked Jenna after all?"

The bag slipped from Leo's hand and thunked to the floor. "Not now, Daniella."

"You mean *not now,* and by the way, *not ever?* When will we have this conversation if not now?" Too annoyed to check her action, she poked a finger in his chest. Being demure had gotten her exactly nowhere. "You've been avoiding me. I want to know why. Am I not performing up to your expectations?"

"I'm not avoiding you." Guilt flitted through his expression, contradicting the statement. "I've got three proposals out, the shareholder value on one of my major investments took a forty percent loss over the last week and a start-up I staked declared bankruptcy today. Is that enough truth for you? The reason we haven't talked is because I'm extremely busy keeping my company afloat."

The Monet on the wall opposite her swirled into a mess of colors as she shared some of that guilt. "I'm sorry. I shouldn't have bothered you about the noise. I just wanted to…" *See you. Talk to you. Find out if you've been thinking of me.* "Not be scared."

Leo's expression softened and he reached out to grip her shoulder protectively. "You shouldn't have been. I had the security system installed as soon as you agreed to marry me and it's top-of-the-line. It would take a SWAT team to breach it. You're safe here. Do you not feel like you are?"

She stared up into his worried blue eyes and her insides liquefied. He genuinely cared about the answer. "I do."

It dawned on her then that Leo did a lot behind the scenes—far more than she'd realized. Almost as if he preferred for no one to know about all the wonderful gestures he made or that he was such a kind person underneath. Was he afraid she'd figure out he cared about her more than he let on?

"Good." The worry slipped from his expression and was

replaced with something that looked an awful lot like affection. "The last thing I want is for you to feel anxious or
insecure."

Perfect segue. They shared a drive for security. Surely
he'd understand her need to settle things. "You know what
would make me feel a lot less anxious? If I knew what was
going on between us." Emboldened by the fact that Leo had
cared enough to rush home for her, she went on. "We're supposed to enjoy each other's company when we cross paths,
but we never cross paths."

"We just went out a week ago," he protested with a glint
in his eye that warned her to tread carefully.

She wasn't going to. If Leo pulled another disappearing
act, this might be her only chance to make her case. Besides, he said they could talk about anything.

"Exactly. A whole week ago and we haven't spoken since
then, other than a terse 'Good morning.' I can't handle your
life if I'm not in it. Besides, our relationship won't ever develop without deliberate interaction. On both our parts."

"Daniella." He put a thumb to his temple. Great, now she
was giving him a headache. "What are you asking of me?"

He said it as if she hoped he'd blow through the door and
ravish her, when all she really wanted was a conversation
over a nice glass of wine. "For starters, call me Dannie. I
want to be friends. Don't you?"

Wariness sprang into his stance. "Depends on your definition of friends. The last time you brought that up, I got the
distinct impression it was a euphemism for something else."

"You mean sex?" Oh, Scarlett had just been chomping at
the bit to get in the middle of this conversation, hadn't she?

Leo gave a short nod. "Well, to be blunt."

Oh, no. There was that word again. Her last fight with
Rob flashed through her mind and she swallowed. Was she
trying to ruin everything?

But Leo wasn't a spineless, insecure guy like Rob who

couldn't handle a woman's honest opinion. Besides, this was her marriage and she was prepared to go to the mat for it.

"Our marriage apparently calls for blunt. Since I might not get another opportunity to speak to you this century, here it is, spelled out for you. My offer of friendship is not a veiled invitation to jump me."

His brows rose. "Then what is it?"

Laughter bubbled from her mouth. "Guess I don't spell as well as I think I do. Didn't we decide our relationship would eventually be intimate?" *Not blunt enough.* "Sorry, I mean, that we'd eventually have sex?"

To Leo's credit, he didn't flinch. "We did decide that. I envision it happening very far in the future."

Gee, that made her feel all warm and fuzzy. "Great. Except intimacy is about so much more than shedding clothes, Leo. Did you think we'd wake up one day and just hop into bed? It doesn't work like that. There's an intellectual side to intimacy that evolves through spending time together. By becoming *friends*. I want to know you. Your thoughts. Dreams. Sex starts in here." She tapped her forehead. "At least it does for me."

"You want to be romanced," he said flatly.

"I'm female. The math shouldn't be that hard to do."

"Math is one of my best skills."

What was that supposed to mean? That he'd done the math and knew that's what she wanted—but didn't care? She stumbled back a step.

With her new distance, the colors of the Monet swirled again, turning from a picture of a girl back into a jumble of blotches.

She and Leo needed to get on the same page. She took a deep breath. "How did *you* think we were going to get from point A to point B?"

"I never seemed to have any trouble getting a woman interested before," he grumbled without any real heat. "Usually it's getting them uninterested that's the problem."

Ah, so she'd guessed correctly from the very beginning. "You've never had to invest any energy in a relationship before, have you?"

Gorgeous, well-spoken, rich men probably never did as often as women surely threw themselves at them. He'd probably gone through a series of meaningless encounters with interchangeable women.

"I don't have time for a relationship, Daniella," he said quietly, which only emphasized his deliberate use of her full name all the more. "That's why I married you."

Blunt. And devastating. She nearly reeled from it.

This was what he'd been telling her since the beginning, but she'd been determined to connect the dots in a whole new way, creating a mess of an Impressionist painting that looked like *nothing* when she stepped back to view the whole. The spectacular kiss, the security system, the gentle concern—none of it had signaled anything special.

He'd meant what he said. He didn't *want* to invest energy in a relationship. That's why he cut himself off from people. Too much effort. Too much trouble. Too much fill-in-the-blank.

There was no friendship on the horizon, no tenderness, no progression toward intimacy. He expected her to get naked, get pleasured and get out. Eventually.

She nodded. "I see. We'll enjoy each other's company when we cross paths and then go our separate ways." *He'd* been the one euphemizing sex and she'd missed it.

Her heart twisted painfully. But this wasn't news. She just hadn't realized that being in a marriage that wasn't a marriage was worse than being alone.

How could Elise's computer have matched her with Leo? Oh, sure, neither of them had professed an interest in a love match, which was more of a tiny white lie in her case, but to not even be *friends?* It was depressing.

Leo looked relieved. "I'm glad we talked, then. To answer

your earlier question, you're everything I'd hoped. I'm very happy with my choice of wife. Jenna wasn't right at all."

Because she'd inadvisably bucked the rule: don't ask Leo for more than he chooses to give.

"Speaking of which," he continued, "I'd like you to plan a dinner party for twenty guests in about two weeks. Does that give you enough time?"

"Of course."

Two weeks?

Panic flipped her stomach inside out. How would she organize an entire party in two weeks? Well, she'd just have to.

This was why Elise matched her with Leo, and running his personal life was what she'd signed up for. She couldn't lose sight of that. "I'd be happy to handle that for you. Can you email me the guest list?"

He nodded. "Tommy Garrett is the guest of honor. Make sure you pick a date he's available. No point in having the party if he can't be there. Any questions?"

A million and five. "Not right now. I'll start on it immediately."

That was the key to enduring a marriage that wasn't a marriage. Jump into her job with both feet and keep so busy she didn't have time to castigate herself. After all, if she'd begun to believe this marriage might become more than an arrangement because of a few sparks, it was her fault. Not Leo's.

Her mother was being taken care of. Dannie was, too. Furthermore, she'd spoken her mind with as much blunt opinion as she could muster and Leo hadn't kicked her out. What else could she possibly want? This was real life, not a fairy tale, and she had work to do.

She bid Leo good-night, her head full of party plans. It wasn't until her cheek hit the pillow that she remembered the total discomfort on Leo's face when he thought friendship had been code for sex.

If he expected her to get naked, get pleasured and get out, why wouldn't he take immediate advantage of what he assumed she was offering?

Leo's forehead thunked onto his desk, right in the middle of the clause outlining the expiration date for his proposal to finance Miles Bennett's software company.

That woke him up in a hurry.

Why didn't he go upstairs to bed? It was 3:00 a.m. Normal people slept at this time of night, but not him. No—Leo Reynolds had superpowers, granting him the ability to go days without sleep, because otherwise he'd get behind. John Hu had slipped through his fingers at the alumni gala and was even now working with another backer. It should have been Leo. Could have been Leo, if he'd been on his game.

And not spending a good portion of his energy recalling his wife's soft and gorgeous smile. Or how much he enjoyed seeing her on the porch waiting for him, the way she had been tonight.

Sleep was for weaker men.

Younger men.

He banished that thought. Thirty-five—thirty-six in two months—wasn't old. But lately he felt every day of his age. Ten years ago he could have read contracts and proposals until dawn and then inhaled a couple of espressos to face the day with enthusiasm.

Now? Not so much. And it would only get worse as he approached forty. He had to make every day count while he could. No distractions. No seductive, tantalizing friendships that would certainly turn into more than he could allow.

Maybe he should up his workout regimen from forty-five minutes a day to an hour. Eat a little better instead of shoveling takeout into his mouth while he hunched over his desk at the office.

Gentle hands on his shoulders woke him.

"Leo," Daniella murmured as she pressed against his arm. "You fell asleep at your desk."

He bolted upright. Blearily, he glanced up at Daniella and then at his watch. Six-thirty. Normally he was already at work by now.

"Thanks for waking me up," he croaked and cleared his throat. "I don't know how that happened."

She lifted a brow. "Because you were tired?"

Her stylish dress was flowery and flirty, but clearly altered to fit perfectly, and her hair hung loose down her back. Flawlessly applied makeup accentuated her face and plumped her lips and he tore his gaze away from them.

"Besides that." He shuffled the Miles Bennett proposal back into some semblance of order without another glance at his wife. Though he wanted to soak in the sight of her. How did she look so amazing this early in the morning?

"Let me make you a cup of coffee," she offered and perched a hip on his desk as if she planned to stay awhile.

"I have to go. I'm late."

She stopped him with a warm hand on his bare forearm, below his rolled-up sleeve. "It's Saturday. Take ten minutes for coffee. I'd like to make it for you. Indulge me."

The plea in her eyes unhitched something inside. After he'd thrown up barrier upon barrier, she still wanted to make him coffee. How could he gracefully refuse? "Thanks. Let me take a quick a shower and I'll meet you in the kitchen."

The shower cleared the mist of sleep from his mind. He dressed in freshly pressed khakis and a button-down shirt instead of a suit since it was Saturday. A concession he couldn't recall making before. What had possessed him to do it today?

When he walked into the kitchen, the rich, roasted smell of coffee greeted him only a moment before his wife did.

She smiled and handed him a steaming mug. "Perfect timing."

He took a seat at the inlaid bistro table off the kitchen

and sipped. Liquid heaven slid down his throat. He wasn't surprised she'd somehow mastered brewing a cup of coffee to his tastes. "You even got the half-and-half right."

"Practice makes perfect." She slid into the opposite seat and folded her hands into her lap serenely.

Something in her tone piqued his interest. "How long have you been practicing?"

"Since the wedding." She shrugged, and her smile made light of the admission. "I've been trying to get up before you every morning so I could make you coffee. Today's the first day I succeeded."

The coffee didn't go down as smoothly on the next sip. Why had she put so much effort into something so meaningless? "That wasn't part of our agreement. You should sleep as late as you want."

"Our agreement includes making sure your life runs fluidly, especially at home. If you want coffee in the morning, it's my job to ensure you get it."

My job.

Daniella was in the employee box in his head, but he'd never expected her to view herself that way. Of course, why would she view herself any differently when all he talked about was their arrangement?

The cup of coffee—and the ironed clothes, ready at a moment's notice—took on implications of vast proportions. Everything EA International promised, he'd received. Daniella had slipped into her role as if she'd always been his wife. The staff liked her and already deferred to her judgment, which freed him from having to deal with the cook's grocery account or the gardener's questions about seasonal plants.

She was incredible.

If only he'd gotten the wife he really meant for EA International to match him with—one he could ignore—his life would be perfect.

It wasn't Daniella's fault he suffered from all-or-nothing syndrome. Intensity was the major backbone of his temperament. That's why he didn't draw anymore. Once he started, he could fill an entire notebook with landscapes, people's faces—Carmen's beautiful form—and then scout around for a blank book to begin filling that one, too.

If it hadn't been for his calculus teacher's timely intervention, Leo would probably be a starving artist right now, doodling in the margins of take-out menus and cursing the woman who'd been his first model. And his first lover. He'd been infatuated with capturing her shape on the paper, infatuated with her. His teacher had opened his eyes to his slipping grades, the upcoming SATs and a potentially bleak future mirroring his parents' if he didn't stop skipping school to draw Carmen. Fortunately, he'd listened and turned his intensity toward his education, then Reynolds Capital Management, vowing to never again let his obsessive personality loose on anything other than success.

He knew it the way he knew the sky was blue: the second he let himself taste Daniella again, that would be it. He wouldn't stop until he'd filled them both. And once wouldn't be enough. He'd be too weak to focus on anything except her.

"Thanks for the coffee. I should go." Leo shoved away from the table.

Her warm almond-colored eyes sought his. "Before you do, I have a couple of questions about the party for Tommy Garrett."

He settled back into the uncomfortable wrought-iron chair. "Sure."

It was the only subject that could have gotten him to stay. The party was critically important since Garrett had narrowed down the field to two firms. Leo didn't intend to lose out to the other guy.

She leaned forward on her forearms with all the attentiveness of someone about to leap into a negotiation. "What does Garrett Engineering make?"

Not *What china should I use?* or *What hors d'oeuvres should I serve?* "Why does that matter?"

"I'm curious. But also because I'd like to know more about the guest of honor. From you. I'll call his admin but I want your opinion. It will help me plan the menu and the decorations."

There was something hypnotic about Daniella's voice that pulled at him. He could listen to her recite the phone book. "I wouldn't have thought of that."

Her mouth tipped up in a smile that was so sweet, it pulled one from him. "That's why I'm here. Tell me."

"Tommy's a bit of a whiz kid." Leo pursed his lips as he contemplated the most relevant facets of the man—and he used the term *man* in the loosest sense—he wanted to do business with. "One of those geniuses who wears Converse sneakers and hoodies to work. He's just as likely to spout Xbox stats as engineering principles and no one cares because he graduated summa cum laude from Yale. He designed a modification to the way gasoline is consumed in a car that will increase gas mileage by almost double. It's revolutionary."

"You like him."

"Yes." The admission surprised him.

He hadn't thought one way or another about whether he *liked* Tommy Garrett. Leo liked the instant profitability of Garrett's design. He liked the idea of orchestrating the financing and letting Tommy be the face of the venture. Tommy had a lot of spirit, a quick wit and, despite the hoodies, he also had a work ethic Leo respected. It wasn't unusual to have a conversation at eleven o'clock on a Saturday night to brainstorm ideas.

Impressed, he cocked his head at his wife. "How did you ferret that out from what I said?"

"Because I listened with my eyes." Her smile widened as he snorted. "I could see it in your expression."

Leo tried to scowl but he was enjoying the back-and-forth just as much as the sound of Daniella's voice.

"It doesn't matter whether I like him. We stand to make a lot of money together and that's the key to our association. The party is paramount. He's got another potential partner on the hook and I need to convince him to go with Reynolds."

"What percentage stake in his company did you offer in the proposal?" He did a double take and she laughed. "I read up on how venture capital works. How can I help you land the deal if I don't know what I'm talking about?"

Perhaps he should have had a cup of coffee with his wife long before now. "I guess I thought you'd handle the party details and I'd handle Garrett. But I'm reconsidering that plan."

If he unleashed the formidable force of Daniella on Tommy Garrett, the poor guy probably wouldn't even know what hit him.

"You do that. Tell me more."

Her smile relaxed him. She had the best smile, easily given, genuine. He liked seeing it on her, but liked being the one to put it there even more. Making women smile wasn't a skill he felt particular proficient at, though. Maybe he should take a cue from his wife and practice.

"Not only will his design fit new engines, it retrofits to existing engines so it can be sold to both consumers and automobile manufacturers. It's almost miraculous. He might as well have designed a way to print money."

"Sounds like you really believe in the product. I can't imagine why Mr. Garrett would choose another venture capital firm."

"Because it's business. Not personal. And actually, I couldn't care less what the product is as long as the entrepreneur comes to me with a solid business plan and proven commitment."

"All business is personal, Leo," she said quietly. "If you

didn't spend so much time behind the scenes, you might discover that for yourself."

"Behind the scenes is where I function best." Ensuring the players never had to worry about money as they took center stage—that was his comfort zone. He couldn't afford to get truly involved or he'd bury himself.

Her expression softened, drawing him in. "But in the middle of things is where the best experiences are."

He had the distinct impression they weren't talking about Tommy Garrett anymore and had moved on to something he did not want to acknowledge in any way, shape or form.

"Thanks for the coffee. I'm going to head in to the office." He glanced at his watch. Almost seven-thirty, but there was no rush hour on Saturday, so he hadn't lost too much time. "If you have any more questions about the party, don't hesitate to call me."

"Have a good day." She covered his hand with hers and squeezed. "Don't look now, Leo, but I think we just had a friendly conversation. Are you shocked it didn't kill you?"

No, the shock happened when he laughed.

Her return smile stayed with him as he climbed into his car. The gas gauge needle pointed to full. When was the last time he'd even glanced at it? He drove to the office and instead of thinking about whatever else should be on his mind, he thought about Daniella.

Dannie. Maybe she could be Dannie and that wouldn't kill him, either.

No way. He couldn't imagine allowing it to roll from his tongue.

As much as he wished he could ignore his wife, he was painfully aware she conversely wished he wouldn't. They had an agreement, but it didn't seem to be sticking and she was flesh and blood, not a piece of paper. Or an employee.

And agreements could be terminated.

He was getting what he hoped from this marriage. She wasn't, not fully. If he wanted her to be happy, he had to give a little. Otherwise she might walk. A sick worm of insecurity wiggled into his stomach at the idea of losing a woman who fit into his life so well. And who, against all odds, he liked.

Friends. It didn't sound so terrible. Surely he could handle a friendship with his wife.

Six

Dannie hummed as she drew up proposed menus. She hummed as she perused the guest list Leo emailed her and savored the little thrill she got from the short message at the bottom.

You make a great cup of coffee.

She hummed as she waited on hold to speak with Tommy Garrett's admin and later as she checked off several more things on her to-do list. The tune was aimless. Happy. Half of it was due to finally connecting with Leo on some small level, especially after he'd made it clear he wasn't interested in developing their relationship.

The other half had to do with finding her niche. Growing up, her chief source of entertainment had been old movies and TV shows on the free channels, and she'd always wanted to have her own household like the glamorous women of the '50s. It was everything she'd expected. Being in charge of her domain gave her a heady sense of accomplishment and purpose, which popped out of her mouth in song.

When Leo strode through the door at six o'clock that evening with a small, lopsided grin, her throat seized up and quit working entirely.

"I thought we'd have dinner together," he said as she stared at him, wordless. "If you don't have other plans."

Dinner? *Together?* Why?

"Oh," she squeaked and sucked in a couple of lungfuls

of oxygen in hopes it might jar everything else into functioning. "No plans. I'll let the cook know."

Clothes, she thought as she flew to alert the staff Leo would be dining in. She should change clothes. And open a bottle of wine. Her foot tangled on the edge of the Persian runner lining the stairs to the second floor. *And slow down.* A broken leg wouldn't do her any favors.

This was the first time she'd dine alone with Leo since they'd gotten married. It was practically like a date. Better than a date, because it had been his idea and totally a surprise. She wanted it to be flawless and so enjoyable he couldn't wait to do it again.

In spite of a triple-digit pulse and feeling as though her tongue was too big for her mouth, she could get used to that kind of surprise.

Dannie opened her closet and surveyed her small but lovely wardrobe. She'd never owned such amazing clothes and shoes before and never got tired of dressing up. She slipped into a casual black cocktail dress that veed over her breasts, buckled her feet into the sexiest Louboutins she owned and curled her lip at the state of her hair. Quickly she brushed it out and twisted it up into a sleek chignon.

Done. That was as close as she could get to looking like the kind of wife a man would enjoy coming home to. She took her time descending the stairs in her five-inch heels and spent a few minutes in the wine cellar glancing at labels until she put her hand on a sauvignon blanc *Wine Spectator* had talked up. A perfect date-night wine.

She stuck the bottle in a bucket of ice and left it on the formal dining room sideboard to chill until dinner, which the cook informed her would be a few minutes yet. At loose ends, she tormented the place settings until the silverware was either perfectly placed or exactly where it'd been when she started. She couldn't tell, which meant *stop obsessing.*

The cook announced dinner at last. She went to fetch Leo and found him in his study, of course, attention decisively on his laptop. His suit jacket hung on the back of the leather chair. His shirtsleeves were rolled up on his forearms and he'd already removed his tie. Rumpled Leo might be her favorite.

Leaning on the doorjamb, she watched him type in efficient strokes, pause and type again. Mentoring anonymously via chat again, most likely. She hated to interrupt. But not really.

"Dinner's ready."

He glanced up without lifting his head and the way he peeked out from under his lashes was so sexy, it sent a spiral of heat through her tummy.

"Right now?" he asked.

"Um, yeah." She cleared the multitude of frogs camping out on her vocal cords. "We don't want it to get cold."

He typed for another couple of seconds and then closed the laptop's lid with a snick as he stood. "That would be a shame."

Boldly, she watched him approach, aware her body blocked the doorway and curious what he'd do about it. "I'm a believer in hot food, myself."

He stopped a healthy distance away when he apparently realized she wasn't budging. "I'm looking forward to a home-cooked meal. Thought I should start eating better. I've had too much takeout lately."

Whose fault is that? "Just the food, then? The company wasn't a draw?"

"Of course the company was a factor." Something flickered in the depths of his blue eyes and heat climbed all over her.

Oh, that had all sorts of interesting possibilities locked inside. They gazed at each other for a long, delicious moment, and he didn't look away. Or back up.

Then he gestured to the hall. "Shall we, Mrs. Reynolds?"

And somehow, that was far more intimate than calling her Dannie. Deliberate? Oh, goodness, she hoped so.

Leo's capable palm settled into the small of her back as they walked and she felt the contact all the way to the soles of her feet. Something had changed. Hadn't it? Was her coffee *that* good?

In the dining room, Leo drew back the heavy chair and allowed her to sit on the brocade cushion before pushing it in for her. Then he expertly poured the wine to exactly the same level in both glasses on the first try—impressive evidence of how good Leo was with both detail and his hands.

Not that she'd needed additional clues the man hid amazing things under his workaholic shell. Were they at a point where she could admit how outrageously attracted to Leo she was? Or was that going past blunt into another realm entirely?

Placing her glass on the table before her, he took the seat catercorner to hers instead of across the table. "So we can talk without shouting," he said when she raised her eyebrows.

All small, small gestures, but so huge to her romance-starved soul. Flutters spread from her stomach to every organ in her body. Especially her heart.

For whatever reason, he was trying, really *trying,* to give her some of his time. But what was his intent? The friendship she'd hoped for or merely a small gesture toward crossing her path?

She'd keep her wits about her and under no circumstances would she read anything into what was essentially just dinner. As they dug into Greek salads served with crusty bread, she stuck to discussing her progress on the party. The more the wine flowed, the more relaxed they both became.

About halfway through her swordfish, she brought up the one thing she'd been dying to ask since the night of their marriage. "Do you still draw?"

Leo's fork froze over a piece of grilled zucchini. "How did you know about that?"

"Your mother told me."

He grimaced. "I should have guessed. She still has every piece of paper I've ever touched with a pencil."

Which was no answer at all. "Is it a sensitive subject?"

"No." Carefully, he cut a hunk of fish and chewed it in a spectacular stall tactic she recognized a mile away. He didn't want to discuss his art, that much was clear.

"So, never mind then. It's not important," she lied. His reaction said there was more to the story and it was very important, but she didn't want to alienate him. "Tell me something else instead. Why venture capital?"

His expression warmed. "If you're good, you can make a lot of money. You just have to recognize the right opportunities."

"Are you good?"

She already knew the answer but was curious what he thought about the empire he'd built. Most of her research into the complexities of venture capital had been conducted by reading articles about her husband's successful company before she'd even spoken to him on the phone for the first time.

"I'm competent. But I've made my share of mistakes."

As if that was something to be ashamed of. He seemed determined to downplay all his positives. "Everyone makes mistakes. You've recovered from yours quite well. The reputation of Reynolds Capital Management is unparalleled."

He inclined his head with a pleased smile. "It's a work in progress."

Fascinated with the way his eyes turned deeper blue when he engaged, she drained her wineglass and propped her chin on a curled hand. This was exactly what she'd envisioned their friendship would look like. "So how do you recognize the right opportunity?"

The cook bustled in and cleared their empty dinner plates, replacing them with bananas Foster for dessert. She lit the rum and blew it out in an impressive culinary display, then efficiently disappeared.

Leo spooned the dessert into his mouth and murmured appreciatively before answering Dannie's question. "Experience. Gut instinct. A large percentage of success is simply showing up. I create the remaining percentage by getting there first and staying until everyone else has gone home."

"Do you see your job as creative?" Dannie took a small bite of banana, gratified Leo liked the dessert as much as she did, but determined to keep him engaged in conversation. A full mouth wouldn't lend itself well to that.

He pursed his lips. "In a way, I suppose. Without backing, a lot of entrepreneurs' ideas would never see the light of day. I provide the platform for other people to tap into their creativity."

Which was what he'd done for her—given her the opportunity and the means to be exactly what she wanted to be. A wife. If tonight was any indication, Leo had changed his mind about spending time getting to know each other. Maybe she'd get the relationship—in some form or fashion—she craved out of it, too.

"You're the puppet master, then," she said.

"Not at all. I never stick my fingers in the pie. Micromanagement is not the most effective way to do business. I'm the money, not the talent."

"But you have talent," she protested.

His expression dimmed. "You've never seen one of my drawings."

"I meant you have a talent for recognizing the right opportunity." She smiled in hopes of keeping things friendly. "But I have a feeling you've got artistic talent, too. Draw me something and I'll let you know."

She was pushing him, she knew she was. But she wanted to know him, and his mysterious artistic side intrigued her.

"I don't draw anymore," he said, the syllables so clipped they nearly drew blood.

Message received. They hadn't connected nearly as deeply as she'd hoped, but they'd only just begun. One day, maybe he'd open up that part to her. "You've moved on to bigger and better canvases. Now you're creating your art with completely different tools."

Leo pushed his chair back. "Maybe. I've got some work to finish up. Thanks for dinner."

He escaped, leaving her to contemplate whether to open another bottle of wine in celebration of a successful dinner or to drown her disappointment since Leo had abandoned her once again.

Drown her disappointment. Definitely.

She located a bottle of pinot that went better with her mood than white wine and filled her glass almost to the rim. Then she called her mother to talk to someone uncomplicated and who she knew loved her always and forever, no matter what.

"Dannie," her mother cried when she answered. "Louise just told me. Thank you!"

Dannie grinned. Her mother's caregiver had turned into a friend almost instantly, and the two were constantly chattering. "Thanks for what?"

"The cruise, silly. The Bahamas! I'm so excited, I can hardly stand it." Her mother clucked. "I can't believe you kept this a secret, you bad girl."

The wineglass was somehow already half-empty again, but she didn't think she'd drunk enough to be *that* confused. "I didn't know. What cruise?"

"Oh. You don't? Louise said Leo booked us on a seven-day cruise, leaving out of Galveston. Next week. I thought for sure you suggested it. Well, thank him for us. For me, especially."

A steamroller flattened her heart. Her husband was a startling, deeply nuanced man underneath it all.

Dannie listened to her mother gush for several more minutes and managed to get a couple of sentences in sideways in spite of the question marks shooting from her brain. Were Leo's nice gestures indicative of deeper feelings he didn't want to admit for some reason? No man did a complete about-face without a motive. Had he come home for dinner in hopes of developing a friendship—or more?

Regardless, *something* had changed, all right, and her husband owed her a straight answer about what.

Sometimes talking to Leo was worse than pulling teeth, like their conversation after her text about the fake noise. Her marriage didn't just call for blunt—if she wanted to get answers, it apparently called for Scarlett, as well. And Scarlett had been squashed up inside for a really long time.

Three glasses of wine put a good dose of liquid courage in Dannie's blood. She ended the call and cornered Mr. Behind the Scenes in his office.

She barged into the study. Leo glanced up, clearly startled. She rounded the desk to pierce him with the evil eye, not the slightest bit concerned about the scattered paperwork under his fingers.

"About this cruise." Bumping a hip against the back of his chair, she swiveled it so he faced her, swinging his knees to either side of hers.

Not the slightest bit intimidated, he locked gazes with her. "What about it?"

Good gravy, when he was this close to her, the man practically dripped some sort of special brand of masculinity that tightened her thighs and put a tingle between them.

"Are you going to deny you did something nice for my mother?"

"No?" He lifted his brows. "Or yes, depending on whether *you* thought it was nice, I suppose."

His voice hitched so slightly, she almost didn't notice it until she registered the rising heat in his expression. *Oh, my.* That was lovely. Her proximity was putting a tingle in his parts, too.

"It was nice. She's very excited. Thank you."

He sat back in his chair, as if trying to distance himself

from the sizzling electricity. "Why do you seem a little, ah, agitated?"

"Agitated." She inched forward, not about to give up any ground, and her knees grazed the insides of his thighs. "I *am* agitated. Because I don't get why you won't ever acknowledge the wonderful things you do."

His gaze flicked down the length of her body and back up again slowly. "What would be the point of that?"

Her husband was nuanced all right…and also incredibly frustrating. He likely refused to take credit for his actions because that would require too much of an *investment* from him. Someone might want to reciprocate and make him feel good, too, and then there'd be a whole cycle of emotions. *That* would never do.

She huffed out a noise of disgust and poked him in the chest, leaning into it as her temper rose. "You do these things and it's almost like you'd prefer I didn't find out you've got a kind streak. Jig's up, Leo."

He removed her finger from his rib cage, curling it between his and holding it away from his body instead of releasing it. Probably so she wouldn't wound him, but his skin sparked against hers and nearly buckled her knees.

The memory of *that kiss* exploded in her mind and heightened the gathering heat at her core.

But she still didn't know what was happening between them—friends, lovers, more? Maybe it was actually none of the above. If she gave in to the passion licking through her, would he disappear afterward until the next time he wanted sex? Or could this be the start of something special?

"You have an active imagination," he said.

She rolled her eyes to hide the yearning he'd surely see in them. "Yeah, I get it. You're a ruthless, cold-blooded businessman who'd rather be caught dead than disclosing your real name to a couple of students. What's it going to take to get you off the sidelines and into the middle of your own life?"

That was the key to unlocking his no-emotional-investment stance on marriage. It had to be. If he'd only wade into the thick of things and stop cutting himself off, he'd see how wonderful a real relationship could be. How satisfying. Fulfilling. Surely their marriage could be more than an occasional crossing of paths. He needed her to help him see that.

Leo's frame tensed and slowly he rose from the chair, pushing into her space. "I like the sidelines."

Toe-to-toe, they eyed each other, the impasse almost as palpable in the atmosphere as the swirl of awareness. "Why did you book my mother on a cruise?"

He shrugged, lashes low, shuttering his thoughts from her. "I thought she would like it."

"That's only half the truth. You did it for me." A huge leap. But she didn't think she was wrong.

Their gazes locked and the intensity shafted through her. "What if I did?"

Her pulse stuttered. Coffee, then dinner. Now this. What was he trying to accomplish? "Well, I'm shocked you'd admit that. Before you know it, we'll be buying each other birthday cards and taking vacations together. Like real couples."

Like the marriage of her dreams. Just because neither of them had expressed an interest in a love match didn't mean it was completely impossible to have found one. What better security was there between two people than that of knowing someone would love you forever?

He threw up a palm. "Let's don't get out of hand now."

She advanced, pushing his palm into her cleavage, burning her skin with his touch and backing him against the desk. She wanted to bond with her husband in the most elemental way possible. To complete the journey from A to B and see what they really could have together.

"I like getting out of hand."

"Do you have a response for everything?" His fingertips curled, nipping into her skin.

"If you don't like what I have to say, then shut me up."

His expression turned carnal. He watched her as he slid an index finger down the valley between her breasts and hooked the neckline of her dress. In a flash, he hauled her forward, capturing her lips in a searing kiss.

On legs turned to jelly, she melted into it, into him as he wrapped his arms around her, finally giving her what she'd been after since she walked in. Maybe since before that.

Greedy for all of him, she settled for the small, hot taste of Leo against her mouth. With a moan, she tilted her head and parted his lips with hers. She plunged into the heat, seeking his tongue with hers, and he obliged her with strong, heated licks.

His arms tightened, crushing her against his torso, aligning their hips. Need soaked her senses as his hard ridge nudged her. She cupped the back of his neck as his hand snaked under her dress to caress the back of her thigh.

Yes. As seduction techniques went, he could teach a class.

Soft cotton skimmed under her fingers as she explored the angles and muscles of his back. Delicious. Her husband's body was hard and strong, exactly as she liked, exactly perfect to keep her safe and satisfied at the same time.

The kiss deepened and the hand on her thigh inched higher, trailing sparkling warmth along with it. She tilted her hips in silent invitation, begging him to take those fingers wherever he so desired.

But then he pulled away, chest heaving, and spun her to face the wall, his torso hot against her spine.

"Daniella," he murmured in her ear, and his fingertip traced the line of her dress where it met the flesh of her back, toying with the zipper. "I'm about to pull this down and taste every inch of you until we're both mindless. Is that what you want?"

Damp heat flooded her and she shuddered. "Only if you call me Dannie while you do it."

He strangled over a groan and moved her forward a confusing foot, then two. "I can't do this."

"Don't say you don't want me." *So close. Don't back off now.* She whirled and tilted her chin at the bulge in his pants she'd felt branding her bottom. "I already know that's not true. You don't kiss someone like that unless you mean it."

"That's the problem." Breath rattled in his throat on a raw exhale. "You want me to mean it in a very different way than I do mean it. I'd rather not disappoint you and that's where this is headed. Making love will not change the fact that tomorrow I'm still going to work a sixteen-hour day, leaving little time for you. Until both of us can live with that, I need you to *walk away.*"

He was blocking himself off from her again, but for a very good reason. The rejection didn't even bother her. How could it? He was telling her he didn't want to treat her like a one-night stand.

That set off a whole different sort of flutter.

"I'm walking." *For now.* She needed a cooler head— among other parts—to navigate this unexpected twist to their marriage.

She skirted the desk, putting much-needed distance between them.

Raking a hand through his hair, he sank into the chair with a pained grimace. "Good night."

"This was the best date I've ever been on."

With that parting shot, she left him to his paperwork, already plotting how to crack that shell open a little wider and find the strong, amazing heart she knew beat beneath. He thought they were holding off until she was okay with no-emotional-investment sex, but he was already so emotionally invested, he was afraid of hurting her.

That's what had changed. Somehow, she had to help him see what he truly needed from her.

If a large percentage of success happened by showing up and then outwaiting the competition, she could do that. Yes, her competition was an intangible, unfathomable challenge called *work,* but the reward compensated for the effort.

Time for a little relocation project.

Seven

The silky feel of Daniella's thigh haunted Leo for days. And if he managed to block it from his mind, her fiery responses when he kissed her replaced that memory immediately.

It didn't seem to matter how many spreadsheets he opened on his laptop. Or how many proposals for new ventures he heard. Or whether he slept at the office because he lacked the strength to be in the same house with Daniella. Sleeping as a whole didn't work so well when his wife invaded his unconscious state to star in erotic dreams.

There was no neat, predefined box for her. For any of this. It was messing him up.

He hadn't seen Daniella in four days and the scent of strawberries still lingered in his nose.

Fingers snapped before his eyes and Leo blinked. Mrs. Gordon was at his desk, peering at him over her reading glasses. "I called your name four times."

"Sorry. Long night."

Mrs. Gordon's gaze flicked to the other end of Leo's office, where a sitting area overlooked downtown Dallas. "Because that couch is too short for a big, strapping young man like you."

He grinned in spite of being caught daydreaming, a mortifying situation if it had been anyone other than his admin. "Are you flirting with me?"

"Depends. How much trouble are you in at home?" Her

raised eyebrows wiped the smile off his face. "Enough that an old woman looks pretty good right about now?"

"I'm not in trouble at home. What does that even mean? You think I got kicked out?" He frowned.

It bothered him because deep down, he knew he'd taken the coward's way out. Being friends with his wife hadn't worked out so well. She was too sexy, too insightful.

"Au contraire. You're in trouble. It's all over your face."

"That's ridiculous." Leo scrubbed his jaw, not that he believed for a second he could erase whatever she thought she saw there, and fingered a spot he'd missed shaving that morning. The executive bathroom off his office left nothing to be desired, but two hours of sleep had affected his razor hand, apparently.

"Forget her birthday, did you?" Mrs. Gordon nodded sagely.

Soon we'll be buying each other birthday cards, Daniella had said, but he didn't even know when her birthday was. "Our marriage isn't like that."

Mrs. Gordon's mouth flattened. Her favorite way to remind him she had his number. "Why do I get the feeling you and your wife have differing opinions about that?"

He sighed and the hollow feeling in his stomach grew worse because she was right. "Did you hear from Tommy Garrett's people yet?"

"Don't change the subject. I'd have told you if I heard from Garrett and you know it. Just like you know you've got a problem at home that you better address sooner rather than later. I've been married for thirty years. I know things." She clucked. "Take my advice. Buy her flowers and sleep in your own bed tonight."

He had the distinct impression Mrs. Gordon believed his wife would be in the bed, as well. He didn't correct her.

After all, what sort of weakness did *that* reveal?

He couldn't have sex with his own wife because he'd backed himself into an impossible corner. She wanted some kind of intimacy, which he couldn't give her, and he didn't want to hurt her. He'd thought friendship might be enough, but friends apparently talked about aspects of themselves that he just couldn't share. Especially not drawing. It was tied to his obsessive side, which he kept under wraps.

How long would Dannie remain patient before finding someone who *would* give her what she wanted? Women in his life usually lasted about two months before bailing.

He'd never cared before. Never dreamed he'd experience moments of pure panic at the thought of Daniella going the way of previous companions. They had a convenient marriage, but that meant it would be easy to dissolve when it was no longer convenient for her.

By 9:00 p.m., Leo couldn't argue with his admin's logic any longer. His body screamed to collapse in a dead sleep, but he couldn't physically make himself lie down on that couch.

What was he really accomplishing by avoiding his wife? When he'd told her to walk after nearly stripping her bare right there in his study, she had. No questions, no hysterics, no accusations. She was fine with holding off on advancing their relationship.

Daniella wasn't the problem. He was.

He was a weak daydreamer who'd rather scratch a pencil over pieces of paper all day and then spend several hours exploring his wife's naked body that night. And do it again the next day, abandoning all his goals with Reynolds Capital Management in a heartbeat for incredible sex and a few pictures. He'd done exactly that before, and he feared the consequences would be far worse if he did it with Daniella.

If he could resist the lure of drawing, he could resist the Helen of Troy he'd married. As long as he didn't kiss her again, he had a good shot at controlling himself. Of course, the real problem was that deep down, he was pretty sure he didn't want to.

He drove to the house he'd bought with his own money,

where he'd created a safe, secure home that no one could take away. The lights always shone brightly and the boiler always heated water. And Leo would die before allowing that to change.

Daniella wasn't downstairs. Good. Hopefully she was already asleep in her room. If so, he could get all the way to his bedroom without running into her.

As he passed the study, his neck heated as the dream from last night roared into his mind—the one where he finished that kiss from the other night by spinning Daniella facedown onto the desk, pushing up that sexy dress and plunging into her wet heat again and again until she convulsed around him with a cry.

That room was off-limits from now on. He'd buy a new desk and have it moved into his bedroom.

So exhausted he could hardly breathe, he climbed the stairs and stumbled to his bedroom. No lights. Too bright for his weary eyes.

His shin cracked against something heavy and knocked him off balance. He cursed as his hand shot out to break his fall and scraped across…whatever he'd tripped over.

Snick. Light flooded the dark room via the lamp on his bedside table.

"Are you okay?" Daniella asked.

His head snapped up in shock. "What are you doing here? Why are you in my bed?"

His wife, hair swept back in a ponytail and heavy lidded with sleep, regarded him calmly from beneath the covers of *his bed.* "It's my bed, too, now. I moved into your room. If you'd come home occasionally, you might have known I rearranged the furniture."

The throb in his shin rivaled the sudden throb in his temples. "I didn't… You ca—" He sucked in a fortifying breath. "You had no right to do that."

She studied him for a moment, her face contemplative and breathtakingly beautiful in its devoid-of-makeup state.

"You said I should think of this as my home. Anything I wanted to change, you'd be willing to discuss."

"Exactly. *Discuss.*"

The firm cross of her arms said she'd gladly have done so, if he hadn't been hiding out at the office.

"You're bleeding." She threw the covers back, slipped out of bed and crossed the room to take his hand, murmuring over the shallow cut.

As she was wearing a pair of plaid pants cinched low on her slim hips and a skintight tank top that left her midriff bare, a little blood was the least of his problems.

"And you're cold," he muttered and tore his gaze from the hard peaks beneath the tank top, which scarcely contained dark, delicious-looking nipples.

Too late. Heat shuddered through his groin, tightening his pants uncomfortably. Couldn't she find some clothes that she wasn't in danger of bursting out of? Like a suit of armor, perhaps?

"I'll be fine." She tugged on his hand, flipping the long ponytail over her shoulder. "Come into the bathroom. Let me put a bandage on this cut."

"It's not that bad. Go back to bed. I'll sleep somewhere else." As if he had a prayer of sleep tonight.

Adrenaline coursed through his veins. Muscles strained to reach for her, to yank on the bow under her navel and let those plaid pants pool around her ankles. One tiny step and he could have her in his arms.

He tried to pull away but she clamped down on his hand, surprisingly strong for someone so sensuously built.

"Leo." Her breasts rose on a long sigh and under her breath she muttered something about him that sounded suspiciously uncomplimentary. "Please let me help you. It's my fault you're hurt."

It was her fault he had a hard-on the size of Dallas. But it was not her fault that he'd been avoiding her and thus didn't know the layout of his own bedroom any longer. "Fine."

He followed her into the bathroom, noting the addition of a multitude of mysterious girly accoutrements, and decided he preferred remaining ignorant of their purposes.

Daniella fussed over him, washing his cut and patting it dry. In bare feet, she was shorter than he was used to. Normally she had no trouble looking him in the eye when she wore her architecturally impossible and undeniably sexy heels. He hadn't realized how much he liked that.

Or how much he'd also like this slighter, attentive Daniella who took care of him. Fatigue washed over him, muddling his thoughts, and he forgot for a second why it wasn't a good idea to share a bed with her.

"All better." She patted his hand and bent to put the box of bandages under the sink, pulling her pajama pants tight across her rear, four inches from his blistering erection. He closed his eyes.

"About the room sharing," he began.

She brushed his sensitive flesh and his lids flew up. He'd swayed toward her, inadvertently. She glanced up to meet his gaze in the mirror. The incongruity between her state of undress and his buttoned-up suit shouldn't have been so erotic. But it was.

"Are you going to read me the riot act?" she asked, her eyes enormous and guileless and soft. "Or consider the possibilities?"

"Which are?" The second it was out of his mouth, he wished he could take it back. Foggy brain and half-dressed wife did not make for good conversation elements.

"You work a hundred hours a week. Our paths will never cross unless we do it here." She gestured toward the bedroom. "This way, we'll both get what we want."

In the bright bathroom light, the semitransparent tank top left nothing to the imagination. Of course, he already knew what her bare breast looked like and the longer she stood there with the dark circles of her nipples straining against the fabric, the more he wanted to see them both, but this time with no interruptions.

"What do you think I want?"

"You want me." She turned to face him. "All the benefits without the effort, or so you say. I don't believe you. If you wanted that, my dress wouldn't have stayed zipped for longer than five seconds after dinner. Sharing a bedroom offers you a chance to figure out why you let me walk away. It won't infringe on your work hours and it gives me a chance to forge the friendship I want. Before we become physically involved."

That cleared the fog in a hurry. "What are you saying, that you'll be like a *roommate?*"

"You sound disappointed." Her eyebrows rose in challenge. "Would you like to make me a better offer?"

Oh, dear God. She should be negotiating his contracts, not his lawyer.

"You're driving me bananas. No. Worse than that." He squeezed the top of his head but his brain still felt as though she'd twirled it with a spaghetti fork. "What's worse than bananas?"

"Pomegranates," she said decisively. "They're harder to eat and don't taste as good."

He bit back a laugh. Yes, exactly. His incredibly perceptive wife drove him pomegranates. "That about covers it."

"Will you try it my way? Give it a week. Then if you still think sex will complicate our marriage too much, I'll move back to my bedroom. I promise I'll keep my hands to myself." To demonstrate, she laced her fingers over her sexy rear and he swore. She'd done that exact thing in one of his dreams. "If you'll promise the same."

His shin didn't hurt nearly as badly as his aching groin. "Are you seriously suggesting we share a bed platonically?"

"Seriously. Show me you think our marriage is worth it. Sharing a room is the only way we'll figure this out, unless you plan to work less. It's unorthodox, but being married to a workaholic has forced my creative hand, so to speak."

It was definitely creative, he'd give her that, and hit him where it hurt—right where all the guilt lived. If he wanted her to be happy in this marriage and stick with him, he had to prove it.

Her logic left him no good reason not to say yes. Except for the fact that it was insane.

Her seductive brown eyes sucked him in. "What are you going to do, Leo?"

Somehow, she made it sound as if he held all the cards. As if all he had to do was whisper a few romantic phrases in her ear and she'd be putty in his hands. If only it was that easy.

And then she shoved the knife in a little further. "Try it. What's the worst that can happen?"

He groaned as several sleepless nights in a row hit him like a freight train. "I'm certain we're about to find out."

Fatigue and a strong desire to avoid his wife's backup plan if he said no—that was his excuse for stripping down to a T-shirt and boxer shorts and getting into bed next to a woman who blinded him with lust by simply breathing. Whom he'd agreed not to touch.

Just to make her happy. Just for a few days. Just to prove he wasn't weak.

He fell into instant sleep.

Dannie woke in the morning quite pleased but quite uncomfortable from a night of clinging to the edge of the bed so she didn't accidentally roll over into Leo's half. Or into Leo.

She'd probably tortured him enough.

But her will wasn't as strong as she thought, not when her husband lay mere feet away, within touching distance, breathing deeply in sleep. The alarm on his phone had beeped, like, an hour ago, but hadn't produced so much as a twitch out of Leo. Who was she to wake him when he obviously needed to sleep? A good wife ensured her husband was well rested.

The view factored pretty high in the decision, too.

Goodness. He was so gorgeous, dark lashes frozen above his cheekbones, hair tousled against the pillow.

How in the world had she convinced him to sleep in the same bed with her *and* agree to hold off on intimacy? She'd thought for sure they'd have a knock-down-drag-out and then he'd toss her out—bound and determined to ignore his own needs, needs he likely didn't even recognize. But instead of cutting himself off from her again, he'd waded right into the middle of things like she'd asked, bless him.

Because his actions spoke louder than words, and his wife was an ace at interpreting what lay beneath.

If this bedroom sharing worked out the way she hoped, they'd actually talk. Laugh over a sitcom. Wake up together. Then maybe he'd figure out he was lying to himself about what he really wanted from this marriage and realize just how deeply involved he already was.

They'd have intimacy—physically and mentally. She couldn't wait.

She eased from the bed and took a long shower, where she fantasized about all the delicious things Leo would do when he finally seduced her. It was coming. She could feel it.

And no matter how much she wanted it, anticipated it, she sensed she could never fully prepare for how earthshaking their ultimate union would truly be.

When she emerged from the bathroom, Leo was sitting up, rubbing the back of his neck, and her mouth went dry. Even in a T-shirt, he radiated masculinity.

"Good morning," she called cheerfully.

"What happened to my alarm?" He did not look pleased.

"I turned it off after listening to it chirp for ten minutes."

"Why didn't you wake me up?"

"I tried," she lied and fluttered her lashes. "Next time would you like me to be a little more inventive?"

"No." He scowled, clearly interpreting her question to mean she'd do it in the dirtiest, sexiest way she could envision.

"I meant with a glass of water in your face. What did you think I meant?"

He rolled his eyes. "So this is what roommates do?"

"Yes. Until you want to be something else."

With that, she flounced out the door to check off the last few items on the list for Tommy Garrett's party. It was tomorrow night and it was going to be spectacular if she had to sacrifice her Louboutins to the gods of party planning to ensure it.

Leo came downstairs a short while later, actually said goodbye and went to work.

When he strolled into the bedroom that evening, the hooded, watchful gaze he shot her said he'd bided his time all day, primed for the showdown about to play out.

"Busy?" he asked nonchalantly.

Dannie carefully placed the e-reader in her hand on the bedside table and crossed her arms over her tank top. What was it about that look on his face that made her feel as if she'd put on Elise's red-hot wedding night set? "Not at all. By the way, I picked up your dry cl—"

"Good." He threw his messenger bag onto the Victorian settee in the corner and raked piercing blue eyes over her, all the way to her toes tucked beneath a layer of Egyptian cotton. They heated, despite the flimsy barrier, and the flush spread upward at an alarming rate to spark at her core.

What had she been talking about?

He shed his gray pin-striped suit jacket and then his tie. "You caught me at a disadvantage last night. I had a few other things on my mind, so I missed a couple of really important points about this new sleeping arrangement."

Her relocation project had just blown up in her face. He was good and worked up over it.

"Oh? Which ones?" The last syllable squeaked out more like a dolphin mating call than English as he dropped his pants, then slowly unbuttoned his crisp white shirt. What had she done to earn her very own male stripper? Because she'd gladly do it fourteen more times in a row.

"For starters, what happens if I don't keep my hands to myself?"

The shirt hit the floor and her jaw almost followed. Her husband had quite the physique hidden under his worka- holic shell.

So maybe he wasn't mad. But what was he?

Clad in only a pair of briefs, Leo yanked the covers back and slid into his side of the bed. She peeled her gaze from his well-defined chest and refixed it on his face, which was drawn up in a slight smirk, as if he'd guessed the direction of her thoughts. Her cheeks flamed.

"I'll scold you?" She swallowed as he casually lounged on his pillow, head propped on his hand as if settling in for a nice, long chat instead of using those hands to do some- thing far more…intimate. "I mean, it wouldn't be very sport- ing of you."

"Noted." He stretched a little and the covers slipped down his torso. "What happens if *you* don't keep your hands to yourself?"

He was toying with her, seeing if he could get her to break her own vow of chastity. In his thoroughly male mind, he'd be in the clear if *she* made the move. His eyelids dropped to a very sexy half-mast and sizzled her to the core.

"And Daniella? Be sure you spell really well so it's all very clear for those of us who didn't barge into someone else's bed and start slinging rules around."

Actually, the relocation project might be working bet- ter than she'd assumed. At least they were talking. Now to get him to understand this wasn't a contest. Their relationship was at a crossroads and he had to choose which fork he wanted to take.

"There are no rules," she corrected. "I don't have a list of punishments drawn up if you decide you're not on board with being roommates, whether you want to go back to separate bedrooms or strip me naked right now. You're calling the shots. You're the one who shut it down after dinner the other night. *Walk away,* you said, and I did, but that's not what either of us wanted."

"Yeah?" Lazily, he traced the outline of her shoulder against the propped-up pillow at her back, carefully not touching her skin but skating so close the heat from his finger raised every hair on her body. "What would you rather I have told you to do?"

"No games, Leo." She met his gaze squarely. "I'm giving us an opportunity to develop a friendship. But I also readily admit I want you. I want your mouth on me. Here." Just as lazily, she traced a line over her breast and circled the nipple, arching a little. "I want it so badly, I can hardly stand it."

She watched him, and went liquid as his expression darkened sinfully.

"No games?" he asked and cleared the rasp from his throat. "Then what is this?"

"A spelling lesson." And she obviously had to really lay it out for him. She dropped her hand. "You want me, then come and get me. Be as emotionally naked as you are physically. Strip yourself as bare as your body and let's see how fantastic it can be between us."

Stiffening, he closed off, his expression shuttering and his body angling away. "That's all? You don't ask for much."

"Then forget I mentioned it. We don't have to hold out for a connection that may not ever happen. If either of us becomes uninterested in the hands-to-yourself proposition I laid out, it's off." She flung herself back against the pillow, arms splayed wide. "Take me now. I won't complain. We'll have sex, it'll be great and then we'll go to sleep."

He didn't move.

"What's the matter?" she taunted, glancing at him sideways. "It's just sex. Surely you've had just sex before. No brain required. I have no doubt a man with your obvious, um...*talent* can make me come in no time at all. In fact, I'm looking forward to it. I'm hot for you, Leo. Don't make me wait a second longer."

"That's not funny. Stop being ridiculous." Translation: he didn't like being thoroughly trounced at his own game.

She widened her eyes. "Did you think I was joking? I'm not. We're married. We're consenting adults. Both of us have demonstrated a healthy interest in getting the other naked. We'll eventually go all the way. It's your choice what sort of experience that will be."

This had never been about withholding sex. She'd be naked in a heartbeat as soon as he made a move. All the power was in his hands and when that move came, it would be monumental. And he'd be so very, very aware of exactly what it meant.

He shoved both hands through his hair. "Why is it my choice?"

Poor, poor man. If he was too clueless to know she didn't have a choice, far be it from her to fill him in. This was something he had to figure out on his own. Besides, he was the one with the crisis of conscience that prevented him from making love to her until something he probably couldn't even articulate happened.

But she knew exactly what he needed—to let himself go. She'd exploit this situation gladly in order to get the marriage she desperately wanted and help him find the affection and affinity he so clearly yearned for.

She smiled. "Because. I'm—" *Already emotionally invested.* "—generous that way."

She was going to drag Leo off the sidelines kicking and screaming if that's what it took to have the love match she sensed in her soul Elise had actually orchestrated.

Eight

By nine o'clock, the party hummed along in full swing, a success by anyone's account. Except perhaps Leo's. In the past hour, he'd said no more than two words to Dannie.

She tried not to let it bother her as she flitted from group to group, ensuring everyone had a full glass of champagne and plenty to talk about. The final guest list had topped out at twenty-five and no one sent their regrets. Chinese box kites hung from the ceiling, artfully strung by the crew she'd hired. Their interesting geometric shapes and whimsical tails provided a splash of color in the otherwise severe living room. A papier-mâché dragon lounged on the buffet table, breathing fire under the fondue pot in carefully timed intervals.

Tommy's admin had mentioned his love of the Orient and the decorations sprang easily from that. More than one guest had commented how unusual and eye-catching the theme was, but Tommy's signature on the dotted line was the only praise she needed.

Well, she'd have taken a "You look nice" from Leo. The ankle-length black sequined dress had taken three shopping trips to find and a white-knuckle twenty-four hours to alter. She'd only gotten it back this morning and it looked great on her.

Not that anyone else had noticed.

She threw her shoulders back and smiled at the knot of

guests surrounding her, determined to be the hostess Leo expected.

Hyperawareness burned her back on more than one occasion, and she always turned to see Leo's piercing blue eyes on her and his expression laced with something dangerous.

The bedroom-sharing plan was a disaster. He hated it. That had to be his problem—not that she'd know for sure, because he'd clammed up. Was he waiting until the party was over to give her her walking papers?

Turning her back on Leo and the cryptic bug up his butt, she came face-to-face with Leo's friend Dax Wakefield. "Enjoying the party?" she asked him brightly.

Not one person in this room was going to guess she had a mess of uncertainty swirling in her stomach.

"Yes, thank you." Unfailingly polite, Dax nodded, but his tone carried a hint of frost. "The buffet is wonderful."

Her radar blipped as she took note of the distinct lack of a female on Dax's arm. A good-looking guy like Dax—if you liked your men slick and polished—was obviously alone by choice. Was he no longer dating Jenna? Or had Leo asked him not to bring her in some misguided protective notion?

"I'm so glad." She curved her lips graciously and got nothing in response. Maybe he was aloof with everyone. "Congratulations again on the distinguished alumni award. Leo assures me it was well deserved."

"Thank you." Not one hair on his perfectly coiffed head moved when he granted her a small nod. "Took me a little longer to achieve than Leo. But our industries are so different."

What did that mean? There was an undercurrent here she couldn't put her finger on, but Dax definitely wasn't warming up to her. *Problem alert*. Dax and Leo were old friends and a wife was a second-class citizen next to that. Was Dax the genesis of Leo's silent treatment?

"Well, your media empire is impressive nonetheless. We watch your news channel regularly." It wasn't a total lie—

Leo had scrutinized stock prices as they scrolled across the bottom of the screen last night as she pretended to sleep after the spelling lesson.

Dax smiled and a chill rocked her shoulders. If Leo wanted people to believe he was a ruthless, cold-blooded businessman, he should take lessons from his friend. That guy exuded *take no prisoners*.

One of the servers discreetly signaled to get her attention and she pounced on the opportunity to escape. "Will you excuse me? Duty calls."

"Of course." Dax immediately turned to one of Leo's new partners, Miles Bennett, and launched into an impassioned speech about the Cowboys roster and whether they could make it to the Super Bowl this time around.

The server detailed a problem in the kitchen with several broken champagne bottles, which Dannie solved by pulling out Leo's reserve stash of Meunier & Cie. It was a rosé, but very good and would have to do in a pinch. Most of the guests were men and such a girly drink had definite potential to go over like a lead balloon.

Mental note—next time, buy extra champagne in case of nervous, butterfingered staff.

She poured two glasses of the pink champagne and sought out Tommy Garrett. Something told her he'd take to both an out-of-the-norm drink and being roped into a coconspiracy.

Maybe because of the purple canvas high-tops he'd worn with his tuxedo.

"Tommy." Grateful she'd caught him alone by the stairs, she handed him a champagne flute. When Leo had introduced them earlier, they'd chatted for a while and she'd immediately seen why her husband liked him. "You look thirsty. Humor me and drink this. Pretend it's beer."

A brewery in the Czech Republic exported Tommy's vice of choice, which she'd gleaned from his admin. But he'd already had two pints and hopefully wouldn't balk at her plea.

The young man flipped chin-length hair, bleached almost white by the sun, out of his face. "You read my mind. Talking to all these suits has parched me fiercely."

Half the champagne disappeared into Tommy's mouth in one round and he didn't gag. A glance around the room showed her that others weren't tossing the rosé into the potted plants. Crisis averted.

"Thanks, Mrs. Reynolds." She shot him a withering glare and he winked. "I mean Dannie. Sorry, I forgot. Beautiful women get me all tongue-tied."

She laughed. "Does that geek approach actually work?"

"More often than I would have ever imagined. Yet I find myself devoid of promising action this evening." Tommy sighed dramatically and waggled his brows, leaning in to murmur in her ear. "Wanna see my set of protractors sometime?"

Her grin widened. She really liked him, too, and was almost disappointed he hadn't worn a hoodie to her fancy party. "Why, Thomas Garrett, you should be ashamed of yourself. Hitting on a married lady."

"I should be, but I'm totally not. Anyway, I couldn't pry you away from Leo with a crowbar and my own private island. Could I?" he asked hopefully with a practiced once-over she suspected the coeds fell for hook, line and sinker.

"Not a chance," she assured him. "I like my men all grown-up. But feel free to keep trying your moves on me. Eventually you'll become passable at flirting with a woman."

Tommy clutched his heart in mock pain. "Harsh. I think there might be blood."

That prickly, hot flash traveled down her back an instant before Leo materialized at her elbow. His palm settled with familiarity into the groove at her waist and she clamped down on the shiver before it tipped him off that such a simple touch could be so affecting. *Why* had she worn a backless dress?

"Hey, Leo." Tommy lifted his nearly empty glass in a toast. "Great party. Dannie was telling me how much she likes protractors."

"Was she, now?" Leo said easily, his voice mellower than the scotch in his highball.

Uh-oh. She'd never heard him speak like that.

Swiping at Tommy with a flustered hand, she glanced up at Leo and nearly flinched at the lethal glint in her husband's eyes. Directed at her or Tommy? "Protractors. Yes. They get the job done, don't they? Just like Leo. Think of him as a protractor and Reynolds's competitor, Moreno Partners, as a ruler. Why not use the right tool for the job from the very beginning?"

Tommy eyed her. "Moreno is pretty straight and narrow in their approach. Maybe that's what I need."

Good, he'd picked up on her desperate subject change.

"Oh, no." Dannie shook her head and prayed Leo's stiff carriage wasn't because he didn't like the way she was sticking her nose in his business with Tommy. This was absolutely what she was here for and she absolutely didn't want to blow it, especially with Leo in such a strange, unpredictable mood. "Reynolds can help you. Leo's been doing this far longer than Moreno. He has connections. Expertise. You know Leo has a degree in engineering, too, right?"

Leo's hand drifted a little lower. His pinky dipped inside her dress and grazed the top edge of her panties. Her brain liquefied into the soles of her sparkly Manolos and she forgot to mention he'd actually double majored in engineering and business.

"Daniella," Leo murmured. "Perhaps you'd see to Mrs. Ross? She's wandering around by the double glass doors and I'm afraid she might end up in the pool."

"Of course." She smiled at Tommy, then at Leo and went on the trumped-up errand Leo had devised, likely to avoid saying outright in front of a prospective partner that he could handle his own public relations. Which she appreciated.

As she guided Mrs. Ross toward the buffet, she laughed at the sweet old lady's jokes, but kept an eye on Leo and Tommy. They were still talking near the stairs and Leo's expression had finally lost that edge she so desperately wanted to understand.

If she'd gone too far with the bedroom-sharing idea, why didn't he just tell her?

This party was a measure of how effectively she could do her job as Leo's wife and how well she contributed to his success. Coupled with the high-level tension constantly pulsing between them, her nerves had stretched about as tight as they could without snapping.

Dannie showed the last guest to the door and spent a long thirty minutes with the auxiliary staff wrapping up postparty details.

Leo was nowhere to be seen.

Around midnight, she finally stumbled to their bedroom with the last bottle of champagne, uncorked, intending to split it with him in celebration of a successful party. Surely Leo shared that opinion. If he didn't, she really should be told why.

Darkness shrouded the bedroom.

She set the champagne bottle and two glasses on the dresser and crossed to the freestanding Tiffany torchiere lamp in the corner. She snapped it on and bracing against the wall, fingered apart the buckle on one shoe.

"Oh, you should leave those on." Leo tsked, his voice silky as scotch again.

She whirled. He was lounging on the settee, tie loose and shirt unbuttoned three down. Not that she was counting. "What are you doing sitting here in the dark?"

"Seemed appropriate for my mood."

That sounded like a warning. She thumbed off the other shoe in case she had to make a run for the door. "Would you like me to turn off the light?"

He contemplated her for a long moment. "Would darkness make it easier for you to pretend I was Tommy Garrett?"

She couldn't help it. The laugh bubbled out.

It was a straight-from-the-bottle kind of night. Retrieving the champagne from the dresser, she gulped a healthy dose before wiping her mouth with the back of one hand. "Jealousy? That's so..." *Cliché*. Well, it seemed like a tell-it-like-it-is night, too. "...cliché, Leo."

His gaze scraped her from head to toe, darkening as he lingered at the vee of her cleavage. "What should I feel while watching my wife flirt with another man?"

"Gratitude?" she offered. "I was working him for you."

Leo barked out a laugh. "Shall I call him back, then? See if he's up for a threesome?"

This was going downhill fast. Not only was he not thrilled with her party, he'd transformed into a possessive husband. "Are you drunk?"

Maybe she should catch up. If she downed the entire bottle of champagne, her husband might make a lot more sense. Or it would dull the coming rejection—which this time would no doubt include an annulment. Alcohol had the potential to make either one more bearable.

"Not nearly drunk enough," he muttered. Louder, he said, "Since you're so free with your favors this evening, perhaps you'd do me another one."

Her eyes narrowed. "Like what?"

"Show me what's under that dress."

Okay, *not* the direction she'd anticipated him going.

More champagne, STAT. She swigged another heady gulp and set the bottle on the dresser. "Why? So you can stake your claim? Jealousy is not a good enough reason to strip for you."

His mouth quirked. "What would be?"

"Diamonds. A trip to Bora-Bora. A Jaguar." She ticked

them off on her fingers airily. If he was going to be cliché, she could, too. "The typical kept woman baubles."

"What if I called you…Dannie?" He drew it out and in that silky voice, it swept down her spine and coalesced in her core with heat. "It's the key to intimacy, isn't it? You let Tommy call you that. The two of you were very cozy."

She cursed under her breath. How dare he turn her on while accusing her of dallying with Tommy? "He's twenty-four, Leo. I'm old enough to be his…older sister. Stop being such a Neanderthal."

"So that's your objection to Tommy? His age?" Leo slid off the settee and advanced on her, slowly enough to trip her pulse. "What about Dax? He's my age. Maybe you'd like him better."

"What's this really about?" Boldly, she stared him down as he approached, determined to get past this barrier she sensed he'd thrown up to avoid the real issue—she'd failed at being the wife he needed, on all levels. Somehow. "You're not threatened by Tommy. Or Dax. You've been weird all evening. If you've got a problem with me, lay it out. No more smoke and mirrors."

Only a breath away, he halted, towering over her. Without heels, she wasn't that much shorter than he was, but his presence—and his dark, intense mood—overwhelmed her.

"You know, I do have a problem with you." His gaze traveled over her and that's when she saw the vulnerability he'd hidden behind a mask of false allegations. "You're still dressed."

Baffled, she cocked her head and studied him. Hints of what he was so carefully not telling her filtered through. All at once, she realized. He *was* threatened by other men and conversely paralyzed by his conscience, which had dictated that he wouldn't touch her until she was okay with what he could give.

His body language was equally conflicted. His fingers

curled and uncurled repeatedly, as if he wanted to reach for her but couldn't.

She was his wife. But not his wife, in the truest sense.

Her heart softened. He wanted something he had no experience with, no vocabulary to define. And she'd been trying to force him into admitting his needs by sharing his bed and denying him the only outlet for his emotions that he understood, assuming her way was best.

Well, this was all new to her, too, but she wasn't above changing course to give him what he needed.

Their connection was already there. Instead of waiting on some murky criteria she doubted either of them could verbalize, she'd just show him.

That was a good enough reason to strip for him.

Dannie locked her gaze on his and reached up to her nape to unclasp her dress.

Leo was acting like an ass.

Knowing it didn't give him any better ability to control it, or to eliminate the constant spike of lust when he caught sight of his wife. Seeing her laugh with another man had generated something ugly and primal inside.

He didn't like it.

He didn't like how he'd focused so much energy and attention on this deal with Tommy Garrett and then spent the night sulking in the corner instead of using the opportunity to do his job. His wife had picked up the slack. *His wife.* Once again, she'd kept the importance of the evening front and center while he wallowed in jealousy.

How dare she be so perfect and imperfect at the same time?

A few more fingers of scotch might have dulled the scent of strawberries. But he doubted it. When he was this close to his wife, nothing could dilute the crushing awareness.

Daniella's fingers danced across the back of her neck. His gut clenched as he realized what she was doing, but the protest died in his throat as her glittery dress waterfalled off her body, catching at the tips of her breasts for one breathless second. Then it puddled on the floor, baring her to his greedy gaze.

A beautiful, half-nude vision stood before him. Daniella, in all her glory. Fire raged south, ravaging everything in its path to his center, numbing his extremities and nearly bringing him to his knees.

It would be fitting to kneel before a goddess.

"Daniella." His raw voice scraped at his throat and he cleared it. "What are you doing?"

He knew. She was doing what he'd been pushing her to do. But she was supposed to slap him. Or storm out. Or push him in kind, the way she always did. As long as she punished him for being an ass, any response would have been fine.

Except this. And it was a far more suitable penance to get exactly what he asked for.

"I'm eliminating the problems," she said, head held high. "*All* the problems."

That was impossible, let alone this way. "Put your clothes back on. I'm—"

Actually, he had no clue what he was. Nothing could have prepared him to feel so…ill equipped to be in the same room with a woman who radiated power and sensual energy.

He shut his eyes.

Strip yourself as bare as your body, she'd suggested. But his wife's simple act of disrobing, of making herself vulnerable, had accomplished that for him, even while he was still fully dressed.

Everything about her touched him in places no one had ever dared tread.

This night was not going to end well. She wanted something he couldn't allow himself to give her. Once that bottle was uncorked, he'd focus on nothing but Daniella and lose his drive to succeed. Then he'd fail her—and himself—on a whole different level, which he could not accept.

"Leo." The softness in her voice nearly shattered him. "Open your eyes. Look at me."

He did. God help him, but he couldn't resist. His gaze sought hers, not the gorgeous bare breasts there for his viewing pleasure. His eyes burned with effort to keep them trained straight ahead.

"I would never—" she emphasized the word with a slash of her hand "—dishonor you with anyone else, let alone a friend or a business partner. I respect you too much. I'm sorry if I behaved in a way that made you question that."

Her words, sweetly issued and completely sincere, wrenched that hollow place inside. He'd been treating her horribly all night for who knew what reason and she was apologizing. "You didn't. You were just being a good hostess."

A very poor depiction of how absolutely stellar a party she'd thrown. She deserved far more than degradation at the hands of her husband. Far more than the absent, unavailable man she'd cleaved to.

"I really hope you think so." Her expression warmed. "You're the only man I want. Forever. That's why I married you."

The sentiment flowed like warm honey through his chest. This was the kind of romantic nonsense he'd gone to EA International to avoid. But then, wasn't she describing exactly what he'd asked for? Fidelity and commitment? It just sounded like so much *more* than that from her mouth, so deep and profound.

What was he supposed to do with that? With her?

"Don't you want me, too?" she asked, her voice dropping into a seductive whisper that funneled straight to his erection.

"So much more than I should," he muttered and regretted saying it out loud.

"Then come over here and show me."

His feet were rooted to the carpet. It wasn't going to be just sex. Maybe just sex wasn't possible with someone he'd made his wife.

Regardless, he'd married Daniella, and consummating their relationship meant they were embarking on forever at this very moment.

Part of him strained to dash for the door, to down the rest of the scotch until the unquenchable thirst for Daniella faded from memory. Then he wouldn't have to deal with the other part that compelled him to accept everything she was offering him, even the alarming nebulous nonphysical things.

"So the touching moratorium is lifted?" he asked. "Or is this the precursor to another round of rules?"

Apparently he wasn't finished lashing out at her. If he infuriated her enough to leave, they could go back to circling each other and he'd put off finding out exactly how weak he was.

He didn't want her to leave.

"This is about nothing more than being together. Do whatever feels right to you." She spread her arms, jutting out her perfectly mounded breasts. His mouth tingled and he imagined he could taste one. "Standing here in nothing other than a tiny thong is turning me into Jell-O. I'd really like it if you'd kiss me now."

"A thong?" He'd been so focused on her front, the back hadn't even registered. The feel of silk beneath his pinky when he'd pushed past the fabric at her waist during the party rushed back and he groaned.

Slowly, she half turned and cocked a hip, bare cheek thrust out. "I wore it for you. Hoping you'd pick tonight to make me your wife in more than name only."

He was so hard he couldn't breathe. Let alone walk. Or kiss. Neither was he ready to cross that line, to find out how far she'd suck him down the rabbit hole if he gave in to the maelstrom of need.

Her lips curved up in a secret, naughty smile. Palms flat against her waist, she smoothed them downward over the curve of her rear, down her thighs. "If you're not going to touch me, I'll just do it myself."

Provocatively, she teased one of her nipples with an index finger. Her eyes fluttered halfway closed in apparent pleasure and he swore. Enough was enough.

She was serious. No more choices, rules, games or guidelines. She wanted him.

It was too late to address all the lingering questions about the status of their relationship or how this would change it. It was too late to imagine he'd escape, and far too late to pretend he wanted to.

Daniella was going in the lover box. Now.

In one stride, he crossed the space between them and swept her up in his arms. He swallowed her gasp a moment before his lips captured hers. Crushing her against him, he leaped into the carnal desire she'd incited all night. Actually, since that first glimpse of her on the stairs at their wedding. Every moment in between.

Their mouths aligned, opened, fed. Eagerly, she slid her tongue along his, inviting him deeper. He delved willingly, exploring leisurely because this time there'd be no interruptions.

He was going to make Daniella his, once and for all. Then he'd recover his singular concentration and no more deals would slip away as he daydreamed.

The taste of her sang through his veins and instead of weakening him, she gave him strength. Enough strength to pleasure this woman until she cried out with it. Enough to grant her what she'd been begging for. Enough to make love to her all night long.

He'd hold on to that strength, because he'd need it to walk away again in the morning. It was the only outcome he'd allow, to delve into the physical realm without losing himself in it. Just tonight, just once.

Leo broke the kiss long enough to pick her up in his arms. Carefully, he laid her out on the bed and spent a long moment drinking in the panorama of his wife's gorgeous body. All that divine skin pleaded for his touch, so he indulged himself, running fingertips down her arms, over the peaks and valleys of her torso and all the way down to her siren-red toenails.

He glanced at her face. She was so sensuously lost in pleasure, his pulse nearly doubled instantly.

She shivered.

"Cold?" he asked.

Shaking her head, she got up on her knees and pulled his tie free. "Hot. For you."

Then she slid off his jacket and went to work on the buttons of his shirt, watching him as she slipped them free.

Finally, she'd completely undressed him. Taking her in his arms, he rolled with her to the middle of the bed and picked up the kiss where they'd left off.

Her lips molded to his and his mind drained as her warm body snugged up against him. They were naked together, finally. Physically, at least.

Almost naked. He skimmed a hand down her spine and fingered the thong. Silky. Sexy. She'd worn it for him. If he'd known that, the party would have been over at about seven-thirty.

Her palm raced across his skin in kind and her touch ignited an urgency he couldn't allow. He'd take as little pleasure from this as possible. Otherwise he'd never leave the bed. It was a delicate balance, made more complicated by the fact that no matter what she'd said, she still wished for something cataclysmic out of this.

He'd make it as physically cataclysmic as he could. That was the best he could do.

Still deep in her mouth, he yanked off the thong and then explored her torso with tiny openmouthed kisses until he reached her core. There, he licked her with the very tip of his tongue.

"Leo," she gasped, which only drove his urgency higher.

"You taste like heaven." He wanted more and took her nub in his mouth to nibble it gently, then harder, laving his tongue against it until she writhed beneath his onslaught.

Mewls deep in her throat attested to her mindless plea-sure and then she cried, "More. I'm about to come," which was so hot it shoved him to the brink.

His erection pulsed and he clamped down, aching with the effort to keep from exploding. He drove a finger into her wet core, then two, and tongued her and she arched up as she clinched around him, shattering into a beautiful climax.

He rose up and tilted her chin to soak up the sated, satis-fied glint in her eyes as he gave her a minute to recover. But not too long. When her breathing slowed a bit, he guided her hands upward and curled them around the top edge of the headboard.

If she touched him, he'd lose all his hard-won control.

"Hold on," he murmured, and she did, so trusting, so eager.

He parted her thighs and slowly pushed into her. Rap-ture stole across her face, thrilling him. She enveloped him like a vise, squeezing tight. She was amazing, open, wet.

His vision flickered as Daniella swamped his senses.

More. He thrust into her. *Again*.

Desire built, heavy and thick, and he thumbed her nub, circling it. Heat broke over him and he ached to come but needed her to come first. To prove he wasn't weak, and that he could still resist her.

"Daniella," he ground out hoarsely, and she captured his gaze.

He couldn't break free.

Everything shrank down to this one suspended moment and her bottomless, tender irises ensnared him, encourag-ing him to just feel. And he did feel it, against his will, but heaviness spread alarmingly fast through his chest, displacing what should be there. Against all odds, she'd wrenched something foreign and indefinable and magnificent from his very depths.

Only one thing could encapsulate it, one word. "Dannie."

It left his mouth on a broken plea and she answered with a cry, convulsing around him, triggering his release. He poured all his desire, all his confusion—and what he feared might be part of his soul—into her, groaning with sensual gratification he'd never meant to experience.

Daniella had taken his name, taken his body. Taken something primal and physical and turned it into poetry. The awe of it engulfed him, washing through his chest. He wanted to mark every page of her again and again and never stop. And let her do the same to him.

Intellectually, he'd realized long ago that one small taste of her would never be enough. But the actual experience had burst from its neat little box, crushing the sides, eclipsing even his wildest fantasies.

He couldn't allow himself to indulge like that again. Otherwise his wife would swallow him whole and take every bit of his ambition with her.

Nine

Dannie awoke at dawn tangled with Leo. Her husband, in every sense.

Muscles ached and begged to be stretched so beautifully again. Above all, her heart longed to hear him say "Dannie" with such raw yearning as they joined. Like he had last night, in that smoking-hot voice.

The bedroom-sharing plan deserved an award.

Leo was still asleep, but holding her tightly against him with his strong forearms, her back against his firm front. The position seemed incongruous for someone so determined to remain distanced. But in sleep, his body told her what he couldn't say with his mouth.

He craved a relationship with her, too. The yearning bled from him in waves every moment she spent in his company. It was all over the good deeds he did behind the scenes, which she no longer believed were designed to avoid emotional investment.

He just didn't know how to reach out. And she'd gladly taken on the job of teaching him.

As he guided her toward her full potential as his wife, she'd done the same, pushing him to keep opening up, giving him what he needed. She'd keep on doing it until he embraced everything this marriage could be. The rewards of being the woman behind the man were priceless.

She hated to disturb him, but his front was growing

firmer by the moment and it pressed hot and hard against her suddenly sensitized flesh.

Heat gathered at the center of her universe and her breath caught.

Involuntarily, her back arched, pushing her sex against his erection. She rubbed back and forth experimentally. Hunger shafted through her. Oh, *yes*.

Then his whole body stiffened and his hands curled against her hips, forcing her to be still. Awake, and obviously not on board with a round of morning love.

Wiggling backward, she deliberately teased him without words.

"Daniella," he murmured thickly. "Stop. I forgot to set my alarm. I have to go to work."

"Yes, you do." She wiggled again, harder, and he sucked in a ragged breath. "Ten minutes. I'm so turned on, I'm almost there already."

Cool air rushed against her back as he rolled away and left the bed without another word.

Her heart crashed against her ribs as he disappeared into the bathroom. The shower hummed through the walls.

Nothing had changed between them.

Last night had meant everything to her. But she'd vastly overplayed her hand. Instead of viewing it as a precious stepping-stone toward a fulfilling marriage, Leo seemed perfectly content to sleep with her at night and ignore her the rest of the day.

Exactly what he'd warned her would happen.

She had no call to be disappointed. She'd given him what he needed and hoped it would be the beginning of their grand, sweeping love affair. It obviously wasn't. She'd dropped her dress, pushed him into making that final move and, for her effort, got a round of admittedly earth-shattering sex. She'd even given him permission to do whatever felt right.

At what point had she asked for anything more?

Since the *I do*s, she'd put considerable effort into preventing screwups, convinced each successful event or household task solidified her role as Mrs. Reynolds.

It never occurred to her the real screwup would happen when she invented a fictional future where Leo became the husband of her dreams.

Flinging the covers up over her shoulder, she buried herself in the bed, dry-eyed, until Leo left the bedroom without saying goodbye.

Then she let her eyes burn for an eternity, refusing to let the tears fall.

Her stupid phone's musical ringtone split the air. *Leo.*

Bolting upright, she bobbled the phone into her hands. He was calling to apologize. Tell her good morning. That it had been a great party. Something.

A bitter taste rose at the back of her throat when she saw *Mom* on the caller ID. She swallowed and answered.

"Hi," she said and her voice broke in half.

"What's wrong, baby?"

Great, now her mother was concerned. Worrying her mother was the last thing Dannie wanted.

"Nothing," she lied brightly. "I'm still in bed. Haven't woken up yet. How are you?"

"Fine." A round of coughing negated that. "Do you want to have lunch today?"

Oh, that would never do. Her mother would instantly see the hurt in her heart blossoming on Dannie's face. She had to get over the disenchantment first. "I've got a few things to do. Maybe tomorrow?"

"I'm leaving on the cruise tomorrow. Did you forget? I wanted to see you before I go."

Yes, she had forgotten and it was a brutal reminder about what was important—her mother. Not Dannie's bruised feelings.

Suck it up, honey. "I can rearrange my appointments. I'll pick you up around eleven, okay?"

"Yes! I'll see you then."

Dannie hung up, heaved a deep shuddery breath and hit the shower to wash away every trace of Leo from her body. If only she could wipe him from her mind as easily, but his invisible presence stained the atmosphere of the entire house.

She fought tears for twenty excruciating minutes as the car sped toward her mother's.

The driver paused at the curb outside her mother's apartment and Dannie frowned. Paint peeled from the wood siding and weeds choked the grass surrounding the front walk. The shabbiness had never bothered her before. How was it fair that Dannie got to live in the lap of luxury but her mother suffered both pulmonary fibrosis and near poverty?

But what could Dannie do about it? She didn't have any money of her own—everything was Leo's. A nasty voice inside suggested he could pony up alternative living space for her mother in reciprocation for last night.

She hushed up that thought immediately. Leo hadn't treated her like that. He'd told her what would happen on more than one occasion and she'd chosen to create a fairy tale in her head where love conquered all.

Her mom slid into the car and beamed at Dannie. The nurse had done wonders to improve her mother's quality of life with daily pulmonary therapy and equally important emotional support.

"I'm so glad to see you, baby," her mom gushed.

The driver raised the glass panel between the front seat and the back, then pulled out into the flow of traffic to ferry them to the restaurant. Dannie leaned into her mother's cheek buss and smiled. "Glad to see you, too."

What ills could she possibly have that Mom couldn't make all better? The pricking at her eyelids grew worse.

Her mother's hands on her jaw firmed. "Uh, oh. What happened?"

She should have known better—sonar had nothing on a

mom's ability to see beneath the surface. Dannie pulled her face from her mother's grasp and looked out the window in the opposite direction. "Nothing. Leo and I had a little... misunderstanding. I'll get over it."

Probing silence settled on her chest and she risked a glance at her mother. She was watching her with an unreadable expression. "Nothing serious, I hope."

Dannie half laughed. "Not in his opinion."

With a sigh of relief, her mother settled back against the seat. "That's good."

"Well, I don't think he's planning to divorce me, if that's what you're worried about."

At least not yet. By all rights, her desperate mental reorganization of their arrangement should have resulted in a firm boot to the backside long before now. Yet, he hadn't breathed a word about divorce, so apparently he still needed her for reasons of his own.

"Of course that's a concern." Her mother's warm hand found Dannie's elbow. "Fortunately, you married a solid, respectable man who believes in commitment. A very wise choice. You'll never end up brokenhearted and alone like I did."

Yes. That was the purpose of this marriage. Not grand, sweeping passion and a timeless love. This was a job. Wife was her career. Hardening her heart against the tiny tendrils of feelings she'd allowed to bloom last night in Leo's arms, Dannie nodded. "You're right. Leo is a good man."

The muted sound of sirens filtered through the car's interior a moment before an ambulance whizzed by in the opposite direction. She'd ridden in an ambulance for the first time not too long ago, on the way to the hospital, with her mother strapped to a gurney and fighting to breathe. When the bill came, she'd gone to the library that same day seeking a way to pay it.

And now she was riding in the modern-day equivalent

of a horse-drawn carriage, but better because it had air-conditioning and leather seats.

Leo had saved them both, providing security for her and for her mother. She couldn't lose sight of that again. He'd held up his end of the bargain honestly. It was time for her to do the same and stop wallowing in the mire of lost romance that she'd never been promised in the first place.

Love didn't work out for other people. Why would it be any different for her?

"The misunderstanding wasn't over the possibility of children, was it?" her mother asked.

Hesitantly, Dannie shook her head.

They hadn't used protection. Actually, she could be pregnant right now. Warmth soaked through her chilled soul. If Leo gave her a child, his absence would be notably less difficult. Her mother had raised her single-handedly. Dannie could do that, too.

Funny how she hadn't thought about procreation once last night. Yet children had been foremost on her mind when she'd agreed to marry Leo. Back when she assumed there was no possibility of more between them than an arrangement. Now she knew for a fact there was no possibility.

Suck it up. She pasted on a smile for her mother. "Tell me more about the cruise."

Her mother chatted all through lunch and Dannie responded, but couldn't have repeated the content of their discussion for a million dollars. Fortunately, Leo didn't come up again. That she would have remembered.

Leo didn't call and didn't join her for dinner. She got ready for bed, resigned to sleeping alone.

At ten o'clock, he strolled into the bedroom.

Her gaze flicked over him hungrily, searching for small clues to the state of mind of the man who'd put his lips on her body in very inventive ways not twenty-four hours ago.

"Hi," she said politely and flicked off the TV she'd been

staring at for who knew how long with no idea what was on. "How was your day?"

"Fine," he said. "I got you something."

Her eyebrows rose. "Like a present?"

Lifting the small silver gift bag clutched in his fingers, he nodded and crossed to the bed to hand it to her. She spilled out the contents and opened the square box. Diamond earrings sparkled against royal-blue velvet.

The box burned her hand and she threw it on the bedside table. "Thank Mrs. Gordon for me. She has lovely taste."

His face instantly turned into a brick wall. "I spent an hour picking them out myself. To thank you for the party. You were amazing. I should have told you before now."

"I'm sorry." Remorse clogged her throat. What had happened to the quiet, demure girl Elise created? Lately, Dannie rarely thought twice about what came out of her mouth. "That was obnoxious."

"And well earned." He cleared his throat and sought her gaze, his blue eyes liquid. "I'm sorry I left the way I did this morning. That was *far* more obnoxious. And undeserved."

"Oh." He'd robbed her of speech. Which was probably fortunate, since the question on the tip of her tongue was, *Why* did *you leave that way, then?* She didn't ask. If he'd intended for her to know, he'd have told her.

Regardless, he'd apologized. *Apologized.* And bought her a present.

Leo retrieved the box and handed it to her. "Will you wear the earrings? I'll take them back if you don't like them."

A touch of the vulnerability she'd witnessed last night darted across his expression. The earrings represented both a thank-you and an apology and he wanted her to like them. Just when she thought she had the dynamic between them straight in her head, he flipped it upside down.

"I love them." She unscrewed the backs and stuck them in her ears, then struck a pose. "How do they look?"

"Beautiful." His gaze skittered down her body and back up again. He wasn't even looking at her ears.

A wealth of undisclosed desire crackled below the surface. Some of it was physical. But not all. He'd picked out the earrings himself. What did that mean? She'd lay odds *he* didn't even know what the significance of that was.

Last night, she'd learned one surefire way to communicate with him.

She flung back the covers and crawled to him. He watched her, his body poised to flee, but she snagged his lapels before he could. Without speaking, she peeled his jacket from his shoulders and teased his lips with hers as she unknotted his tie.

"Daniella." He groaned against her lips and pulled back a fraction. "The earrings weren't... I'm not—"

"Shh. It's okay." The tie came apart in her hands and she leaned into him, rubbing his chest in small circles with her pebbled nipples.

Almost imperceptibly, he shook his head. "I don't expect sex in exchange for jewelry."

How could such a simple statement sink hooks so deeply into her heart? He was trying so hard to be honorable, so hard to keep from hurting her at great expense to himself. "And I don't expect jewelry in exchange for sex. Now that's out of the way. Shut up and put your hands on me."

His eyelids flew closed and he swallowed. That was close enough to a yes for her. She bridged the gap and claimed his lips with hers.

Winding the ends of his tie around her hands, she pulled him closer and deepened the kiss. A firestorm swept outward from their joined lips, incinerating her control.

Urgently, wordlessly, she undressed him, desperate to bare Leo in the only way he'd allow. He ripped off her pajamas and they fell to the bed already intertwined.

Leo kissed her and it was long and thorough. *This* was the man who'd held her in his sleep. The man who'd whispered her name with gut-wrenching openness. As she'd known beyond a shadow of a doubt, this joining of bodies spoke volumes beyond the scope of mere words. And it said Leo had far more going on beneath the surface than he dared let on.

As she cradled her husband's beautiful body and stared into the depths of his hot-with-passion blue eyes, something blossomed inside. Something huge and reckless, and she tamped it down with no small effort. But it rose up again, laced with images of Leo's child growing in her womb. She imagined the tenderness of his gaze as he looked down on their newborn child and the back of her throat heated.

Suddenly, the fear of Leo tiring of her romantic foolishness wasn't her only problem anymore.

She'd traded it for the painful, diametrically opposite problem of what was going to happen if she fell in love with him and doomed herself to a lifetime of marriage to a man who would forever keep his kind heart buried beneath a workaholic shell.

Tap. Tap. Tap.

Leo blinked and glanced up. Dax tapped his pen a few more times, his face expressionless as he nodded to the laptop screen filled with verbiage regarding the proposed joint venture to finance a start-up company called Mastermind Media.

"Clause two?" Dax prompted and lowered a brow. "They agreed to extend the deadline to midnight. We don't have long. You were supposed to be telling me why you don't like it."

I don't like it because it's standing between me and a bed with my wife in it.

Theoretically, that applied to the entire proposal he and Dax had been tearing apart since four-thirty with only a short break for General Tso's chicken in bad sauce from Jade Dragon.

Leo stole a peek at his watch. Nine o'clock on a Friday night.

If he left the office now, he could be home in twenty minutes. Sixteen if he ignored the speed limit. He might even text Daniella as he drove to let her know he'd be there soon. Maybe she'd greet him wearing nothing but the diamonds he'd given her.

What started as a simple thank-you gift had somehow transformed into something else. Hell if he knew what. He hadn't intended to make love to her again. At least not this soon, not while he was still struggling to maintain some semblance of control around her.

But one minute Daniella was threading the diamonds through her ears, and the next...

The memory of last night and his sexy wife invaded his mind. Again. The way she'd been doing all day.

"The clause is fine." *No.* It wasn't. Leo shook his head and tried to focus. "It will be fine. With a minor tweak to the marketing expectations."

More tapping. Then Dax tossed down his pen with a sense of finality.

"Leo." Dax shrank down in the high-backed chair and laced his hands over one knee, contemplating the ebony conference table. Lines appeared across his forehead. "I'm starting to get the impression you don't think we should do this deal."

"What?" Leo flinched. *No more daydreaming.* What was wrong with him? "I've put in sixty hours on this. It's a solid proposal."

"Then what's up?" His friend eyed him, concern evident in his expression. "We've been looking at Mastermind Media for months. If you're worried about you and me doing business together, you should have spoken up long before now."

Hesitating, Leo rolled his neck. They'd known each other

more than fifteen years—since college. Dax was the one person who'd call him on it if Leo zoned out. "That's not it."

"Is the financing sticky?" Dax frowned, wrinkling his pretty-boy face. "You're not using your own money on this because of our relationship, are you?"

"Of course not." Venture capital relied on other people's money. Leo never risked anything he didn't have to.

"I've run out of teeth to pull. Spill. Or I'm walking."

Walking. As in, he'd purposefully let the deal expire because Leo wanted to go home and sleep with his wife. He sighed. Apparently losing John Hu hadn't been enough of a wake-up call.

"I'm distracted. Sorry. It's not the proposal. Something else."

Something that needed to stop. Leo's will was ironclad and had been since he was seventeen. How had Daniella destroyed it so easily?

Dax smirked. "I should have known. You've been different since you married that woman."

He wasn't the slightest bit different. Was he?

"Watch your tone."

Friendship or not, Dax had no call to refer to Daniella as "that woman," as if Leo had hooked up with a chain-smoker in a tube top, straight from the trailer park. He'd deliberately chosen a classy, elegant woman. Not one who mirrored his childhood neighbors in the near ghetto.

Throwing up his hands dramatically, Dax flipped his gaze heavenward. "It begins. We've been through a lot of women together, my friend. What's so special about this one?"

The answer should be nothing. But it wasn't.

"I married her."

And now he was lying to his best friend. Not only was that just part of the answer, it was the tip of the iceberg. He couldn't stop thinking about her. About how beautifully she'd handled the party. Her laugh. The way she took care of things, especially him, with some kind of extrasensory perception.

When he was inside her, his world shifted. He'd never realized his world *could* be shifted. Or that he'd like its new tilt so much. That he'd willingly slide down Daniella's slippery incline.

Snorting, Dax glanced at the laptop screen positioned between their chairs and tapped on the keyboard. "So? It's not like you have feelings for her. She's a means to an end."

A vehement protest almost left his mouth unchecked. But Dax was right. Why would he protest? Daniella *was* a means to an end, like Leo had told him. It just sounded so cold from his friend's perspective. "Feelings aside, she's my wife. Not a casual date. It's important for her to be happy."

"Why? Because she might leave you? Think again. Gold diggers don't bite the hand that feeds them."

Quick-burning anger sliced through Leo's gut. "She's not a gold digger. Our marriage is beneficial to us both. You know that. Surely you don't believe it's acceptable for me to treat my wife like a dog and expect her to put up with it because I have money."

Dax quirked one eyebrow. "Like I said. This one is special."

Leo rolled his eyes. Dax saw meaning where there was none. Except they knew each other well. The Chinese food churned through Leo's stomach greasily. Or maybe that was a smear of guilt.

His track record with women spoke for itself—he wouldn't win any awards for tenderness, attentiveness or commitment. And maybe he did buy expensive presents to apologize for all of the above.

"Let's have this conversation again when *you* get married."

"Ha. That's a good one. There's no *when* in that statement. There's hardly an *if*. Women are good for one thing." Dax flashed his teeth. "They give you a reason to drink."

Perfect subject-change material. "Things not going well with Jenna?"

Too bad. Dax obviously needed someone in his life who could knock down all his commitment and trust issues. Jenna wasn't the right woman for that anyway.

"What are you talking about? She's great. The sex is fantastic." Waggling his brows, Dax leaned back in his chair. "Well, you know."

Leo's already unsettled stomach turned inside out at Dax's smarmy reference to the fact that she'd been Leo's lover first. Had Leo always treated women so casually, blowing it off as a necessary evil of success?

No. Not always. Daniella *was* special, but not the way Dax implied. Leo had treated her differently from the beginning, demonstrating a healthy respect for the institution of marriage. That's all. He was making an iceberg out of an ice cube.

Dax sat up to type out a few more corrections to the proposal. "Judging by the way you couldn't keep your eyes off Daniella at the party the other night, she must be a wildcat. Let me know if you get tired of her."

The chair's wheels squealed as Leo launched to his feet. Staring down at Dax, he crossed his arms so he didn't punch his oldest friend. "I strongly suggest you close your trap before I do it for you."

"Jeez, Leo. Calm down. She's just a woman."

"And you're just a friend." When Dax glanced up, surprise evident, Leo skewered him with a glare that couldn't possibly be misinterpreted. "Things change. Get over it."

Slowly, Dax rose to his feet. Eye to eye, they faced off and Leo didn't like the glint flashing in his friend's gaze as Dax gave Leo's stiff carriage a once-over.

"I can't believe you'd let a chick come between us. Especially not one you found through a matchmaker." Dax nearly spat the word. "Let the deal with Mastermind expire. When you come back from la-la land and realize you've lost your edge over an admittedly nice pair of boobs, I'll be around to help you pick up the pieces. We've been friends too long."

Dax stepped back and Leo let him, though his fingers were still curled into a nice, fat fist that ached to rearrange that pretty-boy face. "I agree. It's best not to go into business together right now."

"Go home to your wife," Dax called over his shoulder as he gathered his bag, phone and travel coffee mug. "I hope she's good enough in bed to help you forget how much money we just lost."

He strode out the door of Leo's conference room without a backward glance.

Sinking into the nearest chair, Leo stared out the window at the green argon lights lining the Bank of America Plaza skyscraper. Since the building housed the headquarters of Dax's far-flung media empire, the familiar outline drove the barb further into Leo's gut.

Yeah, they'd lost a lot of money. And a friendship.

He didn't imagine for a second this rift would be easily repaired. Not because of the sense of betrayal Leo felt, and not because Dax had said reprehensible things about Leo's wife.

But because Dax was right. Leo had changed since marrying Daniella. No longer could he stomach being that guy Dax described, who treated women horribly but rationalized it away and bought them shiny presents to make up for it. Or that guy who wasn't bothered by introducing an ex-girlfriend to Dax because she hadn't meant anything to him.

Dax didn't see a problem with either. Leo couldn't continue to be friends with someone who held such a low opinion of women. Why hadn't he seen that long before now? And what would it take to get Dax to recognize the problem? Maybe Dax should visit a matchmaker himself. If Elise could find the perfect woman for Leo, she could do it for anyone.

Losing the friendship hurt. Letting the deadline expire

for their proposal to Mastermind Media hurt worse. In his entire professional career, he'd never willfully given up. And one thing hadn't changed, would never change—Leo also didn't want to be that guy who lost deals or worse, lost his edge. For any reason. Let alone over a woman who drove him to distraction.

He'd lost John Hu. Now this deal. Was Tommy Garrett next?

He refused to allow that to happen. Daniella's invisible, ill-defined hold on him had to end. Immediately. He'd tried ignoring her. He'd tried sleeping at the office. He'd even tried going in the opposite direction and allowing himself small tastes of her. None of that had worked to exorcise his wife from his consciousness.

So he'd have to try the only thing left. He was going to spend the weekend in bed with Daniella in full-on immersion. By Monday, she would be out of his system and he'd have his focus back. He could share a house with her at night and forget about her during the day, like he'd planned all along.

It had to work. He'd toiled so hard to build a secure company and he owed it to everyone to maintain it. Especially Daniella. He'd vowed to care for her and he'd scrub floors at a state prison before he'd allow his wife to live next door to a meth lab like his own father had.

Ten

The book Dannie was reading held her interest about as well as the last one. Which was to say not at all. She'd parked on the settee to wait in hopes that Leo might come home soon, but it was already almost ten o'clock.

One more page. The story had to get better at some point. If it didn't, she'd get ready for bed. Leo's alarm went off before dawn and she was still adjusting to his routine.

The atmosphere shifted and she glanced up from her e-reader. Leo stood in the open doorway, one hand on the frame and the other clutching a bouquet of red roses. And he was watching her with undisguised, delicious hunger.

Heat erupted at her center and radiated outward, flushing her whole body. The e-reader fell to the carpet with a thunk, released by her suddenly nerveless fingers.

"Roses? For me?" Her voice trembled, and he didn't miss it. Her temperature rose as his expression darkened.

"In a manner of speaking." Striding to the settee, he held out his free hand and when she took it, he pulled her to her feet. His torso brushed hers and her nipples hardened. "Follow me."

Anywhere.

Mystified, she trailed him into the bathroom, where he flicked on the lights to one-quarter brightness and began filling the bathtub. Over his shoulder, he called, "It probably hasn't escaped your notice that I work a lot. I have very little opportunity to indulge in simple pleasures. So I'm correcting that oversight right now. I have this fantasy involving you, me and rose petals. This time of night, I had to buy them still attached."

He gathered the petals in one hand and wrenched them from the stalks, then released them into the water.

As the red circles floated down to rest on the surface, her heart tumbled along with them. "You have fantasies about me?"

The look on his face shot her temperature up another four thousand notches.

"Constantly."

"What am I doing in these fantasies?" she asked, her tongue nearly tripping over the words.

"Driving me pomegranates, mostly." He grinned and it was so un-Leo-like she did a double take. "By the way, I'm taking the weekend off. If you don't have other plans, I'd like to spend it with you. Maybe we could consider it a delayed honeymoon."

Honeymoon? *Weekend off?* She jammed her hands down on her hips and stared at him. "Who are you and what have you done with Leonardo Reynolds?"

His expression turned sheepish and he shrugged. "Let's say I had a revelation. We're married. I have to do things differently than I've done in the past. I *want* to do things differently," he stressed. "For you. Because you deserve it. You're a great wife."

A hard, painful lump slammed into her throat. He wanted to spend time with her. Romance her, as she'd asked. The roses were reciprocation—one great husband, coming up.

Little stabs at the corners of her eyes warned of an imminent deluge. What was he trying to do to her? She'd just become good and convinced their marriage was enough as it was. Now this.

I will not cry. I will not cry.

"You ain't seen nothing yet."

"Yeah?" He twisted the faucet handle and shut off the water. "You've been holding out on me?"

"Maybe. Talk to me about these fantasies." A good, strong dose of Leo's potent masculinity—that was what she needed to keep the emotion where it belonged. Inside. At least until she figured out where all this was coming from. Her husband had done so many about-faces she couldn't help but be slightly wary. "Have you really had a lot about me? Like what?"

"Oh, I've been so remiss, haven't I?" He tsked and sat on the edge of the garden tub, feet on the lowest step leading up to the rim. "Come here."

Her toes curled against the cold travertine as she approached and then she forgot all about a small thing like bare feet as Leo drew her between his split legs, his gaze heavy lidded with sensuous promise.

"I've been a very bad husband," he told her. "You clearly have no idea how wickedly sexy I find you. Let's correct that oversight, too, while we're at it."

Her insides disintegrated and she had no idea how she was still standing with no bones.

Slowly, he loosened each button on her blouse, widening the vee over her bra until he'd bared it entirely. The shirt slipped from her shoulders and Leo reeled in the fabric, pulling her forward.

"My fantasies are no match for the real thing." His open mouth settled onto the curve of her breast where the edge of her bra met skin. His tongue darted inside, circling her nipple. Pure, unaltered desire flared from her center, engulfing her senses.

Clutching at his shoulders, she moaned his name as he unzipped her skirt, still suckling her, wetting her bra with his ministrations. Impatiently, he peeled the cup from her breast and sucked the nipple between his teeth to scrape it lightly.

She pushed farther into his mouth and drowned in sensation as he lit her up expertly with a combination of hard teeth and magic hands against her bottom.

"Daniella," he murmured against her flesh, abrading it with slight five-o'clock shadow, which felt so amazing she shuddered.

Leo lifted his mouth and she nearly sobbed as it left her skin. He licked his lips in a slow, achingly obvious gesture designed to communicate how delicious he found her. Drinking in the sight of her pale pink bra-and-panty set, he reached around to unhook her bra, letting her breasts fall free.

He cursed, almost reverently. "Beautiful. You're the most beautiful woman I've ever seen. And you're all mine."

Her knees went numb, but his sure hands held her upright as he leaned down to kiss her waist, openmouthed, drawing her panties down simultaneously. His fingers trailed between her legs up the backside, wandering unchecked in some unknown pattern and thoroughly driving her insane.

"Leo," she choked out.

"Right here," he murmured and captured her hand. "In you go."

He led her up the stairs and into the tub, helping her lie back against the incline of the oval. She peeked up at him as he snagged a rose petal, swishing it through the water, through the valley of her breasts, around her already sensitized nipples. The motion shafted biting desire through her flesh.

When he rubbed the petal between her legs, a moan rumbled in her throat.

"Playtime is over." She yanked on his tie. "I want you in here with me."

His irises flared with dark heat.

Clothes began hitting the floor and she shamelessly watched as he revealed his taut body inch by maddeningly slow inch. A smattering of dark hair covered his chest, screaming his masculinity, and hard thighs perfectly showcased the prominent erection she wanted inside her with every shuddering breath.

He splashed into the water. The giant garden tub shrank as gorgeous, vibrant male filled it.

Leo grasped her arms and settled her into place against his chest spoon-style and immediately covered her breasts with his hands, kneading them. She gasped as his thick flesh ground hard against her rear.

Rose petals floated in the water, catching on wet skin, filling the air with their warm floral scent. He murmured wicked things in her ear as he touched her, and in combination with the warm water, his hands felt like silk against her skin, in her core, against her sensitive nub.

She reached behind her to grasp his erection. It filled her palm, hard and hot, and she caressed the slick tip. A groan ripped from deep in his chest.

He tore her hand away and clasped her hips, repositioned her and drove home in one swift stroke.

"Dannie," he whispered, his voice guttural, raw. Beautiful. It crawled inside her, filling her as surely as he filled her body. Clasping her close, he held her, torso heaving against her back as they lay joined in the water. Completed perfectly by the other.

After an eternity, he lifted her hips high enough to yank a long slice of heat from her center and eased her down again. They shuddered in pleasure together.

This *was* different. Leo was different. More focused. Drawing it out, allowing her to revel in the sensations, to feel so much more than the physical. It was a slow ride with plenty of mental scenery along the way.

Intense Leo was her new favorite and his brand of romance stole her breath.

"Dannie," he said again and increased the rhythm, hypnotically, sensuously.

He repeated her name over and over as he completed her. A dense torrent of heat gathered at the source and she split apart with a sob, not the slightest bit surprised he'd made her cry after all. She'd given him what he needed and it had been returned, tenfold.

What he'd started with the diamonds, he ended with the rose petals. She wasn't in the process of falling in love with him. It was done. Irrevocably. Wholly.

Her heart belonged to her husband.

"Leo, I..." What would he say if she told him? Surely he was in the throes, too. That's what this was all about, wasn't it? Their marriage looked different than what they'd originally thought. He wanted it to be different.

"Speechless? You?" He chuckled. "I'm incredibly flattered."

It took every ounce of Elise's personality-makeover training to bite back the words as he drained the tub and helped her out, then dried her with slow, tender swipes of a soft towel. This was too important to let Scarlett off the leash. Too important to screw up.

He'd never said he loved her. Only that he wanted to do things differently. Maybe this pseudohoneymoon was simply about sex. Goodness knew she'd given him permission to make it so often enough.

But honestly. If he didn't want her to fall in love with him, he should stop being so wonderful.

Leo threw on a robe and returned with flutes and a bottle of champagne. They drank it in bed while they talked about nothing and everything.

She kept looking for the right opening to blurt it all out. Shouldn't he know that he'd made her wildly happy? That their marriage was everything she'd ever dreamed of? Her feelings for Leo far eclipsed anything she'd ever felt for Rob. She'd found purpose and meaning in being a wife; she'd married a man who made her body and soul sing in perfect harmony and her mother was being taken care of. Leo was a sexy genie in a bottle, granting all her wishes effortlessly. She wanted to tell him.

The right moment never came.

He didn't shoot her long, lingering glances with his gaze full of love. When he took her glass and set it on the bedside table, then thoroughly ravished her, he didn't whisper the things in his heart while holding her.

Instead, he fell into a dead sleep. She lay awake, but he didn't murmur secret confessions into the darkness. Though he did seek her out while unconscious, sliding his solid thigh between hers and wrapping her up in a cloak of Leo. That part she had no difficulty understanding. He enjoyed having her in his bed. Enjoyed the closeness without the requirement of having to expose himself emotionally.

The feelings, the rush of love and tenderness, were strictly one-sided. For now.

Her marriage was *almost* everything she'd yearned for since she was a little girl. She had forty-eight hours to entice Leo that last few feet to the finish line.

When the early light of dawn through the triple bay window of the bedroom woke Leo, he didn't hesitate to indulge in another fantasy—the one he'd denied himself thus far.

He gripped Daniella's hips and wedged that sweet rear against his instant erection. His fingers trailed over her breasts and she sighed and it was sleepy. Erotic.

"Leo. It's—" One of her eyes popped open and immediately shut. "Six twenty-three. In the *morning.*"

"I know." He nuzzled her neck and she arched sensuously against him. "I slept sinfully late. It's refreshing."

"Thought you were taking the weekend off," she muttered and rolled her hips expertly. The cleft between her bare cheeks sandwiched his raging erection. His eyes crossed.

"Taking the weekend off to—" She did it again. Deliberately.

"Talk a lot?" she suggested sweetly and choked on the words as he skimmed a finger through the swollen folds of her center.

Closing his eyes, he breathed in the scent of crushed roses and the musk of Daniella's arousal. "Not hardly."

He sank into her and it was amazing. There was something about spooning with her that just killed him. They fit together this way, moving in perfect cadence as they had last night, and he savored it.

All her beauty was within easy reach and he made full use of the access, tweaking her gorgeous breasts and circling her nub as he sheathed himself from behind again and again. Hot friction sparked, driving them both faster.

She climaxed with a sexy moan and he followed in a brilliant chain reaction of sensation that didn't quit.

Playing hooky from work had a lot going for it. He was slightly ashamed at how much he was enjoying his weekend off, especially given that it had essentially just started. There was a lot more indulgence to be had. A lot more fantasies to enact. A lot more dread at the imminent reel back Monday morning.

How was he going to forget Daniella and concentrate on work? It was like ordering your heart not to beat so your lungs could function.

Eventually, they rolled out of bed and he let his wife make him pancakes. It beat an energy bar by quadruple. Her coffee, as always, was amazing. He hadn't enjoyed it with her since the first time she'd made it after he fell asleep at his desk. But he never left the house without a full travel mug. Somehow it had become part of his routine to drink it on the way to work. The empty mug sat on his desk all day and the sight of it made him smile.

"What should we do with all this borrowed time?" he asked her and forked another bite into his mouth as they sat at the bistro table in the breakfast nook.

Daniella peered at him over her coffee mug. "Is that what it is? Borrowed?"

"Well…yeah." Something in her frozen posture tipped him off that he might have stumbled into quicksand. "The initiatives I have going on at the office didn't magically disappear. I'm putting them off until Monday."

"I see."

"You sound disappointed." The next bite didn't go down so well. He could stand a lot of things, but Daniella's disappointment was not one of them.

She shook her head, long brown hair rippling the way it had this morning over his shoulder. "Just trying to interpret your phrasing. *Borrowed* implies you'll have to pay it back at some point. I don't want you to have to do that."

"I made the decision to spend the weekend with you. I wanted to. Don't feel guilty."

Her eyebrows lifted. "I don't. I mean I wish you didn't have to choose. Like you've got a lot of balls to juggle and I'm the one you happened to grab."

"What other choice do I have, Daniella?" Suddenly frustrated, he dropped his fork into the middle of his half-eaten pancakes. "I have a company to run. But I'm here with you now, aren't I? I'm juggling the best I can."

It was the voice of his worst fears—that he would drop a ball. Or all of them. He was horrible at juggling.

She laughed. "Yes, you're here, but it doesn't seem like either of us are fond of the juggling. Isn't there a way to whittle down the number of balls until you can hold them all in your hand? Maybe you can hire some additional staff members or change your focus."

"You're telling me to scale back my involvement in Reynolds Capital. Take on fewer partners."

His gut clenched at the mere thought of how quickly the company would dissolve if he did what she suggested. Venture capital was a carefully constructed illusion of leveraged moving parts. Like a Jenga puzzle. Move one piece the wrong way and the whole thing crashed into an ugly pile.

"I don't know what would work best. But you do." Casually, she sipped her coffee. "Why don't you try it? Then you don't have to borrow time from work to spend it with me."

Really? She'd morphed into the opposite of an understanding wife who forgave her workaholic husband's schedule. He'd married her specifically to avoid this issue. Now she'd joined the ranks of every other woman he'd ever dated.

"*I'm* the Reynolds in Reynolds Capital. I spent a decade building the company from nothing and—" Quickly, he squashed his temper. *Give a woman an inch and forget a mile—she'll take the circumference of the Earth instead.*

"Forgive me if I overstepped. You were the one who said you wanted to do things differently and I was offering a solution. Less juggling would be different." She had the grace to smile as she covered his hand with her more delicate one. But he wasn't fooled. She had more strength in one pinky than most men did in their whole bodies. "I only meant to point out we all have choices and you make yours every day. That's all."

"Uh…" His temper fizzled. She'd only been trying to solve a problem *he'd* expressed. "Fair enough."

"Let's forget this conversation and enjoy our weekend."

Somehow, he had a feeling it wasn't going to be that simple. The die had been cast and she'd made a point with logic and style. Much to his discomfort.

True to his word, Leo didn't so much as glance at his phone or boot up his laptop once. He kept waiting for jitters to set in, like an addict deprived of his fix. The absence of being plugged in should be taking a toll. It wasn't.

He wrote it off as a keen awareness that he owed Daniella his attention until Monday morning. And then there was her gift for distraction. By midafternoon, they were naked in the warmed spa adjacent to the pool. He easily forgot about the blinking message light on his phone as they christened the spa.

He'd immersed himself in his wife's deep water and surfacing was the last thing on his mind.

So it was a bit of a shock to join Daniella in the media

room for a late movie and have her announce with no fanfare, "You need to call Tommy Garrett."

"Tommy? Why? How do you know?" Leo set down the bottle of wine and stemware he'd gone to the cellar to retrieve and pulled the corkscrew from his pocket.

"He's been trying to reach you all day. He called my cell phone, wondering if you'd been rushed to the hospital."

About a hundred things careened through his head, but first things first. "How does Tommy have your cell phone number?"

Anger flared from his gut, as shocking as it was powerful.

"Don't wave all that testosterone in my face. How do you imagine he RSVP'd for your party if he didn't have my cell phone number?" She arched a brow. "Pony Express?"

His stomach settled. Slightly. He eased the cork from the bottle and poured two glasses. Wine scraped down his throat, burning against the shame already coating it. "I'm sorry. I don't know where that comes from."

"It's okay. It makes me all gushy inside to know you care." She giggled at his expression. "The movie can wait. Call Tommy. It seemed rather urgent."

Grumbling, he went in search of his phone and found it on the counter in the kitchen. Yeah, Tommy had called a time or twelve. Four text messages, one in all caps.

He hit Callback and shook his head. Kids.

"Leo. Finally," Tommy exclaimed when the call connected. "My lawyers got all their crap straightened out. I'm going with you, man. Let's get started taking the world by storm."

Leo blindly searched for a seat. His hand hit a bar stool at the kitchen island. Good enough. "You're accepting my proposal?"

"That's what I said, isn't it? Why didn't you answer your phone, by the way?" Munching sounds filled a sudden pause. Tommy lived on Doritos and Red Bull, which

Leo always kept on hand at the office in case of impromptu meetings. Thankfully, there'd be a lot more of those in the future. "Took me forever to find Dannie's number again. I didn't save it to my contacts."

"I'm taking some…" Leo's mouth dried up and he had to force the rest. "Time off."

This was it—the Holy Grail of everything he'd worked for. Now Leo would find out if he was as good as he thought he was at selecting a winner. But not today. He'd have to sit on his hands for the rest of the weekend.

"That's cool. We can talk mañana."

It was physically painful for Leo to open his mouth and say, "It'll have to be Monday."

"Seriously?" Tommy huffed out a noise of disgust that crawled up Leo's spine. "Well, I gotta say. I'd tell you to piss off, too, if I had a woman at home like Dannie. They sure don't make many of 'em like that. I'll be by on Monday."

Leo bit his tongue. Hard. Because what could he say to refute that? Daniella *was* the reason Leo couldn't talk shop on a Sunday when normally no hour of the day or night was too sacred to pour more cement in the foundation of Reynolds Capital Management's success.

But dear God, it was difficult to swallow.

Even harder was the task of sitting next to his wife on the plush couch in the media room and *not* asking her for leeway on his promise to spend the weekend with her. He did it. Barely. And insisted Tommy's call was unimportant when she asked.

Why had he told her he was taking the whole weekend off? She would have been happy with just Saturday. It was too late now. After her speech about choices, he couldn't imagine coming right out and saying he was picking work over her.

While the movie played, Daniella emptied almost an entire bottle of wine by herself and then expressed her appreciation for the rose-petal bath the night before with a great deal of creativity. By the time the credits rolled, Leo couldn't have stated his own name under oath.

The whirlpool of Daniella had well and truly sucked him under and he could no longer pretend he was taking the weekend off for any other reason than because he physically ached when he wasn't with her.

He didn't want to pick work over her. Or vice versa. If there was a more difficult place to be than between a woman and ambition, Leo didn't want to know about it. Not just any woman, but one who tilted his world and righted it in the same breath. And not just ambition, but the culmination of banishing childhood fears and achieving adult aspirations.

Sunday, after the last round of sleepy morning indulgence Leo would permit himself to experience for a long, long time, Daniella kissed him soundly and retrieved a flat package from under the bed.

"For me?" An odd ping of pleasure pierced his chest as she nodded, handing it to him.

He tore off the plain brown wrapping to reveal a framed sepia-toned drawing.

"It's one of da Vinci's," Daniella explained quietly. "You probably know that."

He did. Reverently, he tilted the frame away from the light to reduce the glare. It was one of his favorites, a reproduction of da Vinci's earliest drawing of the Arno Valley. "The original hangs in the Uffizi. Thank you. What made you think of this?"

"Da Vinci was more than a painter. He invented. He drew. He was a sculptor and a mathematician. And, like, four other things I've forgotten." With a small laugh, she tugged the frame from his grasp and laid it on the bed, then took his hand. "He was so much more than the *Mona Lisa*. Like you're more than Reynolds Capital Management. I wanted you to know I see that."

The gift suddenly took on meaning of exponential proportions. And he wasn't sure he liked it. "Are you angling for me to show you something I drew?"

The exposure of such a thing was inconceivable. Drawing was for him alone. No one else. It would be like slicing open his brain and allowing his deepest secrets to flow out, then trying to stitch the gray matter back together. It would never heal quite right. There'd always be a scar and the secrets would be out there in the world, unprotected.

"I would have asked if that's what I was after."

"What are you after, then?"

Her expression softened. "No nefarious motives. All my motives are right here." Crossing her heart with an index finger, she sought his gaze, her irises as deep and rich as melted chocolate.

"What does that mean?"

"What do you think it means, Leo?" She smiled. "I gave you the picture because I love you and want to express that in tangible ways."

His insides shuddered to an icy halt.

I love you.

It echoed in his head, pounding at the base of his skull. Where had that *come* from? No one had ever said that to him before. Well, except his mom.

Oh, dear God. His overtly romantic mother would have a field day with this. Leo's arranged marriage had just blown up in his face. His wife had *fallen in love with him.*

What was he supposed to say in response?

"You can't drop something like that on me out of the blue."

"I can't?" She sat up, covers—and her state of undress—forgotten. "How should I have led up to it, then?"

He unstuck his tongue from the desert the roof of his mouth had turned into. "I mean, you didn't have to say it at all. That's… We're not—" He pinched the bridge of his nose and tried to corral his spooked wits before he told her the truth. That he'd liked the sound of those words far more than he would have expected. "That's not the kind of marriage we agreed to."

She recoiled and quickly composed her expression, but not before he saw the flicker of hurt. "I know that. It doesn't erase my feelings. You're a kind, generous man who makes me happy. We spent a romantic weekend together and you kind of pushed me over the edge after Tommy called and you blew him off. Wouldn't you rather I be honest with you?"

Not really, no. Not when it involved sticky emotions he couldn't fathom. Dangerous emotions. Wonderful, terrible emotions that quaked through him. Love was a hell of an indulgence and he could hardly comprehend the ramifications of her blithe announcement.

But it was out there and he couldn't ignore it. Like he couldn't ignore the corkscrew through his gut over what he had to do next. "Since you're such an advocate of honesty, I lost a couple of deals over those fantasies I couldn't get out of my head. I spent the weekend with you so I could go back to work on Monday and finally concentrate."

The pain radiating from her gaze sliced through his chest like a meat cleaver.

Get some distance before you hurt her even worse.

He couldn't reach for her. He wanted to. Wanted to tell her it was all a big lie and *I love you* was the sweetest phrase in the English language. It almost made the Tommy-free weekend worth it and that scared him the most. Because he might do it again.

Curling his fingers under, he said the most horrible thing he could think of.

"The rose petals weren't intended to seduce you into falling in love. It was an exorcism."

One that had just failed miserably. His wife had fallen in love with him. It was all over her face, in her touch. Had been for some time and he'd only just realized how much he liked it on her.

Worse, he had to pretend that her words hadn't lodged in his heart. That his soul wasn't turning them over, examining them from all angles and contemplating grabbing on with all its might. Whispering seductive ideas.

It could be like it was this weekend forever. Forget about work, not your wife. You don't have to surface. Not really.

Said Satan about the apple.

Love was the decisive destroyer of security, the ultimate quicksand that led to the ghetto, and he would not fall prey to the temptations of his weaknesses. He would not become his father. No matter how hard it was to force out the words.

"We have a marriage of convenience, Daniella. That's all."

"I understand," she whispered, and nodded once without looking up from her folded hands.

She wasn't going to slap him and storm out. The relief he'd expected to feel didn't materialize. Instead, the juggling act had grown exponentially harder. Now he had the Herculean task of continuing to push her away so she didn't utter *I love you* in his presence again. He couldn't take that raw devastation on her face, knowing that he was hurting her, knowing that he'd hurt her even more later if he slipped and said it back.

And neither would Leo allow Dax to be right. He still had his edge and that wasn't ever changing.

Eleven

The pill was so tiny. How could such small packaging prevent such a huge thing like pregnancy?

Dannie stuck the birth control pill in her mouth and swallowed, the action serving the dual purpose of getting it down her throat and keeping the tears at bay. The pill was both functional and symbolic. Not only was she preventing pregnancy, but she was giving up on grand, sweeping passion and love. Forever.

Her heart was too bruised to imagine having a baby with Leo. Not now. Maybe at some point in the future she'd get those images of him smiling tenderly at their child out of her head. Leo didn't have an ounce of tenderness in him.

Okay, that wasn't true. He had it, he just used a great deal of judiciousness in how and when he allowed it to surface. She couldn't willingly give birth to a child who would one day want his or her daddy's attention. No child deserved to be fathered by a man who refused to participate in his own life.

Scratch a baby off the list. Yet another sacrifice she'd make. She understood people didn't always get their heart's desire. But she'd about run out of dreams for her non-fairy-tale real life to strip away.

She'd had an entire weekend to show Leo how wonderful their marriage could be. And she'd failed. He didn't find the idea of opening his heart to her the least bit appealing. In her most spectacular screwup to date, she'd assumed they'd grow to care for each other. Maybe not at the same rate, but they'd eventually catch up, right? It had never occurred to her he'd refuse to show even a tiny bit of affection for his wife.

She was simply a convenience. Exactly as he'd always said. Reading unmet needs into his actions and pushing him into intimacy hadn't gotten her anywhere but brokenhearted.

Wife was her identity, her essence. Work was his. Cliché indeed.

So he went back to his sixteen-hour days and she made a doctor's appointment. After three days of falling asleep before Leo came home, the pills were unnecessary insurance thus far. Apparently telling her husband she loved him was birth control in and of itself.

The music of her stupid phone's ringtone cut the silence in the bathroom.

She glanced at it. Elise's name flashed from the screen. What in the world?

"Hello?"

"It's Elise. I'm sorry to bother you, but I'm in a bind and I need your help."

"Of course. Whatever you need, it's yours."

There was very little Dannie wouldn't do for the woman who had changed her life, broken heart notwithstanding. Elise had helped her find a secure marriage. This was the "for worse" part—so much worse than she'd predicted, and she'd expected it to *suck* if she fell in love with Leo and he didn't return her feelings.

"Thank you. So much. I've got a new applicant for the program and I'm totally booked. But I can't turn her away. Will you go through the preliminary stages with her?"

"You want *me* to teach someone else how to do her hair and makeup?"

Elise chuckled. "Don't sound so surprised. You're highly qualified."

That was only because her fairy godmother had no idea

how solidly catastrophic Dannie's match had become. "As long as it's just preliminaries. I couldn't do any of the rest."

"Oh, I'll pay you."

"I wasn't talking about that." But now she was thinking about how it was almost like a short part-time job. Good timing. That might get her mind off the empty house. "I'd do it for free."

"I insist. Can you help me out or am I imposing on your new marriage?"

Dannie bit back maniacal laughter. "I can do it. Be there in thirty minutes."

She ended the call and finished getting ready for the day. She'd stopped rolling out of bed before dawn and making Leo's coffee. What would be the point? He probably hadn't even noticed.

Elise's elegant two-story town house in uptown brought back bittersweet memories. Inside these walls, Dannie had transformed from an outspoken, penniless—and hopeless—woman into a demure, suitable wife for the man Elise's computer had matched her with.

Well, not so demure. Scarlett sometimes took over, especially when Dannie's clothes came off. And when Leo made her mad, or smiled at her or—okay, Scarlett was here to stay. Dannie sighed. The suitable part was still true. She'd orchestrated a heck of a party and Tommy had signed with Reynolds Capital. Clearly, *some* of Elise's training had taken root.

Elise answered the door and threw her arms around Dannie in an exuberant hug that knocked her off balance, despite the fact that Dannie had six inches on Elise in height. But what she lacked vertically, Elise more than made up for in personality and heart.

"Look at you," Elise gushed. "So gorgeous and sophisticated. Thanks, by the way. Come meet Juliet."

Dannie followed Elise into the living room where she'd married Leo. It seemed like aeons ago that she'd stood at that fireplace, so nervous about entering an arranged marriage she could barely speak. Never had she imagined as she slipped that ring on Leo's finger that she'd fall in love and when she told him, he'd so thoroughly reject it.

Not just reject it. He'd *exorcised* her. As if she'd been haunting Leo and he hoped to banish the grim specter of his wife from the attic in his head.

If she had known, would she have still married him? Her mother's face swam into her mind. Yeah. She would have. Her mother was too important to balk at a little thing like a broken heart.

Dannie turned her back on the fireplace.

The woman huddled on the couch unfolded and stood to greet her.

"Juliet Villere," she said and held out a hand.

Even without the slight accent, her European descent was obvious. She had that quality inherent in people from another country—it was in the style of her shoes, the foreign cut of her clothing and light brown hair, and in the set of her aquiline features.

Dannie introduced herself and smiled at the other woman. Curiosity was killing her. As Dannie did, surely Juliet had a story behind why she'd answered Elise's ad. "You're here to let Elise sprinkle some magic dust over you?"

"Magic would help."

She returned Dannie's smile, but it didn't reach her eyes and Dannie was sold. No wonder Elise hadn't turned her away. The woman radiated a forlorn aura that made Dannie want to cover her with a warm quilt and ply her with hot chocolate. And it was eighty-five degrees outside.

Elise nodded. "Juliet is a self-described tomboy. I couldn't think of anyone more ladylike than Dannie and I've already taken on more candidates than I can handle. It's a perfect match."

Heat climbed into Dannie's cheeks. She *was* ladylike when it counted. What had happened between her and Leo in the media room after he ignored Tommy's call was nobody's business but hers. Besides, he liked it when she put on her brazen side.

At least she excelled in that area of her marriage.

"Thank you for helping me, Ms. Arundel. I had nowhere else to turn." Juliet bobbed her head first at Elise and then at Dannie. "I would be grateful to find an American husband."

"Did your computer already spit out some possibles?" Dannie asked Elise.

Elise shook her head. "She's not entered yet. Makeover first, then I do the match. The computer doesn't care what you look like, but I find that the makeover gives women the confidence to answer the profile questions from the heart instead of their head. Then the algorithm matches based on personality."

"Wait." Dannie went a little faint. "External characteristics aren't part of the profile process?"

"Of course not. Love isn't based on looks."

"But…" Dannie sank onto the couch. "You matched me with Leo because he was looking for certain qualities in a wife. Organized. Sophisticated. Able to host parties and mingle with the upper crust."

Which had everything to do with external qualities. Not internal.

"Yes. That covers about four of the profile points. The rest are all related to your views on relationships. Love. Family. How you feel about sex. Conflict. You and Leo fit on all forty-seven."

"That's impossible," she countered flatly.

"Name one area where that's not true and I'll refund Leo's money right now."

"Love. I believe in it. He doesn't." Saying it out loud made it real all of a sudden and a breakdown threatened Dannie's immediate future.

"That's totally false." Elise's brow puckered as she paused. "Unless he lied on his profile. Which I suppose is possible but highly improbable."

"It can't be that foolproof."

Why was she arguing about this? The computer had
matched her with Leo because they'd both agreed a marriage based on mutual goals made sense. Neither of them
had expressed an interest in love from the outset and Elise
was absolutely correct—Dannie had answered the profile
questions from her heart. She loved her mother and marrying Leo had saved her. End of story.

"It's not. But I am." The flash of Elise's smile did not
temper her self-assurance. "I administer the profile test myself and I wrote it."

Juliet watched the exchange as though it was a tennis
match, eyelids shielding her thoughts. "But something is
amiss or you would not be having this discussion, right?"
she suggested.

Something as in Dannie had created this mess by forgetting love didn't create security, but honoring your word did.
Her mother's stance on relationships had never steered her
wrong before, and if she'd tried a little harder to embrace the
idea of a loveless marriage, she could have avoided all this.

Elise deflated a little. "Yes, of course you're right. I'm
sorry. I have to shut down my analytical side or it takes
over."

Yeah, Dannie knew all about shutting down inappropriate emotional outbursts. "I'm just disappointed and mad at
myself for thinking I could entice him away from his dollar signs with promises of fulfillment. It's not your fault."

Elise put a comforting hand on Dannie's arm. "My point
is that you totally can. I'm sorry he's being difficult about
accepting all that you have to offer beyond the ability to
schedule personal appointments. But you've got what he
needs emotionally, too."

Did she?

And did she have what he really needed or only what he
thought he needed? For a long time, she'd smugly believed
she knew the difference and her job was to guide him into

understanding how to express his true desires. But really, her own pent-up needs had messed that up. And how.

Dannie took Juliet upstairs to Elise's war room, complete with a long lighted mirror and counter, racks of clothing and more hairstyling and makeup tools than a Vegas show-girl dressing room.

"All this is necessary?" Juliet's gaze darted around the room, her nostrils flaring. "What is *that?* Will it hurt?"

The panicked questions lightened Dannie's mood. "It's a straightening iron. For your hair. We don't stick your fingers between the plates unless you fail at balancing a book on your head." The other woman's cheeks blanched and Dannie laughed. "I'm kidding. Sit down in that chair and let's get started. Drink?"

Dannie crossed to the small refrigerator stocked with water, lemons, cucumbers and ice packs, the best beauty accoutrements on the planet behind a good night's sleep.

"Thank you. I'm not thirsty."

"You need to drink plenty of water. It's good for your skin and helps you stay full so you don't feel as hungry." Elise's lessons rolled out of Dannie's brain effortlessly. "Lemon gives a little bit of taste, if you prefer."

"I prefer to be sailing or swimming." The frown had no trouble reaching Juliet's eyes, unlike her smile. "I miss the water."

"Where are you from?" Dannie asked as she plugged in the hair dryer, straightening iron, curling iron and hot rollers. She hadn't decided yet how Juliet's long hair would best be styled, though it would surely benefit from a more elegant cut. And she'd definitely need a facial. Dannie mentally ticked off a few more details and realized she was humming.

It was the happiest she'd felt all week.

"South of France. Delamer." Juliet spat out the country's name as if it had the reputation of being a leper's colony instead of a Mediterranean playground for the rich and beautiful.

"That's a lovely place. And you've got those two gorgeous princes. I read that Prince Alain is getting married soon. I hope they televise it." Dannie sighed a little in what she assumed would be mutual appreciation for a dreamy, out-of-reach public figure and his royal romance.

Juliet instead burst into tears.

Dannie gathered the other woman into a wet embrace and patted her back. "Oh, honey. What's wrong?"

Juliet snuffled against her shoulder. "Matters of the heart. They can undo us like no other."

She had that right. "Is that why you left Delamer? Someone broke your heart at home?"

With one last sniff, Juliet pulled out of Dannie's arms and dragged the back of a hand under both newly steeled eyes. "I want to forget that man exists. In Delamer, it's impossible. They splash his picture on everything. If I marry an American husband, I don't have to return and watch him with his perfect princess."

Dannie finally caught up and sank into the second director's chair. "Prince Alain broke your heart?"

This story called for chocolate and lots of red wine. Unfortunately, it wasn't even lunchtime and Elise kept neither in the house.

With a nod, Juliet twirled a brush absently, her thoughts clearly thousands of miles away. "There was a scandal. It's history. I can't change it and now I have to move on. What should we do first to transform me into a woman who will attract an American husband?"

Dannie let her change the subject and spent the next two hours teaching Juliet the basics of makeup and hair. It was a challenge, as the woman had never learned an iota about either.

"If you line only the bottom lip with a pencil that's a shade darker than your lipstick, it'll create an illusion of fuller lips." Dannie demonstrated on Juliet's mouth.

"Why would I want to do that? I can't sleep in lipstick. In

the morning, my husband will realize I'm not pouty lipped, won't he?" Juliet pursed her newly painted lips and scowled at her reflection in the mirror.

"Well, figure out a way to distract him before he notices," Dannie suggested and moved on to eye-shadow techniques. There was no polite way to say Juliet needed some style.

Tomboy she was, down to her bitten-off fingernails, Mediterranean sailor's tan and split ends. The tears had unlocked something in Juliet and she talked endlessly with Dannie about her life in Delamer, minus any details about the prince.

Dannie bit back her questions, but she'd love to know how such a down-to-earth woman without an ounce of polish had gotten within five feet of royalty, let alone long enough to develop a relationship with a prince. Then there was the briefly mentioned scandal.

She didn't ask. The internet would give up the rest of the tale soon enough.

Elise checked in and offered to have lunch delivered. Since Dannie had nowhere else to be, she stayed the rest of the day. She took Juliet shopping at the Galleria in North Dallas and by the time they returned to Elise's house, Dannie had made a friend. Which, she suspected, they both desperately needed.

Before Dannie left to go back to her empty house, Elise pulled her aside. "You did a fantastic job with Juliet. If you're in the market for a permanent job, I would hire you in a second."

Dannie stared at the matchmaker. "Are you serious?"

"Totally." Elise flipped her pageboy-cut hair back. "It takes time to groom these women, and I've got more men in the computer than I ever thought possible. Successful men don't have a lot of patience for sorting out good women from bad and I provide a valuable service to them. Business is booming, in short. If you've got spare time, it would be a huge help to me."

Elise named a salary that nearly popped Dannie's eyes from their sockets. "Let me think about it."

Her job was Leo Reynolds's Wife. But suddenly, it didn't have to be. She could make money working for Elise and take care of her mother.

Leo was married to his company, first and foremost. He made that choice every day. And now, Dannie had choices, too.

She didn't want a divorce. She wanted to be Leo's wife and have the marriage of her dreams, but Leo was half of that equation. Before she made a final decision about how she'd spend the next fifty years, he should have the opportunity to fully understand what her choices were. And how they'd affect him. He might give her the final piece she needed to make up her mind.

Maybe she'd get an exorcism of her own out of it.

The exorcism was not only a colossal failure, but Leo had also learned the very uncomfortable lesson that he couldn't find a method to erase the scent of strawberries from his skin.

He'd tried four different kinds of soap. Then something called a loofah. In one of his less sane moments, sandpaper started looking very attractive. It was totally irrational. The scent couldn't actually still be there after so many days, but he sniffed and there it was. Essence of Daniella.

Leo clenched the pencil in his hand and pulled his gaze from the Dallas skyline outside his office window. The garbage can by his desk overflowed with crumpled paper. He balled the sheet on his desk and threw the latest in another round of useless brainstorming on top. It bounced out to roll under his chair. Of course. Nothing was happening as it should. Normally, paper and pencil was his go-to method when he needed to unblock.

Surprise. It wasn't working.

Tommy Garrett was very shortly going to be furious that

he'd signed with Leo instead of Moreno Partners. This deal represented the pinnacle of venture capital success and Leo's brain was fried. He had nothing to show for his half of the partnership. He was supposed to provide business expertise. Connections in manufacturing. Marketing. Ideas.

Instead he'd spent the past few days mentally embroiled in about a million more fantasies starring his wife, whom he'd deliberately driven away. For all the good it had done.

His pencil trailed across the paper and in seconds, graphite lines appeared in the form of a woman. He groaned and shut his eyes. Then opened them. What the hell. Nothing else was coming out of his brain.

As his long-suppressed muse whispered halting, undisciplined inspiration, his hand captured it, transforming the vision into the concrete. Details of Daniella's shape flowed onto the paper. Glorious. Ethereal. So beautiful his chest ached. The ache spread, squeezing his lungs and biting through muscle painfully.

Sweat broke out across the back of his neck and his hand cramped but he didn't stop. He yanked more minutiae, more emotion, from a place deep inside until he was nearly spent.

Another. More paper. Draw.

As if the drawing conjured the woman, Leo glanced up to see his wife standing in the doorway of his office. In the flesh. Dear God, Daniella was luminous in a blue dress and sky-high heels that emphasized the delicate arch to her feet.

Heart pounding, he slipped a blank sheet over the drawing and shoved everything he'd just freed back into its box. He glanced at the clock. It was eight-thirty. And dark. When had that happened?

"What are you doing here?" he asked her and stood. *Nice greeting for your wife, moron.*

"I came to see you. Do you have a few minutes?" She waltzed in as if he'd said yes.

He hadn't seen her awake since Sunday, but his body reacted as if she'd slid up against him into that niche where she fit like clinging honey instead of taking a seat on the couch in his sitting area.

"Would you like to sit down?" she offered politely, every bit the queen of the manor despite the fact that his business acumen paid the rent on this office space. Or it used to. He was this close to selling caricatures on the street if something didn't change ASAP.

He sat on the other couch. Good. Distance was good. Kept their interaction impersonal. "How are you?"

"Fine. Elise offered me a job today."

She smoothed her skirt and crossed her legs, which he watched from the corner of his eye. It was so much more powerful a blow to witness those legs sliding together when he knew what they felt like against his. What he felt like when she was near him, even when they weren't touching.

"A job? As a matchmaker?"

"As a tutor. She asked me to help her polish the women she accepts into her program. Hair, makeup. That sort of thing."

"You'd be a natural. Are you here to ask my permission? I certainly don't mind if you—"

"I'm here to ask if there's the smallest possibility you could ever love me."

A knot the size of a Buick hardened in his chest. All his carefully constructed arguments regarding the status of their relationship had ended up forming a bridge to nowhere. Probably because he could hardly convince her of it when he'd failed to convince himself.

"Daniella, we've been over this."

"No, we haven't." She clasped her hands together so tightly one of her knuckles cracked. "I told you I loved you and you freaked."

That was a pretty accurate assessment. "Well, I don't want to rehash it. We have an arranged marriage with a useful design. Let's stick with it."

"Sorry. We're rehashing it right now. Extenuating circumstances caused me to give up what I really want in a marriage. And extenuating circumstances have caused me to reevaluate. I love you and want you to love me. I need to know if we can have a marriage based on that."

I love you. Why did that settle into so many tender places inside all at once?

"You make it sound simple. It's not," he said, his voice inexplicably gruff. All the emotions drawing had dredged up weren't so easily controlled as they would have been if he'd resisted the temptation in the first place.

"Explain to me what's complicated about it."

Everything.

"You want me to choose you over my company and that's an impossible place to be."

"I'm not asking you to do that. I would never presume to take away something so important to you. Why can't you have both?"

It was the juggling-act conversation all over again. As if it was simple to just choose to have both. This would always be a problem—he saw that now. And now was the time to get her crystal clear on the subject. Get them both clear.

"I'm not built that way. I don't do anything halfway, something you might better appreciate after this past weekend. Surely you recall how thoroughly I threw myself into pleasuring you." He raked his gaze over her deliberately to make the point and a gorgeous blush rose up in her cheeks. Which made him feel worse for God knew what reason. "I went to a matchmaker to find a wife who would be happy with what I could provide financially and overlook the number of hours I put into my company. Because I don't do that halfway, either. One side is going to suffer."

All or nothing. And when it came to Daniella, he was so far away from nothing, he couldn't even *see* nothing.

Her keen gaze flitted over his expression and it wasn't difficult to pinpoint the exact instant she gleaned more than he'd intended. "But that doesn't mean you don't have feelings for me, just that you're too afraid to admit something unexpected happened between us."

"What do you want me to say, Daniella?" His voice dipped uncontrollably as he fought to keep those feelings under wraps. "That you're right? That of all the things I expected to happen in our marriage, this conversation was so far down the list it was nearly invisible?"

Her bottom lip trembled. "I want you to say what's in your heart. Or are you too afraid?"

She didn't get it. He wasn't afraid of what was in his heart; he just couldn't give in to it. The cost of loving her was too high.

"My heart is not up for discussion."

Nodding, she stood up. "Security is vitally important to me and I married you to get it. It was the only way I could guarantee my mother would be taken care of. Elise changed that today. I can support my mother on the salary she'll pay me."

An arctic chill bit into his skin, creeping through the pores to flash freeze his whole body. "Are you asking me for a divorce?"

Please, God, no.

If he lost her, it was what he deserved.

She shook her head. "I'm telling you I have a choice. And I'm making it. I took lifetime vows I plan to honor. Now I'm giving you a chance to make a choice as well as to how that marriage will look. Get off the sidelines, love me and live happily ever after. Or we'll remain married, I'll manage your personal life but I'll move back into my own room. Separate hearts, separate bedrooms. What are you going to do?"

Panic clawed at his insides, a living thing desperate to get out and not particular about how many internal organs it destroyed in its quest. She wanted something worse than a divorce. The one thing money couldn't buy—him. His time. His attention. His love.

"That's ridiculous," he burst out and clamped his mouth closed until he could control what came out of it. "I told you what I need, which is for you to be happy with what I can give. Like I've told you from the very beginning. You're throwing that back at me, drawing a line. You or Reynolds Capital Management."

A tear tracked down her cheek. "Don't you see, Leo? *You* drew that line. Not me."

"My mistake. The line you drew is the one where you said I can't sleep with you anymore unless I'm in love with you."

"Yes. That is my fault." Her head dropped and it took an enormous amount of will to keep from enfolding her in his arms. But he was the source of her pain, not the solution. "My mother…she's an amazing woman, but she has a very jaded view of marriage and I let it fool me into believing I could be happy with a loveless arrangement. And I probably would have been if you were someone different. Someone I couldn't love. Be the husband I need, Leo."

She raised her head and what he saw in the depths of her shiny eyes nearly put him on his knees, prostrate before her in desperate apology, babbling, "Yes, I will be that husband," or worse, telling her he'd do anything as long as she'd look at him like that forever: as though he was worthy of being loved, even though he'd rejected her over and over again.

The overflowing trash can taunted him.

Lack of focus is what happens when you let your wife swallow you. Other venture capital firms have fewer dominoes, more liquid assets, less leveraged cash. One push and it'll all vanish.

He could never do what she was asking.

Once and for all, he could resolve it. Right here, right now, give her that final push away before he gave in to the emotions and forgot all the reasons he couldn't have his company *and* love Daniella.

"I stay on the sidelines for a reason. It's how I balance my obsessive personality." His heart thumped painfully. This was the right thing, for him and Reynolds Capital. Why didn't it feel like it? "I need you to be the wife I thought I was getting from EA International."

Which was impossible. Daniella could never be the out-of-sight, out-of-mind wife he'd envisioned. He'd given up on categorizing her and forcing her into a box when she insisted on being in all the boxes simultaneously. His multi-talented wife was the only woman alive who could do that.

Her expression went as stiff as her spine. "Then that's what you'll get. I'll schedule your appointments and host your parties and make you look good to your associates. I won't be in your bed at night, but I'll give you a hundred percent during the day and never mention how many hours you work."

It was everything he'd asked for. And the polar opposite of what he wanted. He vised his throbbing temples between his middle finger and his thumb but his brain still felt as though it was about to explode. How had she managed to twist this around so that they were back to their original agreement but it felt as if she'd kicked him in the stomach?

"I wish…" She crossed her arms as if holding herself in. "Love creates security, too. I wish you could see that. But if it's your choice for me to be nothing more than a glorified personal assistant, I hope it makes you happy. Just keep in mind that your company *and* your wife bear your name. You will always be a part of both."

And then she walked out, heels clicking on the stained concrete in perfect rhythm to the sound of his soul splitting in two.

Twelve

"Dorito?" Tommy offered and stuck out the bag.

Leo shook his head. Doritos didn't sit well on an empty stomach. Nothing sat well on an empty stomach, especially not the dreck in his coffee cup. Mrs. Gordon had remade it four times already and the look on her face said he'd better be happy with this round.

He shoved the half-full mug to the far end of the conference table, wished it was a travel mug filled by his wife and scrubbed his jaw. Rough stubble stabbed his fingers. *Forgot to shave. Again.*

"So, amigo." Tommy crunched absently and nodded to the TV on the wall, where Leo's laptop screen was displayed. "I've redone this schematic twice. The prototype passed the CAD analysis. What's it going to take to get you happy with it?"

Hell would probably freeze over before Leo was happy about anything. He'd officially labeled this funk Daniella's Curse, because until she'd said she hoped his choice made him happy, he'd never given a thought to whether he was or not. And this funk was the opposite of happy.

He missed his wife. Her invisible presence invaded every last area of his life, including his car, which never dipped below half a tank of gas. And smelled like strawberries.

"The schematic is still wrong. That's why I keep telling you to redo it." Leo flipped the drawing vertically inside the CAD program and glanced up at the TV. "Look, you can't take this to manufacturing as is. We have to shave another two cubic centimeters somewhere to meet the price point. Otherwise the markup will be too high and the distribution deals will fall through."

Leo's phone beeped. Daniella's picture flashed and he snatched it up. Text message. He frowned at the concisely worded reminder of his appointment for a haircut that afternoon. Of course she hadn't called to talk to him.

"Why does this have to be so complicated?" Tommy complained. "I designed the thing. That should be enough. Why don't *you* figure out where to shave off whatever you think makes sense?"

Leo fiddled with the pencil in his fingers, weaving it through them like a baton, and counted all the way to fifteen for good measure. It did not calm him. "You're the designer. You have to redesign when it's not ready." His fingers sought the leather portfolio on the table. The picture he'd drawn of Daniella was inside. It equaled serenity in the midst of turmoil. Oddly enough. "I help you on the back end. We've been over this."

Shades of the last real conversation he'd had with Daniella filtered through his mind. Why did he have to constantly remind people of things they should already know? Leo had a specific role to fill—in the background. Always. Nobody remembered that he stayed out of the middle, except him.

"I don't know how to get it to your specifications!" Tommy burst out in recalcitrant five-year-old fashion, complete with a scowl and crossed arms. "I've tried. I need help. That's why I signed with you."

"I'm your financial backer. I'm only talking to you about the schematic now because we're behind schedule and I need a good design today." With a short laugh, Leo shook his head. "Why would you assume I could do anything to help?"

Tommy flipped hair out of his face. "Dannie. She believes in you. She totally convinced me you walk on water daily and in your spare time you invest in people's potential. As far as she's concerned, you're the messiah of everything."

His gut spasmed. What exactly had his wife told Tommy to give him such a ridiculous picture of Leo? "That's entirely too fanciful for what I do."

Entirely too fanciful for a mortal man who'd made plenty of mistakes. But it didn't stop the low hum of pleasure behind his rib cage. Did Daniella really think of him like that, as someone heroic and unfailing? Or had she said those things for Tommy's benefit, playing her part as a dutiful wife?

Leo had the distinct, uncomfortable realization it was probably both. And he didn't deserve either.

Eyebrows raised, Tommy crossed his feet casually. "Yeah? If you tell me you don't know exactly what needs to happen with that schematic, I'll call you a dirty liar. You've been trying to lead me to it for an hour and I can't see it."

Leo sighed and thought seriously about driving the pencil through the table, but it would only break the wood, not solve his mounting frustration. Before he could count the reasons why it was a stupid, ridiculous path, he centered a piece of paper under the graphite and drew the first line.

Tommy's purple high-tops hit the floor as he leaned forward to peer over Leo's shoulder. The fuel-converter schematic took shape on the paper. With each new line, he explained to Tommy where he varied from the original design, why the modification was necessary, what the downstream manufacturing effect would be.

Occasionally Tommy interjected questions, objections and once, a really heartfelt "Dude. That's righteous."

One of Tommy's objections was sound and Leo reconsidered his stance on it. He erased that part of the drawing and incorporated Tommy's suggestion. Mrs. Gordon left for the day, shaking her head and mumbling about creative minds. After several hours, many heated exchanges and a few moments of near-poetic collaboration, they had a design they could both live with.

The last time Leo could honestly say he'd had that much fun was during the weekend he'd spent with Daniella. Before that—never.

Once Leo had scanned the finished product into his laptop and displayed it on the TV, Tommy whistled. "A work of art. I have to use every tool known to designers to put something that beautiful together. I can't believe you freehanded that. With a pencil, no less."

"A pencil gets the shading right," Leo muttered with a shrug. "I guess you could say it's a talent."

"I knew you had it in you," Tommy said smugly. "If I'd gone with Moreno Partners, I'd be screwed right now. Kiss your wife for me. She knows her stuff."

If only. Ironically, his current interaction with Daniella wasn't too different from how their marriage had started out, before they'd begun sharing a bedroom. If she hadn't barged in and demanded he start sleeping with her, would they still be exchanging text messages with no clue how much more there could be between them?

"She does have some kind of extrasensory perception," Leo said. "I'm afraid she's the one who walks on water."

No, *he'd* be clueless. She wouldn't. From the beginning, she'd seen possibilities, pushing their relationship into realms deeper and stronger than he'd ever imagined could be between any two people, let alone when one of them was Leo Reynolds.

How had that happened when he wasn't looking? And why did the loss of something he'd never asked for haunt him?

He'd done everything he could to drive her away so she wouldn't be hurt and instead of leaving him, his wife had stayed. Why didn't she get the message already?

With a grin, Tommy nodded vigorously. "Dannie's awesome."

His wife's nickname lodged in his gut, spreading nasty poison.

Leo liked Tommy. He was enthusiastic, tireless, brilliant. So what was it about Tommy simply saying his wife's name that burned Leo up? It was more than jealousy, more than a fear either Tommy or Daniella had less than pure intentions toward each other.

It was because Tommy held up a mirror and Leo hated his reflection.

This Dorito-crunching, Red Bull–slurping wonder kid was a younger, unrestricted, better version of Leo. Tommy could call a woman Dannie and think nothing of it, whereas Leo couldn't descend into that kind of intimacy unless he was drunk on Daniella's powerful chemistry.

And he wished he could be more like Tommy.

Tommy polished off the bag of Doritos. "You're awesome, too. I'm over here soaking it all up like SpongeBob."

A cleansing laugh burst out of Leo's mouth, unchecked. "Thanks. It's nice to have an appreciative audience."

"Dude, you talk and I'll listen, no matter what you say. I'm in awe of you right now. I think I learned more today than I did in four years at Yale. What else can you teach me?"

Oh, no. That was beyond the realm of his role. He and Tommy were financial partners, with a carefully constructed agreement separating their interests into neat boxes. That should be the extent of their relationship.

Should be. Everything should fit into a neat box. And nothing did, despite all of Leo's efforts.

"What do you want to know?"

With a lusty sigh, Tommy grinned. "Everything. Lay it on me."

And that was it. For the first time in his life, Leo had become an in-the-flesh mentor and for whatever reason, it felt right. It was a connection with his profit margin, one he'd never explored but suddenly wanted to.

All business is personal.

His wife had pointed that out long ago and he'd brushed it off as foolish sentiment. But it suddenly made brilliant sense. He hadn't lost the deal for Mastermind Media because he'd lost his edge, but because he'd willfully chosen not to enter into a partnership with Dax, for whom he'd lost a great deal of respect. His relationship with Daniella merely highlighted it, but hadn't caused it.

Leo's relationship with Daniella shone into all of his corners and scared away the excuses, the fears. She hadn't left him because she'd already figured out what Leo should have seen long ago.

Their arrangement was dead. Now they had an opportunity to make their marriage something else.

Instead of being like Tommy, maybe Leo should be a better version of himself. One that could be worthy of a woman like Daniella Reynolds.

Leo's morose mood lightened. After setting aside two afternoons a week for Tommy to bring his best SpongeBob absorption skills, Leo kicked his new disciple out of his office so he could leave.

When he got home, Leo paused outside Daniella's closed bedroom door and placed his palm flat against it, as he did every night. Sometimes he imagined he could feel her breathing through the door. The scent of strawberries lingered in the hall, wrapping around him.

He'd built this home as a fortress, a place that represented all the stability he'd never had as a child. Daniella had become an inseparable part of that. How could he ever have lived here without her? How could he explain to her what value she'd brought to his life?

Guilt gnawed a new hole in his gut. She deserved so much more than what he'd given her.

She should have left him.

The main goal of marriage was security. Odd how he

felt as though the ground was disappearing beneath him at an alarming pace the longer he had a wife in name only.

Instead of standing there like a stalker, he knocked and shifted the bulky package in his hand before him like a peace offering. He prayed it might change things but he had no clue how, or what that change might look like.

He just knew he couldn't do marriage like this anymore. The ball was in his court. Had been the entire time. Hopefully he'd picked up the proper racket.

Daniella opened the door, shiny hair down around her face and clad in a skintight tank top and loose pajama bottoms with her flat midriff peeking through. The swift, hard punch to his solar plexus nearly rendered him speechless.

Somehow he managed to choke out, "Hi."

Her luminous brown eyes sought his and a wealth of unexpressed things poured from them. "Hi."

"A gift. For you." He handed her the wrapped package and laced his fingers behind his back before he pulled her into an embrace she probably wouldn't welcome. But oh, dear God, did he want to touch her. "You gave me one. I'm returning the favor."

She ripped it open and his thudding heart deafened him as he waited.

Silently, she evaluated the basket of pomegranates. "What does this mean?"

She tilted the basket as if to show him, which was unnecessary. He'd placed each one in the basket himself, positioning it just so to interlock with the others. "You're still driving me pomegranates. Sleeping in separate bedrooms hasn't changed that."

The tension spiraled between them, squeezing his lungs, and he smiled in hopes of loosening it.

"I got that part. *Why* are you giving them to me?" Her gaze probed his, challenging him and killing his smile. She wasn't going to make this easy. She always had before, using her special powers to figure out exactly how to help him navigate.

Not this time. He shifted from foot to foot but couldn't find a comfortable stance. "Because I wanted to give you something that had special significance."

Her expression didn't change. "So it's nothing more than a gift designed to buy your way out of giving me anything emotional."

What did she want from him? A pound of flesh? She held in her hands one of the most emotional things he'd ever done. Somehow he had to make her see that.

"It's not just a gift, like jewelry. It's better than that."

Frozen, she stared at him for an eternity, long enough for him to realize he'd devalued the diamonds he'd given her for the party. Which were in her earlobes at this moment.

This was not going at all how he'd envisioned. She was supposed to make the first move. Fall into his arms and tell him this separation was killing her, too.

At the very least, she should be giving him a choice between two impossible options and then pretending it was okay when he picked the wrong one. The way she always did.

Floundering, he cast about for a lifeboat. "I'm sorry. I didn't mean it that way."

"How did you mean it? Or do you even know?"

"I do know!" At her raised eyebrows, he faltered. It had been an off-the-cuff protest. And a lie. Nothing between them was tangible. Or quantifiable. Which made it impossible to define the bottom line.

This was like a bad joke. What did the guy who had never hung on to a woman longer than a few weeks say to his wife? If only she'd tell him the punch line, they could move past this.

"What do you want me to say?"

"That's for you to figure out. I'll be here when you do. Thank you for the pomegranates."

With that, she closed the door in his face. Because at the end of the day, she knew the truth as well as he did. Jewelry. Pomegranates. Same difference. He still hadn't given her the one thing she really wanted—everything.

If he truly hoped to change their marriage, he had to dig much deeper. And it was going to hurt.

Dannie slid to the ground, the wood of her door biting into her back, and muffled a sob against the heel of her hand. *Pomegranates.*

Why did this have to be so hard?

Her mother was right: love was the stupidest thing of all to base a marriage on. It hurt too much. All Leo had to do was say, "I brought you a gift because I love you."

If his inability to do so wasn't bad enough, she had the awful feeling that the basket was indeed symbolic of his inner turmoil. Only supreme will suppressed her desire to knuckle under.

He'd tried. He really had. It just wasn't good enough, not anymore. Once upon a time, she'd believed they were a good match because they both valued security. It was how they went about achieving it where they differed.

Leo was an intense, focused man who cut himself off from people not because he didn't want to invest emotionally, but as some kind of compensation for what he viewed as a shortcoming of his personality. She couldn't spend a lifetime pretending it was okay that he refused to dive headlong into the game. She'd already compromised to the point of pain.

His mother had warned her how challenging Leo would be to love. Dannie should get a medal. So should Leo's mother.

Sleep did not come easily. She glanced at the time, convinced she'd been lying there for an hour but in reality, only four minutes had passed since the last clock check. She gave up at quarter past two and flipped on the TV to watch a fascinating documentary about the Civil War.

Her favorite historical time period unfolded on the screen. Women in lush hoopskirts danced a quadrille in the Old South before everything fell apart at the hands of General Sherman cutting a swath through Georgia on his way to the sea.

Dannie's heart felt as if it had taken a few rounds from a Yankee musket, too.

But where Scarlett O'Hara had raised a fist to the sky and vowed to persevere, Dannie felt like giving up.

A divorce would be easier. She could take care of her mother, live with Elise and try to forget about the man she'd married who refused to get out from behind the scenes.

But she'd taken vows. Her stomach ached at the thought of going back on her word. Her heart ached over the idea of staying. Which was worse?

All she knew was that she couldn't do this anymore.

In the morning, she took a bleary-eyed shower and spent the day at Elise's working with Juliet. They were both subdued and honestly, Dannie didn't see the point in giving Juliet a makeover when the woman was already beautiful. Besides, it wasn't as though a manicure and hot rollers would give Juliet what she most desired.

Or would it?

"What if your match is someone you can't fall in love with? Would you still marry him?" Dannie asked Juliet as she showed her how to pin the hot roller in place against her scalp. Some people didn't care about love. Some people found happiness and fulfillment in their own pursuits instead of through their husbands.

But Dannie wasn't some people, and she'd lied to herself about which side of the fence she was on, embracing her mother's philosophy as if it were her own.

Juliet made a face. "I would marry a warthog if he had

the means to keep me in America. Arranged marriages are common in Europe. You learn to coexist."

"But is it worth it to become someone else in order to have that means?"

The other woman shot her puzzled glance in the mirror. "I'm still me. With fingernails." She stuck out a hand, where a nail technician had created works of art with acrylic extensions.

Dannie glanced at her own reflection in the mirror. She'd been polished for so long, it was no longer a shock to see the elegant, sophisticated Mrs. Reynolds in the glass instead of Dannie White. Except they were one and the same, with a dash of Scarlett.

Elise had done the makeover first, but the computer had matched her to Leo because she was perfect for him. As she was. Not because Elise had infused Dannie with some special magic and transformed her into someone Leo would like.

I'm still me, too, but better.

Leo provided the foundation for her to excel as his wife and let her be as brazen, outspoken and blunt as she wanted. He was okay with Dannie being herself.

Their personalities were the match. She'd heard it over and over but today, it clicked.

She'd been so focused on whether Leo would kick her out if she screwed up it had blinded her to the real problem. They both had come into this marriage seeking security, but struggled with what they said they wanted versus what they'd actually gotten. And they were *both* trying to balance aspects of their incredibly strong personalities *for no reason.*

They wanted the same thing deep in their hearts—the security of an unending bond so strong it could never be broken.

The open-heart lavaliere around her neck caught the light as she leaned over Juliet's shoulder to arrange her hair. Elise had given Dannie the necklace when she'd agreed to marry Leo, as a gift between friends, she'd assumed.

Now she saw it as a reminder that marriage required exactly that—*two* open hearts.

Had she been too harsh with Leo about the pomegranates? Maybe she should find a way to coexist that didn't involve such absolutes. Security was enough for Juliet. A fulfilling partnership had been enough for Dannie once.

She'd pushed intimacy in an attempt to fulfill Leo's unvoiced needs and ignored the need he'd actually voiced—a wife he could depend on, who would stick with him, no matter what. Even through the pain of a one-sided grand, sweeping love affair.

One thing was for sure. Real life wasn't a fairy tale, but Dannie wanted her happily ever after anyway. Cinderella might have had some help from her fairy godmother, but in the end, she'd walked into that ball with only her brain and a strong drive to make her life better. What was a fairy tale but a story of perseverance, courage and choices?

It was time to be the wife Leo said he needed, not the one she assumed he needed.

Leo's car was in the garage when Dannie got home. She eyed it warily and glanced at her watch. It was three o'clock on a Tuesday. Someone had died. Someone *had* to have died.

Dannie dashed into the house, a lump in her throat as she triple checked her phone. She'd have a call if it was her mother. Wouldn't she?

"Leo!" Her shout echoed in the foyer but he didn't answer.

The study was empty. Her stomach flipped. Now she was really scared.

Neither was he in the pool, the kitchen, the media room, the servants' quarters around the back side of the garage or the workout room over the garage.

Dannie tore off two nails in her haste to turn the knob on

his bedroom door, the last threshold she should ever cross, but he could be lying a pool of his own blood and need help.

Curtains blocked the outside sunlight and the room was dark but for the lone lamp on Leo's dresser. It shone down on him. He sat on the carpet, hunched over a long piece of paper resting on a length of cardboard. Clawlike, he gripped a pencil in his hand, stroking it over the paper swiftly.

"Leo?" She paused just inside the door frame. "Are you okay?"

He glanced up. The light threw his ravaged face into relief, shadowing half of it. "I don't know when to stop. I tried to tell you."

"Tell me what? What are you talking about? What do you need to stop?"

"Drawing." He flipped a limp hand toward the room at large and that's when she realized white papers covered nearly every surface.

"How long have you been in here?" There were hundreds of drawings, slashes and fine lines filling the pages with a mess of shapes she couldn't make out in the semidark. *Hundreds.* Apparently she'd massively misconstrued what he meant by not doing things halfway.

"Since the pomegranates." His voice trembled with what had to be fatigue. He'd been holed up in here since last night?

"But your car was gone this morning."

"Needed a pencil sharpener. Is it enough? Look at the pictures, Daniella. Tell me if it's enough."

Her heart fluttered into her throat. "You want me to see your drawings?"

In response, he gathered a handful and clambered to his feet to bring them to her. The half light glinted off the short stubble lining his jaw and dark hair swept his collar. Not only had he skipped the haircut she'd scheduled, but he'd obviously not shaved in several days. His shirt was untucked and unbuttoned and this undone version of Leo had a devastating, intense edge.

As if presenting a broken baby bird, he gingerly handed off the drawings and waited silently.

She glanced at the first one and every ounce of oxygen in the room vanished.

"It's you," she whispered. She flipped through the pages. "They're all of you."

Gorgeously rendered. Drawn by the hand of a master who knew himself intimately and who was unashamed to show the world all the glorious details of what made up Leonardo Reynolds.

And he was completely naked in every single one.

He shut his eyes. "I stripped myself bare. Emotionally, physically, spiritually. For you. I cannot possibly explain what it cost me to put all of it on the paper. But it's there. Tell me it's enough."

Oh, my God.

"Leo," she croaked through a throat suddenly tight with unshed tears. This had all been for her. "Yes. *Yes*. It's enough."

More than enough. She clutched the pages to her abdomen. It was the deepest expression of his love she could possibly imagine and these pictures were worth far more than a thousand words. They told the story she'd yearned to hear, lifting his shell once and for all, revealing everything important about the man she loved.

Artist Leo touched her deep in her soul with invisible, precious fingers.

He deflated, almost collapsing. But then he opened his eyes and caught her in his arms, binding her to his strong, solid body. Her knees weren't too steady either as she let the drawings flutter to the floor and burrowed up against him.

Warm. Beautiful. Hers.

Her brain was having trouble spitting out anything coherent. And then he kissed her and she stopped thinking at all.

It was hungry, openmouthed, sloppy and so powerful. As he kissed her, he mouthed words she couldn't understand.

He broke away and murmured into her hair. And the phrase crystallized. "I want to be the husband you need."

"Oh, darling, you are." In every sense. He had been from the first moment, providing a safe, secure place for her to bloom into his wife. He was her match every bit as much as she was his.

He shook his head. "I haven't been. I don't deserve you. But I want you. So much."

"You have me. Forever. We're married, remember?" She smiled but he didn't return it.

"Not like this. No more agreement. No separate bedrooms. No separate hearts." He put his palm flat against his breastbone like a pledge. "I could've hired a personal assistant. But I didn't. I went looking for a wife because I needed one. I need a wife who sees past all my faults and loves me anyway. It's not too late, is it?"

She placed her palm on top of his. "Never. But, Leo, you didn't go to work today. You're not throwing away your company's success for me. I won't let you."

"I can't—so tired." His knees buckled and he fell to the carpet, taking her with him. He pulled her into his lap and cupped her jaw in his strong hands, fiercely, passionately, as if he'd never let go. "Like you said. You didn't draw the line. I did. It's what I do."

With a lopsided half smile, he jerked his head at the hundreds of drawings decorating the bedroom behind him. "You weren't trying to force me to make impossible choices. The choices weren't yours to present. You were simply helping me see what options had been there all along. Reynolds Capital Management is a part of me I can't give up. So are you."

"You want both? Me and your company?" Hope warred with reality. The drawings were a big, flashing exhibit A of what happened when Leo focused on something. His preferred spot on the sidelines made troubling sense.

"I want it all." His eyes closed for a beat, a habit she'd noticed he fell into when he struggled with what was going on inside. "I don't know how to balance. But I want to. I have to try."

His voice broke, carving indelible lines in her heart.

This was the open, raw, amazing man she'd fallen in love with. But she and Leo were the same, with facets of their personality that weren't always easy to manage.

"You can do it. We'll do it together." Who better to help him figure it out than the woman standing behind him, supporting him? "I love your intensity and I don't ever want you to feel like you can't be you. If you want to hole up on a Saturday because you've got a hot new investment opportunity to work, do it. Just don't expect to get much sleep that night. Don't ever deny any piece of yourself. I need all of you. As long as we both shall live."

Her job as Mrs. Reynolds was so simple: provide a foundation for him to blossom, the way he'd done for her.

"That sounds promising. If I have to work on a Saturday, will you still make me coffee?" he asked hopefully.

She smiled. "Every time. We'll both give a little and balance will come."

Nodding slowly, he cleared his throat. "I think it must be like when you have children. You love one with all your heart. Then another one comes along. Somehow you make room. Because it's worth it."

Children. Leo was talking about having children in the same breath with trying to balance.

The tears gathered in earnest this time. He'd transformed before her very eyes, but instead of a pirate or Rhett Butler or even a battered Mr. Fourpaws before her, he was wholly Leonardo and 100 percent the love of her life. "Yeah. I think it must be like that. We have stretchy hearts."

"Mine's pretty full. Of you." He was kissing her again

like a starving man, murmuring, but this time, she had no trouble deciphering what he was saying—*I love you*.

Then he said, "My hand hurts."

She laughed as she kissed it. "Wait right here. I have pills to throw in the trash and a red-hot wedding night outfit to wear for you. I guarantee you'll forget all about your sore hand."

Technically, it wasn't her wedding night. But in her book, every night was her wedding night when she was married to a man who loved her as much as Leo.

Epilogue

Leo Reynolds wished he could marry his wife, but they were already married and Daniella refused to divorce him just so he could have the fun of proposing to her in some elaborate fashion.

"Come on, you can't fool me," Leo teased her as they gripped the railing of the observation deck on the third level of the Eiffel Tower. Nine hundred feet below, the city of Paris spread as far as the eye could see. "You missed out on the proposal *and* the wedding of your dreams. You wouldn't like to do it all over again?"

Daniella kissed his cheek with a saucy smile, throwing her loose brown hair over her shoulder. "I'm getting the honeymoon of my dreams. And the husband. All that other stuff pales in comparison."

Sure it did. His wife suffered from an affliction with no cure—overt romanticism. Since he loved her beyond measure, he took personal responsibility for ensuring she never lost it. "Then you'll have to forgive me when I do something pale and lackluster like…this."

He slipped the ring box from his pocket and popped it open to reveal the rare red diamond ring inside. "Daniella Reynolds, I love you. Will you promise to be my wife the rest of our days, always wear that sexy lingerie set and let me make you as happy as you've made me?"

Daniella gasped. "Oh, Leo. I love you, too, and of course I promise that, with or without a ring. But it's beautiful."

"It's one of a kind. Like you. This ring is symbolic of a different sort of marriage, one based on love. The one I want with you. Every time I see it on you, I'll think about how love is the best security and how easily I could have lost it." He pulled the ring from its nest of velvet and gripped his wife's hand, slipping it on her third finger to rest against her wedding ring. And then he grinned. "Plus, the stone is the same color as pomegranates."

A tear slipped down her cheek at the same moment she laughed. "Thank you. Paris was enough but this…" She stuck her hand out and tilted it to admire the ring. "This is amazing. When in the world did you find time to shop for jewelry? You've been cramming for Tommy's product launch for weeks so you could squeeze in this trip."

"Tommy came with me and we strategized in between." Leo rolled his eyes. "Trust me, he was thrilled to be involved. I never imagined when he said he wanted to learn everything that would include how to pick out a diamond for a woman."

Daniella giggled. "With you as his mentor, I'm sure he'll make the future love of his life very happy."

Tommy had trashed Leo's original proposal. Garrett-Reynolds Engineering opened its doors that same week and the payoff for becoming full partners had been immeasurable. Not only did Leo have a lot of fun, but for the first time, his profit flowed directly from his hand instead of via carefully constructed financing agreements. Leo was right in the middle of every aspect of the business and it fulfilled him in ways he could never completely comprehend.

Without Daniella, he never would have taken that step. She'd invested in his potential and given him a makeover from the inside out. He'd gladly spend the rest of his life loving her for it.

"How're things going in there?" Leo spread his hand across Daniella's abdomen and the thought of their child eventually being inside tightened his throat with awe and tenderness.

"Not pregnant yet. Though certainly not from lack of trying." Her grin warmed his heart. Everything about her warmed his heart, touching him in places he didn't even know existed. "It's only a matter of time."

"We must try harder. I insist."

A baby was one of many possibilities he eagerly anticipated, owing to his new perspective on marriage. And life in general.

Leo kissed his wife and it felt like the beginning of something that would take a very long time to finish—forever.

* * * * *

MATCHED
TO A PRINCE

BY
KAT CANTRELL

To Cynthia, because this book was so hard to write and you were there for me every step of the way.
And because TPFKAd had to be in it somewhere.

One

When the sun hit the three-quarter mark in the western sky, Finn aimed the helicopter for shore. It was nearing the end of his shift and, as always, he couldn't resist dipping low enough to let the powerful downdraft ripple the Mediterranean's deep blue surface.

A heron swooped up and away from the turbulence as fast as its wings could carry it, gliding along the air currents with sheer poetic grace. Finn would never get tired of the view from his cockpit, never grow weary of protecting the shoreline of the small country he called home.

Once he'd touched down on the X marking the spot for his helicopter, Finn cut power to the rotor and vaulted from the cockpit before the Dauphin blades had come to a full stop. His father's solemn-faced driver stood on the tarmac a short distance away and Finn didn't need any further clues to recognize a royal summons.

"Come to critique my landing, James?" Finn asked with

a grin. Not likely. No one flew helicopters with more precision and grace than he did.

"Prince Alain." James inclined his head in deference, then delivered his message. "Your father wishes to speak with you. I'm to drive."

Checking his eye roll over James's insistence on formality, Finn nodded. "Do I have time to change?"

It wouldn't be the first time Finn had appeared before the king in his Delamer Coast Guard uniform, but he'd been in it for ten hours and the legs were still damp from a meet-up with the Mediterranean while rescuing a swimmer who'd misjudged the distance to shore.

Every day Finn protected his father's people while flying over a breathtaking panorama of sparkling sea, distant mountains and the rocky islands just offshore. He loved his job, and spending a few hours encased in wet cloth was a small price to pay.

But that didn't mean he wanted to pay that price while on the receiving end of a royal lecture.

James motioned to the car. "I think it would be best if you came immediately."

The summons wasn't unexpected. It was either about a certain photograph portraying Finn doing Jägermeister shots off a gorgeous blonde's bare stomach or about the corruption charges recently brought up against a couple of his running buddies.

A blogger had once joked that Finn's official title should be Prince Alain Phineas of Montagne, House of Scandal. It wasn't so funny to the king, who had tried to combat the negative press with a royal announcement proclaiming Finn's upcoming marriage. A desperate ploy to get his son to settle down.

Hadn't worked so far. Perhaps if his father could actually name a bride, the ploy might get some traction.

Finn paused. Maybe his father had picked someone.

He hoped not. The longer he could put off the inevitable, the better.

But his life was never his own and whatever his father wanted, Finn would deal with it, like always.

Only one way to find out if he'd be announcing the name of his bride soon.

Finn allowed James to show him into the backseat of the town car his father used to fetch people and tried to swallow his dread. The Delamer Coast Guard administrative building disappeared behind them and Finn's homeland unrolled through the windows.

Tourist season had officially started. Bright vendor booths lined the waterfront, selling everything from outrageously priced sunscreen to caricatures quickly drawn by sidewalk artists. Hand-holding couples wandered along the boardwalk and young mothers pushed strollers in the treed park across from the public beach.

There wasn't a more beautiful place on earth, and Finn thanked God every day for the privilege of not only living here but the opportunity to serve its people. It was his duty, and he did it gladly.

Too soon, the car drove through the majestic wrought iron gates of the palace where Finn had grown up, and then moved out of as soon as his mother would allow it. He'd realized early on he was just in the way. The palace was the home of the king and queen, and eventually would house the crown prince and princess, Alexander and his wife, Portia.

Finn was so far down the line of succession, he couldn't even see the head. It didn't bother him. Most days.

A slew of workers scurried about the hundred acres of property surrounding the stately drive. Each employee focused on maintaining the famous four-tiered landscaping that ringed the central fountain bearing a statue of King Etienne the First, who had led Delamer's secession from France two centuries ago.

Another solemn-faced servant led Finn to the office his father used for nonstate business. That was a relief. There'd be no formality then, and Finn could do without royal addresses and protocol any day.

When Finn entered, the king glanced up from paperwork strewn across his four-hundred-year-old desk, which had been a gift from a former president of the United States. Finn preferred gifts you could drink, especially if they came with a cork.

With a small smile, his father pushed his chair back and stood, gesturing to the brocade couch. "Thanks for coming, son. Apologies for the short notice."

"No problem. I didn't have any plans. What's up?"

Since he didn't mistake his father's gesture for a suggestion, Finn perched on the fancy couch at a right angle to the desk.

King Laurent crossed his arms and leaned on the edge of his desk, facing Finn. "We need to move forward with finding you a wife."

Called it in one.

Finn shifted against the stiff couch cushions, determined to find a comfortable spot. "I said I'd be happy with whomever you picked."

A lie. He'd tolerate whomever his father picked.

If Finn and his bride ended up friends as his parents had, great. But it was a lot to ask in an arranged marriage. It wasn't as though Finn could hold out for love, not when it hadn't worked out the one and only time he'd allowed himself to care about a woman.

Juliet's face, framed by her silky light brown hair, swam into his mind's eye and he swallowed. A hundred blondes with a hundred shot glasses couldn't erase the memory of the woman who'd betrayed him in the most public and humiliating way possible. He knew. He'd tried.

"Be that as it may," the king said, "an option I hadn't considered has come to my attention. A matchmaker."

"A what?"

"An American matchmaker contacted me through my secretary. She asked for a chance to earn our business by doing a trial match. If you don't like the results, she won't charge us."

Finn smelled something fishy, and if there was anything he knew after spending the majority of his day in or near the sea, it was fish. "I'm reasonably certain we can afford her fee regardless. Why would you consider this?"

Was this another ploy to get him under his father's thumb? Had the king paid this matchmaker to orchestrate a match with a woman loyal to the crown, who could be easily controlled?

"This matchmaker introduced Stafford Walker to his wife. I've done enough business with him to know his recommendation is solid. If the woman hadn't mentioned his name, I wouldn't have given her idea a moment's consideration." His father sighed and rubbed the spot between his eyes wearily. "Son, I want you to be happy. I liked what she had to say about her selection process. You need someone specific, who will negate all the bad press. She promises to match you with the perfect woman to become your princess. It seemed like a fair deal."

Guilt relaxed Finn's rigid shoulders. "I'm sorry. You've been more than patient with me. I wish…"

He'd been about to say he wished he knew why he courted so much trouble. But the reason wasn't a mystery. She had eyes the color of fresh grass, glowing skin and a stubborn streak wider than the palace gates.

Perhaps this matchmaker might find someone who could replace Juliet in his heart. It could happen.

"I've had this matchmaker, Elise Arundel, thoroughly checked out, but do your own research. If you don't like the idea, don't do it. But I've had little luck coming up with a potential bride on my own." The king smiled, looking like his usual cheerful self for the first time since Finn had entered the room. "There's no shortage of candidates. Just the lack of one who can handle you."

Finn grinned back. "At least we agree on that."

Because Finn took after his father. They both had big hearts and even bigger personalities. And the absolute sense of duty that came part and parcel with being royalty. They shared a love for Delamer and a love for the people they served.

His father managed to do it with grace and propriety. Finn, on the other hand, tended to whoop it up, and photographers loved to capture it. Of course, a photo could never depict the broken heart that drove him to search for a method, any method, to erase the pain.

He got all that and didn't mind the idea of getting married, especially to save himself from a downward media spiral. Finding a woman he could love at the same time was an attractive bonus. Settling down and having babies appealed to him if he could do it with someone who gave him what he desperately wanted—a sheltered place all his own where he could be a man and not a prince, if only for a few hours.

The odds of a matchmaker pulling a name out of thin air who could do that…well, he'd do better betting a thousand on red and letting it ride.

"I'll talk to Ms. Arundel." Finn owed it to his father to figure out a way to stop causing him grief, and he owed it to his country to portray the House of Couronne positively in the international press. If it meant marrying the matchmaker's choice and making the best of it, so be it.

Relief filled the king's eyes and a double dose of guilt swam through Finn's stomach. His father loved him and wanted the best for him. Why couldn't Finn do the right thing as his brother always did? Alexander would be king one day and constantly kept that forefront in his mind. His behavior was above reproach and *he* never caused their parents a moment's worry.

Finn, on the other hand, was the spare heir. Unnecessary. The Party Prince.

An advantageous marriage was a chance for Finn to do something right for once, something of value to the crown. He'd hoped to keep putting it off. But clearly his father was having none of that.

"She'd like you to fly to Dallas, Texas, to meet in person," the king said. "As soon as possible."

Dallas. He'd never been there. Maybe he could pick up an authentic cowboy hat if nothing else.

Mentally, Finn rearranged his calendar for the weekend. He'd committed to attending a couple of charity fund-raisers and had planned to hit a new club in Saint Tropez Saturday night. Looked as if he'd be skipping all of it.

"I've got a shift tomorrow, but I can go the day after."

His father put a gentle hand on Finn's shoulder. "I think it's a good choice."

Ducking his head, Finn shrugged. "We'll see. What's the worst that can happen?"

As soon as the words left his mouth, he regretted them. Scandal followed him like a mongrel dog he'd fed once and couldn't get rid of. Juliet's betrayal had been the first scandal but certainly not the last. It had just hurt the most.

And that was the kicker. She'd hurt him so badly because he'd loved her so much, only to find she didn't feel the same way. If she had loved him, she'd never have participated in a protest against everything he held dear—his father, the military, the very fabric of the governing structure that he'd sworn allegiance to.

The irony. Two things he'd loved about Juliet were her passion and commitment to her family. Without them, she'd be uninteresting and lackluster. Without them, the protest wouldn't have happened.

It didn't matter. She'd killed all his feelings for her. Except the anger. That, he still had plenty of.

Grimly, he bid his father goodbye and let James drive

him back to his Aventador still parked at the coast guard headquarters. His entire life could be summed up in one phrase—dual-edged sword. No matter which way it was wielded, he'd be cut. He would be a man and a prince until the day he died, and it seemed fated that he could never satisfy both sides simultaneously.

Yet he held on to a slim thread of hope this matchmaker might change things for him.

Juliet Villere did not understand the American fascination with small talk. It was boring.

The packed ballroom wasn't her preferred scene anyway, but coupled with a strong desire to avoid one more conversation about the ridiculous game confused Americans called football, the wall had become her friend. It warmed her bare back nicely and provided a great shield from the eyes she'd felt burning into her exposed flesh.

Why hadn't someone told her that a makeover didn't magically transform your insides? All the makeup and fancy clothes in the world couldn't convert Juliet into someone who liked lipstick. Or parties.

But she owed Elise Arundel and her matchmaking-slash-makeover services a huge debt for taking her in when she'd fled Delamer in search of some magic to heal the continual pain of Finn's betrayal. That was the only reason she'd agreed to attend this glittery event full of Elise's clients.

Maybe Elise wouldn't notice if Juliet ducked out the side entrance and walked back to the matchmaker's house in the Dallas district called Uptown, where Juliet was staying until Elise found her an American husband. It was only a couple of miles, and she'd practiced walking in these horribly uncomfortable heels enough times that her leg muscles were used to the strain.

Then she caught sight of Elise heading in Juliet's direction, a determined look on her mentor's face.

Too late.

"Having a good time?" Elise asked, her dark page boy swinging in time to the upbeat song floating above the crowd.

"Fantastic."

The sarcasm clearly wasn't lost on Elise, who smiled. "It's good for you to be in social settings, dressed to kill. I invited you to this mixer so you could practice mingling. Hugging the wall won't accomplish that."

The reminder tightened Juliet's stomach, and she resituated the waistline of the form-fitting green dress her new friend Dannie Reynolds had helped select.

"I have nothing good to say about football." One thing was clear—the American husband she'd asked Elise to match her with would watch it. Therefore, Juliet would likely become well versed in the fine art of faking interest. "So I'm acquainting myself with the benefits of solitude."

Elise laughed. "Dance with someone. Then you don't have to talk."

Juliet shook her head. She'd never danced with anyone other than Finn, and she didn't want to break that streak tonight.

Finn.

Pain, sharp and swift, cramped her stomach. Crossing the Atlantic hadn't dimmed his hold over her one bit.

He'd shredded her soul over a year ago. Shouldn't she be finished healing by now? She wanted desperately to get to that place where he was just some guy she used to date, one she recalled fondly yet distantly.

But the announcement of his upcoming engagement had cut deeply enough to drive her from Delamer all the way to Dallas, Texas. Thank God she'd stumbled over that EA International ad in the back of a fashion magazine she'd thumbed through at the dentist's office back home—it had given her a place to go.

"I don't see the point in dancing with one of these guys." As she didn't see the point in having fake nails or painted lips. But it wasn't her place to argue with the formula Elise used in her matchmaking service.

"None of them will be my match," she continued. "And besides, they've all got sports on the brain. Does scoring more points feed hungry children? Right any wrongs? No. It's stupid."

Juliet started to make a face and remembered she couldn't do that anymore. Actually, she wasn't supposed to be so outspoken either. Her American husband would want a refined wife with the ability to mingle with the upper crust. Not a woman who had little use for propriety and fluff. Or the Dallas Cowboys.

How in the world was she going to pretend *that* much for the rest of her life?

The same way she was going to pretend her heart hadn't broken when she'd lost the man she'd loved, her sweet little brother and her life in Delamer.

Anything was manageable if it matched her with a husband who could keep her in the States, and save her from having to watch Finn marry someone else.

With a laugh, Elise shook her head. "No, no. Don't hold back. Tell me how you really feel. How about if I save you from further suspense and tell you I have your match?"

Juliet's heart stuttered to a stop. This was it. The reason she'd come to America.

What would her future husband be like? Did he enjoy swimming and sailing and could she ask him to take her on trips to the beach? Would he be okay with her family coming to visit occasionally? Did he have a nice smile and laugh a lot?

Most important, would she be able to develop feelings for him that would fill the Finn-shaped hole inside?

Even though Elise guaranteed a love match, replacing Finn was probably too much to hope for.

Contentment would be enough. It had to be.

She swallowed the sudden burn in her throat. "That didn't take long. I only finished your questions yesterday."

Shrugging, Elise turned to face the ballroom, her shoulder bumping Juliet's companionably. "Sometimes when I load the profile, I don't get a match against someone already in the system and then we have to wait until new clients are entered. Yours came back immediately."

Juliet wanted to ask for the name. And at the same time, she wanted to dive under the buffet table.

What was she doing here? This man in Elise's system expected a certain kind of woman, one who could host his parties and mingle with his friends, smiling through boring stories of business mergers and tax breaks. And football. That was so not her.

She wanted to go home.

Then she thought about living in Delamer day in and day out and how often she saw Finn's helicopter beating through the broad blue sky. Or how she'd stumbled over another photograph of him cutting the ribbon at the new primary school—that picture would never die.

A little girl who would attend the school had sneaked up and wrapped her arms around his thigh just before he cut the ribbon. Finn leaned down to kiss her cheek and presto. Instant immortalization via the hundreds of camera phones and paparazzi lenses in the audience.

The pictorial reminder of the prince's sweet and charming nature stabbed her in the stomach every time. He was such a good guy, with a sense of honor she'd once loved—until realizing it was a front for his stubborn refusal to see how much he'd hurt her by taking his father's side. There was no reasoning with Finn, and that trumped all his good qualities.

In Delamer, there were constant reminders of the void her brother Bernard's death had created.

Any husband was better than that.

"What happens if I don't like the man your computer

picked?" Juliet asked, though surely Elise's system had captured her exact specifications.

"There are no absolutes. If you don't like him, we'll find someone else, though it might take a while. However…" Elise hesitated. "I'd like you to keep an open mind about the possibilities. This man is perfect for you. I've never seen two more compatible people. Not even Leo and Dannie were this closely aligned, and look how well that turned out."

Juliet nodded. Dannie and Leo Reynolds were definitely one of the most in-love couples in the history of time and had never even met each other before they signed on with EA International and got married. If Elise said this man was Juliet's perfect match, why doubt it?

"I had an ulterior motive for inviting you to the party tonight," Elise confessed. "Your match will be here too. Soon. I thought it would take some pressure off if you met socially."

Her match. Already.

Juliet had hoped for some time to learn more about him before being thrown at his feet. She touched her pinned-up hair. At least she'd meet her future husband while looking the absolute best she could, a small victory in her mind.

Deep breath. Bernard would want her to be happy, to move on. The memory of her brother's smile bolstered her.

A disturbance in the crowd caught Juliet's attention. People craned their necks to peer over each other, whispering and nodding toward the ballroom entrance.

"What's going on?" she asked.

Elise uttered a very unladylike word.

"I was hoping for a little more time to explain. It's your match." Elise cleared her throat. "He's early. I think that's a good quality in a man. I mean, along with all of his other ones. Don't you think so?"

Her future husband, assuming everything went according to plan, had just walked into the ballroom.

Juliet's pulse took off, throbbing below her ears. "Sure. But why does it sound like you're trying to talk me into it? Does he have two heads or something?"

"I did something a little unorthodox to find your match." Elise bit her lip and put her hand on Juliet's arm. "Something I hope you'll appreciate. It was a test. I figured if the computer didn't match you, I wouldn't say anything. I'd never tell you and I'd find someone else for you both."

"What are you talking about? What did you do?"

Elise smiled weakly as the crowd pressed closer to the entrance, blocking their view of whoever had drawn so much interest. "You talked so much about him. I heard what was still in your heart. I couldn't call myself a matchmaker if I didn't give you an opportunity to rediscover why you fell in love in the first place."

The first wave of unease rolled through Juliet's stomach. "Talked about whom?"

"Prince Alain. Finn." Elise nodded toward the crush surrounding the entrance. "He's your match."

"Oh, my God. Elise!" Juliet wrapped her arms around her waist but couldn't stop the flood inside of…everything. Hope. Disbelief. The unquenchable anger at his inability to side with her. "You contacted Finn? And didn't tell me? Oh, my God."

Finn was here. In the ballroom.

He was her match.

Not a quiet American businessman who watched football and would save her from the heartache Finn had caused.

"Open mind," Elise reminded her and grasped Juliet's hand to propel her forward, parting the crowd easily despite being half a head shorter than everyone else. "Come say hello. Give me ten minutes. Let me explain to you both what I did and then you can blast me for my tactics. Or spend a little while reacquainting yourselves. Maybe give it a chance. It's your choice."

Greedily, Juliet's gaze swept the crowd, searching for a

familiar face. And found a solid figure in black tie, flanked by a discreet security team, moving toward her.

Finn. Exactly as her heart remembered him.

Tall, gorgeous, self-assured. Every bit a man who could support the weight of a crown despite the probability that he never would. Hard, defined muscles lay under a tuxedo that did little to disguise the beauty of the man's body. His short, dark hair that had a tendency to curl when he let it grow was the same. As was the winsome smile.

Until he paused in front of Elise and caught sight of Juliet. The smile slipped a touch as his gaze cut between the two women. "Ms. Arundel. It's nice to see you again."

Finn extended his hand and took Elise's, drawing her forward to buss her cheek as if they were old friends. To Juliet, he simply said, "Ms. Villere. What a pleasant surprise. I wasn't aware you were on this side of the world."

In spite of the frost in his tone, his voice flipped her stomach, as it always had. More so because it had been so long since she'd heard someone speak with the cadence intrinsic to people from Delamer.

"The surprise is mutual," she assured him, shocked her throat hadn't gone the way of her lungs, which seemed to be broken. She couldn't breathe. The ballroom's walls contracted, stealing what air remained in the room. "Though I'm reserving judgment on whether it's pleasant."

Stupid mouth had gotten away from her again. The laser-sharp eyes of the crowd branded her back and she became aware of exactly how many people were witnessing this public meeting between Prince Alain and a woman they no doubt vaguely recognized. Wouldn't take long to do an internet search and find videos, pictures and news reports of the scandal. It had garnered a ton of press.

His expression darkened. "Be sure to inform me when you decide. If you'll excuse me, I have business with Ms. Arundel which is not of your concern."

Finn was in rare His-Royal-Highness mode. She hated it when he got that way.

"Actually," Elise corrected with a nervous laugh and held a palm out, "Juliet is your match."

Two

"What?" Finn zeroed in on Juliet, piercing her with steely blue eyes she remembered all too well. "Is this your idea of a joke? Did you beg Elise to contact me?"

Is *that* what he thought? Her brother was dead and afterward, Finn had abandoned her when she'd needed him most. Juliet would never forgive him. Why would she extend one small finger to see him again?

"I had nothing to do with this!" Hands on her hips, she waded straight into the rising tension, eyes and ears around them forgotten as the emotions Finn elicited zigzagged through her torso. "I thought you were getting married. What happened to your princess? What are you doing signing on with a matchmaker?"

A muscle ticked in Finn's forehead. "My father does want me to get married, as soon as I find a bride. That's what I'm doing here. I was promised the perfect match. Amusing how that worked out."

Finn wasn't engaged? There wasn't even a potential

princess on the horizon? She'd left Delamer based on something that *wasn't even true*.

"Yeah, hilarious. I was promised the same."

In tandem, they turned to Elise. She smiled and escorted
them both to an unpopulated corner, likely so the coming
bloodbath wouldn't spatter her guests. Finn's muscled companions followed and melted into the background.

"Do you remember the profile question about love?"
Elise tucked her hair behind one ear with a let's-get-down-
to-business swipe. "I asked you both what you'd be willing
to give up in order to have it. Juliet, what did you say?"

Arms crossed, Juliet glared at Elise and repeated the
answer. "You shouldn't have to give up anything for love.
It should be effortless or else it's not real love."

No compromise. Why should she have to completely rearrange her entire belief system to appease one very stubborn man? The right man for her should recognize that
she'd tried to upset the status quo only because she'd been
forced to.

The right man for her would know he'd been everything to her.

"Finn?" Elise prompted and he sighed.

His gaze softened and he spoke directly to Juliet. "You
shouldn't have to give up anything. Love should be easy
and natural, like breathing. No one asks you to give up
breathing so your heart can beat."

He had. He wanted her to forget Bernard had died serving the king's ego, wearing the same uniform Finn put on
every day. She slammed her lids closed and shoved that
thought away. It was too much.

"Right. Easy and natural. That part of us wasn't hard."

And with the words, the good and amazing and breath-
stealing aspects of her relationship with Finn lit up the
darkness inside her.

Everything had been effortless between them. If Bernard

hadn't had that accident, she and Finn would probably be married by now and living happily ever after.

"No. Not hard at all." Finn shook his head, his eyes still on her, searching for something that looked a lot like what she constantly wished for—a way to go back in time.

Which was impossible and the reason she'd fled to the States.

But she'd left Delamer because she thought Finn was marrying someone else. If that wasn't true, what else might she need to reexamine?

Elise put her hands out, placing them gently on their arms, connecting them. "Do you remember what you each said you were looking for in a relationship?"

"The calm in the storm," Juliet said, and her ire drained away to be replaced by the tiniest bit of hope.

"A place where I could just be, without all the other pressures of life," Finn said, his voice a little raspy. "That's how I answered the question."

He didn't move, but he felt closer. As if she could reach out and touch him, which she desperately wanted to do. Curled fingers dug into her thigh. Her heart tripped. This was not a good idea.

"So? We answered a couple of questions the same way. That's no surprise."

Finn agreed with a nod. "I would have been surprised if we didn't respond in a similar vein."

They'd always been of one mind, two hearts beating as one. When they sailed together, they never even had to talk, working in perfect tandem to reef the main or hull trim. They'd met while sailing with mutual friends, then fallen in love as the two of them skimmed the water again and again in Finn's boat.

"So," Elise said brightly, "maybe the better question is whether you can forget about the past and see how you both might have changed. You're in America. The divide you had in Delamer doesn't matter here. It's safe. Take some time on neutral ground to explore whether that effortless love still exists."

That was totally unnecessary. She'd never fallen out of love with Finn and being here in his presence after a long, cold year apart solidified the fact that she probably never would.

But that didn't mean they belonged together.

"Are you a relationship counselor or a matchmaker?" Juliet asked Elise without a trace of guile.

"Both. Whatever it takes to help people find happiness."

Happiness. That hadn't been on her list when she came to Elise, broken and desperate for a solution to end her pain. But instead of an American husband, she'd been handed an opportunity for a second chance with Finn.

He was the only man on earth who could rightly be called her match. The only man she'd ever wanted to let into her heart. That had always been true and Elise had somehow figured that out.

That was some computer program Elise used. Juliet had hoped for a bit of magic. Perhaps she'd gotten her wish.

"Elise is right," Finn said quietly. "This is neutral ground, with no room for politics. And it's a party. Dance with me."

Juliet nodded and hoped agreeing wasn't the stupidest thing she'd ever done.

Elise slipped away, not even trying to hide the relief plastered all over her face.

Juliet's eyelids pricked with tears as something shuddery and optimistic filled her empty soul. She would wallow in her few precious hours with Finn, and maybe it would lead to more. Maybe time and distance had diluted their differences.

Maybe he'd finally understand what his support and strength meant to her. She'd lost so much more than a brother a year ago. She'd also lost the love of her life.

* * *

Finn led Juliet to the dance floor, a minor miracle since his knees had gone numb.

This whole thing was ridiculous. He'd known there was something off about a matchmaker approaching his father, but he never could have predicted Elise's actual motivation or the result of his trip to Dallas.

What would the king say when he realized what he'd inadvertently done? Finn had been matched with a woman who'd caused his family immeasurable misery and created a scandal that had spawned countless aftereffects.

Yet Finn and Juliet had met again, paired by a supposedly infallible computer program. Everybody he'd talked to raved about EA International's process. Raved about Elise and how much she truly cared about the people she helped. So yesterday, Finn had walked through Elise's extensive match profile, answered her questions as honestly as he could and hoped for the best.

Only to have Juliet dropped back into his life with no warning.

The smartest move would have been to turn around and leave without a backward glance. Staying was the surest method to end up insane by the end of the night.

He'd asked Juliet to dance only because manners had been bred into him since birth. This was Elise's party and they were business associates. It was only polite.

But now he wasn't so sure that was the only reason.

Seeing Juliet again had kicked up a push-pull of emotions he'd have sworn were buried. Not the least of which was the intense desire to have her head on a platter. After he had her body in his bed.

Fitting Juliet into his arms, they swayed together to the music. It took mere moments to find the rhythm they'd always shared. He stared down into her familiar face, into the green eyes he'd never forgotten, and felt something loosen inside.

It was *Juliet,* but in capital, sparkling letters with giant exclamation points.

She'd been transformed.

The alterations were external, and he'd liked her exactly the way she'd looked the last time he'd seen her. But what if more than her hair had changed?

Could he really fly back to Delamer without taking a few hours to find out what might be possible that hadn't been possible before?

Now that he had her in his arms, the anger he'd carried with him for the past year was hard to hang on to.

"You look different," he blurted out. *Smooth.* Juliet had never tied up his tongue before. "Amazing. So beautiful. You're wearing cosmetics."

She blinked sultry eyes and smiled with lips stained the color of deep sunset. Even her height was different. He glanced down. Sexy heels showcased her delicate feet and straps buckled around her ankles highlighted the shapely curve of her legs. He had the sudden mental image of unbuckling those straps with his teeth.

That was it. Dancing was officially a form of torture.

This was all so surreal. She was still the same girl who'd stabbed him in the back but not the same. Tension coiled in his gut, choking off his air supply.

"Thanks. Elise gave me a few tips on how to be a girl." Juliet extended a hand to show off long coral-tipped nails. "Don't expect me to hoist any sails with these babies."

Finn couldn't help but grin. If she was going to play it as if everything was cool, he could too. "I'll do all the hard work. Looking at you is reward enough for my effort."

Her brows rose as she repositioned her hand at his waist. "Like the new me, do you?"

He could feel those nails through his jacket. How was that possible?

"I liked the old you." Before she'd skewered his heart on

the stake of her stubbornness. "But this you is great too. You're gorgeous. What prompted all of this?"

Long nails, swept-up hair. A mouthwatering backless dress he easily recognized as high-end. She was double-take worthy and then some.

"It's part of Elise's deal. She has a lot of high-powered, influential male clients and they expect a certain refinement in their potential mates. She spends a couple of months enhancing each of us, though admittedly, she spent far more time with me than some of the others. *Voila.* I am a new creation. Cinderella, at your service." Juliet glanced at him with a sweeping once-over. "She didn't tell you how all that worked?"

"Not in those terms. It was more of a general guarantee that the woman she matched me with would be able to handle everything that comes with being a princess."

Which, in Juliet's case, had never been a factor. He couldn't have cared less if she flubbed royal protocol or never picked up mascara. Because he'd loved her, once upon a time.

But that was over with a capital *O* and in an arranged marriage, he might as well get what he paid for—a demure, non-scandal-inducing woman who could erase the public's memory of the past year.

"Are you disappointed you got me instead?"

His laugh came out of nowhere. "I honestly don't know what I am, but disappointed is definitely not it."

Juliet could have been a great princess. She'd always understood his need to escape from his position occasionally. Finn gave one hundred percent to his job protecting Delamer's citizens, gladly participated in charity events and didn't have a moment's guilt over taking time away from the public eye. A lot of women wouldn't support that, would insist on being treated to the finer things in life.

Juliet had been perfectly content with a beach date or

sailing. Or staying in, his own personal favorite. No, it wasn't a surprise the computer had matched them.

The surprise lay in how much he still wanted her despite the still-present burn of her betrayal.

"What about you?" he asked. "Has the jury reconvened on whether seeing me again is a pleasant surprise?"

"The jury is busy trying not to trip over your feet while wearing four-inch heels."

The wry twist of her lips pulled an answering grin out of him.

He relaxed. This was still neutral ground and as long as everyone kept a sense of humor, the night was young.

"Let's get some champagne. I'm dying to know how you ended up in Dallas in a matchmaker's computer system."

As they turned to leave the dance floor, light flashed from the crowd to the left and then again in rapid succession. Photographs. From a professional camera.

Finn sighed. With the time difference, his father's phone call would come around midnight unless the king's secretary somehow missed the story, which was unlikely.

Finn would ask Elise to match him with someone new. Later.

Juliet waited until he'd led her to the bar and handed her a flute of bubbly Veuve Clicquot before responding. "It's your fault I sought out Elise."

"Mine?" He dinged the rims of their glasses together and took a healthy swallow in a futile attempt to gain some clarity. "I didn't even know Elise existed until a few days ago."

"It was the engagement announcement. If you were moving on, I needed to, as well. I couldn't do that in Delamer, so here I am." She spread her hands, flashing coral tips that made him imagine what they'd feel like at his waist once he'd shed his jacket and shirt.

The temperature in the ballroom went sky high as internal ripples of need spread. He'd only *thought* he was uncomfortable before.

"Like I said, there's no engagement. Not yet. My father and I agreed it was time I thought about settling down and he went on the bride hunt. Here I am, as well."

It was a sobering reminder. They'd both been trying to move past the scandal and breakup by searching for someone new. Was that what she truly wanted?

The thought of Juliet with another man ripped a hole in his gut. A shock considering how angry he still was about what she'd done.

"As much as I've tried to avoid it, I've seen the pictorial evidence of why your dad thought you needed to settle down. You've become the Party Prince." She shot him a quizzical glance, her gaze flat and unreadable. "It seems so unlike you. Sure, we had some fun dancing at clubs and stuff, but we usually left after an hour or so. Did I miss the part where you wanted to stay?"

"I never wanted to stay. I was always thinking about getting you alone."

"Some of the pictures were really hard to take," she admitted quietly, and he didn't need her to elaborate.

Heat climbed up his neck and flushed across his ears.

He'd always known she'd probably see all the photographs of him with other women and hear about his exploits, but he'd honestly never considered a scenario where they'd have an actual conversation about them. There wasn't a lot about the past year that filled him with pride.

"As long as we're handing out blame, that was *your* fault."

To her credit, she simply glanced at him with a blank expression. "How so?"

She *had* changed. The Juliet of before would have blasted him over such a stupid statement. "Well, not your fault, per se, but I was trying to drown out the memories. Focus on the future. Moving on, like you said."

"Did it work?"

"Not in the slightest."

Their gazes crashed and his lips tingled. He wanted to pull her against him and dive in. Kiss her until neither of them could remember anything other than how good they felt together.

She tossed back the last of her champagne as if she hadn't noticed the heavily charged moment. He wished he could say the same as all the blood rushed from his head, draining southward into a spectacular hard-on.

"What do we do now?" she asked.

"Have dinner with me," he said hoarsely. "Tomorrow night. For old time's sake."

Neither of them thought this match was a good idea. He knew that. But he couldn't resist stealing a few more forbidden hours with Juliet. No matter what she'd done in the past, he couldn't walk out of this ballroom and never see her again.

"I should have my head examined. But okay."

Her acceptance was fortuitously timed. A svelte woman and her friend nearly bowled Juliet over in an enthusiastic attempt to get a photo with him.

It was a common-enough request and he normally didn't mind. But tonight he wanted to be selfish and spend as much time with Juliet as he could, before his father interfered. Before all the reasons they'd split in the first place surfaced.

She'd always be the woman who burned a Delamer flag at the palace gates. The people of his country had long memories for acts of disloyalty to the crown.

And so did he.

There was no way crossing an ocean could create a different dynamic between two people. Because Juliet would never see he couldn't go against his father, and never understand that as the second son, Finn had little to offer the crown besides unconditional support.

If she ever did finally get it, all her sins would be forgiven. By everyone, including him.

That would happen when it snowed in Delamer during July.

Until then, he'd indulge in Juliet, ignore the rest and then ask Elise to match him with someone else.

Three

Juliet stared in the mirror and tried to concentrate on applying eye shadow to her lids as Dannie and Elise had shown her. Multiple times. Her scrambled brain couldn't focus.

Dazed and breathless well described the state Finn had left her in last night, and it hadn't cleared up in the almost twenty-four hours since. Finn's clean scent lingered in her nose, evoking painfully crisp memories of being with him, loving him.

And suffering the agony of finally accepting that he cared nothing for her. Cared nothing for her pain at losing the brother she'd helped raise.

All Finn cared about was zipping himself into the uniform of Delamer's military and wearing it with nationalistic pride.

Madness. Why had she agreed to this date again?

Elise stuck her head in the door of Juliet's room.

"Almost ready? Oh. You're not even dressed yet. What are you wearing?"

A flak jacket if she was smart. And if they made one you could wear internally. But she'd come to America in hopes of finding a new direction. She'd stay open to the possibility that time had dulled Finn's zealous fervor.

One date. One night. What did she have to lose?

Her eyes narrowed. She'd stay open, but that didn't mean Finn didn't deserve to suffer for his sins.

"I want to wear something that will show Finn what I've endured in your makeover program because of him. The sexier and more painful for him, the better." Hours and hours of hot rollers, facials and balancing on four-inch heels were about to hit his royal highness where it hurt.

"Yellow dress, then. I brought you something." Elise held out a velvet jewelry box.

Mystified, Juliet opened the lid to reveal a silver heart charm dangling from a matching chain, and another heart dangled from the first, one clutching the other to keep it from falling. "It's beautiful. Thank you."

Simple but elegant, perfect for a tomboy who'd rather be doing something athletic than primping.

Elise clasped it around Juliet's throat. "I give all my makeover clients a necklace. I'm glad you like it."

When the hired car with dark windows rolled to a stop outside Elise's house, Juliet was slightly ashamed to realize she'd been haunting the window for nearly fifteen minutes waiting for its appearance. How pathetic.

She swung open Elise's front door, and the sheer heat in the pointed once-over Finn gave her swept everything else away.

"Hi."

"Wow," was all he said in response.

Little pinpricks worked their way across her cheeks in a stupid blush. "Yeah? It's okay? Elise picked out the dress."

And what was under it, but odds were slim this date would go well enough to model the silk lingerie.

In answer, he grasped her hand and led her out of the house. "I like what I see so far. Come with me so I can properly evaluate the rest."

Her arm tingled from his touch against her palm, warming her in places Finn had always affected quite expertly.

Whom was she kidding? Finn was nothing if not talented enough to get her out of the sunny yellow dress and ivory alligator sandals in less than five minutes if he so chose.

She let him hold her hand down the walk. Partially because she wanted to pretend things were somewhat normal. That this was a date with an exciting man who was whirling her off to a night of possibilities.

He tucked her into the backseat of the luxurious town car and settled in next to her, his heavy masculine presence overwhelming in such close confines. She almost jumped out of her skin when he leaned forward, brushing her arm and setting off a throng of iron-winged butterflies in her stomach. But he only pressed the button to raise the dividing panel between the driver and the back, lingering far too long for such a simple task.

The car slid smoothly away from the curb and flowed into traffic.

"Where are you taking me?" she croaked and cleared the awareness and heat from her throat. "Some place trendy and hip?"

"Not on your life. I'm not sharing you with hordes of paparazzi and gawkers."

Oh. "Are your bodyguards in another car? They're never far away unless you're working."

He squeezed the hand he was still holding. "Worried? I'll keep you safe."

Without a doubt. It was what he did. Most people ignored those in distress, but he reveled in protecting people. Always had.

They chatted about inane topics such as Dallas weather, but thankfully, he did not mention football. The only sport he'd ever followed was Formula 1 racing, but he respected her complete boredom with cars looping a track and seldom talked about it.

"We're here," Finn pronounced as the car stopped under a tree.

Juliet took in the scene through the window. Beyond the roadway lay a secluded private park, where a single table and chairs had been set out with a perfect view of the sunset. A man in a tall white chef's hat stood off to the side, chopping with a flashing knife on a temporary work surface.

"Nice," Juliet acknowledged with a nod and peeked up at Finn from under her lashes. "Out of curiosity, what would you have done if it was raining?"

"We'd get wet. Or we'd ride around and look for a drive-through with decent takeout and eat in the car."

She smiled at his pragmatism. He'd never let a little thing like a change of plans put a hitch in his stride. "Then I'm glad it's a clear night."

His answering grin warmed her neglected parts far past acceptability.

"After the obscene amount of money I paid to rent this park for the night, including an added fifteen percent to buy out the existing reservation, it wouldn't dare rain."

No, it wouldn't. Rain didn't fall on the head of the privileged. Once, he'd made her feel as if the evils of the world couldn't reach them, as if he'd always be the one person she could count on. Until he wasn't.

Finn jumped from the car and helped her rise from the low leather seat. The driver sped away after being told to return in two hours. They were alone.

Juliet started to walk up the path to the center of the park.

Finn tugged on her hand, swinging her around face-to-face. "Maybe we should get something out of the way."

"What's that?" The words were half out of her mouth when the sizzle between them and the glint of anticipation in his blue eyes answered that question.

He was going to kiss her.

Involuntarily, her tongue came out to wet suddenly dry lips and his eyes lingered on them before he met her gaze squarely.

"This."

Juliet froze as Finn's mouth descended.

A part of her screamed to break his hold, to run before it was too late. Her legs wouldn't move.

Then his lips claimed hers, taking her mouth powerfully, demanding a response. It was *Finn*. So familiar and hot and everything she'd been missing for a very long time. She moaned and leaned into it, desperate to taste the divine, to plunge into him.

Euphoria rushed through her veins, deluging her senses with sharp, slick desire. Pushing eager fingers through his short hair, she held his head in place as the kiss exploded with incandescent energy.

Their bodies melded, aligning just right, just as always. *Yes.* Oh, yes, she'd missed him.

Missed how he never held back, missed his intoxicating presence and missed how his strength enabled hers.

His hand slipped beneath a spaghetti strap at her shoulder and he skimmed silky fingertips down her back. If he kept this up, her lingerie would be making an appearance after all, very shortly.

He pulled away before she'd even begun to sate herself on the thrill of his touch. Breathing heavily, he rested his forehead on hers. "That didn't quite do what I hoped."

It had certainly done plenty for her. "What were you hoping for?"

"That it would allow me to eat in peace instead of thinking about whether you still taste the same. Now I'm pretty sure a repeat is all I'll be thinking about."

She hid a smile. "If dinner goes well, a repeat might be on the menu."

His eyelids dropped to a sexy, slumberous half-mast. "I'll keep that in mind. Shall we eat?"

"If you insist." He might be able to eat. The flip-flopping in her stomach didn't bode well for her.

There were still plenty of sparks between them. Not that she'd wondered. But that kiss had at least answered one lingering question—whether they could pick up where they'd left off.

The answer was a resounding yes.

As long as they could sort through the past. The scandal. The utter sense of betrayal he'd left her with.

Suddenly, she didn't want to think about it. There weren't any laws that said they had to immediately hash out how abandoned she'd felt.

Finn led her to a chair and helped her sit, then took his own seat. As the chef served a delicious first course of tomatoes drizzled with balsamic vinegar, Finn mentioned the queen's bout with appendicitis and Juliet murmured appropriate well-wishes. She then shared that her second-youngest sister was expecting a baby and nodded at Finn's hearty congratulations.

A very pleasant conversation all the way around. Thankfully, at least some of the social graces Elise had tirelessly drilled into Juliet's head had held.

Except she couldn't get that kiss out of her mind, and watching him talk wasn't helping. It had been a very long time since she'd been kissed. Since the scandal.

Finn hadn't let any grass grow under his feet in the female companionship department, but she'd taken the ostrich approach. If she stuck her head in the sand long enough, all those feminine urges would dry up and go away.

She'd been pretty successful thus far. Yet in two seconds, he'd done a spectacular job of reminding her sheer will couldn't stop the flood of longing for the tender affections of one very talented prince.

"Did you quit your job in Delamer?" Finn asked once the chef finished serving the main course of corvina sea bass and asparagus over quinoa.

"I did."

The short phrase communicated none of the grief she'd experienced over resigning her position teaching English to bright young minds. She loved the children she taught and had hoped to find a way to continue teaching in America.

Then she remembered.

She hadn't been matched with an American husband. If things worked out with Finn, she could go home, go back to her job, back to the sea. Back into his arms.

Was such a fairy tale actually possible?

With renewed interest, she swept her gaze over the man opposite her. "Are you still flying helicopters?"

"Of course. I'll do that until the day I die. Or until they ground me. Whichever comes first."

No shock. He'd always loved flying as much as he did the search and rescue part of his job. The source of contention wasn't *what* he did but whom he did it for.

"Hmm," she said noncommittally and forked up a bite of fish. "I wasn't going to jump right into this, but I'm on uncertain ground here. Tell me what you hoped to gain from Elise's match. Are you really looking for a wife?"

Finn set his wineglass down firmly and focused on her, the warmth in his expression all too easy to read. "I can't keep being the Party Prince. The best I thought I could do was an arranged marriage, like my parents. Means to an end, and I'm okay with that. What about you?"

That focus unleashed a shiver she couldn't quite control. "I was prepared to marry whomever Elise picked. I couldn't stay in Delamer. Not with the way things fell apart between us. Marriage was a means to an end for me, as well."

She'd like to stop there and just enjoy this date. But there were too many unanswered questions for that.

"What is this dinner all about? We aren't having a first date like we would with the matches we'd envisioned for ourselves. This is something else. We have history we're avoiding. Important history. History that has to be resolved."

Finn's gaze grew keen. "You want to throw down? Go for it."

"No, I don't." She shook her head, though he was certainly the only man who could take whatever she dished out. "We've fought enough in our relationship. I want to work things out like adults. Can we?"

With a smile, Finn picked up her hand and rubbed a knuckle with his smooth thumb. "Let's hold off on history with a capital *H*. Dinner is about me and you reconnecting. That's the part of our history I prefer to remember."

"Okay."

She'd waited this long. What were a few more hours? The time would be well spent working through what she'd realized she'd done wrong a year ago. Instead of fighting so hard to convince Finn to talk to his father, she should have gone about this a whole different way.

If Finn was truly looking for a wife, what was stopping her from marrying him in order to bring about change from inside the palace gates? Princess Juliet would have far more power to influence the king away from mandatory military service than plain old Juliet Villere.

And then maybe she could finally be rid of the crushing guilt she felt over Bernard's death.

Dinner forgotten, Finn nearly swallowed his tongue when Juliet pushed back her chair and waltzed to his side of the table wearing a sultry smile and sporting a very naughty glint in her eye. She extended a hand, which he took silently, and then he stood, allowing her to lead him up the path into a more heavily wooded section of the park.

"Interested in the native fauna and flora?" he asked when the silence stretched on.

"More interested in how well the flora conceals us." She backed him up against a tree and stepped into his torso deliberately, rubbing her firm breasts against his chest.

Oh, so *that's* what she had in mind. Obviously, she remembered how good it had been as well as he did. And apparently she had no problem rekindling that part of their relationship, impending matches to other people notwithstanding. Fantastic.

"That earlier kiss was good. Make this one better," she commanded.

Instantly, he complied, yanking her into his arms and exploring her back flat-handed. Their mouths met, aligning perfectly, and heat arced between them.

Juliet.

Desire thundered through his body, soaking him with a storm of need. She was in his arms, overpowering his senses as if he'd jumped from his helicopter without a parachute.

Thank God Elise had pulled her devious stunt to put them in each other's path again, if only for one night. Tomorrow, he and Juliet could both be matched with more suitable mates.

The kiss deepened and Juliet snuggled against him as if she'd never been away. Heat swept along his skin, craving the perfection of Juliet's beautiful body against it. He groaned and shifted a knee between her legs, and his thigh hit the sweet spot immediately.

That was some dress. The high-heeled and insanely sexy shoes helped too.

He lifted his lips a fraction and murmured, "I've missed you. Can we take this someplace more private?"

Her smile curved against his cheek and she nodded.

Grasping her hand, he pulled her in the direction of the newly returned town car, settled her in the backseat and nearly dived in after her.

He'd never been able to resist her, and now he didn't have to.

Somehow, Finn had been granted a reprieve. The king hadn't phoned him to demand an explanation for the photographs from last night. Now he had this one chance to recapture a small slice of heaven before submitting to an arranged marriage.

He'd hoped, against all logical reason, that the woman Elise matched him with could heal his broken heart. The odds of that happening with the woman who'd smashed it in the first place were zilch. Especially since he'd never in a million years give it to her again.

So he'd grant EA International another chance. Once he had a new bride by his side, the public would forget about the Party Prince and he could become known for something worthwhile.

The People's Prince. He liked the sound of that.

In the meantime, he could have Juliet...and all the good things about their relationship. Without getting into the painful past.

"So I take it you thought dinner went well?" he asked with a grin he couldn't have wiped off his face for anything. "You know, since you agreed to a repeat of the kiss."

Her hair was a little mussed from his fingers. He itched to pull out all the pins and let those silky locks tumble over him.

"I'm staying open to where the night leads. But it's been good so far." She studied him speculatively. "We're not fighting. We're connecting, like you said."

They weren't fighting because they'd thus far avoided the problem. And he was totally prepared to keep avoiding history with a capital *H* for as long as possible. "If this driver would step on it, we'd be connecting a whole lot more."

She laughed. "We have all night. But while we're on the subject, does connecting mean you're open to being on my side this time around?"

Apparently she did not subscribe to the same desire for avoidance of the past. "I've always been on your side."

"If that was true, you'd never have taken the stance you did." Her expression closed in. "You'd have supported me and my family when we tried to talk to your father."

That was the Juliet he'd last seen in Delamer. His stomach dipped. The connection part of the evening appeared to be over.

"You say that like I had no choice, like I had to agree with you or it equaled lack of support." But that's how he'd felt, as well. As if she couldn't see his side. Instantly, it all came roaring back. All the hurt and anger he'd been living with for a very long year. "You didn't support me either. And I never asked you to go against everything you believed in."

She yanked her hand from his. The heat in her expression reminded him she got just as passionate about taking his head off when they clashed.

So much for dinner going well.

"That's exactly what you wanted me to do." A lone tear tracked down Juliet's face and his gut clenched. It hurt to see someone as strong as Juliet crying. "Forget about Bernard and support you every day as you put on the uniform of the Delamer military. Every day, I'd be reminded Bernard died wearing the same uniform and I did nothing to avenge that. Every day, I'd be reminded you chose to stand with the crown instead of with me."

The car stopped at the private entrance to his hotel. It was positioned discreetly in the secluded rear section of the property, off to the side of the underground parking garage.

Finn didn't get out. This wasn't finished, not even close.

"Vengeance well describes it. You humiliated me. That protest garnered the attention of the entire world. Juliet—" Finn pinched the bridge of his nose. They should have recorded this conversation and played it back, saving them the trouble of having it again. "I'm a member of the House of Couronne. You burned the flag of the country my family rules *while we were dating*. How can you not see what that did to me?"

Not to mention the man she'd vilified was his *father*. He loved his father, loved his country. She'd wanted him to choose her over honor.

"My family is forever changed because of your father's policies. Bernard is gone and—" Her voice seized, choking off the rest. After a moment, she stared up at him through watery eyes laced with devastation. "A man who claimed to love me would have understood. He would have done anything to make that right."

But he wasn't just a man and never would be. He could no sooner remove the royal blood in his veins than he could fly blindfolded.

The tearing in his chest felt as if it was on repeat, as well. "A woman who claimed to love me would have realized I have an obligation to the crown, whether it's on my head or not. I don't get the choice to be someone other than Prince Alain Phineas of Montagne, Duke of Marechal, House of Couronne."

He belonged to one of the last royal houses of Europe and he owed it to his ancestors to preserve the country they'd left in his care. No matter how antiquated the notion became in an increasingly modern world.

Now he was ready to get out of the car. To be somewhere she wasn't. That was one thing that hadn't changed—Juliet causing him to feel a touch insane as he veered between extreme highs and lows very quickly. She followed him to the curb, clearly determined to continue twisting the spike through his heart.

"I never wanted you to be someone else. I loved *you*."

Past tense. It didn't escape his notice.

"You meant everything to me, Finn. But it's peacetime. The mandatory military service law is ridiculous. Why can't you see that your royal obligation is to stop being so stubborn and think about people's lives?"

"For the same reason you can't see that the military is mine," he said quietly.

He'd never wear the crown. Flying helicopters was the one thing he could do that Alexander, as the crown prince, couldn't. Juliet's refusal to get out from under her righteous indignation prevented *her* from taking *his* side.

She was the stubborn one.

Anger coated the back of his throat. Juliet was still the same crusader under the cosmetics and sexy dress. She was still determined to alter the heart of the institution to which he'd sworn loyalty.

Suddenly, it was all too easy to resist her. He didn't have the slightest interest in rehashing all of this for the rest of the night, regardless of the more tangible rewards. He'd never bowed to anyone before and he wasn't about to start now.

Arms crossed against her abdomen, Juliet stared dry-eyed at the unoccupied valet booth behind Finn. "I think it's safe to say the date was not a success."

"I'll have the driver take you back to Elise's house." Finn tapped on the passenger-side window.

The squeal of tires on cement reverberated through the quiet underground lot. A van sped down the ramp and wedged tight against the rear bumper of Finn's hired car. Four men with distinctly shaved heads, beefy physiques and dark clothing jumped out, trouble written all over them.

"Juliet, get in the car," Finn muttered, angling his body to shield her as the men advanced on them.

He never should have given his security guys the night off.

It was the last thing he registered as the world went black.

Four

Grit scraped at Juliet's eyeballs. She tried to lift a hand to rub them. And couldn't.

Heavy fog weighed down her brain. Something was wrong. She couldn't see and her hands weren't working. Or her arms.

Rapid blinking didn't improve her eyesight. It was so *dark*.

She never drank enough alcohol to be this fuzzy about her current whereabouts…and how she'd gotten there… and what had happened prior to.

"Juliet. Can you hear me?" Finn's voice. It washed over her, tripping a hodgepodge of memories, most of them X-rated.

Finn's voice in the dark equaled one activity and one activity only. Pleasure, the feel of his skin on hers, urgency of the highest order to fly into the heavens with him—

Wait. What was *Finn* doing here?

"Yeah," she mumbled thickly. "I hear you."

Pain split through her brain the moment her jaw moved, cutting off her speech, her thoughts, even her breath. Inhaling sharply, she rolled to shift positions—or tried to.

Her muscles refused to cooperate. "What's…going on?"

"Tranquilizer," Finn explained grimly and spit out a nasty curse in French. "I think they must have used the same dose on both of us."

The sinister-looking men. An unmarked van. The date with so much promise that ended badly. And then got worse.

Juliet groaned. "What? Why did they give us tranquilizers?"

"So they could snatch us without a fight," Finn growled. "And they should be thanking their lucky stars they did. Otherwise I would have removed their spleens with a tire iron."

Snippets of dinner with Finn flashed through her mind. Okay, good. So she hadn't lost her memory and she wasn't suffering from the effects of a hangover. "We were kidnapped? Stuff like that only happens in the movies."

"Welcome to reality." The heavy sarcasm meant he was frustrated. And maybe a little worried. That didn't bode well. Finn always knew what to do.

Shifting along her right side indicated his general vicinity. Not too far away. "Can you move? Are we tied up?"

It was hard for her to tell. Everything was numb. That's why she couldn't move. She'd been *drugged*. And blinded, maybe forever.

What sort of scheme had she stumbled into simply by being in the wrong place at the wrong time with the wrong companion?

A strong, masculine hand smoothed hair from her face, throwing her back to another time and place where that happened with frequency.

"Nah," Finn said. "They shot us up with enough narcotics that they didn't need to tie us up. I'm okay. The cocktail didn't affect me nearly as long as it did you."

Gray invaded her vision and got lighter and lighter with each passing moment. Thank goodness. "Where are we?"

"Not sure. In a house of some sort. I was afraid to leave you alone in case you needed CPR, or the welcoming committee showed up, so I didn't do more than look out the window."

A fuzzy Finn swam through her eyesight, along with a few background details. White walls. Bed.

Finn held her hand. She squeezed, gratified that her fingers had actually responded, and then licked dry lips. "Guards?"

"Not that I can tell. I haven't seen anyone since I regained consciousness." Finn nodded to a door. "As soon as you can walk, we'll see what's what."

"Help me sit up," she implored him.

Finn's arm came around her waist and she slumped against him. Two tries later, her legs swung off the bed and thumped to the floor.

Barefoot. Had they taken her shoes? She wasn't even completely over the sticker shock at the price of those ivory alligator sandals and now they were probably in a Dumpster somewhere. And she'd actually kind of liked them.

"Now help me stand," she said. Their captors might return at any moment and they both needed to be prepared. Sure Finn was stronger and better trained, but she was mad enough to take out at least one.

Finn shook his head. "There's no prize for Fastest Recovery After Being Tranquilized. Take your time."

"I want to get out of here. The faster we figure out what that's going to take, the better." Throbbing behind her eyes distracted her for a moment, but she ignored it as best she could. "How far do you think they took us from your hotel?"

Elise would be worried. Maybe she'd already called the

police and even now, SWAT teams were tearing apart Dallas in search of Prince Alain.

Or…Elise might be smugly certain she'd staged the match of the century and assume they'd gotten so wrapped up in each other, Juliet had forgotten to call. The matchmaker probably didn't realize they were missing yet.

"There's only one way to find out where we are. Come on." Finn took one step and her knees buckled.

Without missing a beat, he swept her up in his strong arms and she almost sighed at the shamefully romantic gesture.

Except he was still the Prince of Pigheadedness. Why had she ever thought she could marry him—even under the guise of changing Delamer policy from the inside?

Finn deposited her easily on the pale blue counterpane and kept a light but firm hand on her shoulder so she couldn't sit up. "It's early afternoon, if the daylight outside the window is any indication. We've probably been captives for about eighteen hours. The entire Delamer armed forces are likely already on their way to assist the local authorities. Stay here and I'll go figure out the lay of the land."

"You're not the boss just because you're a boy."

He scowled. "I'm not trying to be the boss. I'm trying to keep you from cracking your stubborn head open. If you think you can walk, be my guest."

With a flourish, he gestured toward the door.

Now she had to do it, if for no other reason than to prove His Highness wrong. Slowly, she wobbled upright and took excruciatingly slow steps, one in front of the other.

The door opened easily, despite her certainty that she'd find it locked. It swung open to reveal a bare hallway. "Let's go."

She'd almost taken an entire step across the threshold when Finn leaped in front like her own personal bulletproof vest.

She rolled her eyes. Of course. Bullets bounced off the perpetually arrogant all the time, right?

"Don't you have any sense?" he growled in her ear. "This is a dangerous situation."

If the kidnappers had wanted to harm them, they would have. Finn was more valuable alive than dead. "If anything dangerous is lurking in these halls, it's going to get you first. Then who will protect me?"

"What makes you so certain I'd lose?" he whispered over his shoulder as he flowed noiselessly away from the bedroom. He'd always moved with elegant flair, but this cloak-and-dagger-style grace was sexier than she'd like to admit.

She dogged his steps, tearing her gaze from his spectacular backside with difficulty. "A hunch. If the kidnappers had tranquilizers, they probably have guns. Unless you think they're in this for the opportunity to have afternoon tea with royalty."

"Shh." He halted where the hallway ended in a large room and poked his head out to scan the space with a double sweep. "All clear."

An inviting living area with a fireplace and high-end furniture opened up around her as she stepped out of the hall. "This is not what I would have envisioned as a place to keep captives."

A breathtaking panorama of sparkling sea unfolded beyond a wall of glass. The house perched on a low cliff overlooking the water. That particular shade of blue was etched on her heart, and her breath caught.

"We're not in Dallas anymore," Finn announced needlessly. "And those were some serious drugs the kidnappers used if they brought us clear across the Atlantic without me realizing it."

"We're on an island."

She was home. Back on the Mediterranean, close to everything she loved. She'd sailed these waters often enough to recognize the hills rising behind the city, the coastal landscape.

Home. She never thought she'd see it again. The small ripples in the surface of the water. The wheeling birds. The sky studded with puffy clouds. All of the poetic nuances of the sea bled into her chest, squeezing it, nearly wrenching loose a sob.

"Yeah." Finn skirted the large couch and squinted at the shoreline visible in the distance. "About two miles off the coast of Delamer. There are, I don't know, at least four or five different islands in this quadrant. It's hard to tell from the ground which one we're on."

"There can't be more than a handful of people who own houses on these islands. It would be pretty easy to figure out who kidnapped us." She shook her head. "We were taken by the dumbest kidnappers ever. They dumped us right in our own backyard."

"Dumb—or really smart. Who would think to look for us here? We're both supposed to be in Dallas."

"Well…good point."

So if all the search efforts were concentrated on the other side of the Atlantic, they were going to have to rescue themselves.

"And leaving us on an island means they don't have to stick around," she said. "Very difficult for us to escape. I assume they took both our cell phones."

He nodded. "And I'm sure the kidnappers did a full sweep to remove all devices with access to the outside world."

Gingerly, he gripped the handle of the sliding door and pulled. It slid open, and the swift Mediterranean breeze doused her with its unique marine-life-drenched tang.

Goodness how she'd missed it.

She followed Finn outside onto the covered flagstone patio, set with wicker outdoor furniture around a brick fire pit. The cry of gulls overhead was like hearing a favorite song for the first time in ages. There were worse places to be held captive than in a cliff-side villa in the south of France during early summer.

But they were still captives.

Finn gripped the wrought iron railing surrounding the patio and peered down the cliff to the rocky shore below. "The slip is empty."

Sure enough, the dock was boat-free. "Maybe there's a kayak or something in storage that the kidnappers forgot about."

"We should definitely check around. I'm still not convinced we're alone." Finn grimaced. "Why would they leave us unsupervised in what's essentially a vacation spot? None of this makes any sense."

"Kidnapping as a whole doesn't make any sense. How is kidnapping you, and by extension me, going to achieve changes in the king's policies?"

Even in the midst of her lowest point of grief over Bernard's death, she'd have never willingly put another human in harm's way to promote her political agenda.

"One would assume we're being held for ransom." Finn shot her a wry sideways glance. "Not everyone is a crusader, you know. Though I find it a bit endearing you immediately jumped to the conclusion that the motive here is political gain."

Her spine stiffened. Why didn't he call her naive too, while he was at it? "You don't have to make fun of me. I get that you don't agree with me."

"I'm not making fun of you. I was being dead serious. Your passion for your principles is one of my favorite things about you."

He tipped her chin up to force her gaze to his.

She let him and blamed it on her half-tranquilized brain. But no quantity of numbing agents could stop the flutter in her chest when he looked at her with his eyes all liquid and bottomless and beautiful. Worse, it was clear he was telling the truth.

She looked away without comment. Because really, what could she say to that? It was the perfect encapsulation of their relationship. He appreciated her passion but not what she was passionate about. She loved his sense of loyalty but not what he swore allegiance to.

His hand fell to his side and he stared out over the water as if engrossed by the view.

The endless vicious circle they'd been plunged into could never be broken, and the crushing sadness of it gripped her insides anew.

Maybe she should catch a clue from the kidnappers. They'd exhibited a ruthless determination to reach their goals—whatever those goals might be—and she could do the same.

Not everyone was a crusader, but it took only one to upset the status quo.

For Bernard.

If she eliminated her emotions from the equation, perhaps she could still figure out a way to get the reform she wanted. First, she had to figure out how to get off this island.

Finn laced his fingers at the back of his neck to keep from reaching for Juliet again. She obviously didn't welcome his touch. He understood why—the storm of last night's argument still lingered between them.

But he'd been forced to watch her ashen face for an eternity, praying she'd wake up soon. Praying their captors didn't return with unsavory appetites. He didn't have a problem doing others bodily harm to protect Juliet, but he liked it better when he didn't have to.

Now that she was awake, he had a nearly incontrollable urge to fold her into his embrace and assure himself she was really okay.

She cleared her throat. "We should split up and search the property for a boat."

Obviously she was on the road to recovery.

"Are you out of your mind? Why on earth would you think I'd let you out of my sight?"

She'd just made an excellent point about men with guns, and she thought splitting up was a good plan?

Scowling, she tied her hair up in messy knot, as if preparing to wade into a brawl. "Because we need to get off this island in a hurry and we'll search faster if we do it separately."

"We're not splitting up," he growled. "Walk fast and that'll achieve the same end."

With a withering glare, she took off down the stairs bolted to the cliff side, and her pace was a clear dare-you-to-keep-up. He scrambled after her, easily matching her long-legged stride until they hit sea level. Wordlessly, they tramped over the rocky shoreline and he clamped his mouth closed lest he accidentally show some concern for the sharp rocks digging into her bare feet.

If she'd slow down a minute, he might have volunteered the location of her shoes—in the closet of the room where she'd slept off the tranquilizer. Though the sexy spiked heels probably weren't the best choice for beach-tramping.

"There's nothing here," she said, hands on her hips. The breeze pulled stands of hair from the knot at her nape, wrapping them around her face and neck.

His blood pumped faster as he took in the sight.

Did she have any idea how beautiful she was? Especially framed by the homeland and sea he loved.

He still wanted to sweep her into his arms and forget everything else but pleasure.

He glanced away. "There's a lot of island left to cover. Don't give up yet."

"I wasn't giving up. I was reevaluating. We should be looking for some way to start a fire. Surely there are people out on the water, and someone is doing your job in your place, right? Smoke signals are a better bet than searching for a boat."

"That's a good idea," he lied.

It would never work. Everyone knew the dozens of small islands off the coast of Delamer were owned by wealthy, influential people. Who would dare intrude on someone's private domain to investigate what they'd assume was a bonfire on the beach?

But it was better than doing nothing.

They climbed the stairs to the patio. In the lavishly appointed kitchen, Finn slung open cabinets and drawers in search of matches or a lighter.

Juliet poked her head out of the walk-in pantry. "Well, if we aren't rescued soon, at least we won't starve. Come see this. There are enough provisions in here to feed all your coast guard buddies for a month."

It was the second time she'd mentioned his job in less than ten minutes, and derision laced her tone without apology. She didn't see anything wrong with disparaging a profession he loved.

He wanted to wring her neck as much as he wanted her naked. Push-pull. Seemed as if he'd never escape it.

He swallowed the frustration and joined her. True to her description, boxes and jars lined the shelves of the well-stocked pantry. Cereal, pasta, canned beans and fruits—nearly every variety of dry goods he could imagine.

Curious now, he exited to the kitchen and pulled open the double doors of the stainless steel refrigerator. "Same here. Our captors went to great lengths to ensure we'd have three square meals a day."

The refrigerator held steaks, chicken breasts, fresh vegetables and staples such as milk and butter, all unopened and unexpired.

Juliet brushed his arm as she came up beside him to

peer into the interior. "It makes me uneasy. How long are they expecting to keep us here?"

Worry lined her face, which was still a little white. Most of her makeup had worn off, allowing her true beauty to shine through. He hated seeing it marred by stress.

"Wish I knew." Frustration returned in a rush. With it came the "if-onlys": *If only I hadn't given Gomez and La-Salle the night off. If only I'd invited Juliet to dinner in my hotel room. If only I'd had five more seconds to react when the van pulled up.*

That was a sure way to get his temper in a knot and resolve exactly nothing.

"Why don't you check over near the fireplace for matches?"

The farther away she was, the less she could affect his senses.

As she left the kitchen, he shoved both hands in his pockets. Paper crinkled under his knuckles and he withdrew an envelope with the king's seal prominently displayed in the center. An envelope that hadn't been in his pocket last night.

A strange sense of foreboding slid along Finn's spine.

He slipped an index finger under the seal and withdrew the folded page, his mind already piecing together aspects of this odd kidnapping plot into a whole he didn't like.

Exactly as he suspected, the page bore a note written in his father's bold hand.

Sorry to inconvenience you, blah, blah, but unexpected events caused me to reevaluate blah, blah.

Finn's gaze zeroed in on the last paragraph:

The Villere family is gaining traction in turning public opinion against my rule. Use this time I'm giving you with Juliet well. Patch things up with her and use your relationship to influence both her and her family into dropping their inflammatory political campaign. Marry her and en-

sure it's clear the Villere family sides with the crown. It's the most advantageous match for everyone.

Now Finn knew why he'd never heard from his father about the photographs from Elise's party.

The king had orchestrated a kidnapping plot instead.

Finn's throat tightened. No wonder their captors had left them unsupervised in paradise. It was forced seclusion so Finn had the opportunity to seduce Juliet into siding with him instead of her family. Kidnapping allowed Finn to claim innocence in the deal, and furthermore allowed them to commiserate as they endured their circumstances.

It was fiendishly ingenious. And insane.

The paper crumbled in Finn's fist. His father had gone too far. Juliet had been drugged, not to mention frightened. For what? So Finn could perform a miracle and make Juliet an advocate of the crown? If that was possible, he'd have done it a year ago.

"Found the matches," she called with the most cheer she'd exhibited since coming out of unconsciousness.

Matches were totally unnecessary given this new development. No one was looking for them.

No one would take the slightest bit of notice of a plume of smoke coming from this island, which he now knew for certain was Île de Etienne, where Alexander and Portia owned the only house occupying the entire hunk of rock. This luxurious cage doubled as a lover's retreat for the crown prince and his wife, which was why Finn had never been invited to check it out.

Was his brother in on the plot too? Was everyone in the royal family waiting to see how Finn would handle this twist?

The best way to combat the king's underhanded tactics was to tell Juliet exactly what was going on.

"A fire isn't going to help. Listen, you need to—"

"No, you listen." She scowled. "You don't know everything because you're in the military. You can sit around here and wait for your buddies to show up, but I'm not going to. I want to go home."

Turning on her heel, she flounced from the kitchen, her gorgeous backside swinging under her crinkled but still very sexy yellow dress. The shush of the sliding door opening and then being shut—likely with Juliet on the outside—reverberated in the suddenly quiet house.

Finn sank onto a bar stool with a groan and put his aching head in his palms. What an obstinate, hardheaded woman. Those very qualities had caused him immeasurable pain a year ago, and only an idiot would step up for a repeat.

The last thing he wanted to do was chase after her, and the only silver lining in this situation was that he didn't have to. If nothing else, the king's note reassured Finn they weren't in any danger from zealous criminals who might return at any moment to start slicing off fingers.

What had the king been thinking? Well, that wasn't a mystery. It was all there in blue fountain pen. Finn had an opportunity to make an advantageous match, exactly as his father had discussed before sending Finn off to Dallas. It was merely the definition of "advantageous" that had changed.

If it hadn't been happening to him, Finn might have appreciated the brilliance of the move. With no access to the outside world, Juliet wouldn't realize her family was turning the tide in their quest to see someone pay for Bernard's death. Furthermore, the king surely knew he was playing to Finn's sense of honor and duty to the crown.

Hands flat on the bar, Finn shoved to his feet. He would not be an active party to deceiving Juliet, especially not to the point of marrying her and then influencing her to side against her family. *Influence* was code for *coerce*. Their differences could only be truly resolved if she chose him willingly.

And that wasn't happening. She was far too stubborn and she still made him far too angry.

Finn went outside, determined to tell Juliet what the king had done. Then, they could work together to escape this ridiculous plot.

Smoke plumed from the rocky shore. He peered over the cliff's edge. Juliet stood near a blazing wood patio chair, turned upside down on the ground. Apparently his brother would be short a piece or two of furniture the next time he was in residence, which was Alexander's due for lending the house to their father's scheme.

"Any luck?" Finn called as he descended the stairs.

"Yeah, can't you see the Delamer armed forces storming the beach?" she retorted, throwing his earlier words back at him. "You must not be as important as you think since no one's come to rescue us yet."

Actually, he was *more* important than he'd thought, which was why they were both in this situation. "I tried to tell you a fire wouldn't work."

"Feel free to come up with a plan that will work, Genius."

He opened his mouth to blurt out the truth. Something in her posture, or the wind, or something beating through his chest stopped him.

He was important.

More important than he'd realized.

The king wasn't pushing chess pieces across his royal board—this situation had been carefully constructed to allow Finn to shape the future of Delamer. His brother couldn't do this. Neither could his father. Only Finn had a prayer of swaying Juliet and her family away from their attacks on the king and the Delamer military.

Finn, the second son, wasn't useless after all.

The king possessed a sharper mind than Finn had credited. If Finn told Juliet about the king's involvement in the kidnapping, it would only fuel her ire. Who knew what she'd do to retaliate? The goal was to get her to stop disparaging his family, not make it worse.

Furthermore, if Finn *didn't* do as his father asked, the king might find another way to handle the problem of Juliet and her family, a way that could potentially destroy their lives.

Finn alone held all the winning cards.

If he did as his father asked, he'd save his country and have Juliet again. In his life, in his bed. But never in his heart. That part of their relationship was over.

Juliet stared out over the water, her face troubled.

"I'm racking my brain for a plan," he told her. Which was true enough…but it wasn't a rescue plan. It looked a lot more like a seduction plan. But could he really go through with it?

Glancing at Juliet, he fingered the crushed note out of his pocket and dropped it into the fire. The paper curled, turned black and then burst into flames.

If only his misgivings about the task before him were so easily destroyed.

Five

Finn coughed away a bit of smoke. "So, here's a plan. Let's go back to the house and eat. We'll talk about next steps once we've fueled up."

The reprieve would also give him time to think through what he wanted to do. Could he really seduce Juliet out of her position against the king's military policies?

He'd been convinced at dinner last night she hadn't changed, but in their year apart, she'd quit a job she loved, flew across the Atlantic and enrolled in a matchmaker program with the intent to marry an American.

Obviously *some* things had changed. But enough things? Things he hadn't begun to uncover during their short dinner last night?

Crossing her arms, Juliet met his gaze. "We should stay here, by the fire. If someone comes, they might put it out and leave, never realizing there are captives in the house."

He bit back a groan. Of course she would still be concerned about rescue, and unless he clued her in, she'd continue to be. But he couldn't tell her yet, not until he figured out what he wanted to do.

Such was the problem with deception. One small omission became many big lies.

"Fine, then I'll make us something and bring it down. We'll have a picnic on the beach."

She eyed him. "You can't cook."

"I'm not talking about a four-course meal complete with soup and appetizers. Will a sandwich work for your delicate palate?"

"Sure." With a small smile, she plopped down onto a large rock. "I'll be waiting."

Angry—and not entirely sure at whom—Finn slapped peanut butter and jelly on wheat bread and wrapped the sandwiches in napkins. This whole situation grated on him. Food was not going to soften the rock or the hard place he was smack in the middle of.

A quick search revealed a tray worthy of balancing a couple of water glasses down a steep flight of stairs, and he was back by the fire in ten minutes. With a less-than-perfect solution to his screaming conscience.

"Eat your sandwich, and then we'll start fires all around the perimeter of the island," he advised her. "I'm pretty sure this is Île de Etienne. If anyone with half a brain is paying attention, several fires will be cause for investigation."

He'd forgotten how Juliet constantly challenged him to be better, smarter, faster. In the past year, he'd floundered without her influence, something he'd only recently recognized. The blondes should have been a clue.

Eyebrows raised, Juliet gulped water from her glass and swallowed. "That's a great idea. Thanks for the sandwich."

Finn nodded and shoved his own sandwich in his mouth. The faster he finished, the faster they could get off this island—because no one said he had to wait around for his father to come get them. He could seek rescue on his own. Then he wouldn't be catering to the king's mad plan, but neither did he have to tell Juliet about it and risk damaging relations with her family further.

In the meantime, if they could find a way to spend time together without fighting, which was doubtful, marriage might seem like more of a possibility.

Finn and Juliet clambered up the stairs to the patio and threw as many wooden objects to the beach below as they could pick up. Alexander could bill their father for the damages as far as Finn was concerned.

The cliff went halfway around the island's perimeter and gradually sloped to sea level on the side facing south toward Africa, but they agreed their odds were best suited to fires along the shore closer to Delamer. Deep-water fishermen and cargo boats would pass by in the morning, and if the fires along the Delamer side didn't generate interest, they'd focus efforts to the south tomorrow.

The first patio chair burned a few yards from the stairs. Broken pieces of the rest of the patio set littered the shoreline beyond it. They rounded the fire and began spreading out piles of wood along the northern shore. The process was effortless. No speech required. She seemed to read his mind, leaning the boards into a cone shape, then stepping back so he could light it.

Finn had a strange sense of déjà vu or the feeling that the past year had been a horrible nightmare he'd woken from, sighing in relief because he and Juliet were together and still in love. Still happy.

At the same time, the pain of her betrayal rode in his chest, right where his heart was supposed to be. The protest had happened. They weren't together.

It was that push-pull paradox he didn't enjoy.

Juliet's hair had blown loose from the messy knot long ago and her cheeks had turned bright pink under the afternoon sun. She'd never say a word, but he'd bet her feet were cut and bloody too.

That was how she challenged him—with silent strength

he couldn't help but admire. Couldn't help but strive to match.

"Let me finish setting these fires. Why don't you go back to the house?" he suggested after they torched the third patio chair.

"What for?" She tossed a glance over her shoulder, already off to the next pile of wood—a side table.

"So you can rest. Take a long, hot bath. I'm sure you can find some jazz music to play in the bathroom." He followed her and cut to the chase. "You're getting sunburned and it doesn't take two people to set these small fires. Don't worry. If someone comes, I'll make sure they don't leave without you."

She halted in her tracks and they nearly collided. His arms came up to steady her, but she spun, eyes bright and searching. "You remember that I like to listen to music while I'm taking a bath?"

The sheer hopefulness in her tone uncoupled something in his chest, and the caustic scent of smoke sharpened a sudden memory of roasting marshmallows in the fireplace of his living room one evening when they'd opted not to brave the paparazzi.

"I remember everything about you."

The way she'd looked in the firelight that night. The way she'd felt in his arms when he'd made love to her right there on the floor. How he hadn't cared about anything but being with her; the obligations of his position, job, family—everything—eliminated for a blissful few hours.

He wanted that back. Wanted to forget all about the scandal for a while and indulge in the paradise around them. The paradise of neutral ground, no hurt, no past. The paradise of Juliet.

Marriage might be off the table, but maybe romance wasn't.

Her breathing changed, ever so slightly, and a hint of hunger bled into her expression. As if she'd read his thoughts. The throb of awareness spread, coiling through him.

As if she hated the separation between them as much as he did, she swayed into his space. Their lips played at meeting, hovering in hesitation. Then he closed the gap, taking her mouth firmly.

She flooded him, drenching him with need. Hands to her jaw, he angled her head, deepening the kiss, tasting the fire of her mouth. She moaned under him, building the pressure of sheer want in his system.

He slid a palm down her spine to cup her sweet rear, molding her body to his as he hiked that sexy yellow dress up so he could feel her bare skin. Like satin. He groaned and blindly went for the hem to remove the dress completely. Fingers ready to whip it off, he paused to give her a chance to stop him, seeking an answer to his unvoiced question.

With the scent of the sea, of fire and of Juliet engulfing his senses, he prayed the answer would be yes.

The weight and pressure of Finn's amazing lips on hers dissolved Juliet's knees. Never at a loss, he tightened his arms around her, supporting her against his body. *More, more, more.*

All the anxiety and fear she'd carried around since awakening in a strange bed in a strange place vanished. Finn was here, with her. Nothing mattered except losing herself in the sensations of a sea breeze and him. It was very welcome. Effortless, as it had always been between them.

No other man had ever made her feel as this one did, as if a tide of power had swept through her. Her body electrified as his energy zipped into her very blood.

Her dress bunched up at her waist and his fingers teased her flesh, brushing against her thighs, then her stomach. Yes. She wanted his hands everywhere.

As the kiss drew out, her heart soared.

And then plummeted.

She couldn't let him affect her this way. This wasn't an opportunity for a second chance. She'd tried at dinner last night and it hadn't worked.

No emotions. Ruthless determination.

Breaking loose—with incredible effort—she shook her head and pulled her dress back in place. "Um, we have to…"

What? The man scrambled her brains like a double heatstroke. The cuts on her feet weren't even as painful after Finn's mouth had numbed all her extremities. No more kissing. Or other stuff. It was too mind-altering.

He let her go and jerked his head toward the house, his expression blank. "Go inside. I'll finish here."

How very Finn-like to turn bossy when she didn't respond to his original suggestion. "I'm not taking a bath when I could be putting effort toward rescue."

His huff of frustration nearly made her smile. "Then go back to the house and see if you can get on the internet through the TV. I'm pretty sure I saw a video game console too. Try both."

"Aye, aye, Lieutenant." She gave him a saucy salute to hide her relief at the perfect excuse to remove herself from his overwhelming presence. Before she kissed him again.

She had to keep her wits about her and keep focused on escape, not her humming girl parts and desperately lonely soul.

She left him on the beach and limped up the stairs to the house, her mind turning over the kiss.

One minute they were setting fires, and the next she couldn't have stepped away from him at gunpoint. They'd both agreed in the car after dinner that they didn't make sense together. Somehow, she'd given him the wrong signals. Or they'd both been caught up in the heat of the moment, like two survivors in a disaster movie, inexplicably drawn to each other over shared circumstances.

Either way, it didn't matter. If it hadn't been for the kidnapping, she'd never have seen Finn again. Being held captive together didn't change facts. She could never marry him solely to promote her agenda. It would be too painful, too difficult.

And when he kissed her, she forgot all that.

She had to get off this island and away from him. It was best for them both.

The TV wasn't the kind with an internet connection, but it did have satellite cable service, offering more than three hundred channels, including all the premium movie ones. Quickly, she cued up a news channel to see how much coverage their disappearance was receiving.

After fifteen minutes of zero mentions of the missing Prince of Delamer, Juliet gave up. No one realized they'd been kidnapped yet. What kind of kidnappers waited so long to make their demands?

The credenza did indeed house a Wii console on the bottom shelf, tucked way in the back. Only Finn's sharp helicopter-pilot eyesight could have spotted it.

She hit the power button, but despite many attempts, the console couldn't connect to the internet. No service, likely. The kidnappers had been quite thorough. Absently, she flipped through the hundred or so games lining the shelf next to the console, hard-pressed to think of a title not present and accounted for.

They certainly wouldn't suffer from boredom here in this gilded cage.

Heaving a sigh, she turned off the electronics and spent several minutes opening cabinets and drawers looking for a laptop or cell phone or *something* that could be used to contact help.

The sliding glass door to the patio opened and shut, announcing Finn's return.

"Shouldn't one of us stay on the beach in case someone comes?" she asked with raised eyebrows. "I'll go back down if you don't want to."

She definitely didn't need to be in the same room with him, not while he looked all deliciously windblown and wild from being out in the elements.

His jaw tightened as he pushed his rolled sleeves up over his elbows. "It's late. I doubt there are many boaters out on the water. If one of the guys is doing my rounds, he'll land on the south side of the island to investigate. The sound of a helicopter would be hard to miss. I think it's okay to be in the house."

There was no argument for that. Her feet could use a break anyway.

Gingerly, she crossed to the couch and plopped down to contemplate. "I guess we should think about dinner."

"A shower wouldn't be out of line either."

"Are you suggesting I need one?" she teased, and nearly bit her tongue.

It came so automatically to joke around with Finn, when really, there was nothing funny about being kidnapped. Nothing funny about being stuck on a small island with him when things were so impossible between them.

His smile did nothing to ease her consternation. "*I* need the shower. But if you want to join me, I'd be okay with that."

Accompanied by an exaggerated eyebrow waggle, the invitation was clearly not intended to be taken seriously, but of course now she was thinking about Finn's unclothed body, water sluicing down his sinewy muscles as he soaped himself.

"Uh…" She shut her eyes for a blink. It didn't help. Images danced across her mind's eye, growing increasingly erotic. "Thanks. I'm good."

He chuckled as if he'd guessed the direction of her thoughts. "I'm taking the bedroom at the end of the hall. You can have the one where you woke up. See you in a few."

Moments after he blew from the room, water hummed through the pipes in the walls. *I will not think about Finn naked. I will not think about Finn naked,* she chanted silently as she heaved off the couch to see about dinner.

Naked was actually better than thinking of him fully clothed and gazing at her with his heart in his eyes. She missed that far more than sex.

Listlessly, she rooted around in the refrigerator and then the pantry, but inspiration did not strike. She'd spent two months enduring hours upon hours of wife training under Elise's and Dannie's expert hands, including many sessions in the kitchen. Proper wives learned far more than how to cook, Elise had explained. They knew ingredients, how to pair food and wine, the true cost of a meal…even if they had professional chefs or the funds to eat out regularly. Otherwise, lack of knowledge gave caterers a license to rob you blind, or the charity fund-raiser you helmed ended up way over budget.

Surely some of the lessons had stuck. After all, the entire time, Juliet had assumed she'd be matched with an American businessman, as Dannie had been. She'd paid close attention, she really had.

Instead of trying to pull information from her brain that clearly wasn't there, she spent far too long searching for a cookbook. Zilch. The gourmet kitchen with its stainless steel appliances and stone countertops either typically accommodated a chef who knew what she was doing or it was strictly for show.

Chicken breast. That seemed easy enough to pop in the oven and cook at…some temperature. When in America, the conversion between Fahrenheit and Celsius had confused her, and now here she was cooking in Europe with an oven using Celsius after all. It was enough to drive her to drink.

Well, that sounded like a plan. She hunted for the wine cellar, and sure enough, it was off the kitchen and fully stocked with labels even she could tell were pricey and rare. The cool stone walls held the chill, promising perfectly temperate wine. With no small amount of glee, she plucked an aged Bordeaux from the rack and hoped the kidnappers had a stroke when they realized the thirty-year-old bottle was gone.

Back at the maddening stove, but fortified with a full glass of the deep red wine, she hummed as she plunked chicken into a dish with one hand and drank with the other.

"Now there's a sight. I do believe that's a happy tune you're humming."

She glanced over her shoulder. Finn lounged at the kitchen entrance, one shoulder against the wall, watching her. His dark hair was still damp and he wore a pair of jeans with a navy T-shirt, which fit as if they'd been custom made for his lanky frame.

"The kidnappers brought your luggage?" She perked up. Half a glass of wine had already gone a long way toward improving her mood, but clean clothes would be a very nice bonus indeed. "Did they bring mine?"

Her sunny yellow dress had become more the shade of ten-year-old linoleum, and a long brown streak of something she'd rather not identify marred the skirt.

His high-watt smile could have baked the chicken by itself. "Afraid not. I found these clothes in the closet of my bedroom. There were some girl outfits too, so I put one on your bed for you. What are you making?"

"Chicken."

After a long pause, his eyebrows rose. "And what else?"

"There has to be more? What's wrong with just chicken?"

"Nothing's wrong with just chicken, but I'm starving. What about some bread or..." He rummaged around in the refrigerator and held up a head of romaine. "A salad?"

"Feel free to contribute whatever you like to the meal. Have some wine," she offered magnanimously. "It's a Bordeaux. Might as well take advantage of our kidnappers' hospitality."

"Don't mind if I do. Alexander's always championing the merits of that label. Let's see what all the fuss is about." He poured himself a glass and bustled around the kitchen alongside her, throwing salad in bowls and slicing hunks from the baguette he'd pulled from the pantry.

Juliet pretended not to watch but *oh, my God,* what was it about a man in the kitchen that was so sexy? Or maybe it was just *this* man, with his fluid grace and his gorgeous, muscled butt that his borrowed jeans showcased as if they'd been stitched together deliberately to induce drool.

The oven timer dinged, startling her out of an X-rated fantasy starring the tabletop, her dress around her waist and Finn's jeans on the floor.

Gah, wasn't she supposed to be *not* thinking about him naked?

Quickly, before he noticed naughty guilt plastered all over her face, she plated everything and they sat at the breakfast nook overlooking the patio. A spectacular sunset splashed the sky to the west and nearly made dinner with the former love of her life bearable.

Finn chatted about nothing and earned major points for failing to mention the dry, tasteless lump of plain chicken on his plate. And she had the nagging thought that poultry and red wine weren't supposed to go together, which someone who regularly attended formal dinners with heads of major countries probably knew like the back of his hand. He didn't make another move or even flirt with her, and he'd helped her set the fires, despite originally hating the idea.

Maybe it wasn't so bad to be stuck here with Finn.

"This is the second night in a row we've had dinner together," she commented and wished she could take it back. Why had she brought that up? She didn't want him to think she approved of the idea.

"Yes." He gave her a long look, and the heat in it meant he'd definitely interpreted her observation the wrong way. "We used to eat together all the time."

"Well, hopefully this is the last time." She cringed. "I don't mean because you're such a horrible dinner companion. But because I hope we're rescued soon."

"I knew what you meant." He stuck a bite in his mouth and chewed thoughtfully. "Once we're home, are you planning to stick around?"

"I haven't really thought that far ahead."

"You could ask Elise for a different match." His smile flattened and he put his fork down in favor of drinking deeply from his wineglass. "If you still wanted to find an American husband."

"I don't."

It was a bit of a shock, but she recognized it as truth, despite not having consciously made any decision of the sort. Her flight from Delamer had been driven by Finn's false engagement announcement. Even if it hadn't been, she'd taken the coward's way out, and that didn't sit well with her anymore.

She rushed on lest he think *he* had something to do with her decision.

"Being back here…I can't leave Delamer again. But I don't have a job, or a place to live."

He shrugged. "That's easily rectified. The new school is short on qualified teachers, and I'm pretty sure I could lean on a few people to find you an apartment."

"Why would you do that?"

Because he thought she was on board with a second chance? That kiss on the beach had led him down the wrong path.

But it hadn't meant anything. The man was a good kisser. *That's* why she couldn't quite put it out of her mind.

"Don't sound so suspicious. I saw your face on the beach. I know what the water means to you. Frankly, I was shocked you'd leave in the first place." He stared out at the sunset for a long moment. "I talked my father into building that new school. For you."

Her wineglass bobbled, nearly spilling the contents, but she caught it with only a few splattered drops sacrificed to her clumsiness. "What? You did not. The existing school was overcrowded. Everyone knows that."

She'd had thirty students in her class last year and mourned letting them go on to the next grade without having given each of them more attention. The new school had been on everyone's mind. Tourism received the majority of the government's consideration at budget time, as it should, since foreign dollars filled the coffers.

"Yes, but it's been overcrowded for a long time with little action. How do you think the powers that be became convinced a new school was critical for the future of Delamer?"

The ribbon-cutting picture of Finn and the little girl sprang into her mind. Prince Alain had cut the ribbon because he'd made the school possible. When she stumbled over the picture, she'd always been too quick to click away the painful reminders to read any of the articles. "You never said anything. I've been complaining about the size of the classes since we first met."

His gaze captured hers, and she couldn't tear her heart away from the depths of his clear blue eyes.

"It was a surprise. I wanted to be sure it was a go before I mentioned it. They'd just broken ground when we split up."

"I don't...but that means..." Her brain and tongue seemed to be operating independently of each other, and a deep breath didn't help. "The king was opposed and you talked him into it?"

"Not opposed. You know how expensive it is to build in Delamer, when all the materials have to be imported. A school wasn't a top priority. I helped him see it should be.

With all the ammunition you gave me over our dozens of conversations about it, it was pretty easy to do."

"You did that for me?" she whispered.

"For you. And for my people. If I didn't think it was necessary, I wouldn't have supported the idea. But Delamer needs educated children who will grow up and become productive members of society. Who will help us compete in a global marketplace with ever-increasing opportunities. We have to start now if Delamer hopes to stay relevant."

She'd never said any of that. Her chief concern had been doing her job and ensuring the children had the best possible environment to learn. He'd drawn his own conclusions, creating a refined, big-picture angle that someone in her position wouldn't have considered.

But he had. Because of his role in the ruling family, he had a different perspective and a greater scope of concern than simply an overcrowded building.

Her head went a little fuzzy. Finn had conspired with the king to solve a problem she'd expressed.

But not the one she'd implored him to take to his father.

She braced for the familiar rush of anger—but it wasn't as harsh as normal.

How could she be mad at Finn? Together, they'd achieved something worthwhile. Of course, she hadn't been an active participant, but what if she was? How much more could they accomplish?

Clearly Finn had been listening to her and had no problem championing a cause once he bought into it. For some reason, he hadn't bought into her impassioned pleas for military reform. Why not?

But to ask might mean answers she didn't like. No reason he could give would make more sense than lifting the mandatory military service law. It couldn't. To believe in his reasons would be a betrayal of Bernard's memory, and that she could never do.

Deep down, she secretly wondered if her brother's death

was her fault. In a family of six children, it had fallen to Juliet, as the oldest, to help with the others. She'd spent so much time with her brother—but she obviously hadn't taught him well enough how to stay safe.

Her parents grieved the loss of their only son, probably more than she could ever imagine. They'd depended on her to ensure the same end didn't happen to another family.

The look on their faces when she told them Finn refused to budge...it had ravaged her. And after losing Bernard and then Finn, she'd have sworn she had nothing left to ravage.

Nothing could possibly fix that except taking this second chance to fulfill the quest her parents expected of her. Somehow, Finn must be persuaded to eliminate the mandatory service law in Bernard's honor. Finn's reasons for not doing so initially were completely irrelevant.

Not even if those reasons led her back into Finn's arms.

<u>Six</u>

The morning dawned with no more progress toward rescue or romance.

Not that Finn had expected much of either. But it was hard to tell his fully alert and female-starved body that yes, Juliet was sleeping in the same house, but Atlantis might rise from its watery grave before she visited his bedroom in the middle of the night.

Finn groaned and rolled over in the huge, lonely bed.

That kiss haunted his dreams. The feel of her flesh, the slide of her tongue.

Dinner last night had been torturous, especially after he'd told Juliet about building the school for her. The look on her face had affected him far more than he'd expected. More than he'd been prepared for.

He'd been about to suggest taking the rest of the wine out on the deck in hopes the evening might take a more passionate turn. But she'd closed off and excused herself for the evening.

"Good morning," Finn called cheerfully from his doorway as Juliet emerged from her bedroom. She had circles under her eyes and appeared to have slept as poorly as he had.

Because she'd been lying awake aching in kind but was too stubborn to admit she wanted him? Because she did want him, regardless of what had made her pull away. No one could kiss a man as she had and not mean it.

"It's morning. That's about all I can say about it," she grumbled before brightening slightly. "At least I got to take a hot shower. Thanks for the clothes."

The light sweater and pants were a little big, but she wore them with panache. Portia's taste ran to the conservative side, but then she was the crown princess and constantly under scrutiny.

"Let's eat breakfast," he said. "And then check out the south side of the island. I have an idea for another way to get someone's attention, but I have to see if it'll work."

"That sounds promising. And mysterious. I can't wait."

Juliet scored a couple of bagels from the pantry and spread them with jam. Finn brewed coffee, ignoring Alexander's lame Colombian brand for the dark roast Finnish label he'd found in the back of the pantry. They took their booty and some slices of cantaloupe outside to the patio, where a gentle breeze from the sea teased Juliet's hair and made him smile. Early-morning sunshine washed the view of Delamer in a silvery cloak and it was so achingly gorgeous, he hardly noticed the missing chairs, gladly sitting on the hard stone to eat.

Finn wanted his own island. Once they got home, he'd see about buying one. His future bride, whoever she was, might like a lover's retreat. Except he couldn't get the image of Juliet out of his mind, standing on the deck with hair falling out of a knot, melding with the background like a gorgeous sea creature too transcendent to catch.

The bite of bagel in his mouth wouldn't go down past the sudden lump in his throat.

Once he finally swallowed, he croaked, "Finished?"

He certainly was.

She held up her mug. "Yeah, if I can take the rest of this to go. I didn't realize how weak and boring American coffee is." She moaned a little in appreciation of the strong version in her cup. "What's the plan? More fires?"

That moan rippled through his still-alert lower half, which hadn't fully recovered from the night alone.

He shook his head. "Rocks. If we can find enough, we can spell out HELP or something that can be seen from the air. If the guys swing out to patrol the shipping lanes, someone will see it. The sooner we get it done, the better."

"Brilliant."

She disappeared into the house and reappeared with a travel mug. She'd also donned a pair of Portia's Timberlands, no doubt in anticipation of tramping along the south side of the island. "We still haven't made the news yet, by the way. Your HELP sign is a good plan since it doesn't even seem like anyone knows we're missing."

He should tell her the truth. But how could he without jeopardizing everything? If rescue came soon, he'd be off the hook.

They set off and soon had a pile of loose rocks from the perimeter of the island. As with the fires, they worked together seamlessly, but this time, Finn opted not to remain silent as they placed the stones in long lines.

"What if you didn't go back to teaching?" he threw out, picking up the threads of last night's conversation. "Could you be happy in some other job?"

Like Princess Juliet.

Where had that thought come from? He frowned. Still thinking about Juliet out on the deck, obviously, and how unhappy his father would be when Finn came home without having proposed to Juliet and without changing her mind.

"I'm sure I could find something I'd be good at besides that." She paused, a rock in each hand.

"What about something you'd like? As opposed to something you'd be good at." It was an interesting distinction, one he'd bet she hadn't consciously made.

With the "H" complete, he moved over to start laying the first branch of the "E." Juliet dropped her two rocks into place after his, clacking them together haphazardly.

"Ow!" She jerked her hand back and examined it.

"Are you okay?"

"Stupid fake fingernails." She frowned at the thin, bloody line splitting her index fingernail into two halves. "One got caught between the rocks and cracked down to the quick. I didn't even know that could happen. Usually I break them off."

"Why have them in the first place then?"

She shrugged and dropped her hand, the nail forgotten even though it had to hurt. "Such is the way of females, I'm told. We're supposed to be polished and put together."

"You don't have to have fingernails to be attractive, you know," he said.

"I know. You never cared about me being ladylike, which I always appreciated. That's why Elise's computer matched us, I suppose."

Actually, they'd been matched because they shared similar beliefs and moral compasses. Which was why he understood that she'd been upset and irrational when her brother died. If their positions were reversed and Alexander had been the one to walk into a live electrical field, Finn would be a wreck.

Polish mattered little in the grand scheme of things, but if he could convince her how wrong she'd been to take the position she had, they'd be dealing with a whole new set of dynamics.

Romance *and* marriage could be on the table.

Time healed wounds and afforded a different perspective. Maybe now she could see facts rationally. Could he really let go of the opportunity to feel her out?

Then he could truthfully tell his father he'd tried.

"You've never been out on the deck of the *Aurélien*," he said casually.

"No." She knelt carefully in the bare dirt where they were working, and placed the next rock with deliberate care, her back to Finn.

And that was the extent of her reaction to his abrupt subject change.

The stiffness of her spine and jerkiness of her movements told him she'd recognized the name of the ship where her brother had taken his last breath.

He almost backed off. His usual method of operation. Why should he have to spell out something she should already know?

But this was too important to stay in his comfort zone.

He sat down next to her and rearranged the already perfectly placed rocks. "It's an air defense frigate. I'm sure you've seen it from shore. Plenty of anti-aircraft guns and missile launchers and general busyness on deck. Extremely complicated equipment and lots of confusing levels."

"Yeah. I've seen it."

She wasn't going to make this easy, which was partly why he'd never talked about this before.

"They go over safety protocol all the time." He'd chosen his words carefully, but some things needed to be said without censor. "It's the responsibility of each private to understand the rules and follow them."

"Are you about to suggest that Bernard didn't?" she cut in, her tone strident.

"I wasn't there," he said as gently as possible. "But the reports were pretty conclusive. They interviewed all the shipmen aboard at the time. You can't go into the electrical rooms without proper protection."

Her head dropped as if too heavy for her neck to support.

"He shouldn't have been on that ship in the first place." She met Finn's gaze, and her ravaged expression tore through him. "He wanted to be in the coast guard. Like you. He worshipped you. Couldn't say enough about your flying skills or how heroically you rescued a swimmer."

That was a double spike to the gut. Finn wasn't a hero, or someone worthy of worshipping.

"The path to the coast guard is three years of mandatory military service," he said brusquely. "I did it too. I hated every second of being a shipman, but Juliet, half of Delamer borders the water. Our naval presence is paramount, and that's where we need men. Our population is so miniscule. How else would we get people on those boats?"

"Do you think the word *help* is enough or should we tack on an exclamation point?" She stood and gathered another pile of rocks with exaggerated movements.

He struggled with whether to drop it or not. Honestly, the subject was a little raw for him too. He'd liked Bernard. Finn could easily imagine having him around on a guy's fishing weekend or eventually becoming the boy's mentor, if he'd gone the coast guard route after serving his three years.

Juliet's broken half sob decided it for him.

Finn yanked her into his arms and snuggled her wet face against his neck. She snuffled for a moment, then her arms clasped him in turn. Her tears flowed unapologetically onto his shoulder, but he didn't care.

He held her, hurting along with her. "Bernard was a great kid. I miss him too."

"I just want to reverse time, you know?" she whispered. "Make it not have happened."

"I know." He breathed in the scent of her hair and the sea and lost a tear or two, as well. "It was a tragedy. But we have to move on, sweetheart."

She stepped out of his arms, and the rush of cool air

burned his Juliet-warmed skin. Obviously that had been the wrong thing to say.

"Move on. Good idea. This is done." She slid a finger under her wet lashes and then waved at the HELP sign stretching across the dirt before them. "You wait here for one of your buddies to make rounds. I'm going to the north side of the island to see if any boats are sailing from the marina to one of the other islands. Maybe I can flag one down."

This time, he let the matter drop. He watched her walk away and cursed.

Somehow, the dynamic between them had grown more complicated. And he had a feeling the longer they stayed on this island together, the worse it would become.

Juliet escaped and willed herself to stop crying. It wasn't working so far.

For brief odd moments, she'd experienced peace while placing stones with Finn, as if things had never become so mucked up. As if they were working together, teasing each other and laughing, then they'd look up and be finished without realizing any time had passed.

Then he'd ruined it.

Why did Finn have to pick at her wounds like that? And then be so understanding and comfortable to cry on? His shoulder was always on offer, always strong, and she'd missed it.

But then, she'd never really had it, not after Bernard died. The reminder was brutal.

The ache in her chest wouldn't ease, no matter how many deep breaths she took or how many times she counted to one hundred. Usually counting put her in a Zen-like state and cleared her mind. Not today.

She had to get away from Finn permanently. He was screwing with her sense of well-being.

"Come on, just one boat," she muttered.

A bright yellow catamaran skipped over the water about two hundred yards off the Delamer marina but no one on board would notice a lone woman waving at them from the shore of an island that was merely a smear on their horizon.

How long would she have to wait for a boat to come close enough to the island?

"I brought you an umbrella from the house."

She whirled. Finn stood behind her, umbrella opened and extended. Summer was typically the dry season in the Mediterranean. Only Finn would have thought to look for an umbrella. Only Finn would think of shielding her from the sun while she stood here waiting for a miracle rescue.

"I didn't hear you come down the stairs," she said.

"You seemed pretty intent on your self-appointed task. Sorry if I scared you."

She shook her head and took the offered shade. "Thanks."

Finn glanced out over the water. "It's a beautiful morning, isn—"

"I thought you were going to wait on the other side of the island."

They weren't doing this casual-conversation thing anymore. She couldn't take it. Not while it still felt as if an elephant was sitting on her chest.

If only he hadn't brought up Bernard. But he had and now it was alive again between them, hanging in that space where their love for each other used to be.

Surprise flitting through his gaze, Finn stared at her. "I can hear a helicopter on the north side as easily as I can hear one on the south. Thought I'd make sure you were okay."

"What, like I can't take care of myself?"

"No, like because you were crying," he corrected mildly. "I didn't mean to upset you."

"I'm fine." Since that clearly wasn't true, she offered the catch-all, noncommittal, leave-me-alone excuse. "Tired. Being kidnapped takes it out of me."

"Yeah, and the subject material too, apparently. Was it better to not talk about it?"

"I don't know."

Sometimes she *did* want to talk about it, and who better understood the anguish she'd endured than Finn? He knew her family, knew her history of helping raise Bernard, knew she was the oldest Villere child in a family of six and how her sense of responsibility had shaped her path.

He knew *her,* through and through. Which was why it hurt so much to be separated.

"What would talking about it solve?"

He shrugged. "Help ease the grief. It's something I didn't get a chance to do the first time. I want to be there for you. Let me."

The idea sprouted inside her, growing and twining through her frozen insides until she could hardly bite back the *yes.*

That had been the hardest part of the past year, that she couldn't turn to Finn during one of the worst periods of her life. She'd spent a lot of time with her parents, of course, but they had each other. Her sisters were understandably lost in their own grieving process, and none of them had helped raise Bernard. They'd lost a brother they loved, but it wasn't the same as losing a boy you'd helped shape and teach.

It wasn't the same as blaming yourself for not teaching him well enough. And then blaming yourself for exposing a sweet, impressionable kid to a man like Finn, worthy of hero-worship, worthy of inspiring Bernard to follow in his footsteps.

But then, no one could understand that. Not even Finn.

And still…the Finn-shaped hole inside yearned to be filled by the man within touching distance, to let him make good on that promise to be there for her. It had always been the two of them, together forever.

Two hearts being as one.

She stepped back, clutching the umbrella with both hands. Finn couldn't grant her absolution. He couldn't even give her the unconditional support she'd desperately hoped for. And then he'd tried to act as if Bernard was to blame for not following the rules.

Latching on to that as a shield against the firestorm of angst raging through her chest, she refused to fall into Finn's arms this time. "It's too late to be there for me. Just like it's too late for us. We're over and so is this conversation."

Finn's mouth clamped into a hard line. Finally, she'd gotten through to him.

If she could only get him to understand it was his stubbornness that stood in their way. All he had to do was lose it and then take her side against his father.

If he did, she was convinced that would be the key to healing. That one thing would allow her to stop blaming herself.

But that was never going to happen.

She sniffed and cleared her throat. "We're short a helicopter patrol and clearly we're too far out to be seen by any boats coming from the marina. The only way off this island is to swim. So that's what I'm doing."

His gaze cut to the sea lapping at the rocky coastline behind her. "Swim where?"

"To shore." She nodded toward the south bank of Saint Tropez. "It's not more than two miles if I head to the French side."

"You've never swam a stretch like that in your life. What makes you think you can do it now?" His tone was deceptively even, but she heard the condescension underneath. He thought she was too weak and too female.

"I can swim two miles. I've done it lots of times." She'd have that drive to succeed in her favor too, born of desperation to get out of this situation at all costs.

"There's a big difference between doing it in shallow

water where we sail and doing it from Île de Etienne to Saint Tropez." He gripped her shoulders earnestly. "Juliet, this is a rocky area. The boating lanes were cleared of submerged obstacles, so I could see you making the mistake of thinking the whole area's clear. It's not. You're talking about swimming in a straight line across open water."

The genuine concern on his face nearly had her second-guessing the plan. But what choice did they have? They were captives and people were undoubtedly worried about them by now.

"I'll be careful."

"It's not a matter of being careful." He shifted from foot to foot, and forked a restless hand through his dark hair. "I rescue people from these waters all the time. You know the number one reason they can't swim to shore on their own? Because they misjudged their strength against the current."

"You don't think I can make it."

She wanted to hear him admit flat out that his concern was about her abilities, not the water she'd been on or in for most of her life.

"This is not about you. It's about being safe and not taking chances. If nothing else, consider that you might get hit by a boat."

The eye roll might have come across a little exaggerated. But who could blame her? "The lack of boats is one of our current problems. At least if I got run over, the boat would notice me."

"You're being flip about this and it's not the kind of thing to be flip about. That's how people die."

The harsh, deep lines of his face hit her all of a sudden. He was worried about her dying.

And then it truly would be too late.

Her heart twisted painfully and she almost reached out to reassure him. Or maybe for another reason, one she could barely acknowledge.

She didn't want it to be too late.

She wanted to find a way to be with Finn again. To recapture the easiness of being in love, the shared smiles, the lazy afternoons, the comfort. To forget about what had happened and move forward.

Her pulse thumped erratically with the realization, scaring her. It was an impossible dream because she *couldn't* forget. They were like two battering rams, pushing each other with all their might but neither giving ground. Look what a disaster their date back in Dallas had become.

Even *thinking* about being with Finn again meant she had to get away from him before she did something she couldn't take back. Something she'd regret.

The umbrella dropped from her shaking fingers.

"Staying here isn't an option."

She jammed her hands down on her hips to hide her consternation. The fact that his concerns were valid was irrelevant.

"We've tried fires. We've tried your HELP sign. No one's come yet and the boats are too far away. We have to try something else."

She twisted her hair up in a knot and kicked off her shoes, but he grabbed her hand before she could flee into the water. "Wait. We're safe here. There's no danger from the kidnappers. They'd have come back by now if they were going to. We have plenty to eat. Why don't we pretend we're on holiday and relax for a few days?"

His earnest blue eyes bored into hers, pleading for her to reconsider. He was serious. "You're insane. We're prisoners. The luxuriousness of the cage doesn't change that. I can't stay here and pretend it's okay that we were kidnapped. I'll send someone for you as soon as I can."

"Juliet, there's something you need to know." Finn squeezed her hand, tight, preventing her from pulling away. "You don't have to swim anywhere because...my father is behind this."

"Behind what?" Her gaze flitted over his dark expression. Suddenly it all came together and she yanked her hand out of his grasp. "The *kidnapping?* Your father kidnapped us?"

Sighing, he laced his fingers together behind his neck, as if his head needed help staying upright. "Yeah."

Her stomach rolled. The king hired those men in the van, who had drugged both her and Finn, then left them here. "Wait a minute. You knew your father had us kidnapped? Since when?"

His jaw worked and then squared. "Since the first day. There was a note in my pocket."

He'd known the whole time and hadn't bothered to tell her. Where was this note anyway?

She cursed. "We've been running around trying to get rescued and setting fires and your father *knew* we were trapped here. He dumped us on this island on purpose. Why in the world would he do something so horrible to his own son? To me?"

"It's complicated." Finn paused and she nearly grabbed his shoulders to shake the rest out of him. "He saw the picture of us together at Elise's party and it snowballed from there."

"So this is an attempt to keep us out of the press." The *nerve* of King Laurent. Apparently a crown gave him license to do whatever he wanted. "Can't have any photos floating around of his precious son by the side of that extremist Villere girl."

"That's not the issue, Juliet. Be quiet for five seconds and listen."

That pushed her over the edge.

"Stop being so bossy! You've known about this all along. You had your chance to talk. Now it's my turn." For once, he clamped his mouth closed and crossed his arms, allowing her to vent every ounce of frustration. "How you sprang from the loins of such a coldblooded man as the king, I'll never understand. He put us in danger, just like he put Bernard in danger, and I'm tired of neither you nor your father seeing the problem. And I'm not going to sit around and wait for him to make the next move."

With that parting shot, she sprinted into the water.

The chill of it stole her breath. The summer was too young to have warmed the temperature, and she hated to admit it was an obstacle she hadn't even considered.

Well, it didn't matter. She could do it. She had to, if for no other reason than to prove to King Laurent that he didn't control her.

Stroking rhythmically, she pulled away from the island slowly, opting to conserve her energy for the middle stretch.

Breathe. Stroke. Breathe, stroke.

It was *so cold*.

She risked a glance around, and saw she'd hardly traveled more than three hundred yards. Checking her progress was a stupid thing to do. It was better not to know how far she still had to go and just swim. She'd hit the distant shore at some point. What did it matter how close she was?

A tingle in her fingers spread up her hands. Oh, no. They were going numb.

She stretched them as she stroked, hoping to increase the blood flow.

Then her side cramped.

And she sucked in a mouthful of seawater.

Coughing and holding her spasming waist, she treaded water mindlessly, frantically, praying the pain would ease as quickly as it had come on.

Water from her hair spilled into her eyes, stinging them. She backhanded the moisture away, but the second she moved her arm, the cramp in her side knifed through her anew, nearly sinking her under the surface.

The sea she loved had turned on her.

No, the sea was the same as always. Her time in America had taken its toll and she was woefully underconditioned for a swim like this. She should have been weight training and doing laps in the pool instead of learning how to balance a book on her head.

Her legs burned with the effort to keep her head above water. She wasn't going out like this, not by drowning in the Mediterranean. Any other body of water but this one, and she'd have considered giving in to the dizzying fatigue.

Gritting her teeth against the pain, she swam a couple of more yards, congratulating herself on each painstaking stroke and kick.

A wave rolled her and turned her head into the swell. Another unwelcome mouthful of seawater went down her throat.

Coughing impeded her progress once again. As soon as she started treading water, a vicious cramp lit up her abdomen, drawing her torso toward her knees involuntarily. Which were underwater.

She had to go back.

Relieved tears pricked at her stinging eyes. She could go back to the island. It didn't feel so much like giving up as survival, and that she could live with.

The decision made, she kicked in the direction of Île de Etienne and counted to five before the cramp in her side jerked her to a halt.

Water burned down her esophagus. When she coughed involuntarily, it shafted into her lungs. Death by drowning became a litany in her head, shouting its presence until she was nearly screaming *no, no, no.* But another mouthful of water contradicted that.

She wasn't going to make it.

This would be her watery grave, precisely as Finn had predicted.

Her tears of relief turned to tears of regret. So many regrets. She hadn't called her mom in a week. She'd never watch another child form his first words in English with her instruction as his guide. Her womb would never grow a child of her own.

Worst of all, she'd never have a chance to tell Finn she still loved him. Why had she clung to her anger for so long?

Just as she thought she'd black out for the last time, Finn was somehow there in the water with her, pulling her into a rescue headlock and towing her to shore.

She went limp and let herself float, desperately sucking air into her body and pushing water out. She wasn't going to die. It wasn't too late.

Seven

Finn tucked Juliet into the larger bed he'd slept in last night and put two blankets over her, cursing Alexander's inability to stock one tiny thermometer in this whole house.

Juliet's skin blazed, almost too hot to touch. She had a fever, no question. He would have liked the confirmation of how high. And whether it was climbing higher or dropping.

Stubborn woman.

Why had she tried to swim to Saint Tropez?

He knew why. She refused to believe he might be right, even about something as important as whether she could actually beat the sea he knew better than his own name. Even telling her about his father's role in the kidnapping hadn't convinced her they were safe and that escape wasn't necessary.

And that was a poor excuse designed to absolve his guilt. It didn't work.

He should have told her sooner about his father's involvement in the kidnapping. If he had, she might not have conceived of the idea of swimming across open water. If anything, his confession had pushed her into it.

No time to wallow in his mistakes. He shed his wet clothes in record time, then threw on some dry ones. Slipping beneath the sheets to lay on the other pillow, he watched her chest rise and fall, telling himself he wanted to be near in case she needed him.

It was a lie.

He couldn't physically separate himself from Juliet after nearly losing her in such a heart-stopping fashion. There on the rocky shore, he'd performed the sloppiest mouth-to-mouth resuscitation on record, but he hadn't been able to stop shaking.

Finally, she had convulsed and started breathing on her own. How he'd managed to haul her up the flight of stairs and into the house with legs the consistency of a wet noodle, he still didn't know.

He held her hand tightly underneath the covers. She was so weak, her fingers slipped from his if he let his grip go slack. Her tangled, still-wet hair draped over the pillow, and he wished he'd thought to grab a towel and dry it before settling in.

The ill-advised feelings stirred up by her unconscious state had to go. But she was so fragile and beautiful, and he couldn't stand the thought of losing her.

Time passed. An hour, then two. Juliet thrashed occasionally and then fell so still, it scared him into pressing his fingertips to a pulse point, just to be sure she hadn't taken her last breath right there in front of him.

Surely the king couldn't have envisioned his plan playing out in quite this way. Despite exhaustion, which ran deep into his bones, Finn found a bit of energy left over to be furious with his father.

Juliet was sick and they had no method of communicating with the outside world. No way of contacting a doctor, of shipping in medicine or shipping Juliet out to a hospital.

Sheer helplessness ran rampant, weighing him down more than the fatigue and concern. It hadn't been easy to swim through the island's natural eddies, then tow another person back to shore, all the while terrified Juliet had already succumbed to the hidden dangers of the sea.

Hunger forced him from the bed as the sun began to set. He dashed to the kitchen, shoved some crackers down his throat, drank two full glasses of water and dashed back to the bed to pick up his vigil where he left off.

A tug on his hand startled Finn into opening his eyes. Automatically, he glanced at the digital clock on the bedside table. Three a.m. Had he fallen asleep?

He glanced at Juliet. The dim light he'd left on in the bathroom spilled over her open eyes. She blinked at him owlishly.

"Hey," he whispered and cupped the side of her face. Still hot, but maybe not as hot as before. "How do you feel?"

She turned her cheek into his hand. Deliberately. As if she actually wanted to be closer to his touch. Then she licked her lips and swallowed a couple of times. "Like someone dropped me in a volcano."

"You have a fever. It was probably something you picked up back in America and it took this long to surface." His thumb trailed over her jaw and his lower half suddenly needed a stern lecture about Juliet's illness and the inappropriateness of being turned on by a woman too weak to respond in kind.

Too late. His body throbbed to life. Exhaustion and stress had lowered his defenses entirely too much for any sort of admonishment to be effective anyway. So now he'd suffer from unrequited sexual frustration in addition to everything else. Fantastic.

Hopefully she wouldn't notice.

"You saved me," she murmured, and the dim light perfectly showcased the tender gratitude beaming from her expression.

"Yeah. What else would I have done?"

"Let me drown. Like I deserved."

He made a face. "Right, that was going to happen."

"How…did you get there so fast? I was way offshore."

Of all the questions—of course she'd ask that one. She was the only swimmer he'd ever rescued who would have even realized the distance he'd traversed to get to her. He sighed and told her the truth, though she wasn't going to like it.

"I was following you. In the water. When you went in, I went in."

"Oh." Her eyes closed for a beat and she dragged them open with what looked like considerable effort. "You didn't think I could make it."

"No." He thought about apologizing. But he wasn't sorry he'd set off after her. Thank God he had.

"Why did you let me go?" she whispered, her voice raw.

"Because I'm not in the habit of forcing women to do things primarily," he said drily. "And also because you needed to try."

A trove of emotions traveled over her face. He couldn't begin to read them all. But he'd bet at least one of them was irritation at his lack of faith.

"That's…interesting," was all she said, and the break in her voice worried him.

"It's the middle of the night. You should be getting rest, not hashing this out. Sleep. I'll be here."

It was an unintentional echo of their earlier conversation, when he'd told her he wanted to be there for her during her grief.

"You don't have to take care of me," she muttered. "I'm the one who should be taking care of you."

"I'm not sick," he pointed out. "Next time I have a fever, I'll let you put me to bed, okay?"

Her hand squeezed his and went slack a few moments later as she drifted off.

Sleep eluded him and by dawn, Juliet hadn't moved so he risked leaving her long enough to take a much-needed shower.

Hot water flowed over his abused muscles, soothing them. He hadn't realized how much he needed a break from the uncomfortable position he'd elected to take in the bed, half hunched against the headboard. But it was the optimal spot for monitoring Juliet.

There in the confines of the enclosed shower stall, finally alone, the sheer terror he'd kept at bay loosened and bled from the center of his chest.

It nearly knocked him to his knees.

He could have lost Juliet. And only now did he realize how much he wanted this second chance his father had given him.

Somehow, he had to find a path to the other side of the huge wall between them. Not because of any advantageous marriage, but because he truly didn't think he could function for the rest of his life without her.

That was the king's ace in the hole. Finn hadn't fallen out of love with Juliet after all, and the kidnapping had brought those emotions to the surface.

What if he *could* find a way to change Juliet's heart? There was no better place or time on earth to try than while trapped together in paradise.

His own heart lurched sweetly at the thought of a future with the woman he loved by his side, all their differences resolved. Marriage. Family. A place where he could achieve some normalcy, away from the public eye.

Unfortunately, a path around that wall between them didn't exist, given that she'd seemed so eager to swim away from a perfectly good island with him on it. She hadn't even given him a chance to explain the rest of his father's plot.

That was the reality clutching his heart in its steely fingers—she didn't want him on her side of the wall. Reconciliation seemed quite impossible. No matter how badly he might now want it.

When he returned to the bedroom, she was propped up against several pillows watching TV. Some color had returned to her face, but not enough for his liking.

"Good morning," she rasped and scowled. "My throat hurts."

"I'll get you a drink, okay?"

She nodded and he fetched a glass of water from the bathroom, which she drank in two gulps. "Better."

"How do you feel?" He touched the back of his hand to her forehead. Still hot.

"Let's cut to the chase, shall we? I'm not getting out of bed for the foreseeable future. Will that make you stop hovering?"

Her bristly tone was back. "I'm not hovering."

She shot him a look and nodded to his side of the bed. "Unless you want to be known as Prince Mother Hen, sit down."

He did, gingerly. "I'm concerned about you. That's all."

"And I appreciate it, but I'm not going to break. I can't swim to Saint Tropez in my current physical condition, but I'm not so fragile that you have to be at my beck and call."

Ah, so this was about her dogged determination to prove she could do whatever she set her mind to. Admirable, but also the reason they weren't married with two kids right now.

She just couldn't admit when she was wrong.

He might have the capacity to love her, but not necessarily the fortitude.

She clicked the remote a few times and tossed it to the bed, then snuggled down into the blankets. Somehow, she'd scooted over the invisible center line, onto his side. "Did I say thank you earlier?"

TV forgotten, she blinked at him with a small smile.

Awareness rolled over him with the force of a powerful whitecap.

He waved it off, his mouth suddenly dry. "You can show your gratitude by getting well and making me a proper meal."

"I'm working on it." She lay back against the pillow. "So tired."

Her legs shifted under the covers, sliding along his until they were flush. She appeared not to notice, had probably even done it accidentally. No matter. Thick layers of fabric separated them, but his skin heated as if all the obstacles between them were gone.

Desperate to get off the bed before he did something foolish, like strip naked and slide under the covers with her, he blurted out, "Do you feel well enough for a bath?"

Her closed eyes fluttered open. "I'd like that. Will you help me?"

Bad idea, his conscience screamed, followed shortly by, *Shut up now.* "I thought you didn't want me hovering."

"It's not hovering if I ask you, silly." Her small, delicate smile blossomed into a larger one that hit him in all the right places. "My skin feels crusty. I don't think I can reach it all."

"I'll help you to the bathroom, but that's as far as I go."

She lifted a wan hand to her forehead. "I need you. Please?"

Coupled with the liquid depths of her pleading gaze, how could he say no?

He fled to the bathroom and ran warm water into the huge marble tub. For good measure, he dumped half a bottle of Portia's oriental bubble bath into the water, hoping the foam would cover enough of Juliet to allow him the possibility of getting through this with his dignity intact.

The exotic scent of sandalwood and jasmine filled the bathroom, and instantly transformed the space from utilitarian to seductive. So much for dignity. He could have plastered the walls with erotic pictures and not achieved such a sensual effect.

Because the torture wasn't already brutal enough, he flipped on the entertainment system mounted to the wall and found a jazz station on satellite radio. The heavy, sultry wail of a saxophone poured through the surround-sound system.

"Finn?" she called from the bedroom, and the sound of his name from her raspy throat spiraled the tension higher.

He shut his eyes for a beat, but it didn't fortify him nearly enough.

Clamping down on his imagination, he hustled to the bed and hustled Juliet out with nary a sidelong glance at the T-shirt he'd haphazardly pulled onto her naked body last night, in place of her drenched clothes.

The simple T-shirt hadn't seemed sexy last night. This morning, it pleaded for a man's hands to lift the hem, just a fraction, revealing all her secrets.

He groaned and turned his back. "Get in the tub. All the way in. Let me know when you're covered up by the suds."

Please take a long time.

"Ready."

"Trying to set the land speed record for bathing?" he muttered and peeked at the bathtub. Sure enough, she'd submerged neck-deep into the water, head thrown back against the tub's lip, eyes closed.

Worst nightmare and hottest fantasy rolled into one.

"Fever, fever, fever," he mumbled and tried to remember the quickest way to break one. He cursed. He should have drawn a *cold* bath—with ice cubes. Or maybe that was the cure for a raging erection. His could use an ice bath the size of Delamer.

Juliet's eyes drifted open. "I know I have a fever. I feel awful."

"I wasn't talk—never mind." Yanking the soap, shampoo and a washcloth from the cabinet beside the vanity, he parked on the edge of the tub. "Let me wash your hair, then you do the rest."

He poured out enough shampoo to wash at least four women's hair—because there was no way he'd have the stamina to do this over if he messed up—and lathered her hair as quickly as possible. "Okay, rinse."

With what looked like considerable effort, she ducked under the water and came up with her eyes closed. He put a towel into her questing fingers and was about to stand and escape when her hand covered his knee.

"Don't go," she murmured. "Scrub my back."

Dark, wet strands of hair covered the area in question, which he could not keep his eyes off of. "I thought we agreed you could do that."

"No, you issued a royal decree. Doesn't make it possible for me to lift my arms that high."

Scootching backward, she presented her bare form for his touching pleasure. Except this was supposed to be a utilitarian process, designed to wash dried seawater from her skin. Not foreplay.

He swallowed and soaped the washcloth. Maybe if he didn't actually touch her, it wouldn't be so bad.

The cloth skimmed down her spine, eliciting a small moan from deep in her throat. Heat spiraled tighter in his abdomen, traveling south whether he wanted it to or not. Body on full alert, he ached to drop the cloth and let his fingertips glide along the ridge of her shoulders instead.

A silver chain around her neck flashed in the low light, and he couldn't stop staring at the place where it met skin. The necklace was new. What did the combination of cool metal on hot flesh feel like?

One little touch. It had been so long. He could reacquaint his senses with the feel of her and wash the grit away at the same time. A practical solution and good for everyone.

But he didn't do it. And not because of the fever.

If they reconciled—*if*—he didn't want it to happen like

this, catering to his father's whims, with the possibility that Juliet might think he wanted to be with her because of her family's politics.

These extraordinary circumstances couldn't possibly create a connection that would translate into a lasting relationship. In his mind, the only real chance they had was to escape first and then see how things went back in Delamer.

If he recalled, the exact words she'd flung at him before trying for a gold medal in cross-country backstroke were, *We're over and so is this conversation.*

He swiped her back, lower, but she moaned again, crossing his eyes. Did she *have* to make that noise as if he'd palmed one of her breasts?

She whimpered and her head fell forward on her knees. "My skin is a little tender. Probably from the fever. Can you hurry?"

"Am I hurting you?" Horrified, he yanked the washcloth away, cursing under his breath.

While he'd been devolving into full-on guy mode, she'd been in pain. None of the names he called himself seemed enough.

"No, not too much. It's just…prickly."

"Do you want me to stop?"

Half of him hoped the answer was yes. The other half prayed it was no.

He missed the simple pleasure of being nothing more than a man touching a beautiful woman. Juliet gave him that. There wasn't a blonde on the planet who ever had or ever could.

She peered over her wet shoulder, eyelids lowered as if she had very naughty thoughts to shield from him. "It's okay. You can keep going."

Sure he could. No problem.

Sweat dribbled between his shoulder blades.

Why was he doing this to himself? The pain of the past year wasn't buried deep enough, the complications on top of that were rampant and she was so very, very naked. Masochism at its finest.

"Thanks," she whispered. "I'm glad you're here."

Warmth of the nonsexual, emotional variety spread through his chest. Yeah. That was why. He wanted to make her feel better, regardless of the cost to himself.

His outdated, inconvenient sense of honor really pissed him off sometimes.

"Me, too. You'd be shark bait otherwise." He swallowed all the squishy, girlie stuff and prayed her fever would break soon. So they could get off this island before he snapped.

After considerable effort, Juliet dressed in another borrowed outfit from the well-stocked closet and allowed Finn to help her to the sofa in the living room. She tucked her feet under the blanket and rested her aching head on Finn's shoulder. For all her grousing, she kind of liked letting Finn take care of her, though she'd deny it to her grave.

She made a face at the TV screen and winced at the stabbing pain through her temples. Everything hurt. Her chest. Her head. Her arms and legs—but that was probably residual muscle fatigue from her unsuccessful escape attempt.

"I'm sorry we're stuck watching this boring movie," she said.

But he couldn't be nearly as sorry as she was.

She hadn't made it to Saint Tropez. And now she was sick and Finn had been forced into caring for her after saving her life.

He'd rescued her. *After* he let her tear off into the water, knowing the odds of her actually making it to the other side were slim to none. He'd let her go anyway. Because he understood what drove her.

The wash of sheer gratitude almost soothed away the bitter taste of failure.

"It's okay. I hate that you feel so bad." His tender grin

looped through her stomach and came out a good bit lower, warming her insides. Okay, it wasn't *just* gratitude.

He'd unearthed something powerful and deep. And it cut through her in a terrible, wonderful way. Finn had been there, right when she needed him.

She hated needing anyone, let alone him. He hadn't been there before when she needed him. What if she let herself trust him and he let her down again?

But she still loved him, that much was clear. And she hated that too.

"I—" A coughing spell cut off the rest and she let it go. What could she possibly say?

I'm conflicted about how you make me feel. Thank you for rescuing me, but can you go to the other side of the island until I figure out how to not be in love with you?

Finn took her hand and held it in his lap, his attention on her, not the movie. Like old times. It kicked up a slow burn in some really delicious places. Places she'd rather he not affect, not when so many unwelcome, baffling things were swirling around in her heart.

"You don't have to talk."

His thumb smoothed over her knuckle, and the contact lit her up. Coupled with the emotional turmoil, watching a movie together sounded less and less like a good idea. But she couldn't face being alone in the bed, aching and wishing for something, or someone, to make her feel better. Someone like Finn.

He'd given her a bath, even though he clearly would have preferred not to. She didn't blame him. She'd been a little snippy on the beach and then he'd had to rescue her. She'd be mad at her too.

"I do feel like death warmed over, but I can still talk." More coughing made a complete liar out of her. Her eyes watered fiercely but not enough to hide Finn's told-you-so smirk.

Her arms were too heavy to lift, let alone smack him one. So she settled for glaring at him.

"Why don't you focus on resting instead of trying to prove me wrong?" he suggested and smoothed a strand of hair away from her face. "The sooner your fever breaks, the sooner we can regroup on the escape effort."

He sounded as exasperated about taking care of her as she felt about him having to. "Look at the bright side. We're stuck together in this beautiful house. There's no danger to worry about. We can hang out while I get better. It'll be fun."

Hang out had a much more superior ring to it than *nursing an invalid.*

His mouth quirked up charmingly. "Seems like that's what I suggested not too long before you waded out into the water."

"And here I am agreeing with you."

"If only that was the start of a long-term trend," he mumbled good-naturedly. "Since this movie is so boring, let's play something on the Wii."

That was why she'd always loved staying in when they'd been dating. Finn's creative streak never ran dry. Everything became fun or a precursor to making love. Usually both.

"Sure." She shoved all the unbidden images behind a blank wall in her mind. The last thing she needed to be thinking about was how much she missed Finn's particular brand of seduction. "As long as it's not too complicated or one of those war games with lots of blood and shooting. Oh, and no zombies. Or aliens."

"That pretty much eliminates…" He flipped through the titles. "All of them. Wait, here's *Super Mario Brothers.* That'll work."

In minutes, Finn set up the game and they began blipping through the levels, laughing as they battled over who got the power-ups. The colorful graphics and lively music infused a sense of peace over them. All their grievances faded away the further they journeyed into the fantastical world of plumbers, walking mushrooms and flying manta rays.

Though Finn and Juliet had never played this particular game together, they were a formidable team and the opposition stood no chance. When he went high, she instinctively went low. When she charged ahead into the thick of enemy territory, he followed, knocking out bad guys right and left, backing her up every step of the way.

As he had in the water yesterday.

Of course if he hadn't brought up Bernard, and then double-whammied her with his father's treachery, she might not have ever set foot in the sea. Yet, he'd been there when it counted, despite being told it was too late.

She couldn't stop thinking about it, about him and all the wonderful things that comprised his character.

It made her question everything.

"Piece of cake," she said after they'd defeated a particularly hard level.

She couldn't swim to France, but at least she could kick the pants off fictional villains. The cartoon monster on the screen fizzled as he died, and his expression made her giggle.

"I'm surprised you're enjoying this." Finn hit the icon to go to the next world. "Given that the object of the game is to rescue Princess Peach."

She scowled. "That's the object? I thought it was to get to the next level."

"The levels have to end sometime. On the last one, Mario rescues the princess from a birdcage."

"So you've played this before."

Disappointment walloped her.

Somehow, she'd built up a scenario where they were playing so well as a team because they were both focusing on the here and now instead of History. Because he really understood what lay beneath her surface.

Obviously their success was instead a product of his familiarity with the game.

"A few times with Portia." He looked away, likely feeling guilty over not having divulged this information before. "It's her favorite but I don't get asked to play very often. Only when Alexander is off doing crown prince duty."

"Figures she'd like it."

Portia was a princess through and through, as if she'd been born to the crown instead of marrying it. Juliet hadn't spent much time with the next queen of Delamer, but when she did, the gracious woman never failed to make Juliet feel gauche and as if they were lifelong friends simultaneously. It was a talent, no doubt.

"It's just a game," Finn said lightly and bumped her shoulder with his.

It was far from just a game. The whole concept encapsulated what was wrong with the world. And poked at her discomfort over the fact that she'd required rescue, as well. Because she hadn't been strong enough to save herself.

"It's sexist and stereotypical. How come Mario didn't get kidnapped?"

Finn glanced at her and did a double take at her expression. "Because Mario and Luigi are the stars. If you want to play something where a woman is the star, go get *Tomb Raider*."

"Why can't there be a setting or something that you flip that changes who gets kidnapped?" She warmed to the idea. "It wouldn't be that big of a deal to switch the characters around and put Mario in a cage."

The more women who believed in themselves and their own strength, the better. Portia could be a princess who liked ball gowns, afternoon tea with the queen and being rescued by her Prince Charming all she wanted.

Juliet didn't like any of that. And didn't that put a knot the size of the crown jewels in her stomach?

Juliet might not like being rescued by the prince, but he'd had to do it just the same. Did he look down on her for not doing what she set out to do? Of course, if she hadn't been coming down with a stupid cold, the swim to Saint Tropez would have been within reach. That was her story and she was sticking to it.

He grinned and put his controller down, settling back against the couch, looking as if he'd humor her until next week if need be. "I'm sure Nintendo would love to hear your thoughts on how to stop perpetuating the stereotype of princesses always needing to be rescued."

"*You're* not even taking me seriously. Let alone a Japanese conglomerate that probably doesn't have one single female executive."

He tucked a lock of hair behind her ear, and she couldn't quite suppress the shiver his touch evoked. She didn't want to. Her stomach clenched. In anticipation *and* fear. Finn's blend of sexiness, solidness and tenderness scared her. Excited her. How messed up was that?

"I'm taking you seriously. I love how passionate you get about…well, everything. Your unwavering opinions define your character."

"You don't like it when I have an opinion. Especially not wh—" She bit down hard on her lip, so hard, the salty taste of blood seeped across her tongue.

Especially not when it's about how you should have acted a year ago.

"I love everything about you, Juliet," he said, and the catch in his voice thrummed through her chest. "I love that as strong as you are, you let me rescue you. I love that despite your seemingly inexhaustible determination, you're willing to ask me to help you take a bath. That's why we're a good team. We each play to the other's strengths and recognize our own limits."

Goodness. If she'd ever wondered why in the world she'd fallen in love with such a draconian, he'd blasted that curiosity to pieces. Where did he come up with such poetry?

"You don't have any limits," she grumbled to hide the thrill his heartfelt words had unfurled.

"That's not true. You almost pushed me past them in the bathtub earlier." The pad of his thumb caressed her jaw, and it was impossible to misinterpret the heat in his gaze.

It was just as impossible to ignore the answering liquid tug in her core. Despite everything, or maybe because of it, she longed to lose herself in the feelings he clearly still had for her and she for him. To lose her inhibitions and fears in his arms, his body, his drugging kisses, so mindless with pleasure, nothing else mattered.

Why did their relationship have to be so complicated? Why couldn't they be together, with all the difficulties of the outside world and their places in it forgotten? Nothing but the two of them, feeding their starving souls with each other. Just for a little while, with no one the wiser, no reminders of their impasse, no public eye to record every nuance of their interaction.

Her pulse beat in her throat.

Wasn't that what was going on *right now?* They were hidden away, held captive on this island, with no hope of rescue anytime soon. She could conceivably be off her stride for several days. Why not take advantage of their time together to enjoy the good parts of their relationship?

No one said they had to kiss *and* make up. Maybe they could just kiss…among other activities. King Laurent didn't dictate the rules. She could be with Finn whether his father liked it or not.

With no future to concern themselves with, no family to disappoint, she didn't have to worry about trusting him. If she kept her heart tucked away, he couldn't break it again. *No emotions. Ruthless determination.*

All they had to do was stay away from the past and focus on now. Piece of cake.

Eight

Later that day, Finn took a short break from monitoring Juliet's condition—or hovering as she liked to call it—and took a cold shower. It went a long way toward easing the ache that had taken up residence in his lower half. But not nearly long enough. He suspected only a naked and willing Juliet could completely eliminate it. That or a coma.

When he emerged from his bedroom, Juliet wasn't ensconced on the couch watching a chick flick where he'd left her. Clanking from the kitchen piqued his curiosity and he wandered into the melee of Juliet attempting to wrangle a pan and some meat into submission.

He watched her struggle for a minute, thoroughly enjoying the backside view of Juliet's slender, barefoot form. Except she was still sick and now he was all hot and bothered again.

"Why aren't you resting?" he finally asked.

The pan clattered to the Italian marble, cracking one

square tile in half. Ouch. Portia was going to have the king's head.

She whirled. "Don't sneak up on me like that."

"Sorry." He stomped in place a few times, mimicking just having arrived. "I'm in the kitchen now. Okay?"

"Okay." She grinned and turned to her stove-top project. "I'm not resting because you asked me to make you dinner."

"I did?" Had he hit his head? Obviously so, if he'd deliberately asked for a repeat of the Chicken With No Taste.

"Earlier. When you said I could show my gratitude by making you dinner." Gingerly, she nodded toward the back of the house and winced.

Ah, yes, on the bed, when he'd been holding on to his sanity by the tips of his fingers. That would definitely explain why he'd done something so unwise as to ask Juliet to make him dinner. "You're nowhere near well enough to be off the couch. Come on."

Sliding his hand into hers, he tugged her toward the living room, ignoring the blistering awareness of skin on skin.

"But you need to eat," she protested and dragged him to a halt between the two rooms.

"I've been feeding myself for twelve years." They were still holding hands but she didn't seem to notice. Far be it from him to bring it to her attention. He liked the feel of her delicate fingers against his. "I'll manage. What about you? Are you hungry? I can heat up some soup."

"Not really, thanks. I ate some crackers. Did I leave the stove on?" Peering over his shoulder, she sank teeth into the plump curve of her bottom lip.

His mouth tingled. That sweet swell of flesh was delicious, as he well knew from personal experience, and he couldn't tear his gaze away from it. "If you did, I'll take care of it."

She made a face. "I'm sure you will. Is there anything you can't take care of?"

Oh, he could think of one thing. A cold shower hadn't

helped his raging hormones catch a clue that first of all, Juliet wasn't in reconciliation mode, and second…

She sighed, pushing her breasts out invitingly. Before he lost his mind, he backed up, inadvertently stretching their locked hands.

She glanced down and tightened her grip, then closed the gap between them. "Wait, don't go. If you won't let me cook dinner, sit with me on the deck and watch the sunset."

Pure desire quickened through his gut.

"I…you probably don't need to be outside." Watch the sunset? Like, together? It almost sounded as if she wanted to spend time with him, in what she probably hadn't even considered would be a romantic setting—a complication he did not need. "You're still sick."

Did he sound as much like a song stuck on repeat to her as he did to himself?

"I don't feel that bad," she muttered, but her face was rosy in all the wrong places and her head tilted listlessly.

Cursing, he picked her up and deposited her on the couch before she could voice another objection. "At least sit down before you fall down. If you're bound and determined to show me your gratitude, get better. That's an order."

"Yes, sir." Flipping him a smart-aleck salute, she burrowed into the cushions and flung the blanket over her body, shoulders to feet. "Happy?"

Not in the slightest. Every nerve in his body ached with unfulfilled need. "Thrilled. We have plenty of time to watch sunsets after you get better."

She blinked up from her nest of blankets, innocent and alluring at the same time. He longed to crawl in with her.

"Sit with me then." She patted the couch and shot him a small smile he couldn't refuse.

In desperate need of a distraction, he sank onto the cushion and hit the power button on the TV remote. A Formula 1 race in Singapore, one of his top five favorite circuits, filled the screen. Automatically, he flexed his thumb to change the channel, but Juliet's hand covered his.

"This is fine," she said, and removed the remote from his suddenly nerveless fingers. "I'd like to watch this with you."

The roar of engines and whine of tires reverberated around them as he glanced at her askance. "I'd ask if you're feeling all right, but I already know the answer to that. Your fever must be worse than I thought if you're willing to watch a Formula 1 race."

"I told you I don't feel that bad. Tell me something. I've always wondered how you know which car is in first when they're going around the same loop over and over." Her temple came to rest on his shoulder as she squinted at the screen.

"The standings are listed in the ribbon across the top." More information about how to gauge the driver's position instantly sprang to his lips, but he bit it back. Surely she didn't actually care.

"Oh. That's easier than I thought it would be. How come some of the cars are identical and some are different?"

"The participants are on teams." Interest in the race completely lost, he tilted his nose toward her hair, inhaling the fresh scent of Juliet and the shampoo he'd used to wash her hair. The memory of her wet and naked under all those bubbles kicked up a slow torture.

She glanced up, puzzled, but clearly engaged.

"The teams have more than one guy driving," he clarified. "Same car, same team."

And for the next fifteen minutes, she asked more questions, patiently listening to his answers and occasionally offering an insightful comment about the ins and outs of the process.

"Planning to apply for a job as a pit crew member?" he asked after her questions tapered off. "You know, instead of teaching? Monaco has a track. You could jet over and back in thirty minutes tops."

She laughed. "Not a chance. I'd be too afraid to touch a million-dollar car."

"Then why all the questions?" An old thorn worked its way loose and poked him. Sporting events bored her and she'd never hidden her contempt for his interests. As she'd never hidden her contempt for his job.

"It's something you like. I wanted to learn more about it." Shrugging, she laced fingers with his casually, as she'd done a hundred times before they split up.

It felt different. Coupled with her nonchalantly tossed-out words, the effect was potent.

Her eyelids drifted halfway closed and she peeked up from under them. "So, what if instead of dinner, I wanted to show my gratitude some other way?"

The question came coupled with Juliet's lazy index finger trailing over his pectoral muscle and left no possibility of misinterpreting "some other way."

What was she doing? First Formula 1 and now this. The fever must be curdling her brain. And the fingertip hold on his sanity was sliding away at an alarming rate.

"You have a fever," he reminded her needlessly since they'd already discussed it at least five times. Or was the reminder more for his well-stirred blood's benefit? "I shouldn't even be this close to you."

"I seem to recall you've kissed me in the last twenty-four hours. More than once and quite thoroughly." She watched avidly for his reaction and he struggled not to give her one.

But he was pretty sure the instant hardening below the belt hadn't escaped her notice. No fabric in existence could disguise it.

"Face it," she murmured and the space between them, what little there was of it, vanished as she threw off the blanket, snuggling up against his chest. "You're already contaminated with my cooties. What's one more little kiss? To show my gratitude."

His gaze snapped to the firm, rosy lips so close to his. "You said we were over. On the beach. Is your near-death experience hindering your decision-making abilities?"

It was certainly messing with his.

This wasn't the plan. Rescue first. Reconciliation later. Too much unsaid lay underneath the surface to go down this path now. How could he even approach the subject of telling Juliet she was his father's choice for Finn's bride? He needed a cooler head, among other things, for that conversation.

She smiled and cupped a hand along his jaw. "Clarifying. Not hindering."

"Clarifying it how?"

How he put actual syllables together to form cohesive words, he'd never know. But *something* had shifted after she almost drowned, and despite protests to the contrary, he suspected it had affected her in a way he didn't fully trust.

"I'm still a prince and y—"

"Shh." Her thumb skated across his lips, silencing him. "Prince Alain isn't here. I only see Finn."

Finn. Yes, here on Île de Etienne, he could forget the complexities of that dual-edged sword and be nothing but a man. That yearning constantly simmered below the surface, and it thundered to life. They could get back to reality after they were rescued. Right now, he could indulge.

Involuntarily, his hands sought her face, determined to touch, desperate to connect. Cool skin met his palms. *Finally.* "I think your fever's gone."

"Is this the part where I get to say I told you so?" She grinned and nuzzled his throat.

"Sure. I can take it."

"Can you take this?"

Drawing him closer, until their breaths mingled, she brushed his lips with hers. Just a whisper of sweet contact, and instantly his mind drained of everything but the sexy, gorgeous woman in his arms.

"Yeah," he murmured against her mouth. "I can take all you've got of that."

Threading his fingers through her hair, he dived into the kiss with every intention of burning off the raging need for Juliet. They could deal with all the implications later.

She moaned and leaned into him as if she couldn't get close enough, her bewitching fingertips sparking across his neck and gliding under his T-shirt to spread at the span of his waist.

Yes, there. And everywhere else. He wanted her hands on him, wanted to touch her in kind, then slake his thirst for the woman he'd missed so very much.

His palms rested lightly against her throat as he angled her head to take her deeper into the kiss. She felt amazing.

The essence of Juliet poured into his senses. She slung a knee across his lap and climbed aboard, breasts teasing his chest, still slaying him with her mouth. Tongues slicked together, twining and seeking. Pleasuring.

He couldn't wait to sink into her tight, wet heat and let all his passion for Juliet explo—

With considerable effort, he twisted his mouth from hers. "We have to slow down, sweetheart."

Slow down.

Two words he'd never uttered in Juliet's presence. He had a bad habit of losing all common sense when she was within touching distance, and that needed to change *tout de suite*.

She lifted her head slightly and wiggled deeper into his lap. "Slow down? Why?"

Her confusion mingled with his frustration, adding weight to the already impossible situation his father had created.

"Because…" Struggling to simply breathe around the sharp desire clogging his system, he raked a hand through his hair before it found its way back into place on her very tempting rear.

Why? *Advantageous marriage. History. Scandal.* All of the above.

And for what was both the best and very worst reason of all. He could never be Just Finn, not even for a few moments, and it had been foolish to pretend he could.

"There's not one single condom in this whole house."

Juliet froze, hands on Finn's chest, as the significance sank in and her mind wheeled off in a dozen directions. "No condoms?"

So much for her plan to seduce Finn out of his clothes and indulge in a short-lived, no-hearts-required reunion. And here she thought the past and future were the complications they should avoid. Now he'd dragged the present into the equation.

"Not one. I've looked. Are you on some form of birth control?" he asked hopefully.

"No. Why would I be on birth control?" She'd spent the past year pretending she had no sex drive.

"Because you'd gone to a matchmaker to find a husband." He shrugged. "It was worth a shot to ask."

In actuality, she'd gone to a matchmaker because she was running away. Intimacy hadn't been forefront in her mind. Thank goodness Elise had saved one of her clients from being matched with Juliet—it would have been patently unfair to some poor man who could never compare with the man sitting next to her.

"So that's it? We can't do *anything?*"

She accompanied the question with a slow finger-walk down Finn's torso and kept going. He sucked in a breath as her nails grazed his still-impressive erection.

"If I'd known those fake nails would feel like that, I'd have bought you some a long time ago." He lifted her hand from his lap and held it against his thundering heart. "So you have to slow down."

"We can be careful." She tilted her hips back and forth, rubbing shamelessly against his rigid length. Heat shafted through her core and she arched involuntarily, grazing his chest with her sensitive nipples.

Thighs quivering, he groaned and thrust upward to meet her hip rolls. "There's no such thing as being careful when I've got you naked, especially if you keep doing that. I've spent the last year at the mercy of tabloids. A surprise pregnancy would be icing on the cake."

A baby. *Finn's* baby.

Sheer longing twisted through her insides, intense and shocking. Where had that come from?

"Sorry, I'll stop." She started to shift but his iron grip held her in place.

"I said slow down, not stop." His sizzling blue eyes sought hers and held them as he slowly circled his hips, grinding his erection against her.

"So," she gasped as the friction lit her up. "If you make love to me really slowly, that's going to prevent conception?"

Slow wasn't going to be an option much longer. She wanted every stitch of clothing between them gone. *Now.*

The wolfish grin on his face shot her arousal up another notch. "I'm more concerned about the out-of-wedlock part, not the pregnancy part."

She shook her head but the ringing in her ears got worse, not better. "What are you saying? That if we were married, it wouldn't be an issue?"

"If you get pregnant, we'd have to get married." His hands slid up both sides of her torso, thumbs hovering near her breasts, almost but not quite circling the aching peaks. "It's non-negotiable."

Her brain couldn't keep up, especially not with Finn's really good parts flush against hers and her nipples straining toward his thumbs, begging to be touched. "Is this a… *marriage proposal?*"

Marriage. Finn was talking about *marriage*. To her. While mere molecules of damp fabric separated her sex from his.

"Not precisely." He pursed his beautifully chiseled lips, and she couldn't tear her gaze from them. "More like a promise of one to come."

A litany of jumbled emotions swirled through her head. Her heart. She wanted him to love her. In the physical sense. In the emotional sense. She flat-out wanted *him* and her body didn't seem to care how she got him.

This was a really bad moment to realize she'd done a poor job of tucking away all her feelings. Why had she thought she could?

"Why can't we talk about this later?" she murmured and leaned into his thumbs until they brushed her taut nipples. Pleasure fluttered her eyelids and flooded her senses. "I just want to be with you. Without all the complications. Is that even possible?"

"Not between us, no."

She almost laughed at the irony. "Because you're Prince Alain. Always."

His gaze sought hers, hot with desire and a significant glint. "Because I'm still in love with you. It messes up everything. If only there was a way to forget about capital *H* history and live right here in this moment, I'd do it, come what may."

She blinked away sudden tears as his confession bled through her body, singing through her pleasure center, heightening everything.

Finn still loved her.

Her heart threw its doors open wide, sucking in the sentiment with glee. Something sweet and wonderful coursed through her.

The concept of an island fling had been a poorly contrived pretext to feel exactly like that—without having to do the hard work of reconciliation. Without having to compromise or deal with her own guilt or risk allowing him to hurt her all over again.

"I shouldn't have said that." He shook his head. "I—"

"It's okay," she whispered, shocked her throat had spit out that instead of the *I still love you too* fighting to work free.

With effort so difficult it drew sweat, she slammed the door on her feelings. She couldn't tell him she loved him. That was how she'd given him the power to hurt her before, by making herself vulnerable.

But this time, she didn't have to.

He'd offered the perfect solution. They didn't have to rehash History or even mention it at all. They could be in the moment, indulge in the pleasure of each other and sort out the future later. Much later—especially the part about their feelings.

Slowly, she lifted the hem of her shirt, watching as his expression darkened.

"Let's forget about what happened a year ago and just be together. If there are consequences, so be it. Right here, right now, be Finn with me, even if you can only do it for one night."

Nine

One night.

Finn watched Juliet reveal her bra-less breasts, pulse beating in his temple in an erratic pattern more closely resembling Morse code than a rhythm designed to keep him alive.

Too much coffee. Too much Juliet. Too much at stake.

The sharp awareness and desire coursing through her expression quickened his blood, drawing his own desire to a fine point. Her breasts were breathtaking, gorgeous, rosy-tipped, and he wanted to run his tongue over the peaks until she cried out.

"Are you sure?" he asked her, his voice thready with anticipation.

If she chose to be with him, it wouldn't matter that the king had thrown them together. It wouldn't matter if she got pregnant as long as she understood marriage would be the next step.

"I'm sure," she said immediately. Decisively. It was heady to know she wanted him that badly.

But she was female and he'd made a cardinal error. "You're not letting the fact that I said I love you cloud this decision, are you?"

The feelings had sort of spilled out in reaction to the moment, without any forethought.

I love you was there in his consciousness, ready to be voiced as if he'd said it to her the day before. He didn't question whether she still loved him too—it was in her touch, in her kiss. In her eyes.

As was the total conflict she felt over it.

Which was why he didn't press her about her feelings. Why the choice had to be hers. This would be a real reconciliation, not one fabricated to serve the king's mandate, or it wouldn't happen at all.

But he was very close to losing control.

"No." A smile played at the corners of her mouth, as if she couldn't quite decide whether to let it flash. "This is about me and you and what we want. Grab hold and don't let go."

He knew exactly what he wanted. Tonight, he wanted to simply be Finn, to experience that harbor Juliet had always offered, where it didn't matter if he was merely the spare heir.

"Can you really forget?" he asked.

She held up a finger. "There's no past. No tomorrow. Just you and me and tonight. That's the only rule."

That sounded like a fine rule. If there was no tomorrow, his father's plan wasn't a factor. Besides, her family would never side with the crown, regardless of what happened between them, so the whole point was moot.

Without missing a beat, she leaned forward and placed her lips on his in a searching, questioning kiss. The heavens opened and poured light into his weakened soul.

Or perhaps that was Juliet's strength infusing his.

He slung his arms around her and clung to the woman he loved, imprinting the moment on his memory, so he could take it out later and savor it. She was the only woman he'd ever held who felt substantial enough to withstand the pressures and difficulties of being with a prince. She'd never crumble.

Unable to hold back a moment longer, he firmed his mouth and kissed her with every ounce of pent-up passion.

She moaned and opened under his onslaught. Eager to taste, he twined their tongues. Eager to touch, he pushed her torso forward, pressing her magnificent breasts to his chest.

"Need this gone," she mumbled and lifted his shirt over his head. As soon as she dropped it to the floor, her hands were back in place at his waist, fumbling with the closure of his pants and nearly ripping them off in her haste.

Yes. Naked. Now.

He lifted her to her feet and slid his pants off and then watched as she did the same with hers. He drew her against his body, peaks and valleys settling into familiar grooves, and finally they were bare flesh to bare flesh. Groaning with the sheer pleasure of her skin heating his, he took her mouth again in a savage kiss, teeth clacking and tongues thrusting.

There was no more need to slow down. And he didn't intend to.

Backing her up against the wall, he slid a thigh between her legs and rubbed her core, up and down, thrilling at the slickness that meant she was hot and ready for him. He knew her body as he knew his own. Knew how to touch her, how hard she liked it, when to let up and when to take her higher.

It was familiar, but that made it only more exciting. No guesswork, no confusion.

"Hurry," she moaned, heightening his own sense of urgency. "It's been so long. I want to feel you."

And he wanted to give her that.

Boosting her up, spine to the wall, he spread her thighs wide and teased her with the tip of his length. Her heat sizzled against his flesh and his eyes slammed shut at the shaft of pure lust spiking through his gut. He couldn't stand it. He eased her hips downward and sheathed himself one maddening centimeter at a time, desperately trying to give her as much pleasure as possible before he exploded.

With no barrier in place, sensation swamped him, rolling over his skin in a heavy tsunami of pleasure and spreading with wicked, thick heat.

Her amazing legs wrapped tighter around his waist, heels digging into his butt, urging him on with matched fervor.

"Unbelievable," she whispered. "You feel unbelievable."

"Tell me about it."

She rolled her hips, driving him deeper, and his knees buckled with the strain of holding back.

"Juliet," he murmured mindlessly and gurgled some more nonsense, unable to hold it all in.

She grabbed his free hand and put it against her nub, lacing her fingers with his to guide him. *Yes,* he loved it when she took charge. When she took her own pleasure. It was powerful, beautiful. Passionate. And it drove him wild.

As he rubbed, she arched, flinging her head back and crying out. She came with powerful shocks that squeezed him so exquisitely, his own release followed.

Sinking to the floor, he gathered her up and held her, slick torsos heaving in tandem. He smoothed her hair back from her forehead and just breathed, his mind, body and soul in perfect peace.

That was what he'd missed the most.

"Maybe next time we'll make it to the couch," she muttered and heaved a contented sigh that he felt clear to his knees. Her head thunked forward to land on his shoulder.

"Maybe next time you'll give me a chance to get near the

couch." Hence his point about the impossibility of "being careful." As if he'd have the capacity to pull out early once Juliet invited him into her slick heat. He'd have a better shot at swallowing the entire Mediterranean.

His lips found her temple and rested in the hollow. For the first time in the history of their relationship, neither of them had anywhere to be. They could make love all day long if they wanted to.

And he wanted to.

Tomorrow, the lack of outside pressures might abruptly end, and what kind of fool passed up an all-you-can-eat buffet?

As long as they were naked, he'd be happy to find a few dozen ways to keep both their brains occupied. Then, the little circle of peace that was Île de Etienne would stay intact. The past didn't exist, and the future wasn't here yet.

Finn didn't have to think about either.

They made it to the bed. Barely.

Juliet flopped back against the pillow and moaned as Finn tongued his merry way up her thigh, leisurely, as if they had all the time in the world. They didn't. Their island paradise was short-lived and besides, she wanted him inside her *now*.

"How do you make that feel so good?" she murmured and then cried out as his lips nibbled her with exactly the right pressure to light her up.

The white-hot pleasure arched her back so fast, her spine cracked. But then he stopped right as a hot wave radiated from her center, the precursor to another amazing orgasm.

Before she could protest, he flipped her onto her stomach, sandwiched her against the mattress and drove in from behind. *Yes, perfect.* It wasn't just his favorite position. It was hers too.

Her eyelids fluttered in ecstasy as he angled her hips to take him deeper, his mouth on her shoulder, chafing her skin with his unshaven jaw. She rolled her shoulder, shoving it between his lips and he complied with her unspoken request, sucking with indelicate pressure.

He eased out and back in again, slowly. Way too slowly.

She locked her ankles together to increase the friction, the way they both liked it. Groaning, he increased the pace, as she needed, at exactly the tempo he knew would launch her into oblivion. She squeezed once and that was it. Stars burst behind her eyes, blinding her for a moment.

He groaned as he collapsed on her back, his climax pulsing inside her deliciously.

She'd lost count of the number of times he'd rendered her boneless. The first one, against the living room wall, had been a near out-of-body experience. The rest had been full-body experiences, a revel in the corporeal as only Finn could deliver.

She remembered that he was good. But reality far eclipsed the memory.

The man was incredible, tireless, physical. When he got excited, he wasn't gentle, but she liked it a little rough, especially because she'd evoked it in the first place. It made a girl feel sexy to have a man slightly out of control over her. Besides, she gave as good as she got, and that only boosted his passion. Which in turn, fed hers.

No wonder they'd been matched. They fit together, like the hearts on the necklace Elise had given her, entwined by passion.

Finally he rolled and they separated. Breathing heavily, he flung an arm over his head and shut his eyes, shamelessly splayed like a bad girl's fantasy across the bed, naked and gorgeous. She drank in the sight and just as shamelessly enjoyed every second of it.

His well-developed chest muscles flexed and relaxed as he breathed. He had a new line of hard, defined ripples across his lower stomach, the result of what must be a new workout routine. She heartily approved of the addition to the contours of his body.

At the same time, sadness crept into her bubble of bliss. He'd developed those muscles over the past year. While they'd been apart. He'd lived a whole year's worth of life that she knew nothing about because his stubborn refusal to open his mind had driven them apart.

Not going there, she reminded herself.

They'd agreed on one rule—forget the past—and already she was trying to break it.

"Let's go outside," she suggested, determined to slide back into a state of mindlessness.

One of Finn's eyes popped open to regard her warily. "It's dark. And I must be rusty at this if you want to go outside instead of staying naked in bed. With me."

She laughed. "I never said anything about getting dressed. One thing we have a distinct lack of is neighbors and paparazzi. It's June, with perfect weather. When else will we have such a unique set of circumstances?"

His brows lifted. "Sex under the stars. I like it."

He rolled from the bed and yanked the comforter along with him, waggling his brows over his shoulder as he dashed from the bedroom.

She followed him, and the view of his bare butt was nice indeed. She sighed. It would be so great if she could count on being able to see it whenever she wanted.

Whose bright idea was it again to be together without thinking about the future? Oh, yeah—*hers.*

She squared her shoulders and shut the sliding glass door to the deck behind her.

A sweeping panorama of stars blanketed the still night, breathtaking in its splendor. The quiet lap of water provided a melodic soundtrack. A bright moon hung in the sky to the west, lighting the way to Spain.

"Wow," she said. "I should get extra points for coming up with this idea."

Finn lay back on the comforter he'd spread on the deck and patted it in a nonverbal invitation to join him. "I was just thinking about all the ways I planned to thank you for it. It's amazing."

She scooted next to him and he curled her into his body, flesh on flesh. His arm lay heavy against her side, fingers stroking the curve of her waist, but it was oddly absent of any sizzle. It felt…comfortable, and tranquility stole over her.

It could be like this back home in Delamer. Surely it could. They were doing a fine job of ignoring the past. Why not keep it up? Maybe not forever, but for a little while at least, dipping back into their relationship slowly.

The stars shone, sending light to Earth that had left years and years ago, before she and Finn had split up. Before life had grown so complicated. If only there was a way to get back to that.

For a long time, she'd considered herself as star-crossed as her name implied. But did it have to be that way? If they loved each other, why couldn't that be enough?

Finn hadn't mentioned marriage or love again, but she knew it wasn't because he'd changed his mind. Finn was nothing if not constant, and she loved that about him. She never had to question whether he'd waffled on an issue or if he'd considered all the facts before forming an opinion. He meant what he said and said what he meant. It was an inexorable part of his character.

For the first time since Bernard died, it seemed like more of a positive than a negative. She'd never have to wonder if Finn would fall out of love with her one day. Never wonder if he'd cheat on her.

"What if I said you could call me?" she blurted out. "At home. After we get off this island."

They could try dinner again, have a civilized conversation and sit on their hands lest they rip each other's clothes off in the cab on the way back to his place, where they'd make love until dawn.

His mouth rested against her forehead, and she felt his lips turn up. "We're a little past that stage, don't you think? By the end of the month, we could be engaged."

An image of Finn on one knee, a diamond as bright as a star extended between his fingers, exploded in her head. Her lungs burned as she held her breath, hoping that would make the image go away.

He didn't want to marry her, but he would—out of duty.

Gee, *that* was romantic. How had this simple night together gotten so messed up? She didn't want Finn to propose to her because he felt obligated to. Neither did she want this idyll to be over.

She sat up and twisted to look at him. "What if I don't get pregnant? That's it? *Au revoir* and don't call me, I'll call you?"

"That's rich, Juliet." He squeezed the bridge of his nose. "You're the one who came on to me, which is like pouring wine down the throat of an alcoholic and daring him not to swallow."

She processed his backhanded compliment. If she'd decoded his analogy correctly, he couldn't resist her. That put a small smile on her face for some unknown reason.

"Should I apologize?"

Finn swore in French. "Is this really the conversation you want to have?"

"I don't know. Everything feels so backward and crazy."

He heaved a sigh that carried all the way into her stomach, rolling it over with its intensity. "Don't you think about being together? Long-term?"

"Yeah," she whispered. She'd be lying if she said no.

"Then let's make that happen—with or without a baby to force the issue. If that's what you want."

That's what I want.

Instantly, the idea took root and she accepted it as gospel truth. A deep, shuddery breath nearly wrenched a sob loose.

But she couldn't have it both ways. Either they'd split up again or they'd be together. He was right—there was no *call me and we'll see how it goes*. Their relationship was too deep for that. Always had been, always would be.

"You can't marry me. Speaking of coronaries, *both* our families would have one."

Her mother would probably have a breakdown right there on the floor. That's why Île de Etienne was so perfect—no one had to know she'd indulged in a little fling with Finn.

Besides, Juliet could never marry Finn, not with the fear she'd find herself capable of using him to her own end fresh on her mind.

She bit her lip. But if she did get pregnant, was she prepared to lie about whom the father was? That wasn't even remotely possible. Finn would never agree to stay silent about having fathered her child.

And honestly, he'd be a wonderful father. She didn't want to raise a child alone or deprive her kid of all the joys of having a nuclear family. Deprive Finn of being able to see his son or daughter every day.

Ice picks of pain stabbed at the backs of her eyes. All she'd sought was an uncomplicated island adventure with a mouthwatering specimen of manhood who made her blood sing. Was that too much to ask?

"That's not true," he countered. "They wouldn't bat an eye if you were carrying my baby. Besides, my father's opinion of you has softened."

"When did that happen?"

"When he saw the photo of us together. It was in the note. He realized there was still something between us."

"Of course." That picture must have captured some serious sizzle to elicit such a drastic ploy as kidnapping.

"That's why he dumped us here, so we couldn't hurt his image any further by being photographed together."

"That's not why. You never gave me a chance to explain. My father had us brought here so we could spend time together, away from everything. See if a relationship was still possible." Sagging a little, he stared at the stars and she caught a hint that something was very off.

"Why in the world would he do something like that?"

"It must have been obvious I didn't want an arranged marriage any longer. But he still wants me to settle down, though I never dreamed he'd...well, that's why I tried so hard to flag down rescue. Spelled out the HELP sign. I didn't want us to reconcile like this, playing right into his hands. I'm sorr—"

"Don't let your father have any more control in our relationship." None of this should be about accidental pregnancy, or Finn's interfering father, but about the future and what making love actually meant for their relationship. "Tonight is just about us. Tomorrow, we can deal with everything else. Including your father, the past and the future. Let it go for now."

She tried to do the same. She really did. But that blanket of peace wouldn't return, no matter what tricks she employed to clear her mind. Because she couldn't stop wondering what was going to make tomorrow different from the past year.

The fates couldn't have conspired to put her and Finn together only to cruelly rip them apart.

Maybe other women waited around for fate to step in, but other women didn't get so much as a first chance with a man like Finn. Juliet Villere didn't leave her future to the hands of fate. And she wasn't blowing her second chance.

Tomorrow, *she'd* be the difference. Somehow.

They had to work through their issues once and for all, create a level playing field and never bring up the past again. She wanted to have their relationship back, intact, exactly as it had been, where she could depend on Finn to put her first above everyone else in his life.

Then she'd know for sure he loved her, for real, for forever.

Ten

When Juliet woke in the morning, she'd hardly opened her eyes before Finn rolled her against his side, intent clear as day in the sizzle shooting from his deceptively sleepy gaze.

"Good morning," she murmured, and snuggled into his warm body for an enchanting moment of pure harmony that had nothing to do with sex. She'd missed the small things that made life so much sweeter—good-night kisses, falling asleep holding hands, waking up together.

A moment was all she got to enjoy it. He thoroughly compromised her in twenty minutes flat, and she had the whisker burn in eight very tender places to prove it. To be fair, she'd left behind a few souvenir teeth marks on him.

"Good morning," he finally responded when he'd caught his breath. Sated and clearly determined to be lazy this morning, he turned on the TV and slung an arm around her companionably as they settled in to watch nothing.

His dark hair was still sleep-and-finger tousled and his chest unashamedly bare, all hard muscle and delicious skin for her tasting pleasure. She could get used to waking up to *that*. She couldn't stop looking at his beautiful form long enough to even register what channel he landed on.

Until he sat up, eyes hard and riveted to the screen. She glanced at the TV. A cable news station flashed a picture of a sinister-looking warship with deadly weapons scattered across the deck.

Finn hit the volume button and the news anchor's deep baritone filled the bedroom.

"...gathering off the coast of Greece, within striking distance of the newly assembled army. World leaders are meeting in Geneva this afternoon to discuss a preemptive hit on the country's forces."

His body tense, Finn glanced at her and she did a double take at the harsh lines around his mouth.

Juliet's pulse slammed into her throat. "What is he talking about?"

"In other news..." The anchor went on to describe a peace rally in Athens protesting the aggression.

"Whatever it is, it's not good," Finn said grimly. "That warship is stationed in the Ionian Sea. I could practically throw a rock and hit it from here."

Her fingers flexed to grab the remote and throw it across the room in kind. Military aggression. Her least favorite hot button.

This was a watershed moment, where she could let the wounds of the past rule or forge a new future. This warship's presence in the Mediterranean was important to Finn, evident in the stiff set of his jaw and the severe tilt of his brows.

"Find another channel talking about it," Juliet suggested softly. "You need to know."

Nodding, he flipped through the channels until he found a news station describing how the government of Alhendra, a small but well-financed country sandwiched between Albania and Greece, had sent missiles into a civilian neighborhood in Preveza, a beautiful Greek coastal region. The casualties were high and world powers' thirst for retaliation was higher. It was an unprovoked act of antagonism that the United Nations couldn't ignore and didn't intend to.

She forced herself to listen alongside him, and when he slid his hand into hers, she stiffened her shaking fingers to keep him from knowing how deeply ingrained her body's response was to seeing warships on the news.

Bernard's death had been reported with similar shots of a ship at full cruising speed, cutting through the dark waters of the sea. Over and over, they'd played that clip, with a scripted spiel about the accident.

A noise of pure disgust growled from Finn's throat. "I can't believe this is happening and I'm stuck here. Delamer might be in jeopardy. Any coastal region could get caught in the crossfire. Our ships can be ready to deploy and stand with our allies immediately. At the very least, we should send someone to Geneva."

Stuck here. With her. He'd rather be back home, reveling in his armed-forces glory.

"Don't you think your father is already on top of it?" she asked with raised eyebrows. "This is his moment in the sun."

Finn's too. It was a golden opportunity to espouse the virtues of his father's military polices. To give her a big, fat I-told-you-so and laugh off her earlier argument that it was peacetime.

He shot her a withering glare. "Of course he's on top of it. But he needs help. He's probably got someone on the way to get me right now. I should be there."

She'd been wrong before. *This* was the watershed moment. She had to accept that his sense of honor would never allow him to side against his father, no matter what the man did. She had to find a way to live with the fact that Bernard's death would not be avenged through reform.

Or she had to not be with Finn.

Which wasn't going to be much of a choice if she was carrying his baby.

Bernard had died but Juliet was still alive, and her brother wouldn't want her to be miserable on principle. He'd loved Finn and would never begrudge Juliet trying to find a future with the prince. Her parents would learn to adjust—or they wouldn't—but her family wasn't the reason her relationship with Finn had fallen apart a year ago.

It was because there was no compromise.

"We should spend the day setting up more signals, just in case your father plans to leave us here a while longer." Her head dropped, suddenly too heavy to hold up. She'd expected the day to unfold with a naked romp in the shower and then another naked romp through a couple of other choice locales. The disappointment melded with the shock, cracking her voice. "If several countries are sending forces to the Ionian Sea, they have to pass right by here. Someone will surely see us this time."

Their island fling-slash-reconciliation-slash-precursor to a marriage proposal had screeched to a halt.

Gently, he tipped her head up to meet his gaze, and she blinked back the moisture she'd been trying to hide. He was watching her with dark intensity that unleashed a shiver.

"I love you," he murmured. "That's not going to change, no matter what happens."

Whether she'd conceived. Whether she hadn't. Whether their families intervened in their relationship or didn't. Whether the world stood at the brink of war or not.

"I know."

Because she loved him like that too. And it messed up everything because she still hated his fervor for the military. Hated that he might die like Bernard and abandon her again, but this time forever.

Recognizing there was no compromise wasn't the same as being okay with it. And she wasn't. She couldn't be. Could she?

Maybe this wasn't real love or else it wouldn't feel so much like one—or both—of them had to give up everything.

Or was this simply proof that love *wasn't* enough?

He shook his head. "No, I don't think you do. I don't think you could possibly understand how completely torn up I am at this moment."

Her laugh wasn't nearly as bitter as she'd have expected. "I have a pretty good idea."

"I know this is hard for you. I know what it cost you to bite back your opinion of my father and of my job. Don't give up your convictions. I don't ever want you to give up, especially not on something you truly believe in."

Her pulse hammered in her throat. He'd never said anything like that before. It almost sounded as if he admired her for taking a stance against his father.

Maybe she'd misjudged his reasons for not siding with her. As many times as they'd argued over the protest, they'd never really talked rationally. Shouted, accused, defended—yes. Well, mostly she did that. Diplomacy wasn't in her DNA.

Worse, when diplomacy wasn't one of her skill sets, how effective of a princess would she really be? If a marriage proposal could potentially be imminent, perhaps she should practice being diplomatic a whole heck of a lot more. What better place to start than with History?

If they could successfully navigate that, they could endure anything and still make it. She'd finally feel safe enough to confess she'd never fallen out of love with him.

Finn shoved food in his mouth, but he couldn't have said what it was for any price.

He kept waiting to hear the sound of rescue approaching. The whine of a boat engine. The drone of helicopter blades. The longer the silence stretched, the worse his muscles knotted with tension.

Surely the king wouldn't leave Finn here marooned on Île de Etienne while warships convened just across the Mediterranean. It was unthinkable.

At the same time, he'd rather keep the real world at bay and stay completely submersed in this new Juliet who watched Formula 1 and didn't slice him open with arguments against military force.

He glanced at her, and she was so gorgeous in a simple red sundress that set off fireworks in her brown hair. She smiled, and it yanked a long slice of warmth from his center. They were sitting at the table, eating breakfast like a normal couple.

Something had happened to get them here. Dare he hope it was enough?

Well, he obviously did dare because hope of the most dangerous kind had begun to live in the back of his mind. Dangerous because he wanted to sweep Juliet off her feet with an outrageously romantic marriage proposal—before she handed him a pregnancy test. Before he had to take up his uniform and rejoin the Delamer Navy in what might devolve into combat. Search and rescue was his day job, but he was still a lieutenant in the armed forces. And his country was worth defending, even with his dying breath.

Securing a "yes" from her before all that other stuff interfered would make everything else bearable. They'd be together, they'd be in love and nothing else could touch them.

But he couldn't propose as he envisioned because they'd done nothing to address capital *H* history, not that he was complaining. He'd rather they didn't talk about that at all, except if they got married, she'd have to understand the obligations that came with being his princess. No more protests.

And she hadn't actually told him she loved him yet.

The timing was wrong. He couldn't propose until all the issues were addressed. *All* of them.

Juliet lifted a lock of hair from her shoulder and twirled it absently as she contemplated him. "You gonna eat that or massacre it?"

He glanced at his hand, which was pulverizing what appeared to have once been a slice of bread. "Both."

Shoving it in his mouth, he chewed and swallowed the evidence, but he barely tasted it.

They *had* to talk. And he'd put it off too long already.

In addition to dealing with History, it was important that she find out about her family's renewed attacks against his father from Finn and not from whoever came to rescue them. The only way this reconciliation would work was if she understood he had no intention of using their relationship to influence her family. But if she loved him, she'd take care of it on his behalf.

"You're so tense, I could cut this butter with your clenched jaw alone," she commented mildly and nodded to his plate. "You done with that?"

"Yeah." If they were both finished eating, now would be the optimal time to get started on that long-overdue discussion. The sooner, the better.

"Good."

Standing so abruptly her chair crashed to the floor, she slid the plate to the other side of the table and nestled into his lap, front to front, fitting into the planes of his body. Instantly, he hardened against her soft core, which radiated heat through her panties.

Or they could talk later. Much later.

Relieved to descend into that place where they connected brilliantly, he snaked a hand under the bright swatch of skirt and palmed her backside, teasing her with light fingertip trails. Then he delved beneath the silky fabric to trace her feminine contours.

Her breath came faster, and desire bloomed across her expression. It thoroughly thrilled him. Hips thrusting and circling, she threw her head back and rode hard against his rigid length. Desperate to get to flesh, he thumbed beneath the scrap of cloth covering her and fused his lips to her throat as he plunged two fingers into her wet heat.

Hot, so hot. Her, the position, his skin.

He wanted to feel her on the inside, let his mind drain of everything but the sensation of loving her.

His spine tingled from holding back his own release. She rocked on his hand faster, then faster still, moaning her pleasure, arching back against the table and spreading her thighs wider.

"That's it," he murmured as her eyelids slammed shut in ecstasy and her core throbbed against his fingers. She came on a cry that shafted through his groin, both painful and erotic at the same time.

She collapsed against his chest and he caught her, binding her close. Her head landed on his shoulder, grinding her core against his inflamed erection.

She made him *insane.*

"Strip," she commanded in his ear without shifting her weight. Or offering to help. Or shedding her dress.

"Easy for you to say." But he lifted her one-handed and wiggled out of his clothes. Gracelessly, for sure, but who cared?

Since she appeared to have lost the ability to work a single muscle group, he hiked up her dress, yanked the panties aside and lowered her onto his shaft. The spiral of heat and light exploded in a whirlwind, sucking him into the oblivion of her body.

Finally, she came alive. Rolling her hips, she took him higher, deeper, faster, and the dual edges of the corporeal and the emotional crashed, culminating in a release of epic proportions that could be fully expressed only with the "*I love you*" that spilled from his mouth, rained from his consciousness, radiated from his soul.

At least he thought he said it out loud. But she didn't say it back.

He willed away the prickliness at the back of his neck. They were just words. Saying them or not saying them didn't make the fact any less true. She loved him. He knew that.

When he found the energy, he stood, easily picking her up along with the motion, and carried her to the bed they'd shared last night. There, he drove them both into the stratosphere again, but it was slightly bittersweet this time. He refused to examine why.

Later, as they lay draped across the mattress, he stroked her hair. "Hey, I'm not so tense anymore."

She turned her head to face him and rested a cheek on the sheets, a grin stretching her lips. "Mission accomplished."

Some perverse tendency compelled him to rock the boat. "You know this is all about to end, right?"

A wrinkle appeared between her brows. "Which part?"

"The island-seclusion part."

"Oh. Yeah, we were supposed to be setting up flares or something, weren't we?" She drew his palm to her lips and mouthed a wet kiss along the crease. "You distracted me."

"Ha. It was the other way around. I was about to bring up another topic entirely."

"We have to talk. I know." She sat up, taking his hand with her and clutching it to her heart. "I think I'm ready."

"You look like you're about to march up the steps to the guillotine."

"We've been putting this off for a reason. It's painful. And it sucks," she whispered. "We haven't dealt with Bernard. Or the protest. And we have to if we're going to be together. I just don't want to. I'm not very good at expressing myself without yelling."

The tension was back, tenfold, cramping his well-used muscles. "What is there to yell about? We agreed to forget about history and move forward."

Obviously that wasn't going to work, not that he'd really believed it would.

"Forget about it for how long? Until they bring you home in a body bag?" She dragged a pillow over her face, but it didn't muffle the heart-wrenching sob as much as she probably hoped.

"Hey." He ran a thumb over her one uncovered shoulder. "That's not yelling. I was promised yelling. Toss that pillow off and let me have it."

Actually, he liked it better when she yelled. That, he understood. They argued, they yelled, they made up. Except for that last epic fight a year ago...

Her laugh eased his tight gut more than he'd expected. They were going to get through this. They were stronger this time. Wiser. More determined.

She peeked out from beneath the pillow. "Rain check? I'd like to look back on this conversation and call it rational. I guess hiding doesn't exactly scream nice and sane." She heaved a sigh and flipped the pillow toward the headboard. "I grew up invisible. Too many kids in the house, I guess. You were the first person who saw *me*. Who loved me for who I was, not what I could do for you. When Bernard died...you refused to listen to me, refused to see I might have valid ideas about changes. It hurt. I felt abandoned and lost. I don't know how to get over that."

She'd told him variations of this before, but never with such brokenness. Never without shouting it, along with as many inventive slurs on his intelligence as she could come up with. He definitely liked the shouting better. It gave him permission to shout back and never deal with the emotions being stirred up.

With that sucker punch ringing in his ears, she twisted the dual-edged sword. "When I see warships on TV, it brings it all back. I want to be with you. But I need you to choose me as well or I can't."

Rational. It was a good goal. And suddenly he wasn't so sure he could comply with it.

"What does that look like, Juliet? How can I help you feel like I'm choosing you?" he said, picking his words carefully lest he lead the witness toward a conclusion neither of them could live with.

"I need to feel like you honor our relationship above all others. Like you're on my side. Especially when it's about an issue that destroyed my family."

There it was. He couldn't pretend to misunderstand. Not this time. But if she could do this without yelling, he could too.

Because he loved her and she was trying to do things differently.

He jackknifed to his knees and took her face between his palms. "I want you to understand something critically important. If I was a regular guy, Finn the helicopter pilot who digs this girl Juliet from down the road, I'd crawl over broken glass for a hundred miles to make you mine forever."

Something equal parts tender and shattered flashed in her eyes, gutting him instantly. Because she knew he wasn't finished.

And he wasn't. He couldn't bow to her demands just because she preferred it.

"But I'm not that guy. I don't want to be that guy because being Prince Alain Phineas of Montagne, Duke of Marechal, House of Couronne is a privilege. One I'm honored to live up to."

"So what are you saying?" she whispered, her gaze darting over his face. "*Au revoir* and don't call me, I'll call you?"

"No." He dropped his hands to his side. "That means I'm standing on the other side of a huge expanse of middle ground. I need you to meet me in the middle if we're going to work outside of Île de Etienne."

There. He'd said it as plainly as he could.

"Compromise." She nodded once. "If that's what it takes, that's something I can work with."

Relief jump-started his pulse. "Then you finally understand. You see how important the military is to me. It's part of me. Part of my identity."

Confusion marred her expression and she crossed her arms. "I thought your title was your identity. That you were honoring your blood. I don't see how the military is suddenly rearing its ugly head into this conversation. One has nothing to do with the other."

So she *didn't* get it. "They have everything to do with each other. Alexander's role is clearly defined. He's going to be king. What am I going to be? Prince Alain, the same thing I am now and always was. There's nothing special about me. Nothing I can do to make a contribution except provide defense for the country my father leads."

That, and marry advantageously. The thought added a ninety-stone weight to his shoulders.

"Oh, my darling." Her lips trembled and she clamped them shut. "You're the most special man I've ever known. Alexander was born to his role, but it's so narrow. You have the opportunity to make yours whatever you want it to be. You can be known as the prince who makes a difference in the lives of his people. By introducing reform to the mandatory service law. Get your recruits the right way, from those who choose it, instead of making it a requirement."

"The military is mine, Juliet," he bit out. "Reform isn't on the table."

Why were they having this conversation again? To prove History always repeated itself?

"I see." Her gaze hardened. "You're all for compromise as long as it's me who's doing the compromising."

"I'm all for both of us showing our respect and affection by honoring the other's position." This was the critical point, the one she had to get through her head. "If you love me, you can't only love part of me. You have to love the whole me, including the part that doesn't agree with you."

"Same goes." She took a deep breath, her bare breasts rising and falling in sync. "Have you ever considered that I am honoring my blood too? Bernard was my brother, and his memory deserves nothing less than my strongest convictions. You said I should never give them up. Are you going back on that now?"

Of course he'd considered that. Finn had a brother too. "No, I meant it. Integrity is important to me. I wouldn't love you if you didn't have those convictions."

"Integrity is important to me too. The fact that you stand so strongly in yours is partly why I'm here having this discussion instead of storming out."

That made two of them. But storming out was sounding better and better the longer they beat their heads against this wall between them. If they couldn't resolve things here without any outside pressures, how could they do it at home?

That was the reason he didn't storm out. Once they left Île de Etienne, it would be too late. They had to break down that wall here and now.

"Family is as important as integrity," he said. "To both of us. Honoring the other's position includes helping our families understand it, as well. You realize if we're together, your family can't continue opposing my father, right?"

From outside the house, the distinctive, unmistakable *thwack, thwack, thwack* of helicopter blades split the air. Juliet whirled toward the sound as if she'd been thrown a lifeline.

No. Not yet.

But willing away rescue didn't work any better than willing it here had. He'd run out of time.

Eleven

The drone of a helicopter cut off the last of Finn's sentence, but Juliet had heard enough of it to be simultaneously sorry and thrilled the king had finally sent someone for them.

Part of her wanted to hop on the helicopter and pretend they'd dealt with all their issues. The rest of her knew that wasn't going to work.

Slowly, she faced Finn, tamping down her rising temper with considerable effort. "My family can't oppose your father or I can't?"

"Neither. I can't take any more scandals. Or protests."

"Or what? Your father won't allow us to be together? This isn't the Dark Ages."

How long did they have until whomever was sent to retrieve them reached the door? They weren't even dressed, something she was happy to take care of. She needed something to do with her hands.

"My father isn't—" Finn thumped the bed in apparent frustration. "This is about you and me and our future. If we're married, you'll be a princess of a country that requires eighteen-year-old males to serve three years in the armed forces."

She paused in the process of slipping on the red dress she'd worn for a grand total of thirty minutes thus far today and glanced at him over her shoulder. "Yeah. That doesn't mean I have to agree with it."

"No, you don't. But you can't freely declare your disagreement. That's the point."

"Fine, then don't marry me." Her chest ached at the pronouncement. "We can be together without getting married. Couples do it all the time, and it solves every problem in one shot, right? It'll even make your father happy."

"It wouldn't make me happy. Besides, this—" his hand cut a zigzag line in the air, indicating the house at large "—was a chance for us to rekindle our relationship, remember? My father wants us to get married."

"What?" The king *wanted* them to get married?

Scooting to the edge of the bed, he pulled on his clothes without looking at her. "I told you that's what this was about."

Something seemed off. She couldn't put her finger on it. "Not the marriage part. I would have remembered that."

"Because it was irrelevant." He yanked his shirt over his head and then raised his eyebrows. "One night. No past, no future. That was your rule. It's tomorrow and we're talking about it."

"Yeah, because yesterday, I thought all we had to work through was the past. Your father wants us married. What don't I know?"

He shut his eyes for a beat, which didn't settle the sudden swirl in her stomach. "Let's just say you're my advantageous marriage."

Like a behind-schedule bullet train, her pulse rocketed into the triple digits. Being dressed didn't provide nearly the shield she'd have expected. "Oh, no, let's *not* just say that. Let's say a whole lot more."

"Your family renewed their attacks against my father." Finn locked gazes with her, his expression dark. Too dark. "If we're a couple, their position is neutralized. It looks like you're siding with the crown."

Dizziness rushed up out of nowhere, knocking her off balance.

This was a setup to get her family to back off. A sharp pain tore through her chest and kept going. Nausea churned up her stomach, and she swallowed against the burn rocketing up the back of her throat.

A *setup*. "And you went along with it."

"I didn't." He fairly bristled with the denial. "I would never use our relationship to influence your family. But if we're married, you see the trouble with continuing to protest Delamer's laws. Don't you?"

That had been the goal all along—get that Villere family to shut up. And she'd fallen for it without a peep of protest. "I slept with you. I was *intimate* with you. Because I thought you wanted to be with me. But it was all a lie. How could you do that?"

"I gave you a choice." His hands flew up in protest, palms out as if he intended to mime his way out of trouble. "I slowed it down even though I absolutely wanted to be with you. For exactly this reason, so you would know you made that choice, not me."

If you get pregnant, we'd have to get married.

A cloud of red stole over her vision and the most unladylike word she knew slipped out, verbalizing her rising distress.

There were no condoms in this house *by design.*

And she'd walked smack into it. This wasn't just his father's plan. Finn had bought into it, made it his own, twisting it into something so brilliantly diabolical, it nearly doubled her over.

"I made that choice without all the facts!" she shouted over the *snap* of her heart breaking.

Oh, God, without *any* of the facts. She'd been so worried about making sure her own motives were pure, that she wasn't using him for her own gain. It never occurred to her that he might not have the same compunction.

He'd been using her. All along.

Unforgivable.

She'd been trying so hard to figure out how to live with his refusal to compromise. Because she'd truly believed that the deficiency was hers. That she couldn't possibly understand the royal pressures he faced and if she wanted to be with him, she'd have to give more than he did.

She'd allowed herself to be vulnerable. To lay out her hurts and fears, trusting that he'd keep her feelings safe.

That might be the worst part of all.

"You had the important facts." His gaze sought hers as if he had a prayer of communicating something nonverbally. "Like that I love you."

Ha. That wasn't a fact. That was the purest fiction.

"*This* is your definition of love? Lying to me and using me?"

He'd used her body, but far worse, he'd used her feelings against her. In the end, it hadn't mattered if she'd told him she loved him or not. He still managed to eviscerate her anyway.

Bang, bang, bang. The helicopter pilot was at the front door.

Finn's forehead wrinkled but it was the only outward indicator that her words had any effect. "I didn't lie to you. I never saw you as my advantageous marriage. Actually, I wasn't even sure we'd work things out, especially not this way. But everything snowballed and I wanted you to hear about your family's renewed fervor from me. I didn't want you to find out from…"

"Finn?" The male voice called out from the living room.

"Alexander," Finn finished.

Crown Prince Alexander of Montagne filled the doorway of the bedroom, larger than life, and a grimace on his face. "What happened to my patio furniture?"

"This is *your* house?" Juliet truly thought she'd lost the capacity to be shocked. But apparently the deception went much deeper than she'd ever guessed. Finn had known that from the beginning too. No wonder the house was stocked with games and food that Alexander and Portia liked.

Alexander, to his credit, didn't flinch at Juliet's version of a royal address. But she wasn't too thrilled with any member of the House of Couronne at this point in time, thank you very much. Royalty earned fealty in her humble opinion, and being a party to kidnapping one of his subjects hadn't endeared Prince Alexander to Juliet in the slightest.

Finn threw up a hand in his brother's direction. "Can you give us a minute, please?"

"Only a minute." Alexander crossed his arms, and it was easy to imagine him piercing the members of Parliament with that same regal glare. Which he could jolly well go off and do. There was no room for another insufferable prince in this horrific situation.

He backed away and disappeared.

"Juliet. For what it's worth, I'm sorry. I could have done this differently." Finn approached her and reached out as if to touch her and then changed his mind at the last minute. Smart man. But not smart enough.

She gathered great gobs of red skirt in both fists before she decked him. "Why didn't you do it differently then? Why didn't you tell me?"

"I—" He sighed. "I honestly didn't think you'd take it like this."

"What, like if I got pregnant, you'd marry me and use that to force every Villere in Delamer to keep quiet?"

His head bowed. "That wasn't the plan. The plan was to get off this island. Then when we got home, I was going to call you and see if we could start over. Things happened. You started coming on to m—"

"I'm going to get in that helicopter with Alexander because I have to." There was *no way* he was pinning this on her. "Once we hit Delamer, I'm going to get out and I never want to see you again."

"Don't say that." His eyes glistened with vulnerability she could hardly stomach. "This reconciliation was real. Don't let the admittedly unusual circumstances take away from that. We can make it work."

Her laugh shot out with surprising ease. "There was no reconciliation. We might have been headed toward one, but don't fool yourself. We still had a lot to work through, and this last bit erased any progress. You still can't see that you not only didn't take my side, you took your father's. There's nothing you can say or do in a million years that would make that okay, that would put us near the realm of 'making it work.' Nothing."

"There's still the possibility of pregnancy."

His trump card. The tips of her ears burned with the mere mention of the word *pregnancy*. That was probably the hardest part—that if she got pregnant, they wouldn't be rejoicing over it together, as she'd stupidly let herself envision.

"Maybe. But it won't involve a wedding or a happily-ever-after. Stay away from me. I mean it."

He'd never know either way. If she'd conceived, she'd never ask him for a single tiny diamond from the crown jewels to support her or the baby.

For the rest of her life, she'd have to see Finn's eyes in her baby's face. That was her punishment for trusting him again.

"You can't mean that. You have the keys to my heart." Finn slapped his chest in the spot where the organ in question was supposed to be—but wasn't—and his mouth softened. "It's not a throwaway cliché. You have the ability to unlock it from the outside and come in without my permission. Rifle around and romp through me intimately. Use that power wisely."

He meant she could hurt him. And she fully intended to ensure he hurt every bit as much as she did.

Finn watched Juliet out of the corner of his burning eyes as she huddled against the helicopter seat without speaking to either him or Alexander.

Fragile and broken, she wore her bruised emotions like a cloak. She hurt and it was his fault.

How had this turned out so badly? They couldn't even talk over the whack of the blades and the rush of air as they flew toward the shore. But what else could he say? She'd made her point quite clearly—she wanted him to choose her, and in her mind, he hadn't.

As soon as Alexander touched down east of the palace, she launched from the helicopter and scurried toward the gatekeeper without a backward glance.

"I'm assuming that didn't go well," Alexander said wryly.

"Shut up. The kidnapping was a stupid idea from the beginning." Finn debated whether to follow Juliet and throw himself at her feet or keep what little of his pride remained and let the gatekeeper call her a taxi.

He turned toward the house, slashing the remainder of his heart from his chest. There wasn't anything else he could do but let her go. She wasn't in love with him. She'd probably never really loved him. After all, someone who loved him wouldn't have participated in the protest in the first place. If she loved him, she would have said so at least once, especially after he said it to her.

Her interest in Formula 1 had probably even been by design—to butter him up so she could get what she wanted.

"I told Father that," Alexander said in his typical matter-of-fact and annoyingly brief fashion.

That answered the question of whether his brother had been in on the king's plan too. Of course Alexander had been the one sent to fetch them. The fewer people who knew about what the king had done, the better, no doubt.

Not many people could fly a helicopter anyway. Alexander had fallen in love with piloting helicopters during his three years of mandatory service but now had to do it on the sidelines. He couldn't fly in combat. But Finn could. And when Finn served his three, he'd vowed to do that one thing better than his brother.

Thus far, he had. It was his calling, his first love. And maybe he tended to be a little protective of it. A long wave unsettled his stomach. Juliet might have recognized that well before he had.

"Why didn't you come get me earlier then if you realized it wasn't going to work?" Finn's fist doubled and he longed to take out his frustration on someone who matched him in strength and skill, who could take whatever he dished out and then some. Someone other than Juliet.

Alexander clapped Finn on the shoulder as they mounted the steps to the palace. "I said it was stupid, not that it wouldn't work. I actually thought you'd pull it off."

And didn't that rub salt in the wound? Not only had he not succeeded, but Alexander's glib comment devalued the emotional aspect of what had happened. As if Finn had merely been trying to land a large account or net a sizable income from an investment. "It was doomed to failure from the start because Juliet is too stubborn."

"Must have been like looking in a mirror then."

"What's that supposed to mean? You think I'm stubborn?"

"As a fish on a line that refuses to come out of the water." Alexander tilted his head. "We don't call you Finn solely for your ability to swim, my brother."

Smirking to hide the bloody trails Alexander had carved

through him, Finn flipped back, "Thanks for the pep talk. It's been hugely helpful."

Even his brother was against him.

Finn ached to take his wounded soul to the kitchen, where the palace cook would look the other way if he stole some leftovers from the refrigerator and a cabernet from the wine cellar. The refuge of his childhood called to him, but he swallowed it away.

Prince Alain didn't have the luxury of hiding or licking his wounds.

"Is Father in residence?" Finn asked instead. "I need to be briefed on the situation with Alhendra."

The crown prince nodded and jerked his head. "In his study."

Finn hadn't lived at the palace in twelve years, but it still welcomed him every time. Footmen called, "Prince Alexander. Prince Alain," as they passed, heads inclined. Maids smiled and bobbed. Finn gave each one a return nod or smile and prayed they didn't take offense if it wasn't entirely heartfelt.

The king glanced up as his sons entered his study. "Excellent timing, Alexander. Finn, good to see you, son."

Respectfully, both men waited for their father to continue speaking in deference to his station.

King Laurent stood and leaned a hip on the desk, as was his habit when doling out difficult news. "Tension is high with our friends in Greece, Italy and Turkey. We're going to send all four of our warships, and it's not going to be well received by the whole of Delamer's population. I trust you have good news for us in that regard?"

Finn shook his head as his stomach rolled. Alexander had excellent timing but Finn's was horrific—now would have been the opportune time to be announcing his engagement to Juliet Villere.

Yeah. He could see how Juliet had taken everything the wrong way.

"Juliet did not find the idea of marrying me to her liking." Finn laced his hands behind his back and spread his legs to brace for the full brunt of the disappointment to come.

His father's mouth flattened into a thin line. Because Finn had failed on every level to deliver to the king's expectations.

"That's unfortunate."

A tiny, inadequate word to describe what it truly was. "Yes, sir."

The king's gaze sliced through Finn and he was seventeen again, being called on the carpet to explain why he hadn't danced with the King of Spain's daughter at a charity ball. Or why he hadn't scored as high on his mathematics baccalaureate as Alexander. Why by age twenty-seven, he hadn't been promoted to captain. The past year had been full of such carpet-treading moments, especially when the photo surfaced of him twined with a leggy blonde on a pool table.

"The relationship is unrecoverable then?" his father asked, his forefinger tapping thoughtfully on his chin, as if they were discussing the budget for the country's infrastructure instead of his son's unhappily-ever-after.

"Yes, I'm fairly certain it's over forever this time."

The cramp in his chest blindsided him and he blinked away moisture from the corners of his eyes. Hopefully no one had noticed him being such a girl.

How was he supposed to get through this? Juliet had a bad habit of breaking his heart and he had a bad habit of letting her. But this time, it wasn't solely her fault. Despite his comment to Alexander, Juliet's stubborn nature wasn't fully to blame.

The die had been cast when the photographer snapped that picture at Elise's party back in the States. Once his father put the kidnapping in motion, things couldn't have played out differently. If his father hadn't kidnapped them,

Juliet never would have spoken to him again anyway—of that, he was certain.

And even if she had, clearly they lacked whatever was needed to finally resolve their history. Worse, she'd never side with the crown. What new disaster might Finn have invited into his life if he'd returned from Île de Etienne engaged, only to have Juliet create another scandal?

"Well, then." The king paused, nodding. "We need to find another way for you to be useful."

Useful. It was the only thing Finn had ever wanted from his father—to be told he wasn't the spare heir but someone with value and importance. Just like Alexander. "I'm happy to do whatever's required of me."

"You're hereby ordered to report to the bridge of the *Aurélien.*" The king's eyebrows drew together over his uncompromising and authoritative gaze. "If you can't inspire a girl to marry you, maybe you can inspire a country to back down."

A second chance. Finn latched on to it with gratitude. He could still make a difference.

"I can." He would, gladly. It was a place to vent his frustration and aggression, spending it all on the backs of Delamer's enemies.

"I wish I could be there." The slight wistfulness in Alexander's tone didn't escape Finn.

"The front line is not your place," Finn said as gently as he could, suddenly glad he had the freedom to take a few more risks.

Alexander was born to his role, but it's so narrow. Juliet's voice floated to him on a wisp of memory. *You have the opportunity to make yours whatever you want it to be.*

Uneasily, he shifted from foot to foot. He'd spent the bulk of his life feeling inferior to the crown prince. Perhaps he'd viewed his birth order with too limited a lens.

Had Juliet broadened his vision that much in a few short

days? They'd dated for nearly a year the first time without any such revelations. Seclusion had positives, too.

Instantly, he was back on Île de Etienne, lying with Juliet on a blanket with the heavens opened above them and talking about making it work long-term. He missed her so much, it weakened his knees for a moment.

"Yes, your brother is needed at home." The king's odd half smile had Finn doing a double take.

"Portia's pregnant," Alexander explained.

The word hit Finn square in the solar plexus. Pure jealousy warred with the joy his brother's announcement evoked. He was going to be an uncle.

But in that moment he wanted to be the one announcing his impending fatherhood, the one with that glint of pure awe and amazement shining from his eyes. At this very moment, Juliet might be pregnant—and Finn had ruined any chance of having a relationship with the mother of his child. Would she even tell him if she'd conceived?

"Congratulations," he choked out.

"Thanks. She's having…complications. It's been a little touch and go. The doctor has her on one hundred percent bed rest and there's still a possibility she could lose the baby." Concern for his wife added a weight to Alexander's voice that Finn didn't recall hearing before.

It never occurred to him that his brother might be walking such a difficult path while Finn had been off frolicking in Alexander's house and drinking his wine.

"Well, of course you can't ship out with the rest of us. Take care of Portia and your child. That's the most important thing you can be doing," Finn said firmly. "I'll take up the mantle of defense."

If that defense required him to lay down his life for his people, he would do that without a whimper. Juliet was one of them after all, and now, he had a whole lot more to defend. Portia was carrying the heir to the Delamer throne.

Finn's only regret was that he would go out with his relationship with Juliet so fractured.

Twelve

Home. Juliet threw her arms around her mom, and the smell of fresh bread and cinnamon in her mother's hair was enough to finally thaw Juliet's flash-frozen internal organs, which had seized up during the interminable helicopter ride with the Royal Duo.

"We've been worried." Her mom smoothed Juliet's hair, as she used to when Juliet was little. "We called your cell phone so many times without an answer. We finally tracked down Elise Arundel and she said you'd gone on an extended vacation with the prince. We were not expecting him to be your match."

Elise. The king must have contacted her and made up some story about Juliet and Finn jetting off to an exotic locale to reconnect, conveniently leaving out the part where they hadn't done so under their own volition.

At least Elise hadn't been left to worry. The king got a tiny minutia of a point for that.

"I wasn't expecting it either," Juliet muttered. "I'm sorry you were worried. But I'm okay."

A total and utter lie. Her insides felt as if she'd sanded them with sharp, grainy silt and then swallowed seawater. She longed for the hollowness she'd carried for the past year. Nothingness was vastly preferable to *this*.

Juliet needed to call Elise immediately and tell her EA International's computer program was fundamentally flawed. She and Finn were not a good match, they weren't meant to be together and if Juliet never saw him again, it would be too soon.

Her mother held Juliet at arm's length, peering over her reading glasses to do a sweeping once-over of her daughter. "Where've you been? Elise said we shouldn't worry, but it was like you dropped off the face of the earth. Did something happen with Prince Alain?"

Finn had insisted it was okay to tell the truth about what had happened, as if he could have stopped her from blabbing to everyone what he'd done, but the righteous burn of anger had so drained her, now that she had the chance to flay him alive to her parents, she couldn't open her mouth.

She just wanted to be here in the circle of her family, where no one had hidden motives and everyone loved her. She wanted to forget, not feed the flames.

"It's a long story. Nothing happened with Finn. Nothing is going to happen with him. I'll tell you the rest some other time."

Collette, her youngest sister and the only Villere sibling still living at home, clasped her hands together with bright anticipation. "Will you be going back to America then, or are you staying here?"

"I'm here for now. I have no idea what my plans are."

"Oh." Collette's face fell. "I got permission to visit you in America. I was hoping you were going back."

Maybe Juliet shouldn't have been so forthcoming with her family about her plans to marry an American. Of course, when she'd left Delamer, she hadn't expected to be back home, heart shredded again courtesy of the Triple Blade Finn Special.

"We're happy you're home, and you may stay as long as you like," her father said gruffly, with a warning glare at Collette, and gave Juliet a one-armed hug. "We have to move fast now that the king's announced he's sending forces to join the other countries standing up against Alhendra."

That hadn't taken long. Finn had probably blown the "all hands on deck" horn the moment he hit the palace doors, firmly in his element.

Her father clapped his hands. "We're organizing a protest and you're our best strategist. It's a shame it didn't work with the prince. We could have used him on our side."

Juliet's legs weakened and she sank to the couch. She'd been home five minutes and they wanted to get started on another protest? Her parents were no better than Finn's.

"I'm pretty tired."

Did *everyone* want her around only for what she could do for them?

"Of course you are, dear. That's enough for now, Eduard." Her mother bustled Juliet into the kitchen to ply her with crepes stuffed with fruit and a steaming cup of Italian coffee. Their best. Because she was the prodigal daughter, returning to the fold after running away to America.

Her family loved her. They weren't glad she'd come home so they could channel her passion against the king or hijack her strategic mind. Finn's betrayal colored everything, but not everyone was like him, using people for his or her own agenda.

No one mentioned Alhendra or protests for the rest of the day, and Juliet's spine slowly became less rigid. But when she stopped bracing for the next round of gleeful hand-rubbing over how to best foil King Laurent, her mind wandered to Finn, and she could still smell him on her skin.

Just a few hours ago, they'd twined their limbs together so tightly, it was a wonder the scent of his arousal and excitement hadn't infused her blood.

Leaping up in the middle of Collette's impassioned speech about why she should get to go to university in America, Juliet fled upstairs to her parents' one narrow bathroom and took a tepid shower, the best the water heater could do. She scrubbed and scrubbed but the scent of well-loved man wouldn't vacate her nose.

She dried off and buried herself in the spare bed, quilts up to her neck. And that's when the tears flowed. Crying. Over a cretin whom she never should have trusted in the first place. Who had systematically broken down her defenses in a plot to discredit her family's position against the king.

But in her mind's eye, she could relive only the absolute relief she'd experienced when he'd pulled her from the water. The care and concern in his expression as he watched over her while she burned with fever. The glint in his eye when he confessed he was still in love with her.

All lies and manipulation. Had to be.

By morning, she'd slept only a few hours and developed a raging need to do something—anything—to wash Prince Alain from her system once and for all. And if it hurt him, so much the better.

She cornered her father in the kitchen. "Let's talk about that protest."

Over the next few days, Juliet routed her energy into managing her sisters, cousins, aunts, uncles, their various spouses and offspring, as well as her parents, into a protest machine of the first order. Even the littlest ones could color fliers or staple pamphlets, and she corralled everyone with a fervor that earned her the nickname General Juliet.

The irony of the military-influenced moniker she could do without.

An organized protest was her first goal and the king's head on a platter her second. Figuratively, of course, but if it happened for real in her dreams, no one else had to know.

If King Laurent would simply call the warships home and show a commitment to staying out of foreign conflicts, that would work too. Then they'd have a shot at softening the remaining military mandates. Finally.

The Villere household buzzed with activity toward that end from dawn until midnight, which Juliet embraced wholeheartedly because she never had time to think. She didn't have the luxury of counting the days until a pregnancy test might yield accurate results, thus determining the course of her future.

At night, she shared her bed with a cousin, sister or niece—sometimes more than one—and the cramped quarters suited her well. If she wasn't alone, she couldn't cry, but the tears were there, waiting for the right tipping point to spill out.

One afternoon, as Juliet argued via phone with the local magistrate about a permit to assemble, Gertrude tugged on her skirt and held up a plain brown paper-wrapped package, proudly clutched tight in her five-year-old hands.

Please be the missing four-color mailers. They'd gotten only half the order from the printer and they had little time to go back to press. The protest was scheduled for tomorrow, at the palace gates.

"Thank you," Juliet mouthed to her cousin's daughter and set the package on the counter, sandwiching the phone between her shoulder and ear to slice the neatly taped lid with kitchen shears. "I'm aware the normal processing time is five days, Mr. Le Clercq," she said into the phone. "I'm asking for an exception."

She flipped the box open. The phone dropped from her shoulder and clattered to the floor.

Shoes. The box contained shoes—*her* shoes. Alligator sandals lay nestled in carefully arranged padding. The same ones she'd worn on her dinner date with Finn, back in Dallas, which she'd donned with a hesitant sense of hope. The same ones she thought she'd lost when she woke up barefooted in the dark, with Finn's voice as her only guide.

The cuts had healed where she'd tramped barefoot across the rocky shore of Île de Etienne. But the internal scars she'd developed there…those she could never be rid of.

"Are you ill?" Aunt Vivian eyed her from across the room, her warm brown eyes magnified by thick glasses.

Juliet waved at her, too numb and speechless to respond.

How in the world had these come back to her? Mystified, she glanced at the return label she hadn't bothered to read because she'd assumed the contents would be something far more innocuous.

Finn. Her heart squeezed. He'd sent them. Which meant he'd had them all along. Something sharp knifed through her chest. If only he could return the rest of what he'd taken from her. The possibility of a different match with EA International. Her ability to trust. Her ability to forget, especially if she ended up pregnant after all.

And now this. A physical reminder of what she'd gambled and lost.

Hands shaking, she smashed the lid closed, covering the sandals, and stuffed the box in the back of the pantry in a place no one would find it. Then she put a sack of potatoes on top.

Unable to quite catch her breath, Juliet fled to the living room, where Uncle Jean-Louis was dozing in front of the lone TV. The simple Villere house sported few of the luxuries she'd experienced while staying in Alexander's house, but she'd take it ten times out of ten over anything else. Especially a residence with a Montagne in it.

She just needed a couple of minutes to get the threat of tears a bit more under control. It wouldn't do for anyone to know she was upset or that a mere man had so negatively affected her. Mindless entertainment would fix her up in a jiffy.

Predictably, the remote was nowhere to be found and the news channel her uncle had tuned to was covering the conglomeration of warships in the Mediterranean off the coast of Greece. Because that was *all* the news stations discussed, as well as her family, she knew Finn was on one. Good. That meant he'd taken her request to stay away from her to heart.

And that was the tipping point. A single tear broke loose, tracking down her cheek. Then another, and suddenly the floodgates busted from their moorings.

This was clearly the wrong place to decompress.

As she was about to stand and flee, Aunt Vivian popped her head into the room and shoved Juliet's phone at her. "Weren't you talking to someone—oh, *cherie*. What's wrong?"

Mortified, Juliet shook her head and motioned the elder woman to go back to the kitchen. There was no way she could speak coherently. Neither did she want to, not even to her favorite aunt.

Vivian ignored the clear "go away" sign and shuffled to the couch to engulf Juliet in a warm hug. "It's not as bad as all that, is it?"

Juliet pressed her face into her aunt's midsection and nodded, too beyond any sense of control to care that she'd wet Vivian's dress through. She was still in love with Finn and apparently nothing he did, no matter how much he hurt her, could erase it.

"Your young man is a fool," Vivian clucked. "You'd think royal DNA would produce more sense."

Juliet's neck jerked involuntarily and she glanced up at her aunt. Had her mother spilled all her daughter's recent activities to her sister? "How did you know I was crying over Finn?"

She smiled and nodded at the TV. "He's a handsome devil but clearly addled in the head if he's given you up."

Finn's handsome face indeed filled the screen as he answered a reporter's questions. Clad in his finest dress uniform decorated with medals of honor, he was breathtaking. Literally. Her lungs hitched and she meant to look away. But couldn't.

Greedily, she searched his face for any clue, no matter how small, to his state of mind. Did he miss her? Was he sorry? She hoped he lay awake at night and suffered. As she did.

Absently, she gnawed on a fingernail. When he smiled at the reporter, it wasn't the same one he always gave Juliet. Fine lines around his mouth and eyes crinkled, aging him. He looked worn out.

When would the urge to soothe him and make sure he took care of himself go away?

Aunt Vivian settled next to Juliet on the sofa, careful not to disturb Uncle Jean-Louis, though a freight train at full speed probably wouldn't wake him. Juliet glanced at her aunt, who seemed content to quietly watch the clip with her.

"The first round of negotiations went well," Finn said into the microphone.

Negotiations?

Warships had assembled in the Ionian Sea to intimidate Alhendra into meekly laying down its arms. Might made right after all, in the minds of those with the might. At what point did anyone ever intend to negotiate?

Finn continued speaking smoothly in his rich public address voice. His royal DNA might have left out any sense, but it certainly afforded him authoritative command under pressure and the ability to look devastating while doing it.

He wrapped up with, "I'm gratified to be a member of the contingent invited into the interior of Alhendra. We hope to have a peaceful cease-fire and an end to this standoff signed and delivered this afternoon."

Finn was a member of the diplomatic committee negotiating with Alhendra? Juliet shook her head, but the banner scrolling across the bottom of the screen reiterated that point in capital letters. Not only was he a member of the committee, but Finn had been instrumental in getting through the ordeal with no discharge of weapons.

He wasn't a diplomat. He was far too pigheaded and obstinate. Wasn't he?

"What was the key to the negotiations?" the reporter asked.

"Meeting in the middle," Finn responded immediately, and the words seared through Juliet's stomach. The same thing he'd asked her to do, but then refused to budge from his side even one little centimeter.

Yet he'd done it successfully with an entire country. How?

The question stayed with her as she tossed fitfully that night. Fortunately, she'd had the foresight to bar any cousins or siblings from her room, citing a need for alone-time. Too much weighed on her mind to sleep. The protest was in the morning, and they'd be doing it illegally since she'd failed to secure the permit to assemble in time.

Juliet would probably be arrested again. At least this time she wasn't publicly linked with Finn, thus saving him the embarrassment of it.

And why would she care? He deserved everything she had to throw at him.

The sentiment rang false in the darkened room.

Regardless of how much Bernard's death had hurt her personally and hurt her family, Finn hadn't deserved the fallout from Juliet's role in the first protest. It had been a mistake. Born of highly charged emotions, sure, but handled very poorly, especially given that she'd claimed to be in love with him.

For the first time, she thought about how he must have felt. How he must have seen it as a betrayal and a clear division of sides. She'd chosen family over Finn. Kind of like what she'd accused him of doing back on Île de Etienne.

Her eyes burned with unshed tears. Finn had hurt her—but that didn't mean he didn't love her. Sometimes people messed up, and trying to forget about their mistakes wasn't the answer.

Her fingers felt for the knob of the bedside table, and she pulled open the drawer to extract the book inside, then snapped on the light. Each page contained a pressed flower, one from every bouquet Finn had given her. Why she'd kept it, tucked away here in her childhood home, escaped her.

Tonight, as she ran a fingertip over first one stalk, then the next, it comforted her. These blooms had once been alive, thriving, stretching toward the sun, and should by all rights have disintegrated into dust by now. It was the sad cycle of life for a flower. But she'd carefully preserved each one, pressing it dry until she had something that would last a very long time.

Was there something similar she should have done—but hadn't—to break the cycle she and Finn seemed destined to travel? All she knew was that she was miserable without him and wanted it to stop.

She clutched the book to her chest and held it until dawn. As the sun rose and light filtered through the curtains, warmth entered her body for the first time since she'd left Île de Etienne. And she was at peace with what came next.

They had to cancel the protest.

Finn had resolved the conflict by influencing everyone to compromise. She could compromise too. For real this time, by not leading a protest against the father of the man she loved. At least half—or maybe all—of her motivation in participating in the protest had more to do with their breakup. Not because she truly believed in the cause.

She'd started the cycle—it was up to her to end it. Her relationship with Finn might never recover from the stupid things they'd both done, but that could be dealt with later.

She had a protest to stop.

People milled through the kitchen, fired up and ready to see heads roll.

"The nerve," her father said, and stabbed a finger at the morning paper's headlines. "The palace is hosting a ball tonight to celebrate Delamer successfully throwing its weight around in Alhendra."

Her mother chimed in. "We're moving the protest to this evening. We'll stand arm to arm across the road by the gates and refuse to let anyone's limousine pass. It'll be very effective as all those wealthy, entitled people wait endlessly in their finery. They'll be forced to read our signs and hear our voices united against the king."

Juliet's sleep-deprived brain had difficulty keeping up with the rapid turn of the conversation. Those *wealthy, entitled people* were the friends and family of Finn, who had resolved what could have been a bloody mess without any loss of life.

"But the conflict is over. They said so on the news yesterday. What are you protesting?"

"It goes against everything we believe in." Her father thumped the table, rattling all the silverware and earning a murmured *here-here* from several of her relatives. "Romanticizing war and aggression with an expensive party and honoring those who traipsed off to perpetuate it is almost worse than forcing young boys into service."

"The king requires mandatory service because Delamer is such a small country," she blurted out. Her father stared at her as if she'd lost her mind, when in actuality, she'd just found it. "The armed forces would be a joke without it."

She'd heard Finn say it a dozen times. But never really listened. She touched the linked hearts fastened to the chain under her dress, one a mirror of the other. She and Finn were matched because they were exactly alike. Passionate. Stubborn. As often as she'd accused Finn of refusing to budge from his side, how many steps had she taken toward his?

He hadn't championed military reform to his father because he hadn't bought into it—and she'd completely discounted his reasons. He loved his people and loved his job. How much had she hurt him by refusing to see that was why he didn't take her side?

The hearts on her necklace clutched each other, one keeping the other from falling. But that worked only if the other reached back. Real love wasn't about what you had to give up but what you gained when you held on. That was Elise's message.

"Half the country borders water," Juliet continued. "Mandatory service leads to a strong naval presence. And maybe that's not the best way to staff the military, but we should be offering alternatives, not protests."

"Juliet!" Her mother's mouth pinched together, trembling. "Your brother died because of that philosophy."

"Bernard's death was an accident. We have to move on. Forgive ourselves and stop blaming the king. It's no one's fault. Which is the very definition of an accident."

The burden she'd carried for over a year lifted. Not completely, but enough. It wasn't her fault Bernard died. It wasn't the king's. It certainly wasn't Finn's, but she'd transferred some of her own guilt to him unconsciously. Guilt because she'd introduced Bernard and Finn. Guilt because she'd not better taught Bernard to listen when his superior officers listed safety regulations. That guilt had driven a lot of her decisions but no more.

She squared her shoulders. "The protest is illegal. We shouldn't do it for that reason alone. But maybe a protest isn't the best way to handle this in the first place. Let's try diplomacy for once."

"The way the king leads should be what's criminal, not a civilized protest. You had a chance to use diplomacy with the prince. That's why we're doing it this way." Her father swept her with his hard, cynical gaze, but she saw only a broken man who'd lost his son. It was easy to forgive him.

"You go ahead with the protest, if that's your choice. But you'll do it without me."

Juliet turned and left the room. She used Skype to contact Elise on the other side of the world, then realized it was still early morning in Dallas. Shockingly, the matchmaker answered almost immediately.

"Juliet. Is everything okay?" Elise had enabled video and Juliet could see her short, dark hair was slightly mussed, as if she'd rolled from bed.

"I was about to disconnect. Sorry to wake you."

"You didn't."

Oh. Elise wasn't alone and worse, had been dragged away from something much more fun than a surprise call. "*Really* sorry to disturb you then."

The matchmaker laughed, but the wistfulness in her expression wasn't hard to read. "I was neck-deep in my budget. I only wish I had a better reason to be awake this early."

In the month Juliet had lived with Elise during her makeover, the matchmaker hadn't dated at all. But she obviously wanted to meet someone and clearly loved a good happily-ever-after. Why didn't Elise enter her own information in EA International's computer and find herself a match? It would only make sense.

"Well, since you're awake, I need your help." Juliet bit her lip and went for broke. It took her ten minutes, but she told Elise the whole horrible story, including the part about her own failings.

It wasn't so easy to forgive herself, but she'd taken the first step. Now she had to take several more, and there was only one place adequate enough, public enough, to do it.

"What can I do?" Elise asked. "Name it and it's yours."

Juliet didn't hesitate. "Wave your fairy godmother wand and make me look like someone worthy of a prince. I'm going to the ball."

Thirteen

Finn's head ached. The limo hadn't moved in ten minutes, but that was okay. The faster it moved, the sooner he'd get to the palace and honestly, he wasn't sure how much more back-clapping and accolades and festivity he could handle.

The conflict with Alhendra was over. But the tension Finn had carried for days wasn't.

With only Gomez and LaSalle for company, Finn had visited the neighborhood in Preveza. Alhendra's missile had decimated twelve blocks, killing four hundred people and leveling buildings. The city would never be the same. It haunted him.

The carnage propelled him to insist on being a part of the diplomatic committee working with Alhendra to put an end to the standoff. His father should have been the one, or Alexander at the very least, but it spoke of Delamer's standing in the United Nations that no one batted an eye when King Laurent announced Finn would be the delegate for his country.

His father's faith in him meant everything. Enough to forgive the king for his role in the kidnapping.

That vivid imagery of the devastated bombing site stayed with him through the cease-fire negotiations. It fueled him, energized him to the point of crystalline determination—Alhendra's leaders would not walk out of that room without agreeing to turn over their weapons. Period. But neither would he allow his ships or anyone else's to fire on Alhendra in retaliation.

Compromise.

It had worked.

He'd intended only to resolve the conflict—and in the process, he'd used the opportunity to expand his role, his usefulness to the crown. He'd made it what he wanted it to be instead of waiting for someone to define it for him. No longer did he feel boxed in by his birth order or as if the military was all he had or could hope to have. The sky was the limit.

The victory was bittersweet because Juliet wasn't there to share it with him.

Finn peered out the limo's front window. The taillights of the town car in front of them flashed as the traffic screeched to a halt again. "What's going on, James?" Finn called to the driver.

"There are several people in the street," James said, eyes trained to the road ahead. "They appear to be blocking traffic."

That's what Finn got for going back to his modest house late last night after arriving in Delamer via plane, well ahead of the ships scheduled to return today. But he'd wanted to be alone and then his mother sprang this ball on him, insisting a party in his honor was the least she could do to show pride in her son. How could he say no?

"I'll walk from here, thanks." Finn reached for the door handle. "If you can get out of this snarl, go have a cup of coffee somewhere. I'll text you when I'm ready to leave."

He hit the pavement and Gomez and LaSalle followed. His bodyguards stayed glued to his side now that Finn had international celebrity for something other than the number of shots he could do in a row. Unfortunately, resolving a conflict with extremists solicited much more dangerous attention than that of paparazzi and socialites.

As Finn neared the palace gates, shouts from the people blocking traffic grew clearer.

Peace not war. No more warships.

The shouting people carried signs, holding them aloft and waving them at those trying to enter the palace gates.

It was a protest. Icy waves cut through Finn's stomach. Not this again, not now.

Almost against his will, he searched the faces, though it was almost unnecessary to confirm his suspicions about the identity of the protesters. But he had to know.

His eyes locked with Collette Villere. Juliet's sister.

The disappointment was sharp. But what had he expected? Of course Juliet was here with her family, standing on her side of the line with pride and stubborn determination. Nonetheless, something died inside, something he'd have sworn had been killed off long ago.

His gaze traveled down the row of Villere protesters but Juliet's brown hair and slight form wasn't among them. A ridiculous and fleeting bloom of hope unfurled. Ridiculous because she was probably perched halfway up one of the stone balustrades flanking the gates, bullhorn in hand, inciting the crowd verbally as her family held signs.

But she wasn't. Juliet was nowhere to be found.

Collette was too far away in the crush of people and vehicles to ask after Juliet's whereabouts. With one last puzzled glance over his shoulder, Finn walked the remaining five hundred yards up the paved entrance to the palace and mounted the steps.

Two footmen opened the wide oak doors, one to each side, and admitted him to the grand foyer. Finn paused at the head of the marble steps leading to the floor below, while another footman announced him, droning out his full title with pomp and ceremony. Necks craned as his name caught the attention of the crowd of partygoers below who had braved the walk to the palace from their boxed-in vehicles.

Applause broke out and Finn took it with a grin. What else could he do? These were his people and he'd walked into negotiations with Alhendra on their behalf. It was nice to know they appreciated his efforts.

Finn mingled with the crowd, accepting the hearty back-slaps and handshakes with as much cheer as he could muster, but his throat burned with each *bonsoir* and *how are you* he said. Unbelievably, no one wanted to discuss Alhendra, but the identity of the protesters outside was on everyone's lips. The sidelong glances and blatant comments about the year-old scandal from every knot of people Finn encountered grew tiresome.

Especially since both Alexander *and* his father got in on that action.

Thankfully, no one mentioned Juliet by name. Obviously she hadn't joined her family yet but the instant she did, placard in hand and shouts for justice raised above the noise of the street, he'd undoubtedly hear about it.

Alexander left to go home to the still-bedridden Portia, and King Laurent abandoned Finn to talk racehorses with his brother, the Duke of Carlier. As they'd competed against each other on the track for over forty years, Finn could have repeated their conversation verbatim without hearing a syllable of it. He was glad to be alone for a moment.

The queen worked her way over to Finn, and he bussed both cheeks. "You look stunning, Mother. This is a great party."

"Go on." She swiped at Finn with a gloved hand, but the tenderness she'd always held for her youngest shone from her eyes. "I'm glad you're home safe. I sent some of the grounds crew to the gates to deal with that…issue. Hopefully they won't disturb us further."

A shadow leached the pleasure from the queen's face.

When would this ever end? Juliet and her family were ruining his mother's party.

Finn excused himself as the Earl of Ghent struck up a conversation with his mother and scouted in vain for a passing tray of champagne. What kind of party was this where the hostess tortured her son with invisible waitstaff?

Finally, he caught up with a beleaguered waiter on the far side of the hall. The crush was stifling; more than a hundred and fifty people milled and laughed and celebrated. Normally Finn loved a good party, but this was overwhelming.

He raised the flute of champagne to his lips as a murmur broke out over the crowd, their gazes cutting toward the entrance. A footman called out, "Miss Juliet Villere."

The name echoed over and over and faded away until dead silence cloaked the room. Then, there she was.

Juliet paused at the head of the stairs, and the flute nearly slipped from Finn's suddenly numb fingers. She was resplendent in a shimmery gown, so light and airy, it looked as if it had been spun from a hundred silver spiders. Fit only for a princess. Hair swept up and pinned, face accented with a hint of color, she stole his breath.

What was she doing here?

She was pregnant. Joy flooded him so fast, his knees turned to jelly.

No, it was too soon to know that. There was only one reason she'd crashed the ball.

His stomach twisting with tension, Finn started toward her, fully intending to personally throw her out on her admittedly spectacular rear end. How dare she waltz in here? If she thought she was going to bring her rabble-rousing, anti-military rants into his mother's party, she had more nerve and less intelligence than he'd ever credited.

Juliet Villere was not going to embarrass or upset his mother.

The crowd parted as he marched through. More than a hundred feet separated him from Juliet, but their gazes locked and something gentle and shiny welled in hers.

"Stop!" she commanded, the word reverberating in the quiet hall.

Finn was so surprised, he did.

"Wait there." Juliet gathered her skirt in one hand and descended the stairs slowly, with a grace he'd never seen. She moved like an apparition, like a vision. Was that what was going on? He'd fallen asleep and dreamed up this scene?

Juliet reached the floor, flanked by wide-eyed guests in beaded gowns and black tie. She watched him as she approached, her gaze steady and unapologetic.

Everything broken inside ached that he couldn't greet her as a lover, with a passionate kiss. That they'd parted with insurmountable differences separating them.

"What do you want?" he called harshly.

Her smile was shaky but for him alone. "For you to stand there while I cross this huge expanse of middle ground."

His eyelids shut and he swallowed, but the tightness in his throat wouldn't ease. When he opened his eyes, she was still moving toward him, beautiful and real and exactly what he'd always wanted. She wasn't compromising—this was something far more profound.

She'd come here to try again, not to embarrass him or bring the protest inside. She wasn't even participating in the protest. She was siding with Finn, not her family. Publicly. It was an apology for participating in the first protest, the very antithesis of what she'd done a year ago.

Something massive welled up and broke over him in a wave, healing so many of his deep wounds instantly.

But then she stopped just past the halfway point. She

glanced down and then back up, her expression clouded. The message was clear.

She wanted him to meet her in the middle.

After her brave entrance to this ball, uninvited and unwelcome, how could he not?

Yet he hesitated, the man and the prince at war, as always.

Juliet's dramatic and public move meant a lot to him. But what had really changed between them? They would be right back in the same boat next week—battling out their opposite agendas and being stubborn and holding grudges. Their families would always be a problem, always interfere with their relationship.

He couldn't do this again, this back-and-forth dance between the duty and privilege of his title and the simple life he wished for where he was just a man who loved a woman.

He couldn't walk across that middle ground.

So Finn sank to his knees and crawled to the woman he loved.

Juliet nearly dissolved into a big puddle of sensations as Finn crossed the remaining expanse of marble on his hands and knees.

The murmurs of the crowd melted away as he reached her and rose up on his knees to take her hand. His beautiful eyes sought hers and out poured the contents of his soul.

"What are you doing?" she asked, emotion clogging her throat.

"I didn't have any broken glass to crawl over. But I'm here to tell you marble is a close second in the pain department," he said wryly with an endearing wince.

"But why are you crawling at all? Here, in front of everyone." The curious crowd pressed in, anxious to catch every word of the drama unfolding around them in all its titillating splendor.

"We can't keep going through the same endless loop,

arguing and hurting each other. It has to be different this time. You did your half, wanting me to meet you in the middle. So I did."

Oh, goodness. Her heart tripped once and settled back in her chest, content and peaceful for the first time in… forever.

He was coming to her as a man, not a prince.

It was symbolic—and so unnecessary. She shook her head. "I'm the one who needed to take those steps. You're who you are by blood, and I selfishly tried to stand in the way of that. Testing you to see if I was more important than your heritage, demanding proof of your devotion by asking you to be someone ordinary. I don't want that. Stand up. I want Prince Alain in all his glory."

Prince, lieutenant, helicopter pilot, lover, friend, rescuer and occasional video game partner—all rolled into one delicious package.

The crowd gasped and tittered and a couple of the women clapped. One was the queen. That seemed like a plus in Juliet's favor.

Still clasping her hand, Finn climbed to his feet, his expression solemn as he called out to the room at large. "Show's over, folks. Go back to the party and enjoy my mother's incredible hospitality."

Dispersing with glacial speed, the crowd drifted back to their conversations and champagne, shooed away largely by the queen herself. Juliet could really learn to like Finn's mother.

To Juliet, Finn simply said, "Dance with me."

Oh, no. Now she had to come clean.

"Is this the part where I should admit the buckle on my shoe broke?" Her mouth twitched and she tried really hard to keep the laugh from bubbling out. "I can't exactly walk."

She stuck her foot out from under the gossamer skirt to show him the offending alligator sandals that she'd rescued from beneath the potatoes. That had probably been the last straw for these poor shoes, which had followed her through thick and thin as she figured out the most important lessons of her life. There was no way she'd have worn any other pair tonight.

"*That's* why you stopped?" A hundred emotions vied for purchase on his face, and he finally picked self-deprecating amusement. "You were going to cross the entire length of the floor, weren't you?"

She nodded. "It was the least you deserved. I'm sorry I was so shortsighted over the last year. And I'm sorry for the protest. It was wrong and I shouldn't have done it. I love you. And did very little to show you how much."

A wealth of emotion swept over his face in a tide, transforming him from merely handsome to magnificent.

"I made mistakes too." He drew her hand to his mouth and pressed his lips to the back of her hand in a long kiss. "My blood may be blue but the organ pumping it belongs to you. Not my father, not Delamer. I love you too, more than I love anything. I'm sorry I didn't honor my relationship with you above them."

The words were sweet and the thrill in her chest even sweeter. That's what made it easy to refute his mixed-up declaration.

"But I'm saying I don't want you to choose me above them any longer. That was our problem all along. Too much pressure to make choices between absolutes. Love obviously isn't enough. Let's find the middle ground."

He grinned. "I take it you liked my speech. I had no idea it would produce all this." He motioned to her dress. "You're the most gorgeous woman here."

A blush that she hoped was becoming fired up in her cheeks.

"It was inspiring. But I think my fairy godmother had more to do with this look than anything. Elise," she clarified when he raised his brows. "You don't think I put this outfit together by myself, do you?"

The benefits of Skype and a webcam for the consummate tomboy could not be overstated. Elise deserved a bonus for working her magic across fiber-optic lines.

"I'm more interested in what's under it than how it came to be."

Heat zigzagged between them and her abdomen fluttered. "What's under it is a woman who's lousy at forgetting the past. Let's try forgiveness instead, shall we? Please, please forgive me for all the horrible hurt I've caused you."

So easy. The answer had been there all along. Forgiveness was the key, not forgetting.

Eyes shiny with tenderness, he smiled. "Already done. Will you do the same for me?"

"Done." She returned the smile and bumped his knee with hers. "That happened the moment you hit the marble. Are we going to make it this time, then?"

"Yes." He nodded decisively. "I couldn't possibly let you get away again. You're going to have to marry me. No pregnancy required, though I'd welcome one at some point in the future."

Princess Juliet. The thought shivered down her spine with equal parts trepidation and awe. "Is this a marriage proposal?"

He shook his head. "More of a promise of one to come, when I'm not so unprepared and dazzled by your sheer beauty." But then he paused and his expression turned earnest. "You'd be a princess for life. A card-carrying member of the House of Couronne. Princess Juliet of Montagne, Duchess of Marechal, along with a ton of other unwieldy titles. Can you do it?"

He didn't mean just the jumble of new names and royal protocol. She'd be choosing him over her family, over her commoner heritage, over Bernard's memory. She'd be far past that middle ground every day, forever. Thank goodness.

Best of all, Elise's efforts toward polishing Juliet's rough edges would actually pay off.

Her grip on his hand tightened. "The better question is, can you? I'm not diplomatic like you. I have opinions and I'll not be shy in giving them to you. The people may never forgive you for marrying me."

"They will. Because they'll see what I see. The People's Princess, who believes passionately in their best interests. You got that new school built. You care about their lives or you wouldn't have protested the mandatory service law."

In his eyes, all the qualities he'd listed reflected back at her. Elise's computer had matched them because they shared a bone-deep belief in their convictions. They were a passionate, stubborn, yet thoroughly formidable team, and together they could change the world.

"Besides," he continued, "when I came across the floor on my knees, it was as public of a declaration as yours. I'm on your side. Everyone will know that by the time the sun rises tomorrow."

"And I'm on your side." The best compromise—instead of giving a little, they'd both gained everything.

He drew her into his arms and said the sweetest words of all. "Let's get out of here."

She smiled, tipping her face up to bask in his potent, wonderful masculine strength. "That's the best royal decree I've ever heard."

She started to follow him and her alligator sandal fell off, broken buckle clattering to the marble. Before her Prince Charming could escape, she thumbed off the other one and left them both in the middle of the ball.

Where she hoped Finn was taking her—straight to heaven—shoes were optional.

Epilogue

Finn slid the patio door open with his hip and stepped out, champagne in one hand and flutes in the other. Île de Etienne spread out around him, its beauty unchanged in the month since he'd left it via helicopter, crushed and hopeless. Head tipped back, Juliet lay on the cushion lining the wooden patio chair they'd selected to replace the ones sacrificed to fire on the rocky shore below them.

She popped an eye open. "I thought you were taking a call. This looks like a celebration."

"It is." He poured her a glass and then filled his, dinging the rims together lightly. "Alexander just texted me. The papers are processed. Île de Etienne belongs to us."

"Well, technically just you," she corrected as he sat on the next chaise lounge. "Your father's horribly outdated laws don't allow us to own property jointly unless we're married."

"About that," he began casually and toyed with the stem of his flute to cover a sudden bout of the shakes.

Nerves? Really? He'd faced down an extremist government without blinking yet freaked out over a little overt display of affection for a woman who deserved the moon.

Their rocky relationship had finally smoothed out. The past could never be forgotten until it was forgiven, and once that happened, they both lost the desire to prove the other wrong or take sides. It made all the difference.

He cleared his throat and nodded toward the west. "You might want to glance in that direction."

She did and gasped. Written across the breathtaking blue expanse of sky were the words *MARRY ME JULIET* in white smoke. His version of an outrageously romantic proposal. Hopefully she'd think so too.

"A skywriter?" She shot him a glance full of her own brand of overt affection. "Is he on call to also post my response for the whole of Delamer to witness?"

Finn grinned. In one small sentence, she'd put them back on comfortable ground. "If you like. We're going to be in the public eye for a long time. Might as well give them their money's worth."

"Do you have to pay by the letter?" Tapping her chin, she pretended to contemplate. "Because a 'no' would certainly be cheaper."

"Not considering how much this set me back." He extended his hand to offer her his heart encased in gold. The ring was a simple band channel set with sapphires, but it was also one of the original Delamer crown jewels, circa the seventeenth century.

"Oh, Finn." Tears welled in her beautiful green eyes as she stared at the ring. "That's not expensive, it's priceless."

"You better believe it. I had to promise my mother you'd give her a grandchild within the year before she'd agree to let this out of the treasury." He held out his other hand, palm up, and she laid her hand in his without hesitation.

His Juliet was brave, bold and loved everything fiercely, especially him. He prayed he could spend the rest of his life returning it tenfold. "You're my calm in the storm and I need you. Will you marry me?"

She blinked back the still-present tears. "Are you sure? I'm not going to give up on convincing your father to pass the law giving kids a choice between mandatory military service and an internship for their eventual career."

The chuckle escaped before he could catch it. The next fifty years promised to be full of arguments and lots of really great makeup sex. "I don't want you to give up. How's this instead? Eighteen months of service and eighteen months of internship, if they want that instead of continued service."

The idea had come to him the instant she'd pleaded her case the night before. Internship allowed the next generation to begin learning their trade much faster, which in turn kept Delamer relevant and able to compete in the expanding global marketplace. The armed forces would continue to be staffed in the meantime.

"Compromise." Her smile lit her from within. "I like it."

He shrugged. "I've tried to tell you what a great team we are. Now, are you going to marry me or will I wither and die waiting around for you to decide?"

"I'll marry you." She squeezed his hand and he felt it clear to his toes. "But only if you promise I'll have the keys to your heart forever."

Something bright flared in his soul. "I'm afraid I don't have much choice in that. You've had them since the first moment I laid eyes on you right over there." He nodded at the shores of Delamer across the wide expanse of the Mediterranean. There, he was a prince. Here on Île de Etienne, with Juliet, he was just a man who loved a woman. The best of both worlds.

"Good. That means I can come in whenever I want and love you exactly as you deserve."

Finn slid the ring on her finger and kissed her to seal the start of their happily-ever-after.

* * * * *

MATCHED TO HER RIVAL

BY
KAT CANTRELL

To Jill Marsal, agent extraordinaire, because you stuck with me through all the revisions of this book and together, we made it great. And because this one was your favorite of the three.

One

In the media business—and in life—presentation trumped everything else, and Dax Wakefield never underestimated the value of putting on a good show.

Careful attention to every detail was the reason his far-flung media empire had succeeded beyond his wildest dreams. So why was KDLS, the former jewel of his crown, turning in such dismal ratings?

Dax stopped at the receptionist's desk in the lobby of the news station he'd come to fix. "Hey, Rebecca. How's Brian's math grade this semester?"

The receptionist's smile widened as she fluffed her hair and threw her shoulders back to make sure he noticed her impressive figure.

He noticed. A man who enjoyed the female form as much as Dax always noticed.

"Good morning, Mr. Wakefield," Rebecca chirped. "He made a C on his last report card. Such an improvement. It's been like six months since I mentioned his grades. How on earth did you remember?"

Because Dax made it a point to keep at least one personal detail about all his employees front and center when speaking to them. The mark of success wasn't simply who had the most money, but who had the best-run business, and no one could do it all by themselves. If people liked working for you, they stuck around, and turned themselves inside out to perform.

Usually. Dax had a few questions for Robert Smith, the station manager, about the latest ratings. Someone was tripping up somewhere.

Dax tapped his temple and grinned. "My mama encourages me to use this bad boy for good instead of evil. Is Robert around?"

The receptionist nodded and buzzed the lock on the security door. "They're taping a segment. I'm sure he's hovering near the set."

"Say hi to Brian for me," Dax called as he sailed through the frosted glass door and into the greatest show on earth—the morning news.

Cameramen and gaffers mixed it up, harried producers with electronic tablets stepped over thick cables on their way to the sound booth, and in the middle of it all sat KDLS's star anchor, Monica McCreary. She was conversing on camera with a petite dark-haired woman who had great legs, despite being on the shorter side. She'd done a lot with what she had and he appreciated the effort.

Dax paused at the edge of the organized chaos and crossed his arms, locking gazes with the station manager. With a nod, Robert scurried across the ocean of people and equipment to join him.

"Saw the ratings, huh?" Robert murmured.

That was a quality Dax fully appreciated in his employees—the ability to read his mind.

Low ratings irritated him because there was no excuse. Sensationalism was key, and if nothing newsworthy happened, it was their job to create something worth watching, and ensure that something had Wakefield Media stamped on it.

"Yep." Dax left it at that, for now. He had all day and the crew was in the middle of taping. "What's this segment?"

"Dallas business owners. We feature one a week. Local interest stuff."

Great Legs owned her own business? Interesting. Smart women equaled a huge turn-on.

"What's she do? Cupcakes?"

Even from this distance, the woman exuded energy—a perky little cheerleader type who never met a curlicue or excess of decoration she didn't like. He could see her dolloping frosting on a cupcake and charging an exorbitant price for it.

Dax could go for a cupcake. Literally and figuratively. Maybe even at the same time.

"Nah. She runs a dating service." Robert nodded at the pair of women under the spotlight. "EA International. Caters to exclusive clients."

The back of Dax's neck heated instantly and all thoughts of cupcakes went out the window.

"I'm familiar with the company."

Through narrowed eyes, Dax zeroed in on the Dallas business owner who had cost him his oldest friend. Someone who called herself a matchmaker should be withered and stooped, with gray hair. It was such an antiquated notion. And it should be against the law.

The anchor laughed at something the matchmaker said and leaned forward. "So you're Dallas's answer to a fairy godmother?"

"I like to think of myself as one. Who doesn't need a bit of magic in their lives?" Her sleek dark hair swung freely as she talked with her hands, expression animated.

"You recently matched the Delamerian prince with his fiancée, right?" Monica winked. "Women everywhere are cursing that, I'm sure."

"I can't take credit." The matchmaker smiled and it transformed her entire demeanor. "Prince Alain—Finn—

and Juliet had a previous relationship. I just helped them realize it wasn't over."

Dax couldn't stop watching her.

As much as he hated to admit it, the matchmaker lit up the set. KDLS's star news anchor was more of a minor celestial body compared to the matchmaker's sun.

And Dax was never one to underestimate star power.

Or the element of surprise.

He strode onto the set and dismissed the anchor with a jerk of his head. "I'll take over from here, Monica. Thanks."

Despite the unusual request, Monica smiled and vacated her chair without comment. No one else so much as blinked. No one who worked for him, anyway.

As he parked in Monica's still-warm chair, the petite dynamo opposite him nearly bowled him over when she blurted out, "What's going on? Who are you?"

A man who recognized a golden opportunity for improved ratings.

"Dax Wakefield. I own the station," he said smoothly. "And this interview has officially started over. It's Elise, right?"

Her confusion leveled out and she crossed her spectacular legs, easing back in the chair carefully. "Yes, but you can call me Ms. Arundel."

Ah, so she recognized his name. Let the fun begin.

He chuckled darkly. "How about if I call you Ms. Hocus-Pocus instead? Isn't that your gig, pulling fast ones on unsuspecting clients? You bibbidi-bobbidi-boo women into relationships with wealthy men."

This interview had also officially become the best way to dish up a side of revenge—served cold. If this ratings gold mine led to discrediting EA International, so much the better. Someone had to save the world from this matchmaker's mercenary female clients.

"That's not what I do." Elise's gaze cut from his face

to his torso and her expression did not melt into the typical sensuous smile that said she'd be happy to further discuss whatever he wanted to talk about over drinks. Unlike most women.

It whetted his appetite to get sparks on the screen another way.

"Enlighten us then," he allowed magnanimously with a wave of his hand.

"I match soul mates." Elise, pardon-me-Ms.-Arundel, cleared her throat and recrossed her legs as if she couldn't find a comfortable pose. "Some people need more help than others. Successful men seldom have time or the patience to sort through potential love interests. I do it for them. At the same time, a man with means needs a certain kind of mate, one not easily found. I widen the potential pool by polishing a few of my female clients into diamonds worthy of the highest social circles."

"Oh, come now. You're training these women to be gold diggers."

That was certainly what she'd done with Daniella White, whose last name was now Reynolds because she'd managed to snare Dax's college friend Leo. Who then promptly screwed Dax over in favor of his wife. A fifteen-year friendship down the drain. Over a woman.

Elise's smile hardened. "You're suggesting women need a class on how to marry a man for his money? I doubt anyone with that goal needs help honing her strategy. I'm in the business of making women's lives better by introducing them to their soul mates."

"Why not pay for them to go to college and let them find their own dates?" Dax countered swiftly.

The onlookers shifted and murmured but neither Dax nor Elise so much as glanced away from their staring contest. An indefinable crackle sliced through the air between them. It was going to be beautiful on camera.

"There are scholarship opportunities out there already. I'm filling another niche, helping people connect. I'm good at what I do. You of all people should know that."

Oh, she had not just gone there. Nearly nose to nose now, he smiled, the best method to keep 'em guessing. "Why would I know that? Because you single-handedly ruined both a business venture and a long-standing friendship when you introduced Leo to his gold digger?"

So, apparently that wound was still raw.

College roommates who'd seen the world through the same lens, he and Leo believed wholeheartedly in the power of success and brotherhood. Females were to be appreciated until they outlived their usefulness. Until Daniella, who somehow got Leo to fall in love with her and then she'd brainwashed his oldest friend into losing his ruthless business edge.

Not that he believed Daniella was 100 percent at fault. She'd been the instigator but Leo had pulled the plug on the deal with Dax. Both he and Leo had suffered a seven-figure loss. Then Leo ended their friendship for no reason.

The pain of his friend's betrayal still had the power to punch quite a hole through his stomach. That was why it never paid to trust people. Anyone you let in eventually stomped all over you.

"No!" She huffed a sigh of frustration and shut her eyes for a beat, clearly trying to come up with a snappy response. Good luck with that. There wasn't one.

But she tried anyway. "Because I single-handedly helped two people find each other and fall in love. Something real and lasting happened before your eyes and you had a front-row seat. Leo and Dannie are remarkably compatible and share values. That's what my computer does. Matches people according to who they are."

"The magic you alluded to earlier," Dax commented with raised eyebrows. "Right? It's all smoke and mirrors, though. You tell these people they're compatible and they fall for it. The power of suggestion. Quite brilliant, actually."

And he meant it. If anyone knew the benefit of smoke and mirrors, he did. It kept everyone distracted from what was really going on behind the curtain, where the mess was.

A red stain spilled across Elise's cheeks, but she didn't back down. "You're a cynical man, Dax Wakefield. Just because you don't believe in happily ever after doesn't mean it can't happen."

"True." He conceded the point with a nod. "And false. I readily admit to being cynical but happily ever after is a myth. Long-term relationships consist of two people who've agreed to put up with each other. No ridiculous lies about loving each other forever required."

"That's…" Apparently she couldn't come up with a word to describe it. So he helped her out.

"Reality?"

His mother had proven it by walking out on his father when Dax was seven. His father had never recovered from the hope she'd eventually come back. Poor sap.

"Sad," she corrected with a brittle smile. "You must be so lonely."

He blinked. "That's one I've never been called before. I could have five different dates lined up for tonight in about thirty seconds."

"Oh, you're in worse shape than I thought." With another slide of her legs that Dax couldn't quite ignore, she leaned toward him. "You need to meet the love of your life. Immediately. I can help you."

His own bark of laughter startled him. Because it wasn't funny. "Which part wasn't clear? The part where I said you were a phony or the part where I don't believe in love?"

"It was all very clear," she said quietly. "You're trying to prove my business, my life's work, is a sham. You can't, because I can find the darkest of hearts a match. Even yours. You want to prove something? Put your name in my computer."

Double ouch. He'd been bamboozled. And he'd never seen it coming.

Against all odds, he dredged up a healthy amount of respect for Elise Arundel.

Hell. He actually kind of liked her style.

Elise wiped her clammy hands on her skirt and prayed the pompous Mr. Wakefield didn't notice. This was not the scripted, safe interview she'd been promised or she never would have agreed to sit on this stage under all these burning hot lights, with what felt like a million pairs of eyes boring a hole through her.

Thinking on her feet was not her strong suit.

Neither was dealing with wealthy, spoiled, too-handsome, arrogant playboys who despised everything she believed in.

And she'd just invited him to test her skills. Had she accidentally inhaled paint thinner?

It hardly mattered. He'd never take her up on it. Guys like Dax didn't darken the door of a matchmaker. Shallow, unemotional relationships were a snap to find, especially for someone who clearly had a lot of practice enticing women into bed. And was likely an ace at keeping them there.

Dax stroked his jaw absently and contemplated her. "Are you offering to find me a match?"

"Not just a match," she corrected immediately and tore her gaze from the thumb running under his chiseled cheekbone. "True love. My gig is happily ever after."

Yes. It was, and she hadn't failed one single couple yet. She wasn't about to start today.

Matching hearts fulfilled her in so many ways. It almost made up for not finding her own match. But hope sprang eternal. If her mother's five marriages and dozens of affairs hadn't squeezed optimism and a belief in the power of love out of her, Dax Wakefield couldn't kill them either.

"So tell me about your own happily ever after. Is Mr. Arundel your one true love?"

"I'm single," she admitted readily. It was a common question from clients who wanted her credentials and the standard answer came easily now. "But it's not a commentary on my services. You don't decide against using a travel agent just because she hasn't been to the resort you're booking, right?"

"Right. But I would wonder why she became a travel agent if she doesn't ever get on a plane."

The crowd snickered and the muscles in her legs tensed. *Oh, spotlight how do I hate thee? Let me count the ways...*

She'd be happy to get on a plane if the right man came along. But clients were always right for someone else, not her, and well...she wasn't the best at walking up to interesting men in public and introducing herself. Friday nights with a chick flick always seemed safer than battling the doubts that she wasn't quite good enough, successful enough, or thin enough for dating.

She'd only agreed to this interview to promote her business. It was a necessary evil, and nothing other than EA International's success could entice her into making such a public spectacle.

"I always fly first class myself, Mr. Wakefield," she responded and if only her voice hadn't squeaked, the delivery would have been perfect. "As soon as you're ready to board, see me and I'll put you on the right plane in the right seat to the right destination.

"What do I have to do?" he asked. "Fill out a profile online?"

Was he actually considering it? She swallowed and the

really bad feeling she'd tamped down earlier roared back
into her chest.

Talk him out of it.

It was a stupid idea in the first place. But how else could
she have responded? He was disparaging not only her profession but a company with her name on it.

"Online profiles don't work," she said. "In order to find
your soul mate, I have to know *you*. Personally."

Dax's eyelids drifted lower and he flashed a slumberous
smile that absolutely should not have sent a zing through
her stomach. "That sounds intriguing. Just how personal
does this get, Ms. Arundel?"

Was he *flirting?* Well, she wasn't. This was cold, hard
business. "Very. I ask a series of intensive questions. By
the time I'm finished, I'll know you better than your own
mother."

Something dark skittered through Dax's eyes but he covered it swiftly. "Tall order. But I don't kiss and tell, especially not to my mama. If I do this, what happens if I don't
find true love? You'll be exposed as a fraud. Are you sure
you're up for that?"

"I'm not worried," she lied. "The only thing I ask is that
you take this seriously. No cheating. If you commit to the
process and don't find true love, do your best to spread
word far and wide that I'm not as good as I say I am."

But she *was* that good. She'd written the matching algorithm herself, pouring countless hours into the code until it
was bulletproof. People often perplexed her, but a program
either worked or it didn't, and she never gave up until she
fixed the bug. Numbers were her refuge, her place of peace.

A well-written line of code didn't care how many chocolate bars she ate. Or how easily chocolate settled on her
hips.

"That's quite a deal." His gaze narrowed. "But it's too
easy. There's no way I can lose."

Because he believed she was pulling a fast one on her clients and that he'd never fall for it. "You're right. You don't lose either way. If you don't find love, you get to tear my business apart in whatever way makes sense to you. If you do find love, well…" She shrugged. "You'll be happy. And you'll owe me."

One brow quirked up and she refused to find it charming.

"Love isn't its own reward?"

He was toying with her. And he wasn't going to get away with it. "I run a business, Mr. Wakefield. Surely you can appreciate that I have expenses. Smoke and mirrors aren't free."

His rich laugh hit her crossways. Yeah, he had a nice laugh. It was the only nice anything he had that she'd admit to noticing. Dannie had certainly hit the mark when she described Dax Wakefield to Elise as "yummy with an extra helping of cocky and a side of reptile."

"Careful, Ms. Arundel. You don't want to give away all your secrets on the morning news."

He shook his head, and his carefully coiffed hair bounced back into place. A guy as well put-together as Dax Wakefield hadn't even needed an hour with a makeup artist to be camera-ready. It was so unfair.

"I'm not giving anything away. Especially not my match-making abilities." Elise sat back in her chair. The farther away she was from Pretty Boy, the better. "So if you find true love, you'll agree to advertise my business. As a satisfied client."

His eyebrows shot up and the evidence of surprise gave her a little thrill that she wasn't at all ashamed to wallow in.

If this had been about anything other than EA International, the company she'd breathed life into for seven years, she'd have been at a loss for words, stumbling around looking for the exit.

But attacking her business made it personal. And for what? Because his friend had broken the guy code? Dax needed someone to blame for Leo's falling in love with Dannie, obviously, not that he'd admit it. Elise made a convenient scapegoat.

"You want me to advertise your services?" Incredulity laced his deep voice.

"If you find love, sure. I should get something out of this experiment, too. A satisfied client is the best reference." A satisfied client who'd previously denounced her skill set in public was worth more than a million dollars in advertising. "I'll even waive my fee if you do."

"Now you've got me curious. What's the going rate for true love these days?"

"Five hundred thousand dollars," she said flatly.

"That's outrageous." But he looked impressed nonetheless. About time she got his attention.

"I have dozens of clients who disagree. I guarantee my fees, too. If you don't find your soul mate, I refund your money. Well, not yours," she conceded with a nod. "You get to put me out of business."

That's when she realized her mistake. You could only find a soul mate for someone who had a soul. Dax Wakefield had obviously sold his a long time ago. This was never going to work. Her code would probably chew him up and spit him out.

She had to get off this stage before all these eyes and lights and camera lenses baked her like a pie.

Rubbing his hands together with something resembling glee, he winked. "A proposition I can't lose. I'm so on board with that, I'll even do you one better than a simple reference. Five hundred K buys a fifteen-second spot during the Super Bowl. If you pull a rabbit out of your hat and match me with my true love, I'll sing your praises right before halftime in a commercial starring *moi*."

"You will not." She let her gaze travel over his smooth, too-handsome face, searching for a clue to his real intentions.

Nothing but sincerity radiated back. "I will. Except I won't have to. You'll need a lot more than smoke and mirrors to win."

Win. As though this was a race.

"Why, because even if you fall in love, you'll pretend you haven't?"

A lethal edge sharpened his expression. "I gave you my word, Ms. Arundel. I might be a cynic, but I'm not a liar."

She'd offended him. His edges smoothed out so quickly, she would have thought she'd imagined it. But she knew what she'd seen. Dax Wakefield would not allow himself to win any other way than fair and square. And that decided it.

This…contest between them was about *her* as much as it was about EA International. As much about Dax's views on love and relationships versus hers. If she matched him with his soul mate—not if, *when*—she'd prove once and for all that it didn't matter what she looked like on the outside. Matching people who wanted to fall in love was easy. Finding a match for a self-professed cynic would be a stellar achievement worthy of everyone's praise.

Her brain was her best asset and she'd demonstrate it publicly. The short fat girl inside who wanted her mother to love her regardless of Elise's weight and height would finally be vanquished.

"Then it's a deal." Without hesitation, she slid her hand into his and shook on it.

Something bold and electric passed between them, but she refused to even glance at their joined fingers. Unfortunately, whatever it was that felt dangerous and the slightest bit thrilling came from deep inside her and needed only Dax's dark gaze to intensify it.

Oh, goodness. What had she just agreed to?

Two

The uncut footage was exceptional. Elise Arundel glowed on camera, just as Dax thought she would. The woman was stunning, animated. A real live wire. He peered at the monitor over the producer's shoulder and earned a withering glare from the man trying to do his job.

"Fine," Dax conceded with a nod to the producer. "Finish editing it and air the interview. It's solid."

Dallas's answer to a fairy godmother was going to wave her magic wand and give KDLS the highest ratings the news show had seen in two weeks. Maybe even in this whole fiscal year.

It was totally worth having to go through the motions of whatever ridiculous process Ms. Arundel cooked up. The failure to find him a soul mate would be so humiliating, Dax might not even go through with denouncing her company afterward.

But that all depended on how miserable Elise deliberately tried to make him. He had no doubt she'd give it her best shot.

Within fifteen minutes, the producer had the interview clip queued and ready. The station crew watched it unfold on the monitors. As Dax hammered the matchmaker, she held her own. The camera even captured the one instance she'd caught him off balance.

Okay, so it had happened twice, but no one other than

Dax would notice—he was nothing if not a master at ensuring that everyone saw him precisely as he meant for them to.

Elise Arundel was something else, he'd give her that.

Shame those great legs were attached to such a misguided romantic, whom he should hate a lot more than he actually did. She'd refused to take any crap and the one-up she'd laid on him with the satisfied client bit...well, she'd done exactly what he'd have done in her shoes.

It had been kind of awesome. Or it would have been if he'd escaped without agreeing to put his name in her computer.

Dax spent the rest of the day immersed in meetings with the station crew, hammering each department as easily as he had Elise. They had some preliminary numbers by lunch on the fairy godmother interview—and they were very good indeed—but one stellar day of ratings would not begin to make up for the last quarter.

As Dax slid into the driver's seat of his Audi, his phone beeped and he thumbed up the text message.

Jenna: You could have dates lined up with five different women? Since you're about to meet the love of your life...which is apparently not me...let's make it four. I never want to see you again.

Dax cursed. How bad was it that he'd forgotten Jenna would most assuredly watch the program? Maybe the worse crime was the fact that he'd forgotten entirely about the redhead he'd been dating for four—no, five—weeks. Or was it closer to six?

He cursed again. That relationship had stretched past its expiration date, but he'd been reluctant to give it up. Obviously Jenna had read more into it than she should have. They'd been having fun and he'd told her that was the extent of it. Regardless, she deserved better than to find out she had more of an investment than Dax from a TV program.

He was officially the worst sort of dog and should be shot.

Next time, he'd be clearer up front—Dax Wakefield subscribed to the Pleasure Principle. He liked his women fun, sexy and above all, unattached. Anything deeper than that was work, which he had enough of. Women should be about decadent indulgence. If it didn't feel good, why do it?

He drove home to the loft he'd bought in Deep Ellum before it was trendy and mentally scrolled through his contacts for just such a woman. Not one name jumped out. Probably every woman he'd ever spoken to had seen the clip. Didn't seem as if there were much point in getting shot down a few more times tonight.

But jeez, spending the night alone sucked.

Stomach growling, Dax dumped his messenger bag at the door and strode to the stainless-steel-and-black-granite kitchen to survey the contents of his cupboard.

While pasta boiled, he amused himself by recalling Elise's diabolical smile as she suggested Dax put his name in her computer. Sweet dreams were made of dark-haired, petite women.

He wasn't looking forward to being grilled about his favorite color and where he went to college so Ms. Arundel could pull a random woman's name out of her computer. But he was, oddly enough, looking forward to sparring with her some more.

The next morning, Dax opted to drive to his office downtown. He usually walked, both to get in the exercise and to avoid dealing with Dallas traffic, but Elise had scheduled their first session at the mutually agreed-upon time of 10:00 a.m.

By nine forty-seven, he'd participated in three conference calls, signed a contract for the purchase of a regional newspaper, read and replied to an in-box full of emails, and drunk two cups of coffee. Dax lived for Wakefield Media.

And now he'd have to sacrifice some of his day to the Fairy Godmother. Because he said he would.

Dax's mother was a coldhearted, untrustworthy woman, but in leaving, had taught him the importance of living up to your word. That was why he rarely promised anything.

EA International resided in a tasteful two-story office building in Uptown. The clean, low-key logo on the door spoke of elegance and sophistication, exactly the right tone to strike when your clients were high-powered executives and entrepreneurs.

The receptionist took his name. Dax proceeded to wait until finally she showed him to a room with two leather chairs and a low table strewn with picture books, one sporting a blue-and-gold fish on the cover and another, a waterfall.

Boring. Did Ms. Arundel hope to lull her clients into a semi-stupor while she let them cool their heels? Looked as though he was about to find out.

Elise clacked into the room, high heels against the hardwood floor announcing her presence. He glanced up slowly, taking in her heels, those well-built legs, her form-fitting scarlet skirt and jacket. Normally he liked taller women, but couldn't remember why just then. He kept going, thoroughly enjoying the trip to her face, which he'd forgotten was so arresting.

Her energy swept across him and prickled his skin, unnerving him for a moment. "You're late."

Her composed expression didn't waver. "You were late first."

Not that late. Ten minutes. Maybe. Regardless, she'd made him wait in this pseudo dentist's office on purpose. Score one for the matchmaker. "Trying to teach me a lesson?"

"I assumed you weren't going to show and took a call.

I am running a business here." She settled into the second chair and her knee grazed his.

She didn't even seem to notice. His knee tingled but she simply crossed her legs and bounced one siren-red pump casually.

Just as casually, Dax tossed the fish book back on the table. "Busy day. The show does not go on without a lot of hands-on from yours truly."

But that didn't really excuse his tardiness. They were both business owners and he'd disrespected her. Unintentionally, but point taken.

"You committed to this. The profile session takes several hours. Put up or shut up."

Hours? He nearly groaned. How could it possibly take that long to find out he liked football, hated the Dallas Cowboys, drank beer but only dark and imported, and preferred the beach to the mountains?

Dax drew out his phone. "Give me your cell phone number." One of her eyebrows lowered and it was so cute, he laughed. "I'm not going to prank call you. If this is going to take hours, we'll have to split up the sessions. Then I can text you if I'm going to be late to the next one."

"Really?"

He shrugged, not certain why the derision in her tone raised his hackles. "Most women think it's considerate to let them know if you're held up. My apologies for assuming you fell into the category of females who appreciate a considerate man."

"Apology accepted. Now you know I'm in the category of woman who thinks texting is a cop-out. Try an actual phone call sometime." She smiled, baring her teeth, which softened the message not at all. "Better yet, just be punctual. Period."

She'd *accepted* his quasi-apology, as if he'd meant to really convey regret instead of sarcasm.

"Personal questions and punctuality?" He *tsk*ed to cover what he suspected might be another laugh trying to get out. When was the last time he'd been taken to task so expertly? Like never. "You drive a hard bargain, Ms. Arundel."

And she'd managed to evade giving out her digits. Slick. Not that he really wanted to call her. But still. It was kind of an amusing turnabout to be refused an attractive woman's phone number.

"You can call me Elise."

"Really?" It was petty repetition of her earlier succinct response. But in his shock, he'd let it slip.

"We're going to be working together. I'd like it if you were more comfortable with me. Hopefully it'll help you be more honest when answering the profile questions."

What was it about her and the truth? Did he look that much like a guy who skated the edge between black and white? "I told you I'm not a liar, whether I call you Elise, Ms. Arundel or sweetheart."

The hardness in her gaze melted, turning her irises a gooey shade of chocolate, and she sighed. "My turn to apologize. I can tell you don't want to be here and I'm a little touchy about it."

It was a rare woman who saw something other than what he meant for her to, and he did not want Elise to know anything about him, let alone against his will. Time for a little damage control.

"My turn to be confused. I do want to be here or I wouldn't have agreed to our deal. Why would you think otherwise?"

She evaluated his expression for a moment and tucked the straight fall of dark hair behind her ear, revealing a pale column of neck he had an unexplainable urge to explore. See if he could melt those hard eyes a little more. Unadulterated need coiled in his belly.

Down, boy.

Elise hated him. He didn't like her or anything she stood for. He was here to be matched with a woman who would be the next in a long line of ex-girlfriends and then declare EA International fraudulent. Because there was no way he'd lose this wager.

"Usually when someone is late, it's psychological," she said with a small tilt of her head, as if she'd found a puzzle to solve but couldn't quite get the right angle to view it.

"Are you trying to analyze me?"

She scowled. "It's not bargain-basement analysis. I have a degree in psychology."

"Yeah? Me, too."

They stared at each other for a moment, long enough for the intense spike in his abdomen to kick-start his perverse gene.

What was it about a smart woman that never failed to intrigue the hell out of him?

She broke eye contact and scribbled furiously in her notebook, color in her cheeks heightened.

She'd been affected by the heat, too.

He wanted to know more about Elise Arundel without divulging anything about himself that wasn't surface-level inanity.

"The information about my major was a freebie," he said. "Anything else personal you want to know is going to cost you."

If they were talking about Elise—and didn't every woman on the planet prefer to talk about herself?—Dax wouldn't inadvertently reveal privileged information. That curtain was closed, and no one got to see backstage.

Elise was almost afraid to ask. "Cost me what?"

When Dax's smoke-colored eyes zeroed in on her, she was positive she should be both afraid *and* sorry. His irises weren't the black smoke of an angry forest fire, but the wispy gray of a late November hearth fire that had just begun to blaze. The kind of fire that promised many delicious, warm things to come. And could easily burn down the entire block if left unchecked.

"It'll cost you a response in kind. Whatever you ask me, you have to answer, too."

"That's not how this works. I'm not trying to match myself."

Though she'd been in the system for seven years.

She'd entered her profile first, building the code around the questions and answers. On the off chance a match came through, well, there was nothing wrong with finding her soul mate with her own process, was there?

"Come on. Be a sport. It'll help me be more comfortable with baring my soul to you."

She shook her head hard enough to flip the ends of her hair into her mouth. "The questions are not all that soul-baring."

Scrambling wasn't her forte any more than thinking on her feet, because that was a total misrepresentation. The questions were designed to strip away surface-level BS and find the real person underneath. If that wasn't soul-baring, she didn't know what was. How else could the algorithm find a perfect match? The devil was in the details, and she had a feeling Dax's details could upstage Satan himself.

"Let's find out," he said easily. "What's the first one?"

"Name," she croaked.

"Daxton Ryan Wakefield. Daxton is my grandmother's maiden name. Ryan is my father's name." He shuddered in mock terror. "I feel exposed sharing my history with a virtual stranger. Help a guy out. Your turn."

This was so not a good idea. But he'd threatened her business, her livelihood. To prove her skills, his profile had to be right. Otherwise, he might be matched with an almost–soul mate or worse, someone completely incompatible. Dax wasn't a typical paying client, and she couldn't treat him like one. What was the harm in throwing him one bone? It wasn't as if she had to answer all of the questions, just enough to get him talking.

"Shannon Elise Arundel."

How in the world had that slipped out? She hadn't told anyone that her real first name was Shannon in years. Her shudder of terror wasn't faked.

Shannon, put down that cake. Shannon, have you weighed yourself today? Shannon, you might be vertically challenged but you don't have to be horizontally challenged too.

The words were always delivered with the disapproving frown her mother saved for occasions of great disappointment. Frowning caused wrinkles and Brenna Burke hated wrinkles more than photographers.

Dax circled his finger in a get-on-with-the-rest motion. "No comment about how your father was Irish and wanted to make sure you had a bit of the old country in your name?"

"Nope. My name is very boring."

Her mother was the Irish one, with milky skin and glowing red hair that graced magazine covers and runways for twenty years. Brenna Burke, one of the world's original supermodels, had given birth to a short Black Irish daughter prone to gaining weight by simply looking at cookies. It was a sin of the highest order in Brenna's mind that Elise had a brain instead of beauty.

Dax quirked his mouth in feigned disappointment. "That's okay. We can't all have interesting stories attached to our names. Where did you grow up?"

"This is not a date." The eye roll happened involuntarily, but the exasperation in her voice was deliberate. "I'm asking the questions."

"It's kind of like a date," he mused brightly as if the

thought fascinated him. "Getting to know each other. Awkward silences. Both of us dressed just a little bit more carefully than normal."

She glanced down at her BCBG suit, which she'd snipped the tags from that morning. Because red made her feel strong and fierce, and a session with Dax called for both. So what? "This is how I dress every day."

Now she felt self-conscious. Did the suit and five-inch stilettos seem as though she was trying too hard?

"Then I'm really looking forward to seeing what you look like tomorrow." He waggled his brows.

"Let's move on," she said before Dax drove her insane. "This is not a date, nor is it kind of like a date, and I'm getting to know you, not the other way around. So I can find you a match."

"Too bad. A date is the best place to see me in action." When she snorted, he inclined his head with a mischievous smile. "That's not what I meant, but since you started it, my favorite part of dates is anticipating the first kiss. What's yours?"

She lifted her gaze from his parted lips and blinked at the rising heat in his expression. The man had no shame. Flirting with his matchmaker, whose business he was also trying to destroy.

"Jedi mind tricks only work on the weak-minded. Tell me more about what you like about dating. It's a great place to start."

He grinned and winked. "Deflection only works on those who graduated at the bottom of their class. But I'll let it pass this time. I like long walks on the beach, hot tubs and dinner for two on the terrace."

Clearly this was slated to be the battle of who had the better psychology degree. Fine. *You want to play, let's play.*

"Why don't you try again, but this time without the *Love*

Connection sound bite? I didn't ask what you liked to *do* on dates. I asked what you like about *dating*."

"I like sex," he said flatly. "In order to get that, dating is a tiresome requirement. Is that what you're looking for?"

"Not really. Plus it's not true." His irises flashed from hearth-fire smoke to forest-fire smoke instantly and she backpedaled. "I don't mean you're lying. Get a grip. I mean, you don't have to date someone to have sex. Lots of women would gladly line up for a roll in the sheets with a successful, sophisticated man."

Who had a face too beautiful to be real, the physique of an elite athlete and eyelashes her mother would kill for. Not that she'd noticed.

"Would you?"

"I don't do one-night stands."

She frowned. When was the last time she'd even been on a date? Oh, yeah, six months ago—Kory, with a *K*. She should have known that one wouldn't work out the instant he'd introduced himself as such.

"There you go. A woman who would isn't worth my time."

Her head snapped back. Was that a compliment? More flirting? The truth?

"So you aren't just looking for sex. You want to put some effort into a relationship. Have drinks, spend some time together. And you want to know things about the women you date, their history, their likes and dislikes. Why?"

He contemplated her as he sat back in his chair, thumb to his jaw, a habit she'd noticed he fell into when she made the wheels in his convoluted head turn. Good.

"You're much more talented than I imagined," he allowed with a jerk of his chin. "I'm so impressed, I'm going to tell you why. It's so I can buy her something she'd genuinely appreciate and give it to her on our next date."

So the woman in question would sleep with him, no

doubt. And it probably never failed. "Another example of a considerate man?"

"Sure. Women like to be treated well. I like women. Ergo, it's no chore to do my best to make them happy."

There had to be something wrong with that, but she couldn't find the fault to save her life. Plus, the glow from his compliment still burned brightly. "If only all men subscribed to that theory. What do you find attractive in a woman?"

"Brains," he said instantly and she didn't even bother to write that down.

"You can't tell if a woman has brains from across the room," she responded drily. "If you walk into a bar, who catches your eye?"

"I don't meet women in bars, and last time I walked into one, I got four stitches right here." He tapped his left eyebrow, which was bisected by a faint line, and his chagrined smile was so infectious, she couldn't help but laugh.

"Okay, you win that round. But I have to note something. Redhead, blonde? Voluptuous, athletic?"

"Would you believe it if I said I have no preference? Or at least that used to be true." He swept her with a sizzling once-over that curled her toes involuntarily. "I might be reconsidering."

"The more you try to unsettle me, the less it works," she advised him and cursed the catch in her throat that told him her actual state far better than her words. This was ridiculous and getting them nowhere. "You promised to take this seriously and all I know about you so far is that distraction and verbal sleight of hand are your standard operating procedure. What are you hiding?"

The flicker of astonishment darting through his expression vanished when a knock sounded on the door. Dang it. She'd hardly begun to dig into the good stuff.

Elise's assistant, Angie, stuck her head in and said, "Your next appointment is here."

Both she and Dax shot startled glances at their watches. When he hadn't shown, she'd scheduled another appointment. How had the minutes vanished so quickly?

He stood immediately. "I'm late for a meeting."

What did it say that they'd both lost track of the hour? She nodded. "Tomorrow, then. Same time, same bat channel?"

He grinned. "You've got yourself a date, Ms. Arundel."

Three

Dax whistled a nameless tune as he pulled open the door to EA International. Deliberately late, and not at all sorry.

Today, he was in charge, and Elise would not get the drop on him again. He'd give her enough information to make it seem that he was going along willingly, simultaneously dragging out their interaction a little longer. Long enough to figure out what about Elise got under his skin, anyway. Then he was done here.

"Morning, Angie." Dax smiled at the receptionist and handed her the vase of stargazer lilies he'd brought. "For you. Is Ms. Arundel's calendar free?"

Angie moistened her lips and smiled in return. "Cleared, just as you requested yesterday. Thanks for the flowers. They're beautiful."

"I'll show myself to Ms. Arundel's office." He winked. "Don't tell her I'm coming. It's a surprise."

When Dax blew through the door of Elise's office, the location of which he'd noted yesterday on his way out, the look on her face was more wary disbelief than surprise.

"Look what the cat dragged in," was all she said and ignored him in favor of typing on her laptop. The clacking was too rhythmic to produce actual comprehensible sentences.

Faking it. For him. Warmed his heart.

"I'm taking you to lunch," he informed her. "Get your handbag and shut that thing down."

That earned her attention. She pierced him with that laser-sharp gaze he suspected had the power to drill right through his skull and read his mind like a book. "Are you this egotistical with all women? I'm shocked you ever get a second date."

"Yet I do. Have lunch with me and you'll find out why." He quirked a brow at her and pulled out the big guns. "Unless you're afraid."

She didn't scowl, didn't immediately negate the statement. Instead, she smiled and clicked the laptop closed. "Can't stand being under the spotlight, can you? If you don't like the setting I use to walk through the profile questions, just tell me."

A spontaneous and unexpected laugh shot from his mouth. Why was it such a surprise that she was on to him?

He held up both hands. "I surrender. You're right. That little room with the fish book is like being in therapy. Restaurants are more relaxed."

Elise opened a desk drawer and withdrew a brown leather bag. "Since my schedule is mysteriously clear, lunch it is. On one condition." She cocked her head, sending her dark hair swinging against her chin. "Don't evade, change the subject or try to outsmart me. Answer the questions so we can be done."

"Aww. You're not enjoying this?" He was. It was the most fun he'd had with a woman he wasn't dating in his life.

"You're quite honestly the most difficult, disturbing, contrary client I've ever dealt with." She swept passed him in a cloud of unidentifiable perfume that hit him in the solar plexus, and then she shot back over her shoulder, "Which means you're paying. But I'm driving."

He grinned and followed her to the parking lot, then slid

into the passenger seat of the sleek Corvette she motioned to. He would have opened her door, but she beat him to it.

New car smell wrapped around him. "Nice ride. I pegged you for more of a Toyota girl."

She shrugged. "Even fairy godmothers like to arrive at the ball in style."

"I'm not threatened by a woman driving, by the way." He crossed his arms so he didn't accidentally brush shoulders with Elise. The seats were really close together. Perfect for lovers. Not so good for business associates. "Just in case you were worried."

Elise selected an out-of-the-way bistro-type place without asking him and told the hostess they'd prefer to sit outside, also without his input. The wrought iron chairs and tables on the terrace added French charm and the wine list was passable, so he didn't mind. But two could play that game, so he ordered a bottle of Chianti and nodded to the waiter to pour Elise a glass whether she wanted one or not.

"To loosen you up?" she asked pertly and picked up her glass to sniff the bloodred wine with appreciation.

"Nah. To loosen you up." He dinged their rims together and watched her drink. Elise liked red wine. He filed that tidbit away. "I didn't actually agree to your condition, you know."

"I noticed. I'm banking on the fact that you're a busy man and can't continually take time away from work to finish something you don't want to be doing in the first place. So don't disappoint me. What's the difference between love, romance and sex?"

Dax choked on the wine he'd just swallowed and spent his time recovering. "Give a guy a warning before you lay that kind of question on him."

"Warning. Question imminent. Warning. Question imminent," she intoned in such a perfect robot voice, he sputtered over a second sip, laughing this time.

For an uptight matchmaker, she had an offbeat sense of humor. He liked it. More than he should. It was starting to affect his focus and the more Elise charmed him, the less he remembered why it was important to punish her for Leo's defection.

"Let's see," he said brusquely. "Fiction, Sade and yes, please."

"Excuse me?"

"The answer to your question. Love equals fiction, Sade is romantic music and critical to set the mood, and I would assume 'yes, please' is self-explanatory in relation to sex."

"That's not precisely what I was looking for."

"Then tell me what you would say. So I have an example to go by."

"You never give up, do you?"

"Took you long enough to figure that out. So?" he prompted with raised eyebrows.

She sighed. "They're intertwined so closely you can't remove one without destroying the value of the other two."

"That's a loaded statement. Tell me more before I proceed to tear it apart." He propped his chin on his hand and ignored the halibut a waiter placed in front of him, which he scarcely recalled ordering.

Her lips mushed together in apparent indecision. Or frustration. Hard to tell with her.

"You can have sex without being in love or putting on romantic music. But it's so much better with both. Without love and romance, sex is meaningless and empty."

As she warmed to the topic, her expression softened and that, plus the provocative subject matter, plus the warm breeze playing with her hair, plus...whatever it was about her that drew him all swirled together and spread like a sip of very old, very rare cognac in his chest. "Go on."

"On the flip side, you can certainly make a romantic gesture toward someone you're in love with and not end up in bed. But the fact that you've been intimate magnifies it. Makes it more romantic. See what I mean?"

"Philosophy." He nodded sagely and wondered if the thing going on inside might be a heart attack. "I see. You want to understand how I feel about the three, not give you examples. Rookie mistake. Won't happen again."

"Ha. You did it on purpose so you could probe me."

That was so close to the truth, the back of his neck heated. Next his ears would turn red and no woman got to have that strong of an effect on him. "Yeah, well, guess what? I like the spotlight. When you accused me of that earlier, it was nothing but a classic case of projection. You don't like the spotlight so you assumed that was the reason I didn't want to sit under yours."

She didn't so much as flinch. "Then what is the reason you went to such great lengths to get me out of the office?"

The shrewd glint in the depths of those chocolaty irises tipped him off that he hadn't been as slick with the schedule-clearing as he believed. Odds were, she'd also figured out that she'd hit a couple of nerves yesterday and lunch was designed to prevent that from happening again.

"That's your turf." He waved at the crowd of tables, people and ambiance. "This is mine."

"And I'm on it, with nary a peep. Cut me some slack. Tell me what your ideal mate brings to the relationship."

"A lack of interest in what's behind the curtain," he said instantly as if the answer had been there all along. Though he'd never so much as thought about the question, not once, and certainly wouldn't have told her if she hadn't made the excellent point about the turf change.

But lack of interest wasn't quite right. It was more the ability to turn a blind eye. Someone who saw through the curtain and didn't care that backstage resembled post-tornado wreckage.

Was that why he broke up with women after the standard four weeks—none thus far had that X-ray-vision-slash-blind-eye quality?

"Good." Elise scribbled in her ever-present notebook. "Now tell me what you bring to her."

When she'd called the questions intensive, she wasn't kidding. "What, presents aren't enough?"

"Don't be flip. Unless you want me to assume you bring nothing to a relationship and that's why you shy away from them." A light dawned in her eyes. "Oh. That's it, isn't it? You don't think you have anything to offer."

"Wait a minute. That's not what I said." This conversation had veered way too far off the rails for comfort.

He'd agreed to this ridiculous idea of being matched only because he never thought it would work. Instead, Elise challenged his deep-seated beliefs at every turn with a series of below-the-belt hits. That was not supposed to happen.

"Then say what you mean," she suggested quietly. "For once. If you found that woman, the one who didn't care what was behind your curtain, what do you have to offer her in return?"

"I don't know." It was the most honest answer he could give. And the most unsettling.

He shoveled food in his mouth in case she asked a follow-up question.

What *did* he have to offer in a relationship? He'd never considered it important to examine, largely because he never intended to have a relationship. But he felt deficient all at once.

"Fair enough. I get that these questions are designed to help people who are looking for love. You're not. So we'll move on to the lightning round." Her sunny tone said she knew she was letting him off the hook and it was okay.

Oddly grateful, he nodded and relaxed. "I rule at lightning rounds."

"We'll see, Mr. Wakefield. Glass half-full, or half-empty?"

"Technically, it's always full of both air and water." Her

laugh rumbled through him and he breathed a little easier. Things were clicking along at a much safer level now, and eating held more appeal.

"That's a good one. Apple or banana?"

"What is that, a Freudian question? Apple, of course."

"Actually, apples have biblical connotations. I might interpret it as you can't stay away from the tree of knowledge," she said with a smirk. "What relieves stress?"

"Sex."

She rolled her eyes. "I probably didn't need to ask that one. Do you believe in karma?"

These were easy, surface-level questions. She should have started with them. "No way. Lots of people never get what's coming to them."

"That is *so* true." She chuckled with appreciation and shook her head.

"Don't freak out but I do believe you're enjoying this after all."

Her smile slipped but she didn't look away. This might not be a date, but he couldn't deny that lunch with Elise was the most interesting experience he'd had with a woman, period. Even ones he was dating.

The longer this went on, the harder it was going to be to denounce her publicly. She was good—much better than he'd prepared for—and to criticize her abilities would likely reflect just as poorly on him as it did her.

Worse, he was afraid he'd started to like her. He should probably do something about that before she got too far under his skin.

By one o'clock, Elise's side hurt from laughing. Wine at lunch should be banned. Or required. She couldn't decide which.

"I have to get back to the office," she said reluctantly.

Reluctantly? She had a ton of things to do. And this

was lunch with Dax. Whom she hated…or rather didn't like very much. Actually, he was pretty funny and maybe a little charming. Of course he was—he had lots of practice wooing women.

Dax made a face. "Yeah. Duty calls."

He stood and gallantly took her hand, while simultaneously pulling her chair away. It was amazingly well-coordinated. Probably because he'd done it a million times.

They strolled to the car and she pretended that she didn't notice how slowly, and she didn't immediately fish her keys from her bag. Dax put his palm on the driver's-side door, leaning against it casually, so she couldn't have opened it anyway. Deliberately on his part, she was sure.

She should call him on it.

"Tomorrow, then?" he asked.

Elise shook her head. "I'm out of the office tomorrow. I have a thing with my mother."

Brenna had an appointment with a plastic surgeon in Dallas because the ones in L.A. stopped living up to her expectations. Apparently she couldn't find one who could make her look thirty again.

"All day?" Dax seemed disappointed. "You can't squeeze in an hour for me?"

No way was he disappointed. She shook her head. The wine was affecting her more than she'd thought.

"I have to pick her up from the airport and then take her to the doctor." Oh, that might have been too much information. "I need to ask for your discretion. She wouldn't like it if she knew I was talking to others about her private affairs."

"Because your mother is famous or something?"

Elise heaved a sigh. "I assumed you checked up on me and therefore already knew I was Brenna Burke's daughter. I should have kept my mouth shut."

Stupid wine.

"Brenna Burke is your mother?" Dax whistled. "I had a poster of her above my bed when I was a teenager. The one where she wore the bikini made of leaves. Good times."

"Thanks, I needed the image in my head of you fantasizing about my mother." That's precisely why she never mentioned Brenna. Not only because of the ick factor, but also because no one ever whistled over Elise. It was demoralizing. "You know she was thirty-five in that photo, right?"

Elise called it her mother's I'm-not-old stage, when the hot runway models were closer to her nine-year-old daughter's age than Brenna's, and the offers of work had all but dried up.

I should have waited to have kids, Brenna had told her. *Mistake Number One talked me into it. Being pregnant and off the circuit ruined me.*

Bitter, aging supermodels took out their frustration on those around them, including Elise's father, dubbed Mistake Number One when he grew tired of Brenna's attitude and left. Adult Elise knew all this from her psychology classes. Still hurt, even years later.

"So?" Dax sighed lustily. "I didn't care. She was smoking hot."

"Yeah. So I've been told." She feigned sudden interest in her manicure, unable to take the appreciation for her mother in Dax's expression.

"Elise." His voice held a note of…warmth. Compassion.

Somehow, he'd steered her around, spine against the car, and then he was right there, sandwiching her between his masculine presence and the Vette.

He tipped her head up with a fist and locked those smoky irises on hers and she couldn't breathe. "Tastes change. I like to think I've evolved since I was fourteen. Older women aren't so appealing anymore."

She shrugged. "Whatever. It hardly matters."

"It does." The screeches and hums of the parking lot

and chatter of other diners faded away as he cocked his head and focused on her. "I hurt your feelings. I'm sorry."

How in the world had he figured that out? Somehow, that fact alone made it easy to admit the truth. She probably couldn't have hidden it anyway. "It's hard to have a mother known for her looks when you're so average, you know?"

He shifted closer, though she would have sworn there wasn't much space between them in the first place.

"You're the least average woman I've ever met, and you know what else? Beauty fades. That's why it's important to use what's up here." He circled an index finger around her temple, oh so slowly, and the electrified feel of his touch on her skin spread through her entire body.

"That's my line," she murmured. "I went to college and started my own business because I never wanted a life where my looks mattered."

After watching her mother crash and burn with Mistake Number Two and then Three without finding the happiness she seemed to want so desperately, Elise learned early on that a relationship built on physical attraction didn't work. It also taught her that outward appearance hardly factored in matters of the heart.

Compatibility and striving to find someone who made you better were the keys to a relationship. She'd built EA International on those principles, and it hadn't failed yet.

Dax was so close; she inhaled his exotic scent on her next breath. It screamed *male—and how.*

"Me, too. Unlike your mother, I never wanted to make a career out of modeling." When her eyebrows shot up, he chuckled. "Figured you checked up on me and knew that Calvin Klein put me through college. Guess you'll be looking me up when you get home."

A lit stick of dynamite between her and the laptop couldn't stop that from happening. "My mother put me through college. Reluctantly, but I insisted."

Funny how they'd both paid for college with modeling dollars and then took similar paths to chart their own destinies. She never would have guessed they had anything in common, let alone such important guiding experiences.

Dax's gaze drifted lower and focused on her mouth. Because he was thinking about kissing her. She could read it all over his expression.

Emergency. This wasn't a date. She'd led him on somehow. They didn't like each other, and worse, he shied away from everything she desired—love, marriage, a soul mate. She was supposed to be matching him with one of her clients.

First and foremost, she'd given him permission to *ruin her business* if he didn't find the love of his life. And she was compromising the entire thing.

All of it swirled into a big black burst of panic. Had she lost her mind?

Ducking clumsily out of his semi-embrace, she smiled brightly. "So I'll call you to schedule the next session. Ready to go?"

His expression shuttered and he nodded. "Sure. I'll leave you my card with my number."

In awkward silence, they rode back to EA International where Dax's car was parked.

Despite knowing he thought happily ever after was a myth, despite knowing he faked interest in her as a method of distraction, despite knowing he stood to lose $500,000 and pretended to misunderstand her questions or refused to answer them strictly to prevent it—despite all that, she'd wanted him to kiss her.

Dax Wakefield was better at seducing a woman than she'd credited.

When Elise got to her office, she locked the door and sank into the chair. Her head fell forward into her cupped

palms, too wined-and-Daxed to stay upright any longer.
If he flipped her out this much without laying those gorgeously defined lips on hers, how much worse would it be
if he'd actually done it?

She couldn't take another session with him.

Match him now.

She had enough information. Dax might have thought he
was being sneaky by probing her for answers to the questions in kind but he'd revealed more about himself in the
getting there than he likely realized.

While the match program booted up, Elise stuck a stick
of gum in her mouth in hopes it would stave off the intense
desire for chocolate. She always craved chocolate, but it
was worse when she was under stress.

Maybe she should take a page from Dax and relieve her
stress with sex.

But not with him. No sir.

Almost of their own accord, her fingers keyed his name
into the browser. Provocative photos spilled onto the screen
of a younger Dax with washboard abs and formfitting briefs
scarcely covering the good parts. Her mouth went dry. The
man was a former underwear model with a psychology
degree, a wicked sense of humor and a multibillion-dollar
media empire.

Who in the world did she have in her system to match
that?

Usually she had a pretty good idea who the match would
be ahead of time. One of the benefits of administering the
profile sessions herself—she knew her clients very well.

A slice of fear ripped through her. What if the program
couldn't find a match? It happened occasionally. The algorithms were so precise that sometimes clients had to wait
a few months, until she entered new clients.

Dax would never accept that excuse. He'd call foul and
claim victory right then and there. Either he'd crow about

proving Elise a sham or worse, claim she'd withheld the name on purpose to avoid the fallout when the match wasn't the love of his life.

Newly determined, she shut down the almost-naked pictures of Dax and flipped to the profile screen. She flew through the personal information section and consulted her notes before starting on the personality questions.

That went easily, too. In fact, she didn't even have to glance at the scribbled words in her notebook.

Do you want to be in love? She typed yes. He did, he just hadn't found the right person yet, or he wouldn't have agreed to be matched. Plus, she'd watched his face when he described a woman who didn't care about whatever he hid behind his curtain. That man wanted to connect really, really badly with someone who got him.

How do you sabotage relationships? She snorted and typed "by only dating women he has no chance of falling in love with."

When she reached the last question, she breathed a sigh of relief. Not so bad. Thank goodness she wouldn't have to see him again. A quick phone call to set up his first meet with the match and she'd be done with Dax Wakefield.

She hit Save and ran the match algorithm. Results came back instantly. Fantastic. She might even treat herself to half a carton of Chunky Monkey as a reward. She clicked on the pop-up link and Dax's match was…*Elise Arundel.*

No! She blinked, but the letters didn't change.

That was so wrong, she couldn't even put words together to say how wrong.

She ran the compiler again. *Elise Arundel.*

Stomach cramping with dread, she vised her temples. That's what she got for not asking him all the questions. For letting her professional ethics slide away in the wake of the whirlwind named Dax.

He'd think she did it on purpose—because she'd started

to fall for his slick charm. If she actually told him she was his match, he'd smirk with that knowing glint in his eyes and…

She'd skewed the results. That had to be it. Talk about your Freudian slipups—she'd been thinking about the almost-kiss and the almost-naked pictures and his laugh and thus answered the questions incorrectly.

Besides, the short, fat girl inside could never be enough to change Dax Wakefield's mind about love. She had to match him with someone else.

Her fingers shook and she could hardly type, but those answers had to change. He didn't want to be in love. Total projection on her part to say that he did, exactly as he'd accused her of earlier. She fixed that one, then the next one and eventually worked her way back through the profile

There. She clicked Run and shut her eyes.

This time, the pop-up opened to reveal…Candace Waters.

Perfect. Candy was a gorgeous blonde with a high-school education. Dax would love running intellectual circles around her and Candy liked football. They'd get along famously.

No one ever had to know Elise had nearly screwed up.

Four

When an unrecognized number flashed on Dax's phone, he almost didn't answer it.

Instead of working, as he should be, he'd been watching his phone, hoping Elise might call today.

He couldn't get that moment against the car out of his head, that brief flicker in her gaze that said she didn't hate him anymore and better yet, didn't see him as a match to be pawned off on some other female. Before he'd had time to explore what she did feel, she'd bolted, leaving him to wonder if he'd imagined it.

He should call her already. It was only a conversation to schedule the next session, which would likely be the last. What was the big deal about calling? It wasn't as if she'd answer the main line at EA International anyway. He could schedule the appointment through Angie and go on with his day.

The quicker they finished the sessions, the closer Elise would be to be finding him a match, at which point he'd prove beyond a shadow of a doubt that Elise's matchmaking service fronted as a school for gold diggers. Then, the cold place inside that had developed during the rift with Leo could be warmed nicely by the flames of EA International roasting on the morning news.

A prospect that held less and less appeal the more time he spent with Elise.

The dilemma ate at him, and if he didn't see her again, he didn't have to think about it. That's why he didn't call.

But Dax answered his phone, mentally preparing to spiel off a contract's status or sales figures—pending the caller's identification. "Wakefield."

"It's Elise Arundel." The smooth syllables hit him in all the right places. "Do you have a few minutes?"

He should have called her. Elise had a sexy phone voice.

Grinning like a loon for who knew what reason, Dax settled back in his chair and put his feet out. "Depends on what for. If it's lightning round two, yes."

Elise's chuckle was a little on the nervous side. "I'm afraid that's not the reason for my call. Actually, I have good news on that front. More sessions aren't required after all. I've got your match."

Oh, wow. This thing had just become nauseatingly real.

"Already? That is good news," Dax said heartily. It *was* good news. The best. He didn't have to see Elise again, exactly as he wanted.

And a little voice inside was singing, *Liar, liar, pants on fire.*

"So," Elise chimed in quickly, "I'm calling to set up your first meet with your match, Candace. She prefers to be called Candy, though."

"Candy." That was something you ate, not someone you dated, and sounded suspiciously like a name for a coed. "She's legal, right?"

"You mean is she over the age of eighteen?" Elise's withering tone put the grin back on his face. "What kind of matchmaker do you take me for? She's twenty-eight and works as a paralegal for Browne and Morgan."

"Just checking. What's the drill? I'm supposed to call her and set up a date or something?"

"That's up to you. I've emailed her picture to you, and

I've sent yours to her. If you're both agreeable to meeting, I'd be happy to coordinate or you can go it alone from here."

Curiosity got the best of him and he shouldered the phone to his ear so he could click through his email. There it was—"Sender: Elise Arundel, Subject: Candace Waters." He opened it and a picture of Candy popped onto the screen.

Holy hell. She was *gorgeous*. Like men-falling-over-themselves-to-get-her-a-drink gorgeous. Not at all what he was expecting. "Is she one of your makeover success stories?"

If so, Elise might have a bit more magic in her wand than he'd credited.

"Not everyone is in need of a makeover. Candy came to me as is."

Nice. Not a gold digger then. He took a closer look. She was blonde-with-a-capital-B, wearing a wicked smile that promised she had the moves to back it up. He would have noticed her across the room in a heartbeat.

For the first time, he got an inkling that this whole deal might be legitimate. "She'll do."

Then he returned to planet earth. There was a much greater chance that Candy had something really wrong with her if she'd resorted to a matchmaker to find a date.

"I had a feeling you'd like her," Elise said wryly. "She's perfect for you."

Because something was really wrong with him too?

Elise was obviously running around wielding her psychology degree like a blunt instrument. She'd probably come up with all kinds of bogus analyses about his inability to commit and his mama issues—bogus because he didn't have a problem committing as long as the thing had Wakefield Media stamped on it. Females were a different story. He'd die before letting a woman down the way his mother had let down his father, and he'd never met someone worth making that kind of promise to.

No doubt Elise had warned Candy about what she'd gotten herself into. Maybe she'd given Candy hints about how to get under his skin. Elise certainly had figured out how to do that well enough. And of course Elise had a vested interest in making sure Candy made him happy. This woman he'd been matched with might even be a plant. Some actress Elise had paid to get him to fall in love with her.

That...*schemer*.

Thank God he never had to see Elise again. A paralegal sounded like a blessed reprieve from razor-sharp matchmakers with great legs.

"I'll call her. Then I expect you'll want a full report afterward, right?"

The line went dead silent.

"Still there, Elise?"

"Not a *full* report."

"About whether she's my soul mate. Get your mind out of the gutter."

For some reason, that made Elise laugh and muscles he hadn't realized were tense relaxed.

"Yeah, I do want that report. I guess we never really laid down the ground rules of how this deal was going to go. Do we need an unbiased third party to verify the results?"

A judge? Suddenly, he felt like a bug pinned to cork. "The fewer people involved in this, the better. I'll call you afterward and we'll go from there. How's that?"

"Uncomplicated. I can get on board with that. Have a good time with Candy. Talk to you later."

The line went dead for the second time and Dax immediately saved Elise's number to his contacts. It gave him a dark little kick to have the matchmaker's phone number when she'd been so adamantly against giving it to him.

Then he dialed Candy's number, which Elise had included with the picture. His perverse gene wanted to find out if Candy was on the up-and-up. If Elise had hired someone to date him, he'd cry foul so fast it would make her head spin. And he'd never admit it was exactly what he'd have done.

Dax handed the valet his Audi's key fob and strolled into the wine bar Candy had selected for their first meet. She wasn't difficult to find—every eye in the room was on the sultry blonde perched on a bar stool.

Then every eye in the room turned to fixate on him as he moved forward to buss Candy on the cheek. "Hi. Nice place."

They'd conversed on the phone a couple of times. She had a pleasant voice and seemed sane, so here they were.

She peered up at him out of china doll–blue eyes that were a little less electric in person than they'd been on his laptop screen. No big deal. Her sensual vibe definitely worked for his Pleasure Principle—she'd feel good, all right, and better the second time.

"You look exactly like your picture," she said, her voice a touch breathier than it had been on the phone. "I thought you'd swiped it from a magazine and you'd turn out to be average-looking. I'm glad I was wrong."

Dax knew what reflected back at him in the mirror; he wasn't blind, and time had been kind to his features. It was stupid to be disappointed that she'd commented on his looks first. But why did his cheekbones have to be the first thing women noticed about him?

Most women. He could have been wearing a paper bag over his head for all the notice Elise had taken of his outward appearance. One of the first things she'd said to him was that he was lonely.

And as Candy blinked at him with a hint of coquettishness, he experienced an odd sense of what Elise meant. Until a woman ripped that curtain back and saw the man underneath the skin, it was all just going through the motions. And Dax dated women incapable of penetrating his cynical hide.

How had he just realized that?

And how *dare* Elise make him question his dating philosophy? If she was so smart, why hadn't she figured out he was dating the wrong women?

Besides, he wasn't. The women he dated were fine. Ms. Arundel was *not* ruining this date with her psychobabble.

He slid into the vacant bar stool next to Candy, swiveled it toward her and gave her his best, most practiced smile. It always knocked 'em dead. "You look like your picture, too. Have you ever modeled?"

Dax signaled to the bartender to bring a wine menu and tapped the Chilean red without glancing at it for more than a moment. Ordering wine was a necessary skill and he'd had plenty of opportunity to develop it. Regardless of whether this woman was his soul mate or Elise's accomplice, she'd appreciate his taste.

She nodded. "Since I was fourteen. Regional print mostly, department stores, catalogs, that kind of thing. Celebrities took over cosmetics so I never had a chance there, but eventually all the offers stopped. My mom made me get a job with benefits when I turned twenty-five."

It had been a throwaway question, one you asked a woman as a compliment, but she'd taken it seriously, reeking of sincerity as she'd talked. "So you're a paralegal now?"

She wrinkled her nose and laughed. The combination was cute. Not perky cheerleader let-me-make-you-a-cupcake cute. Actually, it wasn't so cute at all, in retrospect.

"Yes, I research legal briefs all day," she said. "It's not what I imagined myself doing, but it was so hard to find a job. If a woman interviewed me, I got shown the door immediately. Men were worse. You can bet they made it clear the job was mine if I agreed to 'after hours' work."

Candy shuddered delicately and Dax had no problem interpreting what "after hours" meant. "Discrimination at its finest."

"Most people think it's a nice problem to have. It's not. I get so beat down by people who judge me by my looks." Crossing her legs casually, Candy leaned forward and rested an elbow on the bar to casually dangle her hand an inch above Dax's knee. "That's why I signed up with EA International. I can't meet men the traditional way."

Her body language screamed *I'm into you*. The benefit of understanding human psychology—people rarely surprised him. And Candy was legit. He'd stake his life on it.

"I get that. Who wants to meet someone in a crowded bar, knowing they only came up and talked to you because of your face?" Dax sipped his wine and realized somewhere along the way, he'd actually relaxed. He was on a date with a nice, attractive woman and they had several things in common. It was comfortable ground. "You like football?"

"Sure. It's mindless, you know? Easy to follow."

He did know. That was why he liked it, too. Wakefield Media took 99 percent of his gray matter on a regular basis; it was fantastic to veg out on Sundays, the one day a week he didn't focus on work. "We should catch a game sometime."

Elise might very well be legit, too. Candy was exactly his type, almost to the letter. Dax's neck went a little hot. Wasn't that an interesting turnabout? People in general might not surprise him, but Elise almost never failed to.

"I'd like that." Candy smiled widely enough to display a mouthful of expensively capped teeth. "Tailgating is my favorite part. It's like a six-hour party every Saturday and Sunday."

Dax liked a good party. But *six-hour* parties…every Saturday *and* Sunday? "You watch college ball too?"

"I guess. Is that who plays on Sundays? I forget which one is which. I, um, actually don't watch the game most of the time." Laughing, she shook her head carefully so that strands of hair brushed her bare shoulders and drew attention to her cleavage simultaneously. It was impressive. And it was his turn to give her some signals in kind. He knew this dance well.

Candy's phone beeped. His was on silent, which he considered an unbreakable date rule. Obviously she didn't subscribe to it.

"Oh, pardon me," she tittered in that fake way designed to make it seem like an accident her phone wasn't off, when it was anything but. "I have to check in with my friend so she knows you didn't slip something in my drink and drag me ino a dark alley."

"No problem."

Okay, she got a pass on that one. It did make sense to be safe.

As she thumbed back a reply and then another one, Dax glanced at his own phone while his date texted with her girlfriend.

He had a couple of texts himself. As Candy was still facedown in her phone—likely sending messages to her female posse about Dax with the words "delish" and "rich" in all caps—he glanced at his own messages. They were both from Elise and, for some reason, that made him grin.

How's it going?

Must be going well since you're not answering.

His smile widened as he responded: She's great.

And left it at that. Elise could wait for her full report. While Candy finished texting what must be half the female population of Dallas, Dax sipped his wine and amused himself by imagining a certain matchmaker cooling her jets as she waited for additional details. Which he wasn't going to give her until he was good and ready.

* * *

Elise sat on her hands so she couldn't tap out a reply. Dax was on a date with Candy and she had no business bothering him with inane text messages.

But there was so much riding on this. Of all the women in her database, Candace Waters had the best shot at keeping Dax from vilifying Elise's company. Well, and obviously she wanted Candy to find the love of her life too. Dax was charming, sinfully hot even with his clothes on, and quick on the draw with that intelligent sense of humor. What wasn't to like? If you were into that kind of man, which Candy totally should be.

But what if Dax didn't like Candy? "She's great" didn't really say a whole lot, but then they'd only just met. Elise had to give them both a chance to find out more about each other and trust the process that she herself had created.

To keep her hands busy, she tried typing up copy for an ad campaign that needed to go out immediately. January was just around the corner, which was traditionally a demanding time for EA International. The one-two punch of Christmas and then Valentine's Day got people motivated to find someone special.

Once Dax grilled Candy for all her personal history and figured out what she'd like, what kind of Christmas gift would he buy her?

Yeah, the ad copy wasn't working as a distraction either.

She grabbed her phone and texted Dax back: That's it? Great? Do you like her?

In agony, she stared at the phone waiting for the reply. Nothing.

Dax was ignoring her. On purpose. Not sending a message was as pointed a message as actually sending one.

Butt out, her blank screen said.

Now she really had to stop obsessing. She pushed the

button to power off the phone and tossed it on the couch where she couldn't see it.

Maybe she should comb through some applications for her makeover program. Juliet had been such a challenge and then such a triumph, Elise hadn't taken on a new project yet. There were so many deserving applicants, from the one who'd been caring for her three younger brothers after the death of their parents, to another who'd been in the foster care system her whole life and just wanted to find someone who would love her forever.

Decision made, Elise sat down in her home office to contact them both. These two women had stayed on her mind for a reason, and she could handle two houseguests at the same time. Dannie would help out with the hair and makeup sessions, and after the infusion of cash from Prince Alain's match fee, Elise could afford to feed and clothe two women for a couple of months.

She never charged for her makeover services, instead choosing to gift these destitute women with new lives. Elise's magic wand might be the only opportunity they would have to succeed.

Done. She glanced at the time as she saved the women's information to EA International's database using a remote connection. Eight whole minutes had passed.

Why was she so *antsy?*

Because she'd butchered Dax's profile questions the first time. What if she'd messed it up the second time and Candy wasn't really his soul mate?

Armed with a bowl of grapes and a tall glass of ice water, she opened the algorithm code, grimly determined to sort through how it had arrived at the original match so she could reasonably conclude if it had completed the second match correctly.

After fifteen minutes of wishing the grapes were chocolate and staring at code until her eyes crossed, she couldn't stand it. Retrieving her phone from its place of banishment, she powered it on. And powered it off before it fully booted up.

What was she doing? She might as well drive to the restaurant and peer through the window like a stalker. And worse, she had a feeling she might have done exactly that if she had a clue where Dax and Candy had met.

Ridiculous. She'd check for text messages once and then find a movie or something to watch.

She powered on the phone. Nothing.

That...*man*. She couldn't think of a bad enough word to encapsulate how infuriating Dax Wakefield was. He knew how much this meant to her. Knew she was on pins and needles. How hard would it have been to type, "She's beautiful and fun. I like her a lot"?

Not hard. He wasn't doing it because ignoring Elise was part of the game, to make her think the date was going from bad to worse, so she'd sit here and stew about losing.

In reality, he was laughing it up with Candy, having an awesome time drinking red wine and talking about their similar interests. Right now, he was probably watching her over his wineglass with those smoky bedroom eyes and somehow getting Candy to admit things she'd never told anyone before.

Maybe they'd moved to the parking lot and Dax had Candy cornered against her car, breathless and...that was going too far for a first date. They should be taking things slowly, not jumping right into something physical, the way Dax most assuredly did with all his previous women.

Immediately, Elise pulled up the text app: Candy doesn't go all the way on a first date.

She groaned. Dax had officially fried her brain. She hit the delete button.

Oh, God, had she just hit Send? *Please, please, please*, she prayed, hoping against hope she'd deleted the message as she'd meant to, and scoured her phone's folders for the answer.

Which she instead got in the form of a message from Dax: Speaking from personal experience?

Her stomach flopped at the same time she laughed, quite against her will. He'd made the faux pas okay and comical in one shot. How did he *do* that?

At least she'd gotten him to respond. She replied: You specified no one-night stands. She's in it for the long haul.

Dax: I wouldn't have called her otherwise.

That flopped her stomach in a different way. If this worked, Dax and Candy might very well get married. Most of the couples she matched did. She was in the business of introducing soul mates, after all.

Why did the thought of Dax and Candy falling blissfully in love make Elise want to cry?

The prospect of another round of holidays alone coupled with the stress of dealing with Dax—that was it. They were both killing her. Slowly.

And…if someone as cynical about relationships as Dax found his happily ever after, what did it say that she couldn't find hers?

Five

Candy laughed again and launched into another convoluted story about her dog. Dax was more than a little sorry he'd asked if she had any hobbies. Who knew a dog could be a hobby? Or that a grown woman would actually shop for outfits for said dog?

He signaled the bartender for another round and not for the first time, his attention wandered.

She finally wrapped up her monologue and leaned forward to give him an eyeful of her strategically exposed cleavage, which meant he wasn't paying enough attention to her. It was the fourth time she'd done it in thirty minutes, not that he was counting. Her signals were just so uncomplicated and easy to read.

Despite Elise's warning to the contrary, Candy was most definitely open to ending the night skin-on-skin. She would be energetic and creative in bed and yeah, it would be pleasurable.

But in the morning, she'd wake up intending to pursue a long-term, very serious relationship. Big difference from his usual dates. Regardless, he should embrace the spirit of what Elise had set up here, so when it failed, his conscience was clear.

Time to pay attention to his date. After all, she was supposed to be his soul mate. She certainly had a distinct lack of interest in what was going on behind his curtain. Likely she hadn't noticed he had one.

Giving Candy another practiced smile, he nodded to the door and stood, palm extended. "Shall we find a place to have a bite to eat?"

It was how these things worked—if drinks went well, you asked the woman to dinner. If not, you said you'd call her and escaped. Not that he'd claim drinks had gone particularly well, but maybe over dinner Candy would reveal some hidden depths he couldn't resist.

Without bothering to play coy, she took his hand and slid off the bar stool, rising to her full height. "I'd love to."

Jeez, her legs were long. Too long. She was almost as tall as Dax.

"Pardon me while I powder my nose," she said, and turned to sway across the room with a one-two gait.

Dax was meant to think it was sexy. He *should* think it was sexy. But, all at once, nothing about Candy seemed sexy. The lady had moves and a clear interest in demonstrating them. She was exactly the type of woman he went for in a big way. Something was broken here.

His phone vibrated in his pocket, distracting him totally from Candy's departure. His lips curled up involuntarily. He pulled it out, expecting to see another text from Elise. Which it was.

I hope you're not checking your messages in front of Candy. Because that would be rude.

He laughed, painfully aware it was the first genuine amusement he'd felt all evening. He hit Reply: Then stop texting me.

Elise: .

He groaned through another laugh. A blank message. Her sense of humor slayed him.

Candy materialized in front of him far sooner than expected. "Ready?" she said.

"Sure." He pocketed his phone and followed his date out into the chilly night. She didn't have a coat, deliberately of course, so Dax could offer her his. Then she'd accidentally-on-purpose leave something in the pocket—lipstick, an earring; it varied from woman to woman—so she'd have an excuse to call him.

He shrugged out of his jacket anyway and handed it to her, earning a grateful smile as she slung it around her shoulders.

That's what he had to offer in a relationship—a coat. Nothing more. And it wasn't fair to Candy, who came into this date thinking there might be a possibility of something magical. The back of his neck heated. If Candy was his soul mate, she deserved better.

This was jacked up. He never should have called her. But how else could he have handled this? To prove Elise ran a sham business, he had to go on the date. Who knew said date would be exactly like every other date he'd ever been on, which had worked quite well for a long time, and yet not feel right?

As they walked to the valet stand, Candy stumbled, just a little and with practiced grace. Dax rolled his eyes even as he slung a steadying arm around her waist. She peered up at him in invitation. *Kiss me and let's get this party started,* she said without saying a word.

He could have scripted this date ahead of time and not missed a trick. Wearily, he eyed Candy's plumped lips, knew how good it would feel when she melted into him. On paper, they made sense together, for the short term anyway.

And he had no interest in her whatsoever. The perfect woman wasn't so perfect. What was *wrong* with him?

Elise was wrong with him. She'd set him up on a date with a woman who had all these long-term, soul-mate, mumbo-jumbo expectations and it was seriously cramping his style.

And okay, it pricked at his conscience too. Which had picked a fine time to surface.

Elise had ruined his ability to have fun on a date. She'd pay for that.

"I'm sorry, Candy, but this isn't going to work out."

"Oh." Candy straightened, her face hardening. "But we were matched. By Elise. I was really happy with her choice. But you're not?"

Obviously she'd not been clued in that this date was also part of an experiment. And a wager. Yet another mark against Elise.

"She did a great job matching us. You're exactly the kind of woman I like."

"Then what's the problem?"

"I'm not interested in a relationship, and it would be unfair to you for us to continue." The standard excuse rolled from his tongue.

"You forgot to say it's not you, it's me." Candy had obviously heard the excuse before too. She flung his jacket at him with surprising force. "Thanks for the drinks. Have a nice life."

She flounced to the valet and tapped her foot while the uniformed kid raced to get her car. Then she roared out of the parking lot with a screech.

Not only had Elise ruined him, she'd set him up in a catch-22. There was no way he could have fallen for Candy, not when it meant he'd lose the wager. Plus, all of Elise's profile questions kept getting in the way, making him think about his intentions. *That* was the problem, not the sound bite he'd spieled off to Candy.

The valet pulled Dax's car into the lane and hopped out. Dax slipped him a folded bill and got behind the wheel. The closer he drove to his loft, the deeper his blood boiled. Thanks to a certain matchmaker, he'd be spending yet another night alone, his least favorite thing to do.

He pulled onto a side street and hit the call button on his phone before checking the time. Almost nine.

Elise answered on the first ring, so he didn't worry about interrupting her plans too much.

"Expecting my call?" he said with as much irony as he could. She must have been sitting there watching her phone like a hawk. On a Friday night. Looked like Elise could use a bit of her own magic to find a date.

"Um, yeah," she said, her voice husky as though she'd been running laps, and it sent heat to his blood in a whole different way. "You said you'd give me the full report. Isn't this it?"

He'd totally forgotten about that, but it was absolutely the reason for his call now. "Text me your address. It's an in-person kind of report."

He ended the call and an instant later, the message appeared.

Who said I was at home?

She was *not* allowed to make him laugh when he was still so furious with her.

The address came through a moment later and the grin popped out before he'd realized it. *Let's rock and roll, Ms. Arundel.*

Looked like he wouldn't be returning to his empty loft just yet after all.

Elise answered the door of her uptown condo wearing jeans and a soft yellow sweater, all perky and cupcake-y though she'd only had a few minutes' warning before Dax appeared on her front porch. He tried really hard to not notice how the sweater brought out gold highlights in her eyes. He was mad at her for…something.

"That was fast," she said and raised her eyebrows in that cool, infuriating way that said she had his number. "Did you observe the speed limit at any point on your way here?"

"Gonna give me a ticket?" He crossed his arms and leaned a shoulder on the door frame, because she'd very pointedly not invited him in. That was okay. The view was pretty good from here.

"No, a guess. The date must not have gone well if you were in that much of a hurry to get here."

"You think I wanted to see you instead?"

How had she arrived at that conclusion?

But then hadn't he compared Candy to Elise all night and never found a thing in Candy's favor? Hadn't he anticipated this showdown with Elise during the drive over and looked forward to it far more than he'd anticipated having a naked Candy in his arms?

Well, it was stupid to pretend otherwise, regardless of how ridiculous it sounded. The facts spoke for themselves. He'd wanted to see Elise. He liked baiting her.

She stared at him as if he'd grown an extra nose. "No, ding-dong. Because you wanted to lord it over me that I didn't match you with your soul mate."

"Yeah." He nodded by rote and mentally kicked himself. *Ding-dong.* It might be funny if it wasn't so true. "That's why I sped over here. To tell you Candy was perfect, but it didn't work out."

Perfect for the man he'd shown Elise, anyway. She'd failed to dig beneath the surface and find the perfect woman for the man behind the curtain. *Not as good as you think you are, huh, Ms. Hocus-Pocus?*

Elise cocked her head, contemplating him. "I know she's perfect. I matched you with her. But you never really gave it a chance, did you?"

No point in pretending on that front. "What do you want me to say, Elise? I never made any bones about the fact that I'm not interested in a relationship."

No, that wasn't entirely true. He wasn't interested in a relationship with anyone he'd ever met and part of him was disappointed Elise hadn't pulled someone out of her hat who could change his mind.

But that would have been impossible because she didn't exist.

Dax sighed, weary all of a sudden. "Look, the idea of true love is as bogus as the idea of feeding a bunch of data into a program and expecting something magical to come out."

The porch light highlighted a strange shadow in her expression. "It's not magic. The algorithm is incredibly complex."

"I'm sure the software company told you that when they sold it to you but there's no way a developer can be that precise with intangibles. Admit it, you're—"

"I wrote the program," she interrupted, so softly he had strain to hear her.

Then the words sank in and he forgot all about getting her to admit the matches were actually just random pairings. "*You* wrote the program? You have a psychology degree."

The shadows deepened in her expression and he felt like crap for opening his mouth without censor. He'd hurt her feelings, not once but twice. At what point had she started to care what he thought of her?

"I do have a psychology degree. A master's. My bachelor's degree is in computer science."

"A *master's?*"

"That's right." Her jaw tightened. "I almost went on for the PhD in psychology but decided to take the plunge with EA International instead. I can always go back to school later."

"But…you wrote the program?"

She might very well be the sharpest woman he'd ever met. And not just because she'd earned an advanced degree. Because she defied his expectations in ways he'd only begun to appreciate.

Her slight form held a wealth of secrets, things he'd never imagined might lie beneath the surface. Things he'd never dreamed would be so stimulating—intellectually *and* physically. After an incredibly frustrating night in the company of an inane woman who dressed dogs for fun, he wanted to uncover every fascinating bit of Elise Arundel.

"Is it *really* so hard to believe?" She crossed her arms, closing herself off from him. It was way past time for a heartfelt apology.

"It's not that I don't believe it, it's just so incredibly sexy." That was not even close to an apology and he needed to shut up, like yesterday. "I mean, I wasn't kidding. Brains turn me on."

Her eyebrows drew together. "Really? Because I have one in a jar on my kitchen counter. I've never found it particularly attractive but to each his own."

In a spectacularly unappealing combo, he snorted and laughed at the same time. "Wait. You're kidding, right?"

She rolled her eyes, but a suspicious tug at her lips told him she was having a hard time not laughing. "I do not now, nor have I ever, had a pickled brain in my possession."

"It was worth the clarification." A host of things unsaid passed between them, most of them indecipherable. He wanted to unscramble her in the worst way. "How bad is to admit that a conversation about pickled brains is the most scintillating one I've had this evening?"

With a sigh, Elise butted the door all the way open with the flat of her hand. "You better come in. I have a feeling I need to be sitting down for the full report."

Inside—exactly where he wanted to be, but not to discuss Candy. Dax trailed the matchmaker through a classically decorated condo with rich, jewel-toned accents. "So this is where all the magic happens?"

"The women who go through my makeover program stay here, yes." Elise flopped on the sofa, clearly unconcerned about appearing graceful.

She had no pretense. It was almost as if she didn't care whether he found her attractive. She wasn't even wearing lipstick. The only time he'd ever seen a woman without lipstick was after he'd kissed it off. Women of his acquaintance always put their best face forward.

But Elise hadn't invited him in for any sort of behind-closed-doors activities. She wanted the lowdown on his date with another woman. This was like sailing through uncharted waters during a hurricane.

Slightly off stride, he sank into the plush armchair near the couch.

"Tell me what happened with Candy," she instructed without preamble. "Every last detail. I have to know precisely what didn't work, if anything did work, more abou—"

"Whoa. Why do you have to know all that?" That bug-on-cork feeling was back and on a Friday night in the company of an interesting woman, no variation of this conversation sounded like it would lead to the kind of fun he'd rather be having.

Her stare was nothing short of withering. "So I can get it right the second time."

"What second time?"

"I promised to match you with the love of your life. Admittedly, I like to get it right the first time, but I'm okay with one mistake. Two is unacceptable. So I need details."

Another date? He almost groaned. Somehow he'd thought they could let that lie, at least for a blessed hour or two. The wager was over. She'd lost. Didn't she realize that?

"Elise…"

She gazed across the coffee table separating them, and he couldn't do it. Couldn't denounce her as a fraud, couldn't tell her flat out that she wasn't the fairy godmother she seemed to think she was, couldn't stand the thought of hurting her feelings again.

Then there was the whole problem of this strange draw he felt every time he thought about Elise. Without this mission of hers to match him with his mythical soul mate, he'd have no excuse to see her again, and the thought made him twitchy.

She held up her hand in protest. "I know what you're going to say. You don't kiss and tell. I'm not asking you to."

"I didn't kiss Candy. And that wasn't what I was going to say."

"You didn't kiss her?" Elise looked a little shocked. "Why not?"

"Because I didn't like her. I only kiss women I like."

"But the other day at the bistro, you almost kissed *me*. I know you were about to. Don't bother to deny it."

As Dax did actually know the value of silence on occasion, he crossed his arms and waited until all the columns in her head added up. A blush rose on her cheeks. Really, he shouldn't enjoy that so much.

And he probably shouldn't have admitted he liked her. Not even to himself, but definitely not to her. Too late now.

"Stop being ridiculous," she said. "All this talk about how I'm sexy because I wrote a computer program and trying to throw me off balance with cryptic comments designed to make me believe you like me—it's not going to work."

She thought he was lying. Better yet, she thought he'd told her those things for nefarious purposes, as a way to manipulate her, and she wanted to be clear there was no chance of her falling for it. If he hadn't liked her already, that alone would have clinched it, and hell if he knew why.

Thoroughly intrigued, he leaned forward, elbows on his knees. "What exactly am I working here?"

"The same thing you've been working since moment

one. Distraction. If I'm all flustered and thinking about you kissing me, I'll mess up and match you with the wrong woman. Then I lose. It's brilliant, actually."

And instantly, he hit his stride. The wager, the full report he'd come to deliver, soul mates and matches—all of it got shoved to the back burner in favor of the gem buried in Elise's statement.

He zeroed right in on the kicker. "You're thinking about kissing me?"

Kissing Dax was, in fact, *all* Elise had been thinking about.

Did they make human muzzles? Because she needed one. "I said you were *trying* to get me to think about it. So I'd be distracted. It doesn't work."

Because she didn't need to think about kissing him to be distracted. That had happened the moment she'd opened the door to all that solid masculinity encased in a well-cut body. She didn't know for sure that he still had the washboard abs. But it was a safe bet. And it was easy to fantasize about when she already had a handy image emblazoned across her mind's eye of him half-naked.

Casually, Dax pulled at the sleeve of his date-night suit, which shouldn't have looked so different on him than what he'd worn all the other times she'd seen him. But it was clearly custom-made from gorgeous silk, and in it, he somehow he managed to look delicious and dangerous at the same time.

"Really," he said. It was a statement, not a question, as though he didn't believe her.

Probably because he knew she was skirting the truth. Why had she invited him in? Or given him her address in the first place? This was her sanctuary, and she rarely allowed anyone to intrude.

Dax got a pass because she *had* messed up. "You can't

distract me. I've got a one-track mind and it's set on finding the perfect woman for you. Candy wasn't it. I get that.
But her name came up due to the unorthodox profile sessions. We have to do the last one and do it the right way."

For all the good it would do. Who else did she have
in her database to match with Dax? Mentally, she sorted
through the candidates and tried to do some of the percent-
ages in her head.

And forgot how to add as a slow smile spread across his
face, heavy with promise and a side of wicked. "Shall we
put that to the test?"

"Um…" Her brain went a little fuzzy as he pierced her
with those smoky eyes and raked heat through her abdomen
without moving an inch. "Put what to the test?"

Then he stirred and she wished he'd stayed still.

He flowed to his feet and resettled next to her on the
couch. "Whether I can distract you or not."

Barely a finger width separated them and she held her
breath because oh my God, he smelled like sin and salva-
tion and she had the worst urge to nuzzle behind his ear.

This was not part of the deal. She was *not* attracted
to Dax Wakefield. It was unthinkable, unacceptable. She
had no experience with a predatory man who had a new
woman in his bed more often than he replaced his tube of
toothpaste.

How could this have happened? Did her previously co-
matose libido not understand what a player this man was?
How greatly he disdained long-term commitment and true
love?

The man was her lonely heart's worst nightmare
wrapped in a delectable package. She might as well hand
him a mallet and lie down at his feet so he could get to
smashing her insides flat right away.

He was meant for his true soul mate, who would be the
right woman to change his mind about love. Elise was not it.

Pulse hammering, she stared him down, praying he couldn't actually see her panic swirling. Now would be a great time for some pithy comeback to materialize in her fuzzy brain, but then he slipped his hand under hers and raised it to his lips.

Her fingertips grazed his mouth and his eyelids drifted lower, as if he found it pleasurable. Fascinating. Little old Elise Arundel could make a walking deity like Dax feel pleasure. Who would have thought?

Watching her intently, he pursed his lips and sucked, ever so slightly, on her index finger, and the answering tug between her legs wasn't so slight. Honeyed warmth radiated outward, flushing over her skin, and a hitch in her lungs made it hard to catch a breath.

"What are you doing?" she asked hoarsely.

"Seeing what you taste like," he murmured and slid her hand across his stubbly jaw, holding it against his skin. "And it was good enough to want more."

Before she could blink, his head inclined and his lips trailed across hers, nibbling lightly, exploring, teasing, until he found what must have been the angle he sought. Instantly, their mouths fused into a ragingly hot kiss.

Elise's long-dormant body thundered to life and broke into a rousing rendition of the Hallelujah Chorus.

His hands cupped her neck, tilting her head back so he could take it deeper. Hot and rough, his tongue slicked across hers, and she felt strong responding licks deep in her core. A cry rose up in her throat and came out as a moan.

Those strong and deft hands drifted lower on her back, dipping under the hem of her sweater, spreading across her bare skin at the arch of her waist.

Stop right there.

He did.

She really wished he'd kept going.

They both shifted closer, twining like vines. Then he

pushed with his palm against the small of her back and shoved her torso into his. Oh, my, it was hard against the roused tips of her breasts, which were sensitive enough to feel him through layers of cloth.

This wasn't the PG-rated kiss she'd been thinking about since the almost-kiss of the parking lot. This one had *rated R* slapped all over it. Fisting great wads of his shirt in her hands, she clung to him as he kissed her, shamelessly reveling in it, soaking up every second.

Until she remembered this was all designed as a distraction.

Pulling away was harder than it should have been. Chest rising and falling rapidly, she put a foot of couch between them. Not enough. She hit the floor and kept going, whirling only when the coffee table was between her and the hot-tongued man on the couch.

"Good kisser," she said breathlessly and cursed her fragmented voice. "I'll note it on your profile."

His heavy-lidded gaze tracked her closely. "I wasn't finished. Come back and see what else I'm good at. You want to be thorough on the profile, don't you?"

"I can't do that." If he triggered such a severe reaction with merely a kiss, what would her body do with more?

"Scared?"

"Of you? Not hardly." The scoff was delivered so convincingly, she almost believed it herself.

A light dawned in his expression and she had the distinct impression he'd just figured out exactly how much he scared her. That sent another round of panic into the abyss of her stomach.

"There's just no need," she clarified, desperately trying to counter the effects of being kissed senseless. "We put it to the test, and while the kiss was pleasant, it certainly didn't distract me from the next steps. When do you want to schedule the last session?"

Dax groaned the way someone does when you tell them they have to get a root canal followed by a tax audit. "I'd rather kiss you some more. Why are you all the way over there?"

"We're not doing this, Dax. Hear me now, because I can't stress this enough. You and I are not happening." She held up a finger as he started to speak. "No. Not any variation of you and I. We have a deal, a wager, and nothing more. I have to do my job. It's my life, my business. Let me do it."

He contemplated her for a long moment. "This is important to you."

"Of course it is! You threatened to destroy my reputation, which will effectively ruin the company I've built over the last seven years. How would you like it if I had the power to do that to you and then spent all my time trying to seduce you into losing?"

"Elise." He waited until she glanced at him to continue. "I'm sorry. That was not my intent. I like kissing you. That's all. If you want to do another session, I'll be there. Name the time."

Oh, how *dare* he be all understanding and apologetic and smoky-eyed? "How about if I call you?"

She needed Dax gone before she did anything else stupid, like set off on an exploratory mission to see if he still had underwear-model abs under that suit.

"Sure. I can give you some space. Call me when you're ready to pick up where we left off."

Of course he'd seen right through her and then dumped a heck of a double entendre in her lap. Pick up where they left off with the sessions—or with the kiss? And which way would he interpret it?

Which way would she mean it?

She'd just realized something painful and ridiculous. The text messages during his date, letting him kiss her, the supreme sadness of imagining him blissfully in love with his soul mate; it all rolled up into an undeniable truth—she didn't want Dax to be with anyone else.

And she couldn't let herself be with him, even for what would undoubtedly be the best night of her life. It was the morning after when she woke up alone, knowing she hadn't been enough to keep him, and all the mornings alone from then on, that she couldn't do.

That was the best reason of all to get him matched with someone else in a big hurry.

Six

At precisely seven-thirty the next evening, Elise's door-bell rang. And yes, Dax was exactly who she expected to see grinning at her on the other side of the door, both hands behind his back.

"I said I'd call you."

Not that she'd really thought he'd wait around for the phone to ring, but he could have given her at least twenty-four hours to figure out how to call him without creating the impression she wanted him to pick up *exactly* where that kiss had left off.

Which would be really difficult to convey, when truthfully, she did. And now her house was spotless because every time she considered picking up the phone, she cleaned something instead.

"I know. But I'm taking this seriously. For real. Your office isn't the best place to get answers to your questions. So we're going to do it here."

"Here? At my house?" *Bad, bad idea.* "You want to do the profile session on a Saturday night?"

Didn't he have a new woman lined up already? Candy hadn't worked out, but a man like Dax surely wouldn't wait around for Elise to find him some action. Saturday night equaled hot date, didn't it?

"I don't think you fully appreciated the point I made about getting to know me best while on a date." With a flourish, he pulled something from behind his back. A DVD she didn't recognize. "So we're going to watch a movie."

"The profile session is going to be a date?" *She* was his hot date. How in the world had she not seen this coming?

It was straight out of Psych 101—to get the cheese, she had to complete the maze. But why? What was his motivation for forcing her to navigate a date in the first place?

"More of a compromise," he allowed with a nod. "This is not anything close to what I've ever done on a date. But the setting is innocuous and we can both relax. I don't feel like you're grilling me, you don't feel like it's work."

That sounded remarkably like the excuse he'd used to get her to go to lunch, which had proved to be rather effective, in retrospect. "What if I'm busy?"

"Cancel your plans. You want to know what makes me tick?" His eyebrows lifted in invitation. "I'm offering you a shot. Watch the movie. Drink some wine. If you do that for me, I'll answer any question you ask honestly."

Dax gestured with his other hand, which clutched a bottle of cabernet sporting a label she'd only ever seen behind glass at a pricey restaurant.

She shook her head. "This is a thinly veiled attempt to seduce me again."

The sizzling once-over he treated her to should not have curled her toes. Of course, if he'd given her a warning before he showed up, she could have put on shoes.

"I'm not trying to tilt the scales by coming on to you," he insisted. "Trust me, if I wanted you naked, this is not how I would go about it."

As she well knew his seduction routine, she opted to keep her mouth shut. For once.

"I, Daxton Wakefield, will not touch you one single time this whole evening." He marked the statement by crossing his heart solemnly with the DVD case. "Unless you ask me to."

"You're safe on that front. Not that I'm agreeing to this, but what did you bring?" She nodded at the movie against her better judgment.

He shrugged. "An advanced screening copy of *Stardate 2215*. It's that big-budget sci-fi flick coming out Christmas day."

She eyed him. "That's not in theaters yet. How did you get a copy?"

"I have friends in low places." He grinned mischievously. "One of the benefits of being in the media business. I called in a few favors. You like sci-fi and I wanted to pick something I knew you hadn't seen."

Speechless, she held on to the door so she didn't end up in a heap at his feet. She'd never told him what kind of movies she liked, but somehow he'd figured it out, and then went to great lengths to get one. Her heart knocked up against her principles and it was not cool.

Not a seduction, my foot.

But she really wanted to see that movie. And she really wanted to get Dax Wakefield matched to someone else so she could stop thinking about kissing him.

"Truce?" He held out the DVD and the wine with a conciliatory smile and he looked so freaking gorgeous in his $400 jeans and long-sleeved V-neck, she wanted to lap him up like whipped cream.

If that bit of absurdity didn't decide against this idea for her, nothing would.

"I haven't eaten dinner yet."

"Jeez, Elise." He huffed out a noise of disgust. "You're the most difficult woman to not have a date with in the entire United States. Order a pizza. Order twelve. You may have free rein with my credit card if that's what it takes to get me over your threshold."

"Why are you so dead-set on this? Honestly."

He dropped his arms, wine and DVD falling to his sides.

"Believe it or not, this is me leveling the field. You deserve a genuine chance at doing your thing with the questions and the algorithm. This is an atmosphere conducive to giving you that."

Sincerity laced his words, but to clarify, she said, "Because you don't like my office."

Something flitted through his expression and whatever it was scared her a great deal more than the kiss. "Because I have an extremely full week ahead and daylight hours are scarce. I want to give you my undivided attention, without watching the clock."

Her heart knocked again.

"You've just won an evening with a matchmaker." She stepped out of the door frame and allowed Dax passage into the foyer for the second time in two days.

She should have her head examined.

True to his word, he strolled past her without touching, went to the living room and set the wine on the coffee table.

She fetched wineglasses and he ordered the pizza. They settled onto the couch and three sips in, she finally relaxed. "This cabernet is amazing. Where did you find it?"

"In my wine rack." He handed her the remote without grazing her fingers. It was carefully done. "I was saving it for a special occasion."

"Right. Pizza and a movie is special."

He didn't move, didn't touch her at all, but she felt the look he gave her in all the places his kiss had warmed the night before. "The company is the occasion, Elise."

Prickles swept across her cheeks. The curse of the fair-skinned Irish. She might as well take out a billboard proclaiming her innermost thoughts. "We'll get through the profile session much faster if you quit detouring to flatter me with platitudes."

His head tilted as if he'd stopped to contemplate a particularly intriguing Picasso. "Why do you find it so hard to believe that I like you?"

Because he made a habit of working emotions to his advantage. Because he was a swan and she was not. Because to believe would be akin to trusting him.

But she ignored all that in favor of the most important reason. "You don't ruin the reputation of someone you hold in fond regard. If you really like me, prove it. Let's end this now."

"To be fair, I didn't know I was going to like you when I made that deal. But if you do your job, you've got nothing to worry about, do you?" He lifted his glass in a mock toast.

A part of her had hoped he'd take the opportunity to call it off, and she shouldn't be so disappointed he hadn't. Why—because she'd internalized his pretty words? Thought maybe he'd realized she was actually a very nice person and hadn't deliberately set out to ruin his friendship with Leo?

"Hey."

"Hey, what?" she said a touch defensively, pretty sure she had no call to be snippy.

"It's a compliment that I'm holding fast to our deal. You're a smart, savvy woman and if I didn't respect the hell out of you, I'd have let you bow out long before now."

"Bow out? You mean give up and quit? No way."

When he grinned, she deflated a little. He'd phrased it like that on purpose to get her dander up and allow him to slide the nice stuff by her. How did he know how to handle her so well?

"That's why I like you," he said decisively. "We're both fighters. Why else would I be here to put myself through your profile wringer? I can't claim the matchmaking process is bogus unless I submit to it wholly. Then we both know the victor deserves to win."

Now he'd dragged ethics into this mess. She shook her head in disbelief. Against all odds, she liked him too.

Somehow he'd stripped everything away and laid out

some very profound truths. Of all the ways he could have convinced her he really liked her, how had he done it by *not* calling off their deal?

He respected her skills, respected her as a business woman, and she'd been on the defensive since moment one. It was okay to let her guard down. Dax had more than earned it.

"It's hard for me to trust people," she said slowly, watching him to see if he had a clue how difficult a confession this was. "That's why I give you so much grief."

He nodded once without taking his eyes off her. "I wasn't confused. And for the record, same goes."

He stretched his hand out in invitation and she didn't hesitate to take it. Palm to palm, silent mutual agreement passed between them. Warmth filled her as the intensity of the moment unfolded into something that felt like kinship.

Neither of them trusted easily, but each of them had found a safe place here in this circle of two. At least for tonight.

Dax stopped paying the slightest bit of attention to the movie about fifteen minutes in. Watching Elise was much more fun.

She got into the movie the same way she did everything else—with passion. And it was beautiful. He particularly liked the part where she forgot they were holding hands.

There was nothing sexual about it. He didn't use it as an excuse to slide a suggestive fingertip across her knuckle. He didn't yank on her hand and let her spill into his lap, even though nothing short of amnesia was going to get that hot kiss out of his head.

Far be it from him to disrupt the status quo. The status quo was surprisingly pleasant. He'd agreed not to come on to her, and he'd stick to it, no matter how many more times she gave him a hard-on just by looking at him.

Promises meant something to him and he wanted Elise to understand that.

And oddly enough, when he knew there wasn't a snowball's chance for anything above pizza and a movie, it was liberating in a way he'd never expected.

It was new. And interesting. Instead of practicing his exit strategy, he relaxed and enjoyed the company of a beautiful woman who made him laugh. He couldn't wait to find out what happened next.

The pizza arrived, and he let her hand slip from his without protest, but his palm cooled far too quickly.

Elise set the box on the coffee table and handed Dax a bright red ceramic plate. The savory, meaty smell of pepperoni and cheese melded with the fresh-baked crust and his stomach rumbled. Neither of them hesitated to dig in.

Dax couldn't remember ever eating with a woman in front of the TV. It was something couples did. And he'd never been part of one. Never wanted to be, and furthermore, never wanted to give someone the impression there'd be more couple-like things to come.

But this wasn't a date and Elise wasn't going to get the wrong idea. It was nice.

"Thanks for the pizza," she said around a mouthful, which she couldn't seem to get down her throat fast enough. "I never eat it and I forgot how good it is. You do amazing things with a credit card."

She'd meant it as a joke but it hit him strangely and he had a hard time swallowing the suddenly tasteless bite in his own mouth.

Yes, his bank account could finance a small country, and he made sure the women he dated benefited from his hard work, usually in the form of jewelry or the occasional surprise overnight trip to New York or San Francisco. He'd never given it much thought.

Until now. What *did* he have to offer a woman in a relationship? A coat and a credit card. Thanks to his friendly neighborhood matchmaker, it seemed shallow and not... enough. What if Elise did the impossible and introduced him to his soul mate? She was smart and had a good track record. She could actually pull it off.

By definition, his soul mate would be that woman worth making lifelong promises to.

Did he really want to meet her and be so inadequately prepared?

"You're supposed to be asking me questions." Dax gave up on the pizza and opted to drown his sudden bout of relationship scruples with more wine.

Eyebrows raised, Elise chewed faster.

"I suppose I am," she said and washed down the last of her pizza with a healthy swallow of cabernet, then shot him a sideways glance. "Say, you're pretty good. I did forget about work, just like you predicted."

He crossed his arms so he didn't reach for her hand again. It bothered him that he wanted to in the same breath as bringing up the profile questions designed to match him with another woman. "Yeah, yeah, I'm a genius. Ask me a question."

After pausing the movie, Elise sat back against the sofa cushion, peering at him over the rim of her glass. "What does contentment look like?"

This. His brain spit out the answer unchecked. Thankfully, he kept it from spilling out of his mouth. "I spend my day chasing success. I've never strived for contentment."

Which didn't necessarily mean he hadn't found it.

"What if Wakefield Media collapsed tomorrow but you had that woman next to you, the one who doesn't care about what's behind your curtain? Would you still be able to find a way to be content as long as you had her?"

No surprise that Elise remembered what he'd said at

lunch the other day. How long would it take her to figure out he actually *wanted* someone to care?

Nothing was going to happen to Wakefield Media. It was hypothetical, just like the soul mate. So if this was all theoretical, why not have both?

"What if having the woman *and* success makes me content? Is that allowed?"

Somehow, the idea buried itself in his chest and he imagined that woman snuggled into his bed at the end of a long day, not because he'd brought her home, but because she lived there. And they were together but it wasn't strictly for sex—it was about emotional support and understanding—and making love heightened all of that.

Dax could trust she'd stick around. Forever.

"If that's what contentment looks like to you, then of course."

Her catlike smile drove the point home. She'd gotten a response out of him even though he'd have sworn he'd never so much as thought about how to define contentment.

He had to chuckle. "Well played."

Now that he'd defined it, the image of that woman wouldn't dissolve. She didn't have a face or a body type, but the blurred shape was there in his mind and he couldn't shake it.

What was he supposed to do with that?

With a nod at his concession, Elise sipped her wine and contemplated him. "What do you do with your free time?"

Dax grinned and opted to bite back the inappropriate comment about his after-hours activities. "Should I pick something that makes it sound like I have an interesting hobby?"

"No, you should say what you like."

"I like to people-watch," he said.

"Tell me more about that. What's great about people-watching?"

"Spoken in true therapist fashion." He meant it as a joke and she took it as one. He liked amusing her, and it was easy to do so. "People-watching is the best way to figure out what motivates the masses. And it never gets old."

She was really, really good at this, especially when he wasn't trying to weasel his way out of having his psyche split open. Actually, she had a knack for yanking things out of his brain even when he *was* looking for a way to avoid answering her questions.

So there was no point in being anything less than honest. Plus, this environment, this bubble with only the two of them, created a sort of haven, where it didn't seem so terrible to say whatever he felt.

"Go on," she encouraged with a small wave. "Why do you have to figure out what motivates people?"

"Wakefield Media isn't just a top-grossing media company. It's a top-grossing company, period. That's not an accident. I got a degree in psychology instead of business because it's crucial to have a keen understanding of what brings people back for more, especially in the entertainment space."

Wine and pizza totally forgotten, she listened with rapt attention as if he'd been outlining the secrets of the universe, which she couldn't get enough of. "And people-watching helps?"

For a woman who'd moaned so appreciatively over the pizza, she had amazing willpower. She'd only eaten one piece. She was so interested in what he said, food took a backseat. It was a little heady to be worthy of so much focus.

"People can be notoriously loyal to certain shows, and conversely, very fickle. You'd be shocked at how much you can pick up about why when you just sit and observe how people interact."

Her soft smile punched him in the gut. "Your insights must be something else."

"I bet yours would be as good. Do it with me some time."

Now why had he gone and said that? Hadn't he gotten a big enough clue that she didn't want to hang out with him? Look how hard it had been to get her to agree to pizza and a movie.

The wine must be messing with his head.

"I'd like that. It's a date," she said without a trace of sarcasm and he did a double take.

The wine was messing with her head too, obviously.

"A date that's not a date because we're not dating?" She'd been undeniably clear about that last night. Otherwise, he'd never have agreed to keep his hands off of her.

And look what that promise had netted him—this was bar none the most enjoyable evening he'd had in ages, including the ones that did involve sex.

"Right. We're not dating. We're…friends?" she offered hesitantly.

A denial sprang to his lips and then died. *Friends.* Is that what was happening here? Did that explain why he felt as though he could tell Elise anything?

"I don't know. I've never been friends with a woman. Aren't there rules?"

She made a face. "Like we're not supposed to cancel our plans with each other when someone we *are* dating calls?"

"Like I'm not supposed to fantasize about kissing you again." The answering heat in her expression told him volumes about her own fantasies. "Because if that's against the rules, I can't be friends with you."

She looked down, that gorgeous blush staining her cheeks. "You're not supposed to be doing that anyway. Regardless."

He tipped up her chin and forced her to meet his eyes

again because that heat in hers liquefied him. And he craved that feeling only she could produce. "I can't stop."

As he'd just broken his promise not to touch her, he tore his hand away from her creamy skin with reluctance and shoved it under his thigh.

Elise messed with his head. No wine required.

She blinked, banking all the sexy behind a blank wall. "You'll find it surprisingly easy to stop as soon as I match you with someone else. She'll help you forget all about that kiss, which never should have happened in the first place."

There it was again, slapping him in the face. Elise wasn't interested in him. Her main goal was to get him paired off with someone else as soon as possible.

And that was the problem. He didn't want to be matched with another Candy. The thought of another date with another woman who was perfect for him on paper but not quite right in reality…he couldn't do it.

He wanted that blurred woman snuggled into his bed, ready to offer companionship, understanding. Contentment. Instantly, she snapped into focus, dark hair swinging and wearing nothing but a gorgeous smile.

Elise.

Yes. He wanted Elise, and when Dax Wakefield wanted something, he got it.

But if he pursued her, would this easiness between them fall apart? After all, she wasn't his soul mate and that in and of itself meant she couldn't be that woman in his imagination, with whom he could envision a future.

What a paradox. He'd finally arrived at a place in his life where he could admit he'd grown weary of the endless revolving door of his bedroom. And the woman he pictured taking a longer-term spot in his bed wanted to be *friends,* right after she hooked him up with someone else. Whom he did not want to meet.

Where did that leave the wager between them?

Seven

Bright and early Monday morning, Elise sat in her office and plugged the last of the data into the system. Dax had answered every single question and she firmly believed he'd been honest, or at least as honest as he knew how to be when the content involved elements a perpetual player hardly contemplated. But they'd stayed on track Saturday night—mostly—and finished the profile. Finally.

This would be her hour of victory. She'd built a thriving business using nothing but her belief in true love and her brain. Not one thin dime had come from Brenna, and Elise had fought hard to keep herself afloat during the lean years. She would not let all her work crumble.

She was good at helping people find happiness. Matching Dax with someone who could give him that would be her crowning achievement.

She hit Run on the compiler.

Elise Arundel.

Her forehead dropped to the keyboard with a spectacular crash. She couldn't decide whether to laugh or cry.

Of course her name had come up again. The almost-kiss had been enough to skew the results the first time. Now she had a much bigger mess on her hands because she couldn't get the *oh-my-God* real kiss off her mind. Or the not-a-date with Dax, which should have only been about completing the profile, but instead had eclipsed every evening Elise had ever spent with a man. Which were admittedly few.

They'd bonded over pizza and mutual distrust. And—major points—he'd never made a single move on her. When he confessed he still thought about kissing her, it had been delivered with such heartbreaking honesty, she couldn't chastise him for it.

But his admission served as a healthy reminder. Dax liked women and was practiced at getting them. That's why it felt so genuine—because it was. And once he got her, she'd start dreaming of white dresses while he steadily lost interest. They were *not* a good match.

It didn't stop her from thinking about kissing him in return.

Her mixed feelings about Dax had so thoroughly compromised her matchmaking abilities she might as well give up here and now. It wasn't as though she could fiddle around with the results this time, not when it was so clear she couldn't be impartial. Not after Dax had made such a big deal about ethics.

She groaned and banged her head a couple more times on the keyboard. He was going to have a field day with this. Even if she explained that matchmaking was as much an art as a science, which was why she administered the profile sessions herself, he'd cross his arms and wait for her to confess this matchmaking business was bogus.

But it wasn't, not for all her other clients. Just this one.

The truth was, she abhorred the idea of Dax being matched with another woman so much, she'd subconsciously made sure he wouldn't be. It was unfair to his soul mate—who was still out there somewhere—and unfair to Dax. He was surprisingly sweet and funny and he deserved to be with a woman he could fall in love with. He deserved to be happy.

And she was screwing with his future. Not to mention

the future of EA International, which would be short-lived after Dax crucified her matchmaking skills. That would be exactly what *she* deserved.

How in the world could she get out of this?

A brisk knock on her open door startled her into sitting up. Angie poked her head in, and the smirk on her assistant's face did not help matters.

"Mr. Wakefield is here," she said, her gaze cutting to the lobby suggestively.

"Here?" Automatically, Elise smoothed hair off her forehead and cursed. Little square indentations in the shape of keys lined her skin. "As in, here in the office?"

Maybe she could pretend to be out. At least until the imprint of the keyboard vanished and she figured out what she was going to tell him about his match. Because of course that was why he'd jetted over here without calling. He wanted a name.

"I've yet to develop hologram technology," Dax said smoothly as he strolled right past Angie, filling the room instantly. "But I'm working on it. In the meantime, I still come in person."

Hiding a smile but not very well, Angie made herself scarce.

Elise took a small private moment to gorge herself on the visual panorama of male perfection before her. She'd been so wrong. His everyday suit was anything but ordinary and he was as lickable in it as he was in everything else. And then her traitorous brain reminded her he was most lickable *out* of everything else.

Her mouth incredibly dry, she croaked, "I thought you were busy this week. That's what pizza was all about, right?"

He didn't bother with the chair intended for guests. Instead, he rounded the desk and stopped not a foot from her, casually leaning against the wood as if he owned it.

"I am. Busy," he clarified, his gaze avidly raking over her, as if he'd stumbled over a Van Gogh mural amid street graffiti and couldn't quite believe his luck. "I left several people in a conference room, who are this very minute hashing out an important deal without me. I got up and walked out."

For a man who claimed his company was more important than anything, even contentment, it seemed an odd thing to do. "Why?"

His smoky irises captured hers and she fell into a long, sizzling miasma of delicious tension and awareness.

"I wanted to see you," he said simply.

Her heart thumped once and settled back into a new rhythm where small things like finding his real soul mate didn't matter. The wager didn't matter. The rest of her life alone didn't matter. Only the man mattered.

And he wanted to be with her.

"Oh. Well, here I am. Now what?"

He extended his hand in invitation. "I haven't been able to think about anything other than sitting on a park bench with you and watching the world go by. Come with me."

Her chair crashed against the back wall as she leaped up. She didn't glance at the clock or shut her computer down, just took his hand and followed him.

Most men took her hints and left her alone, more than happy to let her stew in her trust issues. Not this one. Thank goodness. She could worry about how wrong they were for each other and how she had to find someone right for him later.

Fall nipped the air and Elise shivered as she and Dax exited the building. Her brain damage apparently extended to braving the elements in a lightweight wool dress and boots.

"Hang on a sec. I need to go back and get my coat."

She turned when Dax spun her back. "Wait. Wear mine."

Shrugging out of his suit jacket, he draped it around her

shoulders and took great care in guiding her arms through the sleeves. Then he stood there with the lapels gripped in his fists, staring down at her as if the act of sharing his warmth had great significance.

"You didn't have to do that," she said as she rolled up the sleeves self-consciously. But she had to do something with her hands besides put them square on his pectorals as she wanted to. "My coat is right in—"

"Humor me. It's the first time I've given a woman my coat because she needed it. I like it on you."

"I like it on me, too." She hunched down in it, stirring up that delicious blend of scent that was Dax, danger and decadence all rolled into one. She could live in this jacket, sleep in it, walk around naked with the silk liner brushing her skin...

Too bad she'd have to give it back.

They strolled down the block to the small urban park across the street from EA International's office building. Dax told her a funny story about a loose dog wreaking havoc at one of his news station studios and she laughed through the whole thing. Their hands brushed occasionally and she pretended she didn't notice, which was difficult considering her pulse shot into the stratosphere with every accidental touch.

She kept expecting him to casually take her hand, as he'd done Saturday night. Just two people holding hands, no big deal. But he didn't.

No wonder her feelings were so mixed. She could never figure out what to expect. For a long time, she'd convinced herself he only came on to her so she'd lose the wager. Now she wasn't so sure.

Dax indicated an unoccupied bench in the central area of the park, dappled by sunlight and perfectly situated to view a square block of office buildings. People streamed to and from the revolving doors, talking to each other, checking their phones, eyeing the traffic to dart across the street.

She'd opted to sit close, but not too close, to Dax. At least until she understood what this was all about. They might have bonded over the fact that neither of them trusted easily, but that didn't mean she'd developed any better ability to do so.

"How does this people-watching deal go?" She nodded at the beehive of activity around them.

He shrugged. "Mostly I let my mind wander and impressions come to me. Like that couple."

She followed his pointed finger to the youngish boy and girl engaged in a passionate kiss against the brick wall of a freestanding Starbucks.

"Eighteen to twenty-five," he mused. "Likely attending the art school around the corner. They both own smartphones but not tablets, have cable TV but not the premium channels, read Yahoo news but not the financial pages, and can tell me the titles of at least five songs on Billboard's Top 100, but not the names of any politicians currently in office except the president."

Mouth slightly agape, she laughed. "You made all that up."

Dax focused his smoky eyes on her instead of the couple and the temperature inside his jacket neared thermonuclear. "He has a bag with the art school logo and they both have phones in their back pockets. The rest is solid market research for that age group. The details might be slightly off, but not the entertainment habits."

"Impressive. Do you ever try to find out if you're right?"

He gave her a look and stretched his arm across the back of the bench, behind Elise's shoulders. "I'm not wrong. But feel free to go ask them yourself."

Carefully, she avoided accidentally leaning back against his arm. Because she wanted to. And didn't have any clue how to navigate this unexpected interval with Dax, or what to think, what to feel.

"Uh…" The couple didn't appear too interested in being interrupted and all at once, she longed to be that into someone, where the passing world faded from existence. "That's okay."

His answering smile relaxed her. Marginally.

Unfortunately, she had a strong suspicion she could get that into Dax.

"Your turn," he said. "What do you see in those two?"

Without censor, she spit out thoughts as they came to her.

"They're at an age where love is still exciting but has the potential to be that much more painful because they're throwing themselves into it without reservation. They're not living together yet, but headed in that direction. He's met her parents but she hasn't met his, because he's from out of state, so it's too expensive to go home with a girl unless it's serious. Next Christmas he'll invite her," she allowed. "And he'll propose on New Year's because it's less predictable than Christmas Eve."

Dax's lips pursed. "That's entirely conjecture."

He was going to make her work for it, just as she'd done to him.

"Is not. He has on a Choctaw Casino T-shirt, which is in Oklahoma, and if they lived together, they'd be at home, kissing each other in private. The rest is years of studying couples and what drives them to fall in love." She recoiled at the smirk on his face. "So, you can cite research but I can't?"

"Cite research all you want. *Validated* research." As he talked, he grew more animated and angled toward her. "You can't study how people fall in love. Emotions are not quantifiable."

"Says the guy with a psychology degree. How did Skinner determine that mice responded more favorably to partial reinforcement? Not by asking them whether they prefer Yahoo or Google news."

A grin flashed on his face and hit her with the force of a floodlight.

She fought a smile of her own and lost. "You study, you make a hypothesis, you test it and *voilà*. You have a certified conclusion."

Only with Dax could she enjoy a heated argument about her first and only love, the science of the heart.

"So tell me, Dr. Arundel." His gaze swept her with some of that heat in a pointed way she couldn't pretend to miss. "What's your hypothesis about me? Break me down the way you did that couple."

The honks and chattering people filled the sudden silence as she searched his face for some clue to what he was after. Besides the obvious. Clearly he was still thinking about kissing her.

And she was pretty sure she wouldn't utter one single peep in protest.

Great. If she couldn't trust him and she couldn't trust herself to remember why they wouldn't work, why was she still sitting here in the presence of a master at seduction?

"Honestly?" He nodded but she still chose her words carefully. "You don't like to be alone, and women fill that gap. You want her to challenge you, to make it worth your while to stick around, which never happens, so you break it off before she gets too attached. It's a kindness, because you don't really want to hurt her. It's not her fault she's not the one."

His expression didn't change but something unsettled flowed through the depths of his eyes.

"What makes you think I'm looking for the one?" he said lightly. But she wasn't fooled. His frame vibrated with tension.

She'd hit a nerve. So she pressed it, hard.

"You never would have agreed to be matched if you weren't. And you certainly wouldn't keep coming back, especially after it didn't work out with Candy."

He shifted and their knees nested together suggestively. Slowly, he reached out and traced the line of her jaw, tucking an errant lock of hair behind her ear, watching her the entire time.

"I came for the match and stayed for the matchmaker."

"Dax, about that—"

"Relax."

His fingers slid through her hair, threading it until he'd reached the back of her neck. She was supposed to *relax* when he touched her like that?

"You're off the hook," he murmured. "I'm officially calling off our wager. Don't be disappointed."

He'd read her mind. Again.

Relief coursed through her body, flooding her so swiftly, she almost cried. She didn't have to confess that she'd skewed the results. He'd never have to know she'd abandoned her ethics.

But without the wager in place, she had no shield against the onslaught of Dax. No excuse to hold him at arm's length. Much, *much* worse, she had no excuse to continue their association.

"You don't think I can match you?"

"I think you can sell ice to Eskimos. But the fact of the matter is I don't want to meet any more women."

"But you have to," she blurted out. If he didn't, how would he ever meet the love of his life? She might have abandoned her ethics, but not the belief that everyone deserved to be deliriously happy.

Calmly, Dax shook his head. "I *don't* have to. I've already met the one I want. You."

A thousand nonverbal sentiments pinged between them, immobilizing her.

She wasn't right for him. He wasn't right for her. They didn't make sense together and she couldn't let herself think otherwise. Not even for a moment.

The best way to stop wishing for things that couldn't be was to match him with someone else, wager or no wager. Then he could be happy.

Elise froze and forcibly removed his hand from her silky hair.

Now that was a shame. He liked the feel of her.

"Me?" she squeaked.

"Come on. Where did you think I was headed?" Apparently, telling a woman you wanted to see her wasn't enough of a clue that you were into her. "It would be a travesty to continue this matchmaking deal when it's not going to happen."

"What's not going to happen? Finding you a match?" Indignation laced her question.

But then he'd known she wouldn't go down without a fight. He'd have been disappointed otherwise. It had taken him most of Sunday to figure out how to maneuver past all her roadblocks. He still wasn't sure if he'd hit on the right plan. Chances were, she'd drop a few more unanticipated blockades.

That's what made it great.

"The concept was flawed from the beginning. And we both know it. Why not call a spade a spade and move on? We've got something between us." He held up a finger to stem the flow of protests from her mouth. "We do. You can't deny it. Let's see what happens if we focus on that instead of this ridiculous wager."

"I already know what's going to happen." A couple of suits walked by and she lowered her voice. "You'll take me to bed, it'll be glorious and you'll be insufferably smug about it. Hit repeat the next night and the next, for what... about three weeks?"

He bit back a grin. "Or four. So what's the problem?"

His grin slipped as she sighed painfully. "That's not what I want."

"You'd rather I fumble around with no clue how to find your G-spot and then act like it's okay when I come before you? Because I grew out of that before I hit my twenties. The smug part might be a little insufferable, but..." He winked. "I think you'll forgive me."

"You know what I'm saying, Dax. Don't be difficult."

He was being difficult?

"You want promises right out of the gate?" His temper flared and he reined it in. "I don't operate like that. No one does."

"Not promises. Just an understanding that we have the same basic goals for a relationship."

He groaned. "This is not a computer program where you get to see the code before executing it. Why can't we take it day by day? Why can't it be like it was Saturday night?" His thumb found the hollow of her ear again. He spread his fingers against her warm neck and she didn't slap his hand away. "Today is pretty good, too. Isn't it?"

Her eyes shut for a brief moment. "Yeah. It's nice. But we want different things and it's not smart to start something when that hasn't changed. Am I supposed to give up the hope for a committed, loving relationship in exchange for a few weeks of great sex?"

"Who said you have to give up anything? Maybe you're going to gain something." A lot of something if he had his way. He waggled his brows. "What have you got against great sex?"

"I'm a fan of great sex, actually." She crossed her legs, pulling herself in tighter. "It's especially great when I can count on it to be great for a long time instead of wondering when the end is coming."

"Let's break down precisely what it is that you want, shall we?" His head tilted as he contemplated the slight woman who'd had him on the edge of his seat since day one. "You want desperately to find your soul mate but when a guy isn't exactly what you envisioned, you run screaming in the other direction. There's no middle ground."

Her fair skin flushed red. "That's not true."

It was, and she needed someone real to get her over her hang-ups and visions of fantasy lovers dancing in her head. "You have check boxes in your mind, profile questions that you want answered a certain way before you'll go for it. No guy could ever perfectly fit the mold. So you stay home on Saturday nights and bury yourself in futuristic worlds to avoid finding out your soul mate doesn't exist."

"Soul mates do exist! I've seen it."

"For some people." It was a huge reversal for him to admit that much, and she didn't miss it. "But maybe not for me, or for you. Did you ever think of that?"

"Never. Every male I've ever met, that's the first thing I wonder. Is he my soul mate?"

Every male? Even him? "But you don't take that first step toward finding out."

"Just as you evaluate every woman to see if she's the one, decide she can't be, and then don't stick around long enough to let her disappoint you."

Deflection. They were both pretty well versed in it when the subject material grew too hot, and digging into the fact that no one ever measured up—for either of them—was smoking. Escaping unsinged seemed more and more unlikely. But neither of them had jumped out of the fire yet.

She was scared. He got that. It squeezed his chest, and what was he supposed to do with that? After all, *he* was the one who scared her.

"Yeah," he allowed. "But I'm willing to admit it. Are you?"

She slumped down in his jacket, which almost swallowed her. Her wry smile warmed him tremendously. She looked so sweet and delectable sitting there wearing a jacket she hadn't tried to manipulate her way into, and an urgent desire to strip her out of it built with alarming speed.

"It's not fair, you know," she complained. "Why can't you be just a little stupid?"

He laughed long and hard at that and didn't mind that she'd evaded his challenge. He already knew the answer anyway.

"I should ask you the same thing. If you'd relax your brain for a minute, we could avoid all this."

"Avoid what? Psychoanalyzing each other under the table?"

"Hell no. That's the part about us that turns me on the most."

"There's no us," she said and looked away. Her cheeks flushed again, planting the strangest desire to put his lips on that pink spot. "What happened to being friends?"

"Would it make things easier for you to stick a label on this thing between us? I'm okay with calling us friends if you are. But be prepared for an extra dose of friendliness."

She snorted. "Let's skip the labels."

"Agreed. With all the labels off the table, let's just see what happens if I do this."

He tipped her chin up and drew her lips close, a hairbreadth from his, letting her get used to the idea before committing.

Her whole body stilled.

He wanted Elise-on-Fire, as she'd been on the couch the first time he'd kissed her, before she freaked out. And he felt not one iota of remorse in pushing her buttons in order to get her there.

"Scared?" he murmured against her lips. "Wanna go home and watch *Blade Runner* for the four-thousandth time?"

"Not with you," she shot back, grazing his mouth as she enunciated, and it was such a deliberate tease, it shouldn't have sent a long, dark spike of lust through his gut.

He pulled back a fraction, gratified when she swayed after him. "Rather do something else with me? All you have to do is ask."

Her irises flared, and he fell into the chocolaty depths. The expanse between them was an ocean, an eternity, the length of the universe, and he wanted to close the gap in the worst way. Holding back hurt. Badly. But he wanted to see if she'd take the plunge.

"Dax," she murmured and her breath fanned his face as she slid both hands on either side of his jaw. "There is something I want to do with you. Something I've been thinking about for a long time."

Whatever it was, he'd do it. This not-quite-a-kiss had him so thoroughly hot it was a wonder he didn't spontaneously combust. "What's that, sweetheart?"

"I want to beat you at your own game," she whispered and the gap vanished.

Hungrily, she devoured him, tongue slick against his, claiming it masterfully. Her hands guided his head to angle against her mouth more deeply, and fire shot through his groin, nearly triggering a premature release the likes of which he'd not had to fight back in almost two decades.

Groaning, he tried to gain some control, but she eased him backward, hands gliding along his chest like poetry, fingers working beneath the hem to feel him up, and he couldn't stand it.

"Elise," he growled as she nipped at his ear. At the same moment, her fingernails scraped down his abs. White-hot lust zigzagged through the southern hemisphere.

They were in public. On purpose—to prevent anything too out-of-control from happening. Of course Elise had smashed that idea to smithereens.

He firmed his mouth and slowed it down. Way down. Languorously, he tasted her as he would fine wine and she softened under his kiss.

Emboldened now that he had the upper hand, he palmed the small of her back and hefted her torso against his. She moaned and angled her head to suck him in deeper, and he nearly lost his balance. Shifting to the back of the bench, he gripped her tighter, losing himself in the wave of sensations until he hardly knew which way was up.

They either needed to stop right now or take this behind closed doors. He pulled back reluctantly with a butterfly caress of his mouth against her temple.

It had to be the former. It was the middle of the day; he had to get back to work and see about the mess he'd left behind. She probably needed time to assess. Analyze. Work through her checklists and talk herself off the ledge.

Breathing hard, she pursed kiss-stung lips and peered at him under seductively lowered lashes. "Did I win?"

Eight

They held hands as they strolled back to Elise's office and she reveled in every moment of it. Dax didn't pause by his car, clearly intending to walk her all the way back inside. Maybe he was caught up in the rush and reluctant to part ways, too.

Wouldn't that be something? Dax Wakefield affected by Elise Arundel.

What was she *doing* with him?

For once, she had no idea and furthermore, didn't care. Or at least she didn't right now. Dax had a magic mouth, capable of altering her brain activity.

"Don't make plans for tonight," Dax said as they mounted the steps to her office. "I'll bring dinner to your house and we'll stay in."

That worked, and she refused to worry about lingering questions such as whether he intended to seduce her after dinner or if it would be a hands-off night. Maybe she'd seduce him before dinner instead.

She grinned, unable to keep the bubble of sheer bliss inside. This was her turn, her opportunity to get the guy.

"A date that's really a date because we're dating now?" she asked.

Insisting she still had to find him a different match had been an excuse, one contrived to avoid wanting him for herself—and to deny that the whole idea scared her. It still did. But it was her turn to be happy and hopefully make Dax happy at the same time. What could it hurt to try?

He scowled without any real heat. "Dating sounds like a label."

"I'm biting my tongue as we speak."

Unfortunately, she suspected she'd be doing a lot of that in the coming weeks. Somehow Dax had made it seem possible to forgo not only labels, but also guarantees about the future. But that didn't mean her personality had changed. She still wanted a happily ever after. She still wanted Dax to find true love.

The park-bench confessional had revealed more than either of them intended, of that she was sure. It was the only thing she was sure of. But she desperately wanted to believe that the raw revelations had opened them both up to trying something new in a relationship. Sticking around for Dax and day-by-day for her.

It required an extreme level of trust she wasn't sure she had in her. Day-by-day might be a blessing in disguise—it gave her time to figure out if she could trust Dax without wholly committing her fragile heart.

Dax opened the door to EA International and uttered an extremely profane word. She followed his gaze to see four women crowded around Angie's reception desk, all of whom turned in unison at the sound of the door. He dropped her hand without comment.

The park-bench kiss euphoria drained when she recognized Candy. The other three women, a brunette, a blonde and a redhead, weren't familiar but they all had a similar look about them as if they shared a hair stylist. And, like Candy, they all could have stepped from the pages of a magazine.

New clients referred by Candy? That seemed unlikely considering things hadn't worked out with Dax. And Elise had yet to find Candy's soul mate. Guiltily, she made a mental note to go through Candy's profile again to see if she could fix that.

"Is this an ambush?" Dax asked and she did a double take at his granite expression.

"An ambush?" Elise repeated with a half laugh.

That was no way to speak to potential customers. She skirted him and approached the women with a smile. "I'm Elise Arundel. Can I help you?"

"We're here to protest." The redhead stepped to the front and gestured to the other ladies to show she spoke for the group. Not only did these women have similar styles, they also wore identical glowers.

Elise took a tiny step backward in her boots and wished she'd bought the Gucci ones with the higher heel.

"Protest?" Automatically, she shook her head because the word had no context. "I don't understand."

Angie shot to her feet, straightening her wool skirt several times with nervous fingers. "I'm sorry, Elise. I was about to ask them to leave."

Dax took Elise's elbow, his fingers firm against the sleeve of his jacket, and nodded to the redhead. "Elise, this is Jenna Crisp, a former girlfriend. You know Candy. Angelica Moreau is the one on the left and Sherilyn McCarthy is on the right. Also former girlfriends."

These were some of Dax's ex-girlfriends. She couldn't help but study the women with a more critical eye. It seemed Dax had been totally honest when he claimed to have no preference when it came to a woman's physical attributes. The women, though all beautiful and poised and polished, were as different as night and day.

Hard evidence of how truthfully Dax had answered at least one of the profile questions led her to wonder if he'd been forthright on all of them from the very beginning.

Which meant he really did think love was pure fiction.

A funny little flutter beat through Elise's stomach. Dax's hand on her arm was meant to comfort her—or hold her back—and she honestly didn't know which one she needed. "What exactly are you here to protest?"

Had Dax texted them with the news that he was interested in Elise or posted it to his Facebook timeline? He'd have to be very slick to have done so without Elise noticing and besides, why would he? None of this made any sense. It might be upsetting for a former girlfriend to find out Dax had moved on, but surely not surprising—the man was still underwear-model worthy, even fifteen years later, and could give Casanova *and* Don Juan kissing lessons.

Jenna crossed her arms and addressed Elise without glancing at Dax. "We're here in the best interest of your female clients. We're protesting you taking him on as a potential match. Don't foist him off on another unsuspecting woman."

Unable to stop blinking, Elise gaped at Jenna, extremely aware of the other women's hardened gazes. Those lined and mascaraed eyes might as well be spotlights.

"I'm sorry, what?"

A hot flush swept up from her neck to spread across her cheekbones. All those eyes on her, including Dax's and Angie's, had done their job to make her uncomfortable. After all, she was wearing Dax's huge jacket, which told its own story, but also turned her figure blocky, like a stout oak tree in a forest of willows.

"He's not interested in a relationship." Candy cleared her throat. "He told me. Flat out. I thought it was so strange. Why would he go to a matchmaker? Then Jenna and I met by accident at Turtle Creek Salon and I found out he's only in your system as part of some wager the two of you made."

The other ladies nodded and the brunette said, "That's where we met Jenna and Candy too, at the salon."

They *did* share a hairdresser. Elise would congratulate herself on the good eye if it made one bit of difference. Her knees shook and she locked them.

Jenna waved at Dax. "He's a cold, heartless SOB who'll screw you over without a scrap of remorse. No woman deserves that in a match. You have to drop him as a client."

Dax's jacket gained about fifty pounds, weighing heavily on her shoulders. These women had no idea Elise had been kissing Dax not ten minutes ago and making plans to have dinner. But Jenna wasn't talking to her directly. Dax wasn't going to screw Elise over.

"This has gone on long enough." Dax stepped in front of Elise to position himself between her and the ex-girlfriends. "Say anything you like about me, but don't involve Elise in your grievances. She has a right to take on whomever she pleases as a client and you have no call to be here."

Dax's staunch defense hit her in the heart and spread. He was a gentleman underneath his gorgeous exterior, and she appreciated the inside *and* the outside equally.

This was a really bad time to discover she might care about him more than she'd realized.

Jenna glared at Dax, fairly vibrating with animosity. "We were still together when you agreed to be a client. Did you tell her that? One would assume your matchmaker might like to know you weren't actually single."

The bottom dropped out of Elise's stomach. Surely that wasn't true. Jenna was spewing half truths in retaliation for Dax's imagined transgressions. That's what all of this was about—scorned women spewing their fury.

The blonde—Sherilyn, if Elise's beleaguered brain recalled correctly—flipped her curls behind her back and put a well-manicured comforting hand on Jenna's shoulder.

"We were dating, yes." Dax's eyes glittered. "But I was very much single. I did not promise you anything beyond our last date. If you chose to read a commitment into it, that's unfortunate, but it has nothing to do with my business at EA International. Nothing to do with Elise. You're using her to exact revenge on me and it won't work."

Let's take things day by day.

It was almost the same as saying no promises past the last date. Elise suspected Dax gave that speech often.

No, Dax was definitely not a liar. He was a player, exactly as advertised. None of these women had been able to change that and Elise couldn't either, whether she took it day by day or not. Her burden was deciding if she could live with no promises and the likelihood he'd be giving that speech to another woman in a few weeks, after he'd moved on from Elise.

Her fragile heart was already closer to the edge of that cliff on Heartbreak Ridge than she'd like.

All the eyes were back on her, burning into her skin. Jenna's were the hottest as she swept Elise with a pointed look that clearly indicated she found her lacking.

"It has everything to do with what kind of company this is. Are you a matchmaker or a gambler? Do women like Candy come in here expecting to meet a compatible man who's also looking for love, only to be disappointed and out a substantial sum of money?"

It was the TV interview all over again, except this time she wasn't naive enough to offer her matchmaking services to Jenna as a way to prove her skills. She had a hunch that woman ate men alive and then let them beg for more. Except for Dax. He'd truly hurt her.

Elise shook her head, hardly sure where to start slashing and burning Jenna's incorrect and provoking statements.

"I'm a matchmaker. Only. I care about helping people find love, even someone like Dax."

"Someone like Dax?" he repeated silkily as he focused his attention on Elise instead of Jenna. "What's that supposed to mean?"

And now everyone had turned against her, even the one person who'd been on her side. Who *should* have been on her side. She and Dax were embarking on something with no label, but which she'd wanted to explore. Or she had before she walked into this confrontation, this *ambush*.

The room started closing in. "It means you don't believe in love, and I naively thought I could show you how wrong you are. But I can't."

Her heart hurt to admit failure. Not only had she failed to accomplish a reversal in Dax's stance with a soul-mate match, she had almost set herself up for a more spectacular disaster by giving in to his day-by-day seduction routine.

She met the gaze of each ex-girlfriend in succession. It wasn't their fault they weren't the one and she held no hostility toward them.

"Dax is no longer a client as of today. So your protest is poorly timed. Candy, I'll refund your money. Expect the credit to appear on your statement within two days. Please see yourselves out."

She fled to her office and shut the door with an unsatisfying click. Slamming it would have been unprofessional and wouldn't have made her feel any less embarrassed. But it might have covered the sob in her throat.

The door immediately opened and Dax ended up on her side of it. He leaned against the closed door. "I'm sorry. I had no idea they were waiting around to pounce on you. It was uncalled for and entirely my fault."

She let her head drop into her hands so she didn't have to look at him. "It's not your fault. And I was talking to you, too, when I said see yourself out."

"I wanted to make sure you were okay."

The evident concern in his voice softened her. And it pissed her off that he could do that.

"I'm not. And you're the last person who can fix it."

"Elise." His hand on her shoulder shouldn't have felt so right, so warm and like the exact thing she needed. "I have to get back to the office, but I'll make it up to you tonight."

Why did he have to be so sweet and sexy and so hard to pin down?

She shrugged it off—the hand, the man, the disappointment. "I can't do this with you."

"Do what? Have dinner with me? We've eaten plenty of meals together and you never had any trouble chewing before."

That was the problem. He wanted it to be dinner with nothing meaningful attached. In a few weeks, she'd end up like Jenna.

"Dinner isn't just dinner and you know it. It's a start and we have different ideas about what we're starting."

"That's completely untrue. Dinner is about spending time together. Making each other feel good. Conversation."

"Sex," she said flatly.

"Of course. I like sex. What's wrong with that?"

"Because I want to get married! I want to be in love. Not right away, but some day, and I need the possibility of that. I need the man I'm with to want those things too," she shouted.

Shouting seemed to be the only way to get through to him. This was not going to work and he kept coming up with reasons why she should feel differently, as though there was something wrong with her because she didn't want to get in line behind the ex-girlfriends.

He swiveled her chair around to face him. "Maybe I will want that. And maybe you want those things but you'll realize you don't want them with me, and you'll think that's okay. Neither of us knows for sure what's going to happen. Nobody does."

No, but she had a pretty good idea what would happen, and it didn't lead to happily ever after. "Did you imagine yourself marrying Jenna while you were dating her?"

He flinched. "Don't let a few disgruntled women spook you."

The flinch answered the question as well as if he'd flat out said *no*.

"I'm not." That might have been the genesis, but the gang of ex-girlfriends had only brought suppressed issues to the surface. "This was a problem yesterday and the day before that. I let a few hot kisses on a park bench turn my brain off."

"So that's it then. You're done here?"

She didn't want to be. God help her, she couldn't let him walk away forever.

"I have more fun with you than with anyone else I've ever spent time with. If we can't be lovers, what's wrong with continuing to be friends?"

He let his hands fall to his sides. "That's what you want?"

"No, Dax. It's not what I want. But it's what I can offer you." She met his slightly wounded gaze without flinching, though her insides hurt to be so harsh. But what choice did she have? "Go back to work and if you still want to hang out *as friends,* you know where to find me."

Friends.

The word stuck in Dax's craw and put him in a foul mood for the remainder of the day. Which dragged on until it surely had lasted at least thirty-nine hours.

What did Elise want, a frigging engagement ring before they could have a simple *dinner* together? He'd never had so much trouble getting a woman to go on a date, let alone getting her between the sheets. He must be slipping.

"Dax?"

"What?" he growled and sighed as his admin scurried backward over the threshold of his office door. "I'm sorry. I'm distracted."

It wasn't just Elise. The Stiletto Brigade of Former Girlfriends had been brutal, digging barbs into him with military precision. He treated women well while dating them, with intricately planned evenings at expensive venues, gifting them with presents. A woman never left his bed unsatisfied. So why all the animosity?

"You don't have to tell me. I needed those purchase orders approved by five o'clock." Patricia pointed at her watch. "Past five o'clock."

"Why can't Roy sign them? He's the CFO," he grumbled and logged in to the purchase order system so he could affix his digital approval to the documents. Why have a chief financial officer if the man couldn't sign a couple of purchase orders?

"Because they're over five hundred thousand dollars and Roy doesn't have that level of purchasing approval. Only the CEO does. As you know, since you put the policy in place," she reminded him with raised eyebrows. "Are you okay?"

"Fine."

He *was* fine. Why wouldn't he be fine? It wasn't as if he'd lost anything with Elise. They hadn't even slept together yet. A couple of really amazing kisses weren't worth getting worked up over.

Actually, to be precise, he and Elise had shared a couple of amazing kisses and a few good conversations. More than a few. Several.

"Why don't you go home?" Patricia asked.

To his lonely, industrial-size loft? Sure, that would fix everything. "Thanks, I will in a few minutes. You're welcome to leave. You don't have to wait on me."

She nodded, backing away from him as if she expected a surprise attack any second, and finally disappeared.

Dax messed around until well after six o'clock, accomplishing exactly zero in the process, and tried not to think about the Vietnamese place where he'd intended to pick up dinner before going to Elise's house. Vietnamese food warmed up well and he'd fully expected to let it get good and cold before eating.

So Elise hadn't been on board with taking their whatever-it-was-with-no-label to the next level after the run-in with the Stiletto Brigade. They'd freaked her out, right when he'd gotten her panic spooled up and put away.

Fine. He was fine with it.

Elise wanted all her check boxes checked before she'd commit to dinner. It was crazy. She'd rather be alone than spend a little time with a man who thought she was funny and amazing and wanted to get her naked.

Actually, that wasn't true. She was perfectly fine with being friends. As long as he kept his hands to himself and didn't complain when she made astute, painful observations about his relationship track record.

He fumed about it as he got into his car and gunned the engine. He fumed about it some more as he drove aimlessly around Dallas, his destination unclear.

Dax shook his off morose mood and focused on his surroundings. The side-street names were vaguely familiar but he couldn't place the neighborhood. He drove to the next stoplight, saw the name of the intersection, and suddenly it hit him.

He was a block from Leo's house.

House, fortress, same thing when it came to his former friend. Leo had excelled at keeping the world out, excelled at keeping his focus where it belonged—on success. Dax slowed as the car rolled toward the winding, gated drive. The huge manor skulked behind a forest of oaks, bits of light beaming between the branches stripped of leaves by the fall wind.

Was Leo at home? Hard to tell; the house was too far from the street. Once upon a time, Dax would have put money on the answer being no. For as long as he'd known Leo, the man worked until he nearly dropped with exhaustion. Occasionally, when Dax found himself between women, he'd coax his friend out from behind his desk and they'd tie one on at a bar in Uptown.

Case in point—Dax had no woman on call. No plans. It would have been a great night to meet up with a friend who didn't ask him pointed questions about why he never stuck it out with a woman longer than a few weeks.

He didn't call Leo. He didn't drive up to the security

camera at the gate, which was equipped with facial recognition software, and would admit him instantly.

Leo wasn't that friend, not any more. Leo had a new playmate locked away inside his fortress, one he'd paid a hefty chunk of change to meet.

Well, not really a playmate since he'd married Daniella. *Married.* That was a whole lot of forever with the same woman. If Elise could be believed, Leo and Daniella were soul mates.

For the first time, Dax wondered if Leo was happy. Because wasn't that the point of a soul mate? You had someone you wanted to be locked away with, someone you could be with all the time and never care if the world spun on without either of you.

If Dax's soul mate existed, she would care very much what was behind his curtain and furthermore, he'd trust her with the backstage mess—the doubts about whether he actually had something to offer a woman in a relationship. The anxiety over whether he'd find out he had more in common with his mother than he'd like. The fear that he actually lacked the capacity to be with one person for the rest of his life. The suspicion that he was broken and that was why he'd never found someone worthy of promising forever to.

Five hundred thousand dollars seemed like a bargain if it bought a woman who stilled his restlessness. Dax had just spent twice that with the click of a mouse, and barely glanced at the description of the goods Wakefield Media had purchased. Whatever it was—likely cameras or other studio equipment—would either wear out or be replaced with better technology in a few years.

A soul mate was forever. How could that be possible for someone like Dax? What if he'd already met her and didn't realize it? That was the very definition of being broken, and it was exactly what Elise had meant when she'd said "someone like Dax."

Before he did something foolish, such as drive up to Leo's house and demand an explanation for how Leo had known Daniella was his soul mate, Dax hit the gas and drove until the low fuel light blinked on in the dash. He filled up the tank and went home, where he did not sleep well and his mood did not improve.

The next day dragged even worse than the day before. Everyone, including Patricia, steered clear, and while he appreciated their wisdom, it only pissed him off. He needed a big-time distraction.

Because he was in that perverse of a mood, he pulled out his phone and texted Elise.

Have a nice evening by yourself?

Well, that was stupid. Either she'd ignore him, tell him what a fabulous evening she had without him or make a joke that gave him zero information about whether she was in as bad of a mood as he was. And he wanted her to be. He wanted her to suffer for...

Beep. No. It sucked. I miss you.

His heart gave a funny lurch and the phone slipped from his nerveless fingers. God, what was he supposed to do with that?

Nothing. She was trying to manipulate him. She knew he didn't like to be alone and wanted him to crack first. That wasn't happening. He wasn't texting her back with some cheesy message about how he was miserable too. She was probably sitting there on that champagne-colored couch in her condo, phone in hand, waiting for his reply.

They weren't dating. Elise wasn't his lover. It shouldn't be this difficult.

He set the phone off to the side of his desk and proceeded to ignore it for the next thirteen minutes while he read the same paragraph of a marketing proposal over and over again.

The phone sat there, silently condemning him.

"Stop looking at me," he growled at the offending device and turned it over.

Elise wanted him to be some fairy-tale guy who swept her off her feet with promises of undying love, and it was so far from who he was, he couldn't even fathom it. So that was it. Nothing more to say or do.

The phone rang.

Elise. Of course she wasn't going to put up with his stupid text embargo. His heart did that funny dance again as he flipped the phone over to hit the answer button.

"Hey, Dax," a female voice purred in his ear. It was not Elise.

Dang it. He should have at least glanced at the caller ID. "Hey…you."

He winced. He had no idea who she was.

"I've been thinking a lot about you since yesterday," she said.

Sherilyn. He recognized her voice now and if he hadn't been moping around like a lovesick teenager with an atrophied brain, he'd never have answered her call. "Yesterday when you and the rest of your wrecking crew stormed into a place of business and started telling the proprietor how to run it?"

Which wasn't too far off from what he'd done to Elise, but he'd staged his showdown over EA International's formula for success on TV. He swallowed and it went down his throat like razor blades. In his defense, at the time he hadn't known how much she hated being in the spotlight. She'd handled herself admirably, then and yesterday. Because she was amazing.

"Oh, I wasn't really a part of that." Sherilyn *tsk*ed. "I went along because I had a vested interest in seeing that you no longer had a shot at getting matched. I'm in the mood for round two with you."

What a mercenary.

"I'm sorry, Sherilyn, but I'm not interested in a relationship with anyone right now. You heard Candy. It would be unfair to you."

He did not want to have this conversation. Not with Sherilyn, not with Candy, not with any woman. He was sick of the merry-go-round.

"Come on. Remember how good it was?" Sherilyn laughed throatily. "I'm not asking for a commitment, Dax. Just one night."

Her words reverberated in his head, but he heard them in his voice, as he said them to Elise. And of course the idea had seemed as repugnant to Elise when it came from him as it did now to Dax coming from Sherilyn.

Why hadn't Elise slapped him? Instead, she'd offered him friendship, which he'd thrown back in her face because he'd wanted things his way, not hers. And he'd lost something valuable in the process.

Dax sighed. "No, actually, I don't remember. Thanks for calling, but please forget about me. We're not going to happen again."

He hung up and stared out the window of his office. He might as well go ahead and admit he missed Elise, too, and had no idea how to fix it.

The Stiletto Brigade hadn't caused his problem with her. The problem had been there from the beginning, as she'd said. He'd discounted Elise's hopes and dreams because they were based on something he considered absurd and improbable—true love. Yeah, he'd done the profile and gone along, but only to win the wager fairly, not because he believed she had some special ability to prove something that was impossible to prove. Yet she'd built an entire business on the concept, and if someone as smart as Leo bought into Daniella being his soul mate, maybe there was more to the idea than Dax had credited.

Maybe he should give Elise's way a chance.

Or...

Love was a myth and now that some time had passed, the new marriage smell had worn off, but Leo was too embarrassed to admit he'd made a mistake. If Dax gave in to Elise without more information, he could be setting himself up for a world of hurt. After all, he didn't trust easily for a reason. Look what had happened to his friendship with Leo.

Besides, Elise wanted to meet her soul mate and Dax was not it. Their vastly different approaches to relationships—and to life as a whole—proved that. So why pretend?

There was nothing wrong with two consenting adults having fun together. They didn't have to swear undying devotion to take their relationship to the next level.

Why was she being so *stubborn* about this?

Leo might be too ashamed to come clean about how disastrous his relationship had become with Daniella, but Elise had lots of other clients. Surely several of EA International's former matches hadn't lasted. An unhappily ever after was a better way to attest that love was a myth than being matched with another Candy, anyway.

All he needed was one couple who hadn't ended up with their soul mate as advertised. Then he could take the evidence to Elise. She needed to understand how the real world worked, and what better way to convince her? He'd have hard proof that even when people started out wanting a lifelong commitment, sometimes it still didn't happen. Sure, she might be a little upset at first to learn she'd held out for something that didn't exist, but then she'd see his point. She wanted him as much as he wanted her, and it was time to let things between them take their natural course.

Guarantees were for products, not people. By this time tomorrow, he could have Elise naked and moaning under his mouth.

Nine

Saturday night, Elise finally stopped carrying her phone around in her hand. Dax hadn't called, hadn't texted, hadn't dropped by. He wasn't going to. The line had been drawn, and instead of doing something uncomfortable like stepping over it, Dax had hightailed it in the other direction. His loss.

And hers, unfortunately. She couldn't shake a slight sense of despondency, as though she hadn't seen the sun in weeks and the forecast called for more rain.

It was a good thing she'd put on the brakes when she had—imagine how hurt she'd be if things had gone any further. Regardless, she was undeniably disappointed he didn't even want to stay friends, which she had to get over.

She needed to focus on Blanca and Carrie, the two new applicants in her makeover program. They were both due to arrive in a couple of weeks and Elise had done almost nothing to prepare.

She tapped out a quick email to Dannie, who helped Elise with makeup and hair lessons when needed. After years at the knee of a supermodel, Elise had enough fashion and cosmetic tips to fill an ocean liner, but Dannie liked the work and by now, the two women were fast friends.

Elise confirmed the dates and attached a copy of a contract for Dannie's temporary employment. Normally, it wouldn't be a question of whether Dannie would say yes, but she and Leo had just returned from an extended vacation to Bora Bora in hopes Dannie would come home pregnant.

Elise would be thrilled if that was the reason Dannie said no.

Then she made a grocery list as two extra mouths required a great deal of planning, especially to ensure the meals were healthy but not too difficult to prepare. Few of the women in her program came to her with great culinary skills. It was one of the many aspects of training she offered, and after a lifelong love-hate relationship with food, Elise brought plenty to the literal and figurative table.

The remainder of the evening stretched ahead of her, long and lonely. She flipped on a movie, but her mind wandered.

The doorbell startled her and she glanced at the clock. Good grief, it was nearly midnight. It could only be Dax. A peek through the window confirmed it. Despite the shadows, she'd recognize the broad set of his shoulders and lean figure anywhere.

Her heart lightened. She'd missed him, fiercely.

She took a half second to fortify herself. He could be here for any number of reasons. Better to find out straight from the horse's mouth than get her hopes up.

"I wasn't expecting you," she said needlessly as she opened the door and cursed the jumpy ripples in her stomach. He was just so masculine and gorgeous. Then she got a good look at his face. The sheer darkness in his gaze tore through her. "What's wrong?"

Tension vibrated through the air as he contemplated her. "I don't know why I'm here."

"Bored? Lonely? Can't find anyone else who wants to play?" She crossed her arms over her middle. Something was up and it was far more chilling than the frigid fall night.

"On the contrary," he said smoothly, his voice like pure honey. "Women seem to be coming out of the woodwork. Except for the one I really want."

Her?

Why was that so affecting in places better left unaffected? It should irritate her to be thought of as an object of lust. The idea shouldn't feel so powerful and raw. But a week's worth of being on edge and missing their verbal swordplay and dreaming about his abs culminated in a heated hum in her core.

"I…" *Want you too.* "…hoped you'd call."

"Did you?" He hooked his thumbs in the front pockets of his jeans, but the lethal glint in his eye belied the casual pose. "What did you hope I'd say? Let's be friends? Let's paint each other's nails and shop for shoes together?"

She should shut the door. She should tell him to go away and forget she'd ever mentioned being friends.

"I hoped you'd unbend enough to admit there's a possibility you might fall in love one day. Barring that, I hoped you'd still want to have lunch occasionally or—"

"Elise. I don't want to be your friend."

"Not worth it to you?" she snapped.

"It's not enough." His hands fisted against his pockets and she realized he was trying to keep himself under control. "I wasn't going to call. I wasn't going to come over. I found myself within a block of your house five times this week all the same."

"But you kept driving."

He nodded once. "I kept driving. Until tonight."

After a long pause, she voiced the question he obviously wanted her to ask. "What was special about tonight?"

"I can't—I don't know how to give you what you want," he bit out. "And I don't know how to stay away."

Her heart stuttered and shoved all her suppressed feelings to the surface. That's why she'd missed him—when he showed her glimpses of his soul, it was more beautiful than the ocean at sunset.

"I never asked you to stay away. You shouldn't have."

"Yes. I should have. I absolutely should not be here on your doorstep." His chest shuddered with his next deep breath. "But I can't sleep. I can't concentrate. All I can think about is you naked, wrapped around me, and that brain of yours firing away on all cylinders as you come up with more inventive ways to challenge me."

The image of her unclothed body twined with his sprang into her consciousness, sparked through her abdomen, raised goose bumps on her skin. She swallowed against the sudden burn in her throat.

"You say that like it's a bad thing," she joked and nearly bit her tongue as fire licked through his expression.

"It's ridiculous. And I'm furious about it, so stop being so smug."

His glare could have melted ice. All at once, his strange mood made sense. Normally when he wanted a woman, he seduced all her reservations away. But he respected Elise too much to do that to her and he was incredibly conflicted about it. The effect of that realization was as powerful as being the object of his desire.

Combined, it nearly took her breath.

"Poor thing," she crooned. "Did that bad Elise tie you up in knots?"

One brow lifted and every trace of his ire disappeared, exactly as she'd intended. "Don't you dare make a suggestion like that unless you plan to follow through."

"Uh-uh." She shook her head. "This conversation is not devolving into foreplay."

"Not yet." Lazily, he swept her with a half-lidded smoky once-over. "But I appreciate the confirmation that talking dirty to you counts as foreplay."

Now she should slam the door in his cocky face. Except she'd shifted the mood on purpose, to give him a reprieve for confessing more than he'd probably intended. And the last thing she wanted was for him to leave.

But did she want him to stay? This wasn't some random drive-by; it was a showdown.

Between his mercurial mood and the hum in her core, this night could end up only one of two ways—either she'd let him into her bed and into her heart, or she'd give him that final push away.

Dax was still on the porch. Waiting for her to make the decision. And Dax would never let her forget she'd made the choice.

Who was tying whom up in knots here?

"Why are you here, Dax?" She took a tiny step behind the door, in case she needed to slam it after all. Of course there was a good chance he'd slam it for her, once he crossed the threshold and backed her up against it in a tango too urgent and wild to make it past the foyer. "And don't feed me another line. You know exactly why you got out of the car this time."

His reckless smile put her back on edge. "Why do I find it so flipping sexy when you call me on my crap?"

He thought her no-filter personality was sexy. He really did. She could see the truth of it in his expression. The wager was over and there was no reason for him to say something like that unless he meant it.

"Because you're neurotic and deranged, obviously." When his smile softened, she couldn't help but return it, along with a shrug. "We both must be. If you want the real answer, you said it yourself. You like that I challenge you. If it's easy, you don't value it as much."

His irises flashed, reflecting the bright porch light. "I would definitely classify this as not easy."

"And you still haven't told me why you're here."

He crossed his arms and leaned on the door frame. "Have you ever followed up with any of the couples you've matched?"

"Of course. I use them as referrals and I throw parties every few months for both former and current clients as a thank-you for being customers. Many become friends."

"They're all happy. All of them. They've all found their soul mates and say you were one hundred percent responsible." He said it as if Elise had single-handedly wiped out a small village in Africa with a virus.

"You talked to my former clients?"

The shock wasn't that he'd done so, but that he'd *just* done so. Why hadn't he had those conversations at the very beginning, when they were still operating under the terms of the wager?

"Not the recent ones, only those matched over five years ago. They should be miserable by now. Happily ever after doesn't exist." His rock-hard expression dared her to argue with his perfunctory statement.

Except he'd learned otherwise, and clearly it was throwing him for a loop.

He hadn't talked to her clients before now because he'd assumed he didn't need to. That he'd only be told what he already believed to be true.

It was hard to be handed back your arrogance on a silver platter.

"I offer a guarantee, Dax," she reminded him gently. "No one's ever asked for their money back."

Instead of bowing and scraping with apology, he stared at her. "Aren't you going to invite me in?"

"Why would I do that?"

His gaze burned through her. "Because you want to know what else I learned when I talked to your clients."

He'd learned *more* than happily ever after happened to people on a regular basis? Oh, yes, he had and he was going to make her work to find out what, running her through his maze until she dropped with exhaustion. Or solved it and won the prize. It was a ludicrous challenge. And it was working.

But she didn't for a moment believe he only wanted to

tell her about his findings. The prize wasn't simply information and they both knew it.

She held the door open wide in silent invitation and
prayed she wasn't going to be sorry.

She shouldn't have answered the bell. But now she had
to know if talking to happy couples had somehow opened
his eyes. Maybe gotten him to a place where he could see
a future with one woman.

What if she *could* be that woman? She didn't want to
send him on his way before finding out.

"Dax?"

He met her gaze as he stepped over the threshold.
"Elise."

Searching his beautiful face for some small scrap of re-
assurance, she put it all on the line.

"Please don't do this unless you mean it."

Dax shut the door behind him and leaned back against
it, both hands flat against the wood.

The click reverberated in the silent foyer.

Elise's eyes were shiny and huge and he didn't mistake
the look for anything other than vulnerability, which just
about did him in where the last week of awfulness hadn't.

Why had he stayed away so long?

It didn't matter now. He was surrounded by Elise and
everything finally made sense again. He breathed her in
before he hauled her into his arms right there in the foyer.

Tonight wasn't about slaking his thirst in the well of
Elise, though he'd be lying if he said he wasn't hopeful
they'd eventually get there. He'd have sworn this was all
about taking pleasure where pleasure was due. But now that
he was here…it wasn't. He still wasn't sure *what* tonight
was about, what he truly wanted—or what she wanted—
but the fragile quality to her demeanor wasn't doing his
own brittle psyche any favors.

Don't do this unless you mean it.

He didn't pretend to misunderstand. Her voice broke as she'd said it and it echoed in his head, demanding an answer—which he didn't have.

They needed to shake off the heaviness.

"Don't do what?" he asked lightly. "Tell you about the nineteen conversations I had with blissfully happy couples? It was nauseating."

Her quick smile set off an explosion of warmth in his midsection.

"Nineteen? That's a lot of conversations about true love. What I don't get is why you'd subject yourself to that."

He shrugged. "Seek-and-destroy mission. I was sure I'd find at least one couple embroiled in a bitter divorce settlement. Needless to say, no one was. On the heels of that estrogen ambush in your office, I needed to figure out some things."

Guilt flickered across Elise's face. "I'm sorry that happened. Some of that must have been really hard to stomach, especially coming from women you were formerly intimate with. I was selfishly caught up in my own reaction and didn't think about how you must have felt."

"Uh…" He'd been about to brush it away. But this was Elise. She'd see through him in a second. How had she known the whole thing had bothered him so much?

So much for lightening the mood.

"I was more worried about you than me," he said gruffly. "But thanks."

Such a small word to encompass the full generosity of Elise's apology. A lot of women—most women—would have said he'd gotten what was coming to him. And maybe he had. He'd treated Jenna pretty shabbily. He sighed. There was a possibility all of the women had genuine grievances. Relationships were not his forte.

But he wanted that to be different.

Elise motioned him out of the foyer and walked into the living room. "So while talking with my clients, what did you figure out?"

He followed, caught up with her in a couple of steps and grasped her hand to swing her around to face him in front of a gas-log fireplace, the flame lowered to a romantic glow.

Don't do this unless you mean it.

But that was exactly it. He *wanted* meaning, wanted something to finally click.

"I figured out *I'm* the one missing something." And only Elise held the answer. "I got out of the car tonight because I want to know what it is. You're the relationship expert. Tell me."

Her skin was luminous in the firelight and he wanted to trace the line of her throat with his lips, then keep going to discover the delights of the trim body waiting for him under her off-white sweater. But he wanted to hear her response just as much.

She looked up, hand still in his. Flesh to flesh, it sparked and the answering awareness leaped into her expression. Something powerful that was part chemistry and part something else passed between them. He let it, embraced it, refused to disrupt the moment simply because he'd been off balance since the moment this woman insisted he call her Ms. Arundel.

He tightened his grip. He wasn't about to let her step away, either.

"Tell me what I'm missing, Elise."

"What if I show you?" Her voice scraped at him, raw and low.

"What if you did?" he murmured. "What does that look like?"

"It looks like two people connecting on a fundamental level." Without breaking eye contact, she slid her free hand up his chest and let it rest over his heart, which sped up under her fingers. "It looks like the start of a long kiss that you can't bear to end. It looks like a friendship that's made more beautiful because you've opened your soul along with your body. Have you ever had that before?"

"No," he said, shocked at the catch in his throat. Shocked at how much he suddenly wanted something he'd had no clue existed.

"Me, either."

The wistful note of her admission settled over him heavily, binding them together in mutual desire for something meaningful and special.

"How do we get it?"

"It's right here," she whispered, tapping the place over his heart once with an index finger, then touching her own heart. "For both of us. All we have to do is reach out at the same time. That's what makes it wonderful."

Everything inside woke up at once, begging to dive into not just the sensations, but the swirl of the intangible. He'd called off the wager strictly because he'd begun to suspect he was about to lose. Spectacularly. And as he looked into her soul, it was done.

He was lost.

"Elise." He palmed her chin and lifted those luscious lips to his and hovered above them in a promise of pleasures to come. "I mean it."

And then he fell into that long kiss he hoped would never end and wrapped Elise in his arms. When his knees buckled, he took her to the carpet with him, twisting to break her fall, sliding into a chasm of pure joy.

She found the hem of his shirt and spread her palms hot against his back. He groaned and angled his head to take the kiss deeper, to explore her with his tongue, to taste the beauty of her.

This wasn't an urgent coupling, a slaking of mutual

thirst. It was more. Much more. Profound and meaningful. And he couldn't have stopped if his life depended on it.

He wanted Elise. Wanted it all, everything she'd offered, especially the emotional connection.

She lifted her head a fraction. "Dax?"

"Hmm?" He took the opportunity to run his lips down the column of her neck, exactly as he'd envisioned, and yes, it was sweet. She moaned, letting her head fall back to give him better access.

"Don't you want to go upstairs?" she asked after a good long minute of letting him taste her.

Upstairs was far away and required too much effort to get there.

"Not especially. I don't think I can wait that long." That gorgeous blush rose up in her cheeks. Mystified, he ran the pad of his thumb over the coloring. "What's this all about?"

"We're in the living room," she whispered.

"I know," he whispered back and snaked a hand under her sweater to feel the curve of her waist in an intense caress. "I'm becoming very fond of your living room. The fireplace is a nice touch."

"I just...you know. The living room is for watching TV. The bed is for...lying down. In the dark."

More blushing. Despite the rock-hard bulge in his pants and the near-breathless state of desire she'd thrown him into, he recognized a woman in the midst of uncertainty. But over what?

"I'm not a particular fan of darkness. I want to see you."

"There's uh...not much to see." She wiggled a little until his hand fell from her waist, and then she yanked the hem of her sweater down over her exposed skin with a little too much force.

Sitting back on the carpet a bit to give her space, he reached out and took her hand gently. The last thing he wanted was for her to be uncomfortable. "What happened to opening yourself body and soul? Isn't that what this is about?"

"Easier said than done." She made a face. "Especially when I'm up against such stiff competition."

Competition?

Then it dawned on him. The Stiletto Brigade. They'd not only spooked her, they'd given Elise a complex about her appearance. His heart flipped over painfully but when it faded, a strange sort of tenderness replaced it.

"Look at me." When she complied, the earlier vulnerability was back tenfold. "There's not a way to say this without sounding arrogant, but roll with it for a minute. Don't you think I could be in the bed of any woman I chose?"

Her brows furrowed. "Yeah, but that wasn't really in question."

He gave her a minute but her anxiety didn't fade. A smart woman was still susceptible to being deceived by her own self-consciousness, apparently. "Then wouldn't it be safe to assume I'm with the woman I want? And that I think you're beautiful beyond compare?"

Except he'd done almost nothing to convince her of that because their relationship had evolved in such an out-of-the-norm manner. He'd never sent her flowers, never bought her jewelry, and certainly never spent an evening flattering her over dinner.

But he didn't want to do those things with her. He'd done them with other women. A lot. And it had never amounted to more than a shallow bit of nothingness designed to get a woman in bed.

Elise deserved better.

He slid a hand through her hair and smoothed it away from her face. "Instead of telling you how I feel about you, how about if I show you?"

Ten

The corners of Elise's mouth lifted. "What does that look like?"

Obviously she'd recognized her own words as he repeated them back to her.

"It looks like something so stunning, I can hardly breathe." Watching her intently, he fingered the hem of her sweater and lifted it slowly until her stomach was bared. Then he stopped. "Do you trust me with the rest?"

Surprise flitted through her expression. "I...I never thought about this being about trust."

"Of course it is. We're reaching out at the same time, but doing so requires a measure of faith. On both sides."

She stilled, taking it all in, and in a flash, he got the distinct sense she had a lot less experience with men and sex in general than the majority of women he knew. She talked such a good game he'd missed it, but with all the discussion around competition and being embarrassed about the locale he'd chosen, not to mention how often he found her home alone on the weekends...it all fit.

Then she nodded and lifted her arms, silently offering him access to completely remove her top—and placing utter trust in him at the same time. It just about broke him. Sucking in oxygen, which did not settle his racing pulse, he took his time unveiling her, inch by creamy, gorgeous inch.

She wasn't wearing a bra. And her breasts were perfect,

topped by peaks that went rigid under his heated gaze. He muttered a curse as his hands involuntarily balled up, aching to stroke her from neck to belly button. *Take it slow, Wakefield.*

"You're exquisite," he ground out through a throat gone frozen, and tossed the sweater aside, unable to tear his attention from her half-naked form. Nonsense spilled from his mouth, murmured words of praise and awe. So maybe he'd tell her how much he liked her body in addition to showing her.

"Your turn," she whispered.

Immediately he complied, whipping his shirt off as fast as humanly possible because there was no way he was letting fabric block his ability to drink in the sight of gorgeous, uncovered Elise.

"Look your fill," he advised her. "Here in the light."

Look her fill she did, hesitantly at first but then with a hungry boldness that somehow turned erotic instantly. As her gaze traveled over his bare torso, heat flushed across his skin and coalesced at the base of his spine. All the blood in his head rushed south, leaving him slightly dizzy and enormously turned on.

She was going to kill him.

"Get used to me without clothes," he continued. "I'm about to be a whole lot more naked. I want you to see how much you affect me when I look at you. How much I want you, how gorgeous you are to me."

No time like the present to shed his jeans. He stood and with the heat of the fire at his back and the heat of Elise at his front, he flipped the button. She watched, silently, her head tipped up and her lips parted, hands clasped in her lap tightly.

He should have opened with a striptease because she'd totally forgotten her own nakedness. Win-win.

Then he was fully undressed and she huffed out a strangled gasp. It was potent to render a woman with such a quick wit speechless.

"See this?" he pointed at the obvious erection straining toward her. "This is all you, honey. You're not even touching me and I'm about to bust."

He wasn't kidding. Show and Tell was turning into his favorite foreplay game ever.

"What if I wanted to touch you?" she asked coyly. "Is that allowed?"

He strangled over a gasp of his own. "That's more than allowed. In fact, it's encouraged."

Crawling to him, she wiggled out of the remainder of her clothes unprompted and knelt at his feet.

With incredible care, she ran her hands up his legs, fingering the muscles of his thighs, breezing by his erection. She grazed it and his eyelids fluttered with the answering spike of unadulterated pleasure.

She climbed to her feet to continue her exploration and he fought to stay still. Every nerve vibrated on full alert, poised to pounce at the first opportune moment.

"You still have gorgeous abs," she murmured as her fingertips read the muscles of his torso like braille. "They feel like warm, velvet stone."

"Looked me up on Google, did you?" He grinned, pleased for some ridiculous reason. Millions of people had seen those ads and he'd never given it a moment's thought. But the idea of Elise taking secret pleasure in looking at pictures of him—it was hot. "Put your hands a little south of my abs and you'll find something else that feels like velvet stone."

There came the blush again and he should totally be chagrined that he'd provoked it on purpose. But he wasn't.

Glancing at the real estate in question and back up again quickly, she gave a little sigh of appreciation that sang right through him. "I do that to you? Really?"

He groaned in disbelief and frustration. "You have been for weeks and weeks. Years. For an eternity. And now I'm moving on to the 'show' part of this demonstration."

Catching her up in his arms, he fitted hungry lips to her mouth and let all the pent-up desire guide the kiss. Instantly, she melted against him and he took full advantage, winding his embrace tighter to fit her luscious little body against him.

She felt amazing, warm and soft, and he wanted to touch. So he did, running his hands down her back, along the sweet curve of her rear, and he nearly cried out when she responded in kind. Her hands were bold and a bit clumsy with eagerness and combined, it swirled into a vortex of need more powerful than any he'd ever felt before.

This was so far beyond simply taking pleasure and returning it, he couldn't fathom it.

The urge to make this cataclysmic for her became more important than breathing.

He picked her up easily and laid her out on the couch where he could focus on loving every inch of her. Kneeling between her amazing legs, he inched over her until they were skin to skin, but his full weight rested on his elbows on either side of her.

"Talk to me," he murmured as he nuzzled her neck.

"Talk to you about what?" she asked.

He lifted his head so he could speak to her directly.

"Tell me what you like, Elise."

As passionate as she was about connection and relationships, she'd probably be incredibly responsive to anything he did, but he'd prefer to start out educated.

She bit her lip, contemplating. "Shoes. And this is a horrible thing to admit, but I really, really like chocolate."

He couldn't even laugh. She truly had no clue he'd meant for her to tell him what she liked sexually. Probably no one had ever asked her before or she had less experience than he'd assumed. The seriousness of the trust she'd shown hit him in a place inside he'd never realized was there.

"Why is it horrible to like chocolate?"

"Because it goes straight to my hips. I gain weight easily."

"That's impossible." Because he wanted to and he could, he shifted onto his side and ran the back of his hand down the curve of her waist, over the not-chunky hip and around her thigh, and it was nice indeed. "You're so thin you'd have to run around in the shower to get wet."

She snorted. "Thanks, but I didn't always look like this."

The small slice of pizza, the unfinished lunches, came back to him suddenly. She really didn't eat much. And somehow, this fear of gaining weight was tied to her self-image issues.

"You'd be beautiful to me even if you weighed more." In fact, she could stand to gain a few pounds.

"I thought we were doing the show part," she said pertly and slid her leg along his, opening herself without seeming to realize it. It was so unconsciously sexy, he let her change the subject. Plus, the new subject was one he happened to approve of.

"Yeah?" he growled. "You like it when I show you how much you turn me on? Let's begin with exhibit A."

And then he mouthed his way down her stomach to the juncture of her thighs, parting them easily, and she gasped as he tasted her sweet spot, laving it lightly to give her time to adjust to such an intimate kiss.

Her hips rolled, shoving his lips deeper against her wet center, and he sucked. She moaned on a long note and that was it—she pulsed against his tongue with a little cry that he felt clear to his toes. His own release almost transpired right then and there. It took all he had to keep it together.

He couldn't wait to be inside her any longer.

Slipping on a condom with quick fingers, he rose up over

her and caught her gaze, communicating without words, letting all his desire for her spill from his expression. She stared back, eyes luminous with satisfaction.

Slowly, so slowly, he bent one of her gorgeous legs up and nestled between her thighs to complete their connection. She sighed lustily as he pushed. When he'd entered her fully, a wash of pleasure slammed his eyelids shut and he groaned in harmony with her.

It was a dazzling thing to be joined with Elise, and he couldn't hold back. Her name tumbled from his lips, over and over, as he spiraled them both higher. Nearly mindless, he sought to touch her, to caress her, to make her come again before he did...because there were rules. But she shifted, and the angle was so sweet, he lost complete control. Splintering into oblivion, he cried out as answering ripples of her climax sharpened his. The powerful orgasm sucked him under for a long moment, blinding him to everything but the release.

With the fireplace crackling merrily and the warmth of an amazing afterglow engulfing him, he lay there, unable to move. Elise cradled his spent body, both of their chests heaving as one, and he experienced the most profound sense of bliss.

That's what he'd missed.

Happily ever after just might begin with one day of happiness that you found so amazing and wonderful, you woke up the next day aching to repeat it. And didn't let anything stop you.

Elise finally coaxed Dax into bed and they thoroughly christened it in what was the most monumentally earth-shattering experience of her admittedly short list of sexual encounters. So far, she'd managed to keep her total cluelessness from him, but she couldn't let this particular first slide.

She snuggled up against his absolutely delicious body and waited until he'd pulled the sheet up around them to spill it. "You're the first man I've had in this bed."

"Ever?" His voice was soft with a hint of wonderment. As if she'd given him a special gift he'd always wanted but never received.

Was she *that* far gone over a couple of orgasms? She was assigning all kinds of emotions to Dax that she had no business assigning. Her head needed to be plucked out of the clouds really fast, before she got ideas about what was going on here that would only lead to disappointment.

She'd consented to sleep with him, but not to fall for him.

She nodded against his shoulder and opted for candor. "I bought this set about a year ago and I didn't want to sleep here night after night with memories of a past relationship gone wrong still haunting it."

The hand intimately caressing her waist stilled. "Guess that means you figured out how to exorcise the ghosts of past lovers. Or you think I'll be in your bed for the rest of its life."

The post-orgasm high vanished as the heaviness of his real question weighted the atmosphere.

"Um…" Well, she really hadn't thought through how that particular confession was going to go, had she? "Door number three. I thought you were worth it regardless."

He slid a hand up to her jaw and guided her head up so he could look at her. Something misty and tender sprang from his gaze. "That's the best thing anyone's ever said to me."

How could that be? Surely someone had told him he had value before. But his expression said otherwise.

She couldn't look away as a powerful and intangible current arced between them. It was more than the connection she'd told him was possible. More than the deepening of their friendship that she'd sought.

Then he laid his lips on hers in a sweet kiss that went on and on and sent her into the throes of a whole different kind of high. So what if her head was firmly in the clouds?

She was in bed with Dax and he was beautiful and precious and it was the most amazing night in her memory.

And it didn't appear to be ending anytime soon.

"Lay here with me." He spooned her against his warm torso and held her as if he'd never let go, as if it was the most natural thing in the world.

"So are you…staying?" She bit her lip and left it at that, though the question was so much bigger.

"What, you mean overnight?" he mumbled. "Since it's nearly two a.m., I assumed that was pretty much a given. Do you want me to leave?"

"No!" Horrified, she snuggled deeper into him in apology and his arms tightened. The last thing she wanted was to wake up alone. "Just checking. I'm happy with you where you are."

No man had ever slept in this bed, either, and she wasn't sorry she'd waited for Dax to be the first. He fit into it perfectly and if he wasn't careful, she would invite him to spend a good long while in it.

That was actually what she'd hoped to establish by asking whether he planned to stay. Not just overnight, but when tomorrow came, then what? Was it too soon to talk about it? Was it implied that this was the start of a relationship in every sense?

Or was she supposed to know this was one night only?

"Good. Get some sleep. You're going to need it. And Elise," he whispered in her ear. "I might stay tomorrow night, too."

Apparently he'd read her thoughts.

Whether she'd given herself permission or not, it was too late to pretend she wasn't falling for him. She tucked the feeling away and held it close to her heart.

She fell asleep with a smile on her face and woke up with the same smile. Dax made her happy and she wanted to do the same for him. But he wasn't in the bed. Covers thrown back, his side was already cool. Frowning, she strained to hear the shower. Nothing.

He wasn't downstairs either. She sighed and pulled the sash on her robe tighter, cursing herself for thinking...well, it didn't matter. Dax was free to leave. She'd just hoped he wouldn't. He hadn't made promises—false or otherwise—and she hadn't requested any.

But she'd put a lot of faith in him based on his insistence that he meant it and his pretty speech about trust. Perhaps she should have established a better understanding of his definition of "I mean it."

When the front door swung open and Dax called out cheerily, she nearly dropped her freshly brewed cup of coffee.

Dax sauntered into the kitchen all windblown and smiley. It shouldn't be possible to look that delicious after only a few hours of sleep. She didn't bother to hide her openmouthed gaping.

He dropped a kiss on her temple and handed her a bag. "Hey, gorgeous. Bagels. I hope that's okay. Breakfast is the most important meal of the day, after all." He grinned and eyed her robe. "But now I'm wondering what's underneath there. Breakfast can wait a few minutes, can't it?"

"Maybe. Depends on how good the bagels are." She smiled as he glared at her in mock dismay. Then she noticed the other bag, hanging from his shoulder. "That, um, looks like a suitcase. Taking a trip?"

He shrugged. "Picked up a few things while I was out. I don't live far. Figured I'd like to be dressed in an actual suit Monday morning when I show up for work."

Oh, my. Obviously he'd decided to spend Sunday with her. And the whole of Sunday night too. Dare she hope he'd undergone such a miraculous conversion that he was ready to spend every waking second with her?

Or was this blissful weekend the beginning of the end?

"So what are we doing here?" she blurted out, suddenly panicked and quite unable to pinpoint why. "You're staying all day, tonight and then what? I'm sorry, I can't just go with it. I need some parameters here."

The bag dropped to the floor and he leaned against the kitchen counter, his expression blank. "What kind of parameters do you want? I thought this was a pretty good compromise, bringing some stuff over. It's not day by day, but no one's made any promises they can't keep. Were you expecting me to show up with more stuff?"

She'd been expecting *less* stuff, far less. She had no idea what to do with all the stuff he'd unloaded. Relationships were supposed to be structured, predictable. Weren't they? Why hadn't she practiced a whole lot more before this one? The two relationships she'd been in before were vastly inadequate preparation for Dax Wakefield.

"I wasn't actually expecting you to show up at all," she confessed. "I thought you'd bailed."

"I sent you a text. Isn't that our thing?" He grinned. "I thought you slept with your phone in your hand, pining for a message from me. That takes me down a few notches."

Frowning, she scouted about for her phone and finally found it in the side pocket of her purse. On silent. She thumbed up the message.

Don't eat. I'll be back asap with breakfast. Can't wait to see you.

All righty then. She blew out a breath and it turned into a long sigh. She kept looking for reasons not to trust him and he hadn't disappointed her yet. What was her *problem*?

"Hey." He pulled her into his arms and rested his head on top of hers. "You really thought I wasn't coming back? You don't do one-night stands. I respect that. I wouldn't have come here last night if I didn't."

"Sorry," she mumbled into his shirt in case she'd offended him. In truth, he didn't sound anything other than concerned but she'd somehow lost the ability to read him. That scared her. "I'll shut up now."

"I don't want you to shut up." Pulling back slightly, he peered down at her. "Your mouth is the sexiest thing on you."

With that, the tension mostly blew over. Or rather she chose to ignore the lingering questions so she could enjoy spending the day with a man she liked, who liked her back. It *was* a good compromise—for now. She didn't like not knowing the plan or what to expect. But for today, she knew Dax would be in her bed at the end of it and that was something she readily looked forward to.

They had fun giggling together over a couple of Netflix movies and ate Chinese delivery for lunch.

"Let me take you someplace really great for dinner," he suggested as he collected the cartons to dispose of them. "If you'll actually eat, that is."

He hefted her half-full takeout carton in deliberate emphasis.

"I'm not all that hungry," she said out of habit, and then made the mistake of glancing up into his slightly narrowed gaze, which was evaluating her coolly. Of course he hadn't bought that excuse.

Instead of taking the trash to the kitchen as he should have, Dax set the cartons back on the coffee table and eased onto the cushion next to her. "Elise—"

"I ate most of it. There's no crime in not being hungry." Her defensive tone didn't do much for her case.

"No, there's not." He contemplated her for a few long moments. "Except you're never hungry. I didn't press you on it last night when you told me you gain weight easily because, well, I was a little busy, but I can't ignore it forever. Do you have a problem I should know about?"

"Like anorexia?" The half laugh slipped out before she could catch it. This was not funny *at all* but he'd caught her by surprise. "I like food far too much to starve myself entirely, thanks."

How had the conversation turned heavy so fast? And when precisely had they reached a point in their relationship where it was okay to throw it all out there, no censor, no taboos?

"Maybe not *entirely*," he stressed. "But you don't like yourself enough to have a healthy relationship with food either."

Gently, he took her hand and she let him. His concern was evident. But he could stop with all the psychobabble any time now. She didn't have a problem other than an intense desire to never be fat again. Nothing wrong with that.

"Thanks for checking in, but it's okay. My health *is* my concern." She glanced away. He saw too much but it was the price for opening up to him. "This will be hard for you to sympathize with, I realize, but I was an ugly duckling for a long time. A fat girl. When I finally lost all the weight, I vowed never to gain it back. Portion control is my friend."

"Elise." He stroked her knuckles with his thumb in a comforting caress. "I don't know what it's like to be fat. But it's not fair to frame your struggles as if no one else can comprehend them. To deliberately shut me out solely because I have a few strands of DNA that put my face together like this."

He circled an index finger over his cheekbones, and the darkness underneath the motion, in his expression, startled her.

"I'm not trying to shut you out." Was she?

The alternative meant she'd have to let him glimpse her innermost secrets, her deepest fears. It would mean trusting him with far more than her body. It would mean trusting him with her soul.

But hadn't she already done that when she invited him into her bed?

"You may not be consciously trying to. But you are," he said mildly. "And not only that, you're making an assumption about me based on my appearance. Like I can't possibly know what it feels like to have disappointments or pain because of the way I look."

Speechless, she stared into his snapping, smoky eyes. She'd hurt him with her thoughtless comments.

She *had* made assumptions and drawn her fat-girl self around her like a familiar, impenetrable blanket.

Dax had called it during their discussion on the park bench. She ran screaming in the other direction before a man could get close enough to hurt her.

Had she already screwed this up—whatever *this* was—before it started?

"I'm sorry," she said sincerely and squeezed his hand. He squeezed back and her heart lightened a little. "I'm sensitive about food and about being fat. It's an ugly part of me. I'm not used to sharing it with anyone."

"There's nothing ugly about you," he shot right back. "Why in the world would you think a few pounds makes you ugly?"

She debated. It was so much easier to make a joke. But she'd been patiently explaining the components of happily ever after to Dax for weeks, which had everything to do with honesty, vulnerability and trust. Was she really going to balk when it was her turn to lay it all out?

"You've seen my mother. You've been in that world. Surely the pursuit of thinness is not so mysterious an ideal."

He shrugged. "But you're not a model. Neither are you your mother. So your weight is not a requirement for your job."

Easy for him to say. It was different for boys no matter what they looked like.

"It's not that simple. I grew up surrounded by swans and constantly aware I wasn't one of them. In case I didn't feel bad enough about being overweight, my mother made sure I didn't forget it for a moment."

"She's the one who made you self-conscious about being fat?" Dax scowled. "That's horrible."

His unconditional support squeezed her heart sweetly. "It turned out okay. I buried myself in algorithms and computer code instead of hanging out in the spotlight, which was, and still is, cruel. I built a business born out of the desire to shut myself away from all the negativity. Only EA International could have gotten me in front of those cameras where we met. Even now, I give deserving women makeovers because I know how it feels to be in the middle of all those swans, with no one on your side."

"I'm glad you found the fortitude to venture onto my set." Dax smiled. "And I like that you made something positive out of a bad experience."

"There's more." And it was the really important part. "That's why my profile questions dig into the heart of who you are. So my clients can find someone to love them for what's underneath, not what they look like."

Which was not-so-coincidentally what she wanted too—someone to love her forever, no matter what. She'd never had that before.

The smile slipped from his face and he gazed at her solemnly. "I get that."

Of course he did. She'd made sweeping generalizations about him because of his appearance and she'd bet it wasn't the first time someone had done that. Not only did he understand the point about loving someone's insides; of all the people she'd shared her philosophy with, he had the singular distinction of being the only one who'd seen the pain that had created it.

And she was terrified of what he'd do with all this insight.

Eleven

Dax took Elise to eat at the top of Reunion Tower, a place she'd never been despite having lived in Dallas for years. They dined while overlooking the downtown area as the room revolved 360 degrees inside the ball. It should have been a wildly romantic evening.

It *was*. But Elise couldn't quite relax.

When they returned to her house from dinner, Dax took her keys and opened the front door for her, then swept her up in his arms to carry her over the threshold. Solid and strong, he maneuvered through the door frame without hesitation, and it was undeniably sexy.

"What's this all about?" she asked as soon as she unstuck her tongue from the roof of her mouth.

"I seem to have a lot of trouble getting past your front door. This way, I'm guaranteed entrance." He grinned at her cockeyed stare. "Plus, I've got a very special treat planned and thought I'd start it off with a bang."

"Really?" Her curiosity was piqued as her tension lessened. "What is it?"

He let her slide to the ground braced against his gorgeous body and took her hand. "Follow me, Ms. Arundel, and see for yourself."

That made her grin, dispelling more of her strange mood. She trailed him upstairs and the second she entered the bedroom, he whirled her into a mind-numbing kiss.

Her brain emptied as his lips devoured her and heat tunneled into every last crevice of her body. *Oh, yes.*

Bright, white-hot desire flared in a sunburst at her core, soaking her in need and flooding her with Dax, and she couldn't catch her breath. She wanted him to love her exactly as he had last night, perfectly, completely.

Slowly, he backed her to the bed and when she would have stumbled, he tightened his arms. Then he sat her down and drew off her boots, one zipper at a time, and kissed her uncovered calves, all the way to her heels.

She watched him through heavy eyelids, a little unable to process the sight of such a beautiful man at her feet, all his attention on her. He glanced up, his gaze full of dark, sinful promise, and she shuddered as he centered himself between her legs.

With deft, strong fingers, he gathered the hem of her dress and slowly worked it up over her thighs, caressing her bare skin as he went, following the fabric with his mouth and tongue.

A moan rose in her throat and she strangled on it as he licked at her nub through her damp panties.

"I want to see you, Elise," he murmured and slipped off her dress with skill. Quick-like-fox, he had her bra and panties in the same pile as her dress.

As he raked her with a smoldering, hungry once-over, she fought the urge to crawl under the covers.

"You are so beautiful," he croaked, as though he might be coming down with something. Or she'd affected him enough to clog his throat.

Wasn't that amazing? *She* affected *him.*

He stared down at her as he lowered himself to the bed next to her, still fully clothed. "I want to make you feel beautiful."

"You do," she said automatically. Well, actually, he made her feel good. Beautiful was a little more difficult to come by.

His brows arched. "Maybe. But I can do better. Much better. So tonight is about that."

He reached under a pillow and withdrew a bag of Ghirardelli chocolate chips. She'd recognize the bag a mile away. Her mouth started watering. And then her brain caught up. "Why is that instrument of torture in my bed?"

Dax grinned and winked. "You told me you liked chocolate. *Voilà*. We'll get to the shoes another time."

The wall her insides had thrown up crumbled and everything went liquid. "You were paying attention to what I said?"

"Of course." He scowled in confusion. "Why would I have asked if I didn't want to know the answer?"

Heat flamed through her cheeks and she shut her eyes. "I thought you were being polite."

Laughing, he kissed both of her shut eyelids in succession until she opened them. "One thing I am not is polite. But I am interested in giving you an amazing experience. Starting now."

With a wicked smile, he laid her back and tore open the bag, spilling chocolate chips all over her bare stomach.

The chips rolled everywhere, and she jackknifed automatically to catch them, but he stopped her with a gentle hand to her shoulder. Then he grasped a piece of chocolate between his fingertips and traced it between her breasts, up her throat and to her lips, teasing her with it.

The rich, sweet smell of chocolate drugged her senses. She wanted to eat that bite of heaven in the worst way. But she couldn't. A moment on the lips…and it went straight to her hips. She didn't keep chocolate in the house for a reason.

"Open," he instructed. "None of these calories count because honey, I promise you're about to burn them all."

The temptation was humongous. She wrestled with it. And lost.

How could she do anything else but eat it? Chocolate burst on her tongue and a moment later, his tongue twined with hers, tasting the chocolate along with her in a delicious kiss.

The twin sensations of Dax and chocolate nearly pushed her over the edge. She moaned in appreciation. Desire. Surrender.

Trailing chocolate kisses back down her throat, he paused to line up several chips around her nipple and proceeded to lick each one, smearing more chocolate on her breasts than he got in his mouth. He proceeded to suck off the sweetness, sending her into a taut spiral of need that could only be salved one way.

As if he'd read her mind again, he lowered himself between her thighs, opened them and kissed each one. Muscles tight with anticipation, she choked on a breath, waiting for the sweet fire of his intimate kiss.

He didn't disappoint her. She felt a chip graze her nub and then Dax's tongue followed it, and her eyelids slammed closed as her senses pulsed with pleasure.

"You taste delicious," he rasped and stuck another chip under his tongue, laving so hard, she came instantly in a starburst of sparkles that bowed her back and ripped a cry from her throat.

Immediately, he rose up and treated her to a chocolate, musky kiss, twining all the flavors together into an overwhelming, sensual bouquet.

"See how delicious you taste?" he murmured and cupped her with his hand, sliding fingers through her folds and into her damp center, yanking yet another climax from deep inside.

Still in the throes of a chocolate orgasm, she couldn't sort one sensation from the other and didn't want to. Finally the ripples faded, leaving her gasping and nearly blind as dots crowded her vision.

"Delicious," he repeated. "Beautiful."

Then he put the icing on it.

"By the way," he said casually. "In case it wasn't crystal clear, this was me showing you how gorgeous you are. Remember this every time you put chocolate in your mouth, which better be a lot. Because I don't want you to ever, ever forget that you're beautiful or that the sight of you eating chocolate is so hot, I'm about to lose it."

She blinked and focused on his wolfish smile. He'd been trying to psychoanalyze her with this little stunt?

So now every time she thought about chocolate, she'd make all kinds of associations that it should never have, like unbelievable pleasure, a gorgeous man's mouth tasting of sin and sugar, and the pièce de résistance, that watching her eat chocolate turned him on.

It was...brilliant. The benefits of sleeping with a man who understood both psychology and a woman's body couldn't be overstated.

And she wasn't simply falling for him; it was more like being dropped off a cliff, straight into a mess of emotion she had no idea how to handle.

She would have thought herself capable of understanding love, if indeed that's what was going on. Certainly she would have said she could recognize it. And it did not resemble this crazy, upside-down thing inside that was half thrilling, half terrifying and 100 percent Dax.

What if this *wasn't* love but an orgasm-induced hallucination? Worse, what if she went with it, straight into a broken heart? Her fat-girl blanket usually kept that from happening, but she'd lost it.

Or rather, Dax had stolen it from her with chocolate.

And he'd completely piqued her curiosity as to what he planned to do with shoes.

Dax picked up Elise and took her to the bathroom, where he filled the tub and spent a long time washing the chocolate from her body. He wanted to sink into the steaming water and sink into Elise, but he was too busy breathing her in to stop.

She smelled like chocolate and well-loved woman and home, all rolled into one bundle he could not get enough of. He'd only meant to worship her gorgeous body and enable her to eat something she liked at the same time. He had *not* intended to forever alter his perception of chocolate, but he'd never taste it again without getting a hard-on.

Which wasn't necessarily a bad thing.

Finally he couldn't stand being separated from her any longer and stripped to slide into the tub. She watched him unashamedly, ravenous gaze flickering to his rigid erection as he bared it. Last night she'd had a hard time with that, as if nakedness were shocking.

Not so tonight. But he didn't dare say he was proud of her lest he frighten her back into that shell. Besides, the heat in her eyes sent such a shaft of desire spiking through him, he couldn't do anything other than slide into the tub, gather her against his chest and dive in.

He kissed her, openmouthed, sloppy and so very raw. She melted into him, fitting her lithe body into his. Water sloshed out of the tub, which she didn't notice and he didn't point out.

He needed her. Now.

After an eternity of fumbling due to wet fingers and wet body parts and far too much "help" from Elise that nearly set off what would be a nuclear explosion of a release, Dax got the condom in place.

He never had this much trouble. But his fingers were still shaking as he slid into her with a groan and then he simply clung, hands gripping Elise's shoulders. Flinging his head back, he let the sensations bleed through him and only some of them were physical.

That profound sense of what he could only label as *happiness* saturated the experience, lighting him up inside. It felt as if it would burst from his skin and pour out in a river. He savored the harmony, the rightness of it.

Elise, clearly impatient with all the savoring, planted her knees on either side of him and took over the rhythm, and he let her because it was amazing. The faster she moved, the higher he soared, and a growl ripped from his mouth unrestrained as she pushed him to the edge.

Nearly incoherent and almost numb with the effort to hold back, he fingered her in an intimate caress, silently begging her to let go. Instantly, she tightened around him in an answering pulse that triggered his release, and he came in a fountain of blessed relief.

She slumped on his chest, cheek to his skin, and he shut his eyes, reveling in the boneless bliss that he'd only ever experienced at the hands of Elise.

Being with her evoked so many things he had no way to describe, things he hoped never went away. But since he didn't know how it had happened in the first place, what guarantee did he have he wouldn't wake up tomorrow and find himself back in the real world where Elise wasn't "the one"?

Because here in this alternate reality he'd somehow fallen into, it felt an awful lot as though she was a...soul mate.

Against all odds, he wanted to believe the concept existed, that it might be possible for him. For them.

After they dried off and got comfortably snugged together in bed he murmured, "Elise, you have to promise me something."

"Anything. After the chocolate, you name it." She sighed, her breath teasing the hair on his torso.

"Don't stop. Keep doing whatever you're doing and don't stop. Even if I tell you to."

She stirred and raised her head to peer at him in the darkened room, lit only by the moonlight pouring in through the opened blinds. "Why would you tell me to?"

"Because…"

I'm broken.

That's why he'd never found a woman worth promising forever to. Why Elise's matchmaking efforts had failed, despite participating in her profile sessions to the best of his ability. Not because there was something wrong with the women he'd dated, or even Candy, but because something was wrong with him. How could he explain that he pushed women away on purpose, before things got complicated?

But then, he didn't have to explain. Elise knew that already. She had spelled it out in painful detail on the park bench. If he was being honest, that had been the tipping point, the moment he knew she'd snared an unrecoverable piece of him he'd never meant to give up.

He tried again. "Because I'm…"

Falling for you.

His eyelids slammed shut in frustration and fear and God knew what else. What was wrong with him that he couldn't voice a simple sentence to tell this amazing woman how she made him feel? Or at least confess that she made him want to be better than he'd ever dreamed possible?

He wanted to be the man she deserved. For the first time in his life, he didn't want to push her away.

But he knew he was going to anyway.

He couldn't say all those things because Elise wasn't *his* soul mate. She was someone else's and he was in the way. For her sake, he would have to end things eventually.

That realization nearly split him in two. Appropriate to be as broken on the outside as he was on the inside.

"Hey." Her soft hand cupped his jaw and her thumb rested near his eyes, brushing the lashes until he opened them. "What's going on? You're never at a loss for words."

He laughed in spite of himself. She'd been tying him up in knots from day one. Why should this be any different?

"Yeah, this is all kinds of abnormal."

"Start with that. What's abnormal, being in bed to-gether?" She cocked her head and smoothed the sheets over them. "Are you about to tell me your reputation with women is vastly inflated? Because I won't believe you. The things you do to me can only be the result of years of careful study."

"I've had a lot of sex, Elise. Make no mistake," he said without apology. "But it wasn't anything like this. What's different is you. I can't explain it. It feels…bigger. Stron-ger. I don't know what to do with it."

She stared at him, wide-eyed. "Really? It's not like this with other women?"

"Not even close. I didn't know it *could* be different."

If he had, he would have hunted down Elise Arundel about a decade ago. Maybe if he had, before he'd become so irrevocably damaged, things might have worked out between them.

He could have actually *been* the man she needed instead of merely wanting to be.

Wanting wasn't good enough. She deserved someone unbroken and he needed to give her space to find that guy.

But it didn't have to be now. He could wait a few days, or maybe longer.

"But I'm just me." Bewilderment crept over her face. "I'm not doing anything special."

"You don't have to do anything special. It just is. You don't feel it, too?"

Slowly, she nodded and a sense of relief burst through his gut. Relief that this wasn't all one-sided. Guilt because it might already be too late to get out without hurting her.

"I feel it. It scares me and I don't know why." She gripped his hand. "It's not supposed to be like this, all mixed up, and like I can't breathe if you're gone. Like I can't breathe when you're here."

Exactly. That's how he'd felt all week as he'd talked to the couples Elise had matched and then drove around aimlessly, out of sorts, with no clue how to absolve the riot of stuff seething under his skin. Elise was his affliction. And his deliverance.

Maybe she was the answer, the only woman in existence who could fix him. If he wasn't broken anymore, maybe he could find a way to be with Elise forever. Maybe he *could* have her, without pushing her away. But only if he could finally let her behind his curtain.

"I have to tell you something," he said before he lost his nerve. "Your mother made you feel bad about your weight. Well, I understand how mothers can shape your entire outlook on life. Because mine left. When I was seven."

Tears pricked at his eyelids. He'd never spoken of his mother's abandonment and somehow, saying it aloud made it An Issue.

"Oh, honey, I'm so sorry." Elise pressed her lips to his temple and just held him without another word. The odd, bright happiness she evoked filled him.

"It's stupid to still let it affect me. I know that," he muttered and let his muscles relax. He wouldn't flee into the night and not talk about this.

Elise, of all people, understood the twisted, sometimes warped pathways of his mind, often when he didn't get it himself. He could trust her.

"Dax." She gave him time to collect himself and that small act meant a lot to him. "If you don't want to let it affect you, then stop."

"Oh, sure. I'll wave my magic wand and everything will be fine. Better yet, why don't you wave yours?" he said magnanimously. She didn't laugh.

Instead, she leaned forward and pierced him with a somber gaze. "That's exactly what I've been trying to do. By matching you with your soul mate, so you could be happy with someone. I want that for you."

"What if I said I want that too?"

Twelve

She froze, confusion flitting through her expression. "You do?"

"Yeah. Maybe."

She blinked and swallowed several times in a row before speaking. "You mean commitment, emotions, forever?"

Hope shone in her eyes.

For a brief moment, he felt an answering tug of hope in his heart. Forever sounded amazing.

And then reality took over and squelched everything good inside. These feelings would change—or fade—and he'd prove he was just like his mother by walking out the door.

He was wrong for Elise. She had all these visions of true love he could never measure up to. Being with her made him want things he couldn't have, and it wasn't her job to fix him.

That was the final nail. Just because he wanted to be unbroken didn't make it so. Why hadn't he kept his mouth shut and his curtain closed? He couldn't continue this charade, as though there was a future for them.

For once, he'd thought about trying. That's why he'd shared the truth with her. That's why he'd gotten out of the car.

He shouldn't have. And he had a hundred reasons why he should walk out right now before it was too late. He wasn't cut out for this, for relationships. He had to get out now, before he hurt her even more later.

Ruthlessly, he shut off everything inside, especially the part that had started to believe.

"Why do you sound so stunned?" he said instead of answering her question as he scrambled for a way to let her down easy. "This is your area of expertise. Didn't you set out to change my mind about love?"

"I'm not that good," she blurted out and bit her lip.

"Of course you are. The couples you matched think you're every bit the magical fairy godmother you claimed. Take credit where credit is due."

A grin spilled onto her face. "Does that mean I won the wager?"

His chest had the weight of a skyscraper on it and all Elise could think about was the wager? "The wager is over."

"Sorry." Her confusion wrapped around him, increasing the tension unbearably. "What about marriage? Are you on board with that, too?"

The longer he dragged this out, the more hope she'd gather. Heart bleeding, he shrugged and looked away. "Maybe someday. With the right woman."

"Wait a minute." Unease flitting over her face, she sat up, clutching the covers to her bare breasts. "I thought you were talking about having a relationship with *me*."

Carefully, he composed his expression as if this was no more than a negotiation gone wrong and both parties just needed to walk away amicably.

It nearly killed him.

"Come on, Elise. You and I both know we won't work. I got out of the car because I knew I was missing something and I needed you to tell me what. So thanks. I'm good."

She wasn't buying it. Elise was far too sharp to be put off by half truths. That's why it never paid to let anyone behind the curtain.

"Dax, we have something good. Don't you want to see if we work before giving up?"

Her warm hand on his arm shouldn't have felt so right, as though his skin had been crafted specifically for her touch.

"It doesn't matter what I want. I can't make long-term promises. To anyone," he stressed. "I'm all about keeping my word because my mother didn't. I can't stand the thought of caring about someone and then figuring out I don't have what it takes to stick around."

Nothing like the whole truth to make the point. She needed to understand that this was for her own good, so she could move on and find her Mr. Forever, and he could go back to his empty loft.

"But you can make promises to me because I'm your soul mate."

The soft whisper penetrated his misery. "What did you say?"

"*I'm* your soul mate. Your perfect woman. The computer matched us."

Something dark whirled through his chest, squeezing it even tighter, pushing air from his lungs. "That's not true. It matched me with Candy."

She shook her head. "My name came up first. But I thought I'd made a mistake due to the unorthodox profile sessions. So I messed around with the responses until Candy's name came up instead."

Blood rushed to his head and the back of his neck heated. "You did *what?*"

"It was the ethical thing to do. I thought I'd compromised the results because of how I felt about you."

Ethical. He'd been told Candy was his soul mate and therefore he'd believed Elise was meant for someone else. But it had never felt right, never fit…because he'd thought *he* was the problem.

Instead, it was all a lie.

Letting him think he couldn't do happily ever after, letting him think he was broken—that was her definition of *ethical?*

"Let me get this straight." He pinched the bridge of his nose and reeled his temper back. "You had such deep feelings for me it compelled you to match me with someone who isn't my soul mate?"

"I hoped you'd hit it off. Because I do want you to be happy. Candy just wasn't right for you."

"And who is, you?"

The question was delivered so scathingly, she flinched and didn't respond. Fortunately. His mood had degenerated to the point where he was genuinely afraid of what he might say.

He rolled from the bed and scouted around until he found his pants, and then jerked them on, but stood staring at the wall, fists clenched until he thought he could speak rationally.

"Why tell me now? Why didn't you tell me from the beginning?"

The wager. She'd been trying to win and altered the results in order to do so. It was the only explanation. That's why she'd asked if she'd won earlier. Rage boiled up again, clouding his vision.

"It wasn't a secret," she said defensively. "I thought you'd laugh and make some smarmy joke about how I couldn't possibly resist you. Plus, I wanted you to have a shot at finding your real soul mate."

"Who isn't you."

She couldn't be. His real soul mate wouldn't have let him believe all this time that he was the problem. That he was the broken one and that's why Elise's algorithm couldn't find his perfect match.

He'd trusted her. In vain, apparently.

If she'd just told him the truth, everything might be different. But she'd stolen that chance and thoroughly destroyed his fledgling belief in the possibility of happily ever after.

"I am," she corrected softly. "My match process just realized it before I did."

"Pardon me for questioning the results when it seems your process is a little, shall we say, subjective. In fact, I'd say this whole wager was slanted from the beginning. So save the sales pitch, babe."

Oh, he'd been so blind. From the very first moment, all she'd cared about was proving to everyone that she could change his mind about relationships. She didn't want true love, or at least not with him. It had all been an act to gain the upper hand. If Dax had one talent, it was recognizing a good show when he saw one.

"Slanted? What are you talking about?"

"Admit it. This was all an attempt to bring me to my knees, wasn't it? You planned for it to happen this way." He shook his head and laughed contemptuously. "You're far, far better at this than I ever dreamed. To think I almost fell for it."

She'd dug into his psyche with no other intent than to uncover his deepest longings and use them against him. It was unforgivable.

The only bright spot in this nightmare was that he no longer had to worry about how to push her away or whether he'd eventually walk out the door. She'd destroyed their relationship all on her own.

Thankfully, he'd found out the truth before it was too late.

His mistake had been starting to trust her, even a little.

"Fell for what? Dax, you're not making any sense."

Pulse hammering, Elise sorted through the conversation to figure out where this had gotten so mixed up. What had she missed? Up until now, she'd always been able to sort his fact from fiction, especially when he tried to throw up smoke screens, but that ability had disappeared long about midnight yesterday.

She was losing him, losing all the ground she'd gained—

or imagined she'd gained. Clearly, he'd done some kind of about-face but apparently not in her direction. That couldn't be right. She couldn't be this close to getting a man like Dax for her own and not figure out how to get her happily ever after.

He shook his head and laughed again without any humor. "All this time I thought *you* were looking for a relationship and I *wasn't*. You sat right there on that park bench and told me exactly what you wanted. I ignored it." He crossed the room and poked a rigid finger in her face. "'I want to beat you at your own game,' you said. And you know what, you almost did."

She flinched automatically. Oh, God. She had said that. But the way he'd twisted it around...unbelievable. As if she'd cold-bloodedly planned this to hurt him, playing dirty, fast and loose.

"Listen, this wasn't the game I was trying to win."

Except she'd been pretty focused on winning. From the beginning. Maybe she'd been more compromised than she'd assumed. She'd developed feelings for him without really understanding how to love him.

Maybe she didn't really understand male/female dynamics unless they were other people's.

"What game *were* you trying to win, then? Why is this a game at all?" A dangerous glint in his eye warned her to let him finish before she leaped on the defensive again. "Tread carefully, Elise. You clearly have no idea what you're playing around with here."

"This isn't a game," she cried. "When my name came up as your match, I wanted it to be true. I wanted you for myself and I thought those feelings compromised my integrity."

"You're lying." The harsh lines of his face convicted her further. "If that was true, you wouldn't have played so hard to get."

She couldn't fault his logic. Except he was drawing the wrong conclusion. "The truth is I didn't believe I was enough to change your mind about happily ever after."

"Enough?" he spat. "Enough what?"

"Pretty enough, good enough, thin enough. Take your pick," she whispered.

He laughed again and the sound skated down her spine. "I get it now. You said you don't trust easily, but in reality, you don't trust at all. You didn't ever intend to give me a real chance, did you? That's the game you wanted to beat me at. Get me to confess my feelings and then take my legs out from under me. Good job."

"I *did* want to give you a chance. You said we wouldn't work."

He threw his hands up. "This is why I don't do relationships. This conversation is like a vicious circle. With teeth."

She cursed as she realized her mistake. Misdirection was his forte and he was such a master, she'd almost missed it. He *had* developed feelings for her and they scared him. That's what all this was. Smoke and mirrors to deflect from what was going on back stage.

This was the part where she needed to tread carefully.

"Last night," she whispered. "Before you kissed me. You said you meant it. What did you mean?"

The raw vulnerability in his expression took her breath. And when her lungs finally filled, they ached with the effort.

"I meant I was falling in love with you." His expression darkened as her heart tripped dangerously. "I—forget it. It's too late to have that conversation now."

Dax was falling in love with her? The revelation pinged through her mind, through her heart—painfully—because he'd finally laid it all out there while also telling her to forget it. As if she could.

She'd done it. She'd reversed his stance on love and happily ever after. Shannon Elise Arundel *was* that good. Her match program was foolproof. The algorithm had matched them because she had a unique ability to understand him, to see the real him, just as he did her.

Why hadn't she realized it sooner?

"It's not too late." She crawled to her knees, begging him without words for something she had no idea how to express. "Let's figure this out."

"I don't want to figure it out!" He huffed out a frustrated breath. "Elise, I thought I was *broken.* That the reason you couldn't find my soul mate was because there was something wrong with me. I felt guilty for wanting you when your soul mate was supposed to be someone else, someone better. Instead, you were lying all along. You never trusted me."

In one shot, he'd blown all the smoke away and told her the absolute unvarnished truth. While she'd been pushing him away, he'd filed the rejection under *it's not her, it's me.*

Speechless, she stared at the pain-carved lines in his beautiful face. "I didn't know that's how you'd take it when I told you I was your match. There's nothing wrong with you. This is all about me and my issues."

"I get that you have a problem believing I think you're beautiful." He snorted. "You want to find true love but you won't let anyone in long enough to trust that they love you. That's why you've never had a connection with anyone."

"I've been holding out for someone to love me. The real me, underneath."

I've been holding out for you.

He swept her with an angry look. "Yet you're completely hung up on whether you're beautiful enough. If someone loves you solely for what you look like, that's not true love. Neither is it love to refuse to trust. You have a lot of nerve preaching to me about something you know nothing about."

"You're right." Head bowed, she admitted the absolute,

unvarnished truth in kind. "I didn't fully trust you. I don't know how."

"I bought into what you were selling." His bleak voice scored her heart. "Hook, line and sinker. I wanted something more than sex. Understanding. Support. A connection."

Everything she'd hoped for. For both of them. But somehow she'd messed up. "I want those things, too."

A tear tracked down her cheek and he watched it. As it fell to the bed, he shook his head. "You're not capable of giving me those things. This is over, if it ever started in the first place. I can't do this."

Then he stormed from the room, snagging his bag on the way out. She let him go, too numb to figure out how to fix it. Some relationship expert she was.

Dax's ex-girlfriends had been wrong. He wasn't cold and heartless and he hadn't screwed Elise over. She'd done it to him, smashing his fragile feelings into unrecoverable pieces because at the end of the day, she hadn't trusted Dax enough to believe he could really love her. She hadn't trusted herself enough to tell him they'd been matched. And now it was too late to do it all over.

Happily ever after might very well be a myth after all. And if that was true, where did that leave her and Dax? Or her company?

The sound of the front door slamming reverberated in her frozen heart.

Dax nearly took out a row of mailboxes in his haste to speed away from the mistake in his rearview mirror. Astounding how he'd assumed he was the broken one in their relationship. Only to discover she was far more broken.

While he'd naively been trying to get out without hurting her, she'd actually been one step ahead of him the entire time, determined to break him. And she'd done a hell of a job. She'd matched him with the perfect woman all right—the only one capable of getting under his skin and destroying everything in her path.

It was late, but Wakefield Media did not sleep. He drove to the office, determined not to think. Or to feel. He closed it all off through sheer will until the only thing left was a strange hardness in his chest that made it impossible to catch a deep breath.

Shutting himself off behind his desk, Dax dove into the business he loved, the only thing he could really depend on. This company he'd built from the ground up was his happily ever after, the only one available to him. If he put his head down, maybe he'd come out the other side with some semblance of normality. Dawn came and went but the hardness in his chest didn't fade.

At noon, he'd had no human contact other than a brief nod to Patricia as she dropped off a cup of coffee several hours ago. Fatigue dragged at him. Well, that and a heavy heart.

His phone beeped and he checked it automatically. Elise. He deleted the text message without reading it, just as he'd done with the other three. There was nothing she could say that he wanted to hear.

Morosely, he swiveled his chair to stare out over the Dallas skyline and almost involuntarily, his eye was drawn to the building directly across from him, where Reynolds Capital Management used to reside. Dax had heard that Leo left the venture capital game and had gone into business with Tommy Garrett, a whiz kid inventor.

It was crazy and so unlike Leo. They'd been friends for a long time—until Daniella had come along and upset the status quo.

Bad, bad subject. The hardness in his chest started to hurt and the urge to punch something grew until he couldn't physically sit at his desk any longer.

He sent Patricia an instant message asking for the address of Garrett-Reynolds Engineering and the second he got it, he strode to his car. It was time to have it out with Leo once and for all.

Except Leo wasn't at the office. Dax eyed Tommy Garrett, whom he'd met at a party an eon ago. The kid still looked as though he belonged on a surfboard instead of in a boardroom.

"Sorry, dude," Tommy said and stuck a Doritos chip in his mouth. "Leo's still on vacation. But I'm pretty sure he's at home now if you want to catch him there."

"Thanks." Dax went back to his car, still shaking his head. Leo—at home in the middle of the day on a Monday. His affliction with Daniella was even worse than Dax had imagined.

By the time he hit Leo's driveway, Dax was good and worked up. This time, he didn't hesitate, but drove right up to the gate and rolled down his window so the security system could grant him entrance.

Leo was waiting for him on the front steps as Dax swung out of the Audi. Of course the state-of-the-art security system had alerted the Reynoldses that they had a visitor, and clearly Leo was as primed for a throw down as Dax was. Dax meant to give it to him.

"Dax." Leo smiled warmly, looking well-rested, tan and not wearing a suit. "It's good to see you. I'm glad you came by."

Dax did a double take.

Who was this guy? Because he didn't resemble the Leo Dax knew.

"Hi," Dax muttered, and tried to orient. Leo wasn't supposed to be happy. And he wasn't supposed to be nice. They weren't friends anymore.

"Please, come in." Leo jerked his head behind him toward the house. "Dannie's pouring us some iced tea."

"This isn't a social call," he fairly snarled and then heard himself. Where were his manners?

Leo didn't flinch. "I didn't assume that it was. But this is my home, and my wife wanted to serve you a drink. It's what civilized people do when someone comes by without an invitation."

My wife. The dividing line couldn't have been clearer. But then, Leo had drawn that line back in his office when he'd told Dax in no uncertain terms that Daniella was more important to him than anything, including money, the deal between Leo and Dax, and even their friendship.

All at once, Dax wanted to know why.

"I'm sorry," Dax said sincerely. "Tea is great. Thanks."

He followed Leo into a dappled sunroom with a view of the windswept back acreage of the property. The branches were bare of leaves this late into the season, save a few evergreens dotting the landscape.

Daniella bustled in with a tray, smiled at Dax and set a glass full of amber liquid in front of each man. "Nice to see you, Dax. Enjoy. I'll make myself scarce."

Gracious as always. Even to a man who made no secret of his intense dislike and mistrust of her.

Dax watched her drop a kiss on Leo's head. He snagged her hand to keep her in place, then returned the kiss on her lips, exchanging a private smile that seemed like a language all its own. They were so obviously in love, it poleaxed Dax right in the heart.

Because he didn't have that. Nor did he hold any hope of having it.

Against everything he'd ever believed about himself, the world and how he fit into it, he wanted what Leo and Daniella had.

The floodgates had been opened and then shut so swiftly, he'd barely had time to acclimate, to figure out what he was going to do with all the emotions he'd never felt before.

Then *bam!* Betrayal at its finest. The two people he'd let himself care about had *both* betrayed him. And one of them would answer for it right now.

After Daniella disappeared, Dax faced Leo squarely. "I suppose you're wondering why I'm here."

"Not really." Leo grinned at Dax's raised eyebrows. "Dannie and Elise are very good friends. I'm guessing you didn't know that."

Elise. Her name pierced that hard place in his chest and nearly finished what the lovey-dovey scene between Leo and Daniella had started. Death by emotion. It seemed fitting somehow.

And no, he hadn't realized Daniella and Elise were friends. Daniella had probably been treated to an earful already this morning. "And your wife tells you everything, right?"

"Yep."

Dax sank down in the wicker chair, but it didn't swallow him as he would have preferred. If he'd known his spectacular flameout at the hands of Elise had been trotted out for everyone's amusement, he might have gone someplace else, like Timbuktu.

"Last night was really messed up," Dax allowed without really meaning to. It just came out.

"I sympathize." Leo cleared his throat. "Which is more than you did for me when I was going through something similar, I might add."

That hurt. "Is this what you were going through? Because I don't see how that's possible."

Leo and Daniella had an effortless relationship, as if they'd been born for each other and never questioned whether they trusted the other.

"No, it's not the same because we're different people in love with very different women."

"I'm not in love with Elise," Dax broke in.

He might have been entertaining the notion, but she'd killed it. Somehow it was worse to finally embrace the idea that love wasn't just a fairy tale only to have your heart smashed.

Leo just looked at him and smirked. "And that's your problem right there. Denial. That, plus an inability to give someone a chance."

"That's not true," he burst out. "She's the one who didn't give me a chance. She lied to me. I can't trust anyone."

And that was the really painful part. There wasn't one single person in existence he could fully trust. If it could have been anyone, he'd have put his money on Elise, the one person who understood the man behind the curtain. He *had* put his money on Elise—five hundred thousand dollars—and she'd never lost sight of the prize. He should take a lesson.

"I can give you relationship advice all day long if that's what you're after. But you didn't really come here to find out that you guard yourself by pushing people away? You already know that."

Yeah, he did. He ended relationships before he got invested. He left women before they could hurt him. No mystery there. The question was why he'd let his guard down with Elise in the first place.

Dax sipped his tea and decided to go for broke with Leo. "I came to find out why Daniella was such a big deal. I know you married her. But why her? What was special about her?"

Leo's face lit up. "I love her. That alone makes her special. But I love her because she makes me whole. She allows me to be me. She *enables* me to be me. And I wake up every day wanting to do the same for her. That's why Elise matched us. Because we're soul mates."

Dax nearly snorted but caught himself. The evidence stood for itself and there was no need to act cynical about it any longer. No one in this room was confused about whether he believed in it. But believing in soul mates and allowing a woman who professed to be yours to take a fillet knife to your heart were two different things.

"And that was worth ending a friendship over?" Dax asked.

Stupid question. Clearly Leo thought so and at that particular moment, Dax almost didn't blame him. Look what Leo had gotten in return.

"Dax." Leo sat forward in his chair. "I didn't end our friendship. You did. You weren't being a friend when you said disparaging things about my wife. You weren't being a friend when you demanded I choose you over her. I was messed up, wondering how I could love my wife and still maintain the workaholic life I thought I wanted. I needed a friend. Where were you?"

There was no censure in Leo's tone. But there should have been. Hearing it spelled out like that sheared a new layer of skin off Dax's already-raw wounds. He'd been a crappy friend yet Leo had welcomed Dax into his home without question.

"I was wallowing in my own selfishness," Dax muttered. "I was a jerk. I'm sorry."

"It's okay. It was okay as soon as you rolled up the driveway. I've been waiting for you to come by." Leo held out his hand for Dax to shake, which he did without hesitation.

The hardness in his chest lifted a bit. "Thanks for not barring the gate."

"No problem. I had a feeling you'd need a friend after what happened with Elise. It sounded rough. I'd like to hear about it from you, though."

Dax watched a bird hop from branch to bare branch outside the sunroom's glass walls. "Her computer program matched us. But she wasn't interested in me or finding the love of her life. Or professional ethics. Just winning."

"I watched the interview," Leo said quietly. "You were ruthless. Can you blame her for bringing her A game?"

The interview. It felt like a lifetime ago, back when he'd been smugly certain he couldn't lose the bet because love didn't exist. He almost preferred it when he'd still believed that.

"She screwed me over. I can't forget that."

"You reap what you sow. You started out going head-to-head and that's where you ended up. Change it if that's not what you want."

Leo sipped his tea as Dax shifted uncomfortably. "You say that like I had some fault in this, too."

"Don't you?" Leo tilted his head in way that told Dax the question was rhetorical. "I went into my marriage with Dannie assuming I wanted a wife who took care of my house and left me alone. And that's what I got until I realized it wasn't what I really wanted. Fortunately, she was waiting for me to wake up and see what I had. You didn't give Elise that chance. You ended it."

Of course he'd ended it. "I don't make promises I can't keep."

It was an automatic response, one he'd always said was the reason he didn't do relationships. But that wasn't why he'd walked out on Elise.

The problem was greater than the fear of learning he was like his mother, faithless and unable to make promises to one person forever.

He also feared being like his father—pathetic. Mooning over a woman who didn't actually care about him, waiting in vain for her to come back.

Elise hadn't told him the truth and he could never trust her to stay. And if he let himself love her, and she didn't stay, he'd be doomed to a lifetime of pain and an eternity of solitude because he'd never get over losing his soul mate.

Thirteen

When the doorbell rang, Elise's pulse sprang into double time as she flew to answer it.

Dax.

He'd come to apologize, talk, yell at her. She didn't care. Anything was fine as long as he was here. Hungry to see him again after three miserable days, she swung open the door.

Her heart plummeted.

It was Dannie, dressed to the nines in a gorgeous winter-white cashmere coat, matching skirt and heels. Next to her stood Juliet, the new princess of Delamer, wearing a T-shirt and jeans, of course.

"What are you doing here?" Elise glowered at Juliet. "You're supposed to be on your honeymoon."

The princess shrugged delicately and waved a hand full of bitten-off nails. "It was a working honeymoon and you need me more than His Royal Highness. I left my husband in New York with a host of boring European diplomats. I miss him already, but I owe you more than I can ever repay for giving me back the love of my life."

"I need you?" Elise glanced at Dannie. "You called Juliet and told her I needed her?"

"Yes, yes I did." Dannie bustled Juliet into the house, followed her and shut the door, then held up two bags. "This is an intervention. We brought wine and chocolate since you never keep them in the house."

The heaviness Elise had carried since Dax left returned tenfold. "No chocolate for me. But wine sounds pretty good."

The silence had been deafening. He'd ignored her text messages, even the funny ones. He hadn't called. At first she'd thought it was merely pride, which was why she kept reaching out. But he really didn't want to talk to her.

"Come on, Elise. Live a little. When a man acts like an ass, chocolate is the only cure," Dannie called from the kitchen where she'd gone to fetch wineglasses and a corkscrew.

Tears welled up and the ugly-cry faucet let loose. Dannie flew into the living room and enfolded Elise in a comforting embrace while Juliet looked on helplessly.

Murmuring, Dannie smoothed Elise's hair and let her cry. Sobs wrenched Elise's chest, seizing her lungs until suffocation seemed more likely than a cease-fire of emotions.

Her life had fallen apart. But her friends were here when she needed them.

"It's okay, cry all you want," Dannie suggested. "The endorphins are good for you. It'll help you feel better."

"I know." Dabbing at her eyes ineffectively with a sleeve, Elise sniffled and gave up. "But they don't seem to be working."

"Maybe because Dax is more of an ass than regular men?" Juliet suggested sweetly.

Dannie bit back a snort and Elise choked on an involuntary laugh, which led to a fit of coughing. By the time she recovered, the tears had mostly dried up.

"It wasn't working because it's my fault. I'm the problem, not Dax," Elise confessed.

They might be soul mates, but obviously there was more

to it than that. Happily ever after didn't magically happen, and being matched was the beginning of the journey, not the end. And she had no clue how to get where she wanted to be. That's why she couldn't hold on to Dax, no matter how much she loved him.

Everything he'd accused her of was true.

"That's ridiculous." Dannie *tsk*ed.

"I'm not buying that," Juliet said at the same time. "It's always the man's fault."

Elise smiled at the staunch support. She'd had a hand in these two women's becoming the best they could be, in finding happiness with the men they'd married, and it had been enough for so long to be on the sidelines of love, looking in from outside, nose pressed to the glass.

At least then she hadn't known what she was missing.

"Dax has a hard time trusting people," she explained. "I knew that. Yet I didn't tell him we were matched and he took it as a betrayal."

More than a betrayal. She hadn't trusted that he could love the real her. He'd been gradually warming up to the idea of soul mates, putting his faith in her, and she'd forgotten to do the same.

"So what? When you love someone, you forgive them when they mess up," Juliet declared. "People mess up a lot. It's what makes us human."

"And sometimes, you have to figure out what's best for them, even when they don't know themselves," Dannie advised. "That's part of love, too. Seeing beneath the surface to what a man really wants, instead of what he tells you he wants."

"And sometimes," Elise said quietly, "love isn't enough. Sometimes, you hurt the person you love too much and you can't undo it. That's the lesson here for me."

She'd had a shot at being deliriously in love and ruined

it. She'd always believed that if her soul mate existed, then love *would* be enough.

Juliet and Dannie glanced at each other and a long look passed between them.

"You get the wine." Dannie shooed Juliet toward the kitchen and then extracted a jewelry box from her purse.

Juliet returned with the wineglasses, passed them out and perched on the edge of the couch. "Open it, Elise."

After handing the box to Elise, Dannie sat next to Juliet and held her glass of wine in her lap without drinking it.

Carefully, Elise cracked the hinged lid to reveal a silver necklace. A heart-within-a-heart charm hung from the chain. Surprised, she eyed the two women. "Thank you. But what's this about?"

Dannie unclasped the necklace and drew it around Elise's neck. The cool metal warmed instantly against her skin.

"You gave us necklaces during our makeovers," Dannie said and nodded at Juliet. "We were about to embark on the greatest adventure of our lives. We had your guidance from the first moment we met our matches and it stayed with us every day, right here in silver."

"Open heart." Juliet pointed at Dannie's necklace and then at her own. "Hearts holding each other. Simple but profound messages about love. We wanted to return the favor."

"I had no idea those necklaces meant so much to you." Tears threatened again and Elise blinked them back. "What does mine mean?"

Juliet shook her head with a small smile. "That's for you to figure out at the right time. That's how it works."

"We can't tell you. Just like you didn't tell us." Dannie put a comforting hand on Elise's arm. "I wish I could make it easier for you because honestly, working through the issues I had with Leo was the hardest thing I ever did."

Nodding, Juliet chimed in. "Finn and I are so much alike,

it was nearly impossible to compromise. But we found a way and it was so worth it."

Elise fingered the larger heart with the smaller one nestled inside. Her match was a disaster, not like Dannie's and Juliet's. She'd known their matches were solid from the beginning. Of course, it was easier to see such things from the outside.

What was it about matters of your own heart that were so difficult?

That was it. A heart within a heart.

The necklace's meaning came to her on a whisper, growing louder as her consciousness worked through it, embraced it. The large heart was the love between a man and a woman, which had the capacity to be huge and wonderful, eclipsing everything else.

But inside the larger heart lay a smaller heart.

I have to love myself too.

The fat girl inside hadn't vanished when Dax poured chocolate chips over her. Or when he admitted he was falling in love with her. Because it wasn't enough.

She had to be enough, all by herself, with or without a man by her side.

Until she believed she was worthy of loving a man like Dax and allowing him to love her in return, she wasn't his soul mate. She wasn't his perfect match.

Not yet. But she could be.

"I get it. The necklace," Elise clarified, and took the other women's hands in hers, forming a circle. "I know how to get my happily ever after, or at least how to shoot for it. Will you help me?"

"Yes," they said simultaneously.

"You have a plan," Dannie guessed.

Elise nodded slowly as it formed. "Wakefield Media has a box suite at AT&T Stadium, but Dax never goes. He hates the Cowboys." She didn't recall when he'd shared that information. During one of their marathon profile sessions, likely. "But I need him there on Sunday. Can you have Leo make up some reason why they both need to go to a game?"

"Of course." Dannie smiled mischievously. "Leo will do anything I ask. I finally got two pink lines this morning."

"You're pregnant?" Elise gasped as Juliet smiled and kissed Dannie's cheek. "No wonder you told Juliet to get the wine."

"We're not announcing it. I'm only telling you two because I had to tell *someone*." The glow only made Dannie more beautiful. "But enough about me. I'll get Leo and Dax there."

"Thanks." Elise squeezed both of their hands. "You are the finest ladies I've ever had the privilege of meeting."

The last thing Dax wanted to do was go to a Cowboys game. But Leo insisted and they'd only recently resurrected their friendship. How could he say no and not offend Leo?

Dax would much rather spend the day asleep, but that wasn't an option. He hadn't slept well since that last night with Elise. Spending the day alone held even less appeal. So he went.

The stadium teemed with blue and silver and stars aplenty. The world's fourth-largest high-definition video screen hung from the roof, from the twenty-yard line to the opposing twenty-yard line, and only someone in the media business could fully appreciate the glory of it.

The retractable roof was closed today in deference to the late season weather, which boosted the crowd noise to a new level of loud. Once he and Leo arrived in the luxurious box suite, blessed silence cloaked them both as they ordered beer from the efficient waitstaff and then slid into the high-backed suede stools overlooking the field.

Leo held out his longneck bottle and waited for Dax to clink his to it. They both took a long pull of beer.

After swallowing, Leo said, "Thanks for doing this. I thought we should hang out, just us."

"Sure." Dax shrugged, a little misty himself at the catch in Leo's voice. "No one was using the suite today and the Cowboys are playing the Redskins. It'll be worth it if the 'Skins trounce the homeboys."

The spectacle of the teams taking the field began, and they settled in to watch the game. They sat companionably until halftime, when Leo cleared his throat.

"We've been friends a long time. But some major changes have happened in my life. I've changed. I hope you can respect who I am now and it won't affect our friendship going forward." Leo stared out over the field. "On that note, I have to tell you something. It's huge."

Dax's gut clenched. Leo was about to announce he had two months to live. Or Daniella did.

Fate couldn't be so unkind to such genuine people. And Dax had wasted so much time, time Leo may not have, being stupid and prideful.

"I've been hard on Daniella and on you about her. I'm over it." Over his pettiness, over his inability to be happy for his friend. But not over the slight jealousy that Leo had figured out how to navigate relationship waters with such stellar success. "It's great that you found her. She's amazing and obviously good for you."

"She is. And that's good to hear, because—" Leo grinned and punched Dax on the arm "—I'm going to be a father."

"That's what this bro-date was about?" Dax grinned back as his nerves relaxed. "Congrats. I'm glad if you're glad."

Leo was going to have a family.

Jealousy flared again, brighter, hotter. Shock of all shocks. Dax had never once thought about having a family. Never thought he'd want one. Never dreamed he'd instantly imagine a tiny, beautiful face with dark hair and a sharp wit. A little girl who took after her mother.

"Of course I'm glad! It's the second-best thing that's happened to me after marrying Dannie." Leo swallowed the last of his beer and set it down with a flourish. "And no. That's not why I insisted we come to the game. That is."

Leo pointed at the jumbo screen in the middle of the stadium. A woman's face filled it. A familiar, dark-haired woman. *Elise*.

Dax's pulse pounded in his throat. "What's going on?" Audio piped into the suite quite clearly.

"Thanks for giving me thirty seconds, Ed," she said, her voice ringing in Dax's ears, filling the stadium as the crowd murmured and craned their necks to watch. "My name is Elise Arundel and I'm a matchmaker."

What was this all about—advertising? Or much more? He glared at Leo. "You had something to do with this?"

"All her," Leo replied mildly. "I'm just the delivery boy."

Dax's gaze flew back to the screen where Elise was addressing the entire stadium full of Sunday afternoon football fanatics. *Elise* was addressing *80,000 people* voluntarily. If he weren't so raw, he might be proud of her. It must have been difficult for her, given that she didn't like to be the center of attention.

"Some of you saw me on the *Morning Show* a few weeks ago, being interviewed by Dax Wakefield. We struck a deal. If I matched Dax to the love of his life, he'd agree to sing my praises at the Super Bowl. Which is in February and unfortunately, I lost the wager."

Lost? She'd been quite gleeful over the fact that she'd won the last time he'd seen her. His mind kicked into high gear. She was up to something.

"So," she continued. "Congratulations, Dax. You win. You get to put me out of the business of happily ever after. I'm such a good loser, I'm going to let you do it at a football game. All you have to do is join me on camera. Tell these people I didn't change your mind about true love and that you still don't believe soul mates exist."

"How can I do that?" Dax muttered. "I don't know where you are."

"I'm here," Elise said. But in the flesh, not through the stadium's sound system.

He whirled. And there she was, gorgeous and real, and her presence bled through the air, raising heat along his neck. She was within touching distance. He'd missed her, missed her smile, her quirky sense of humor. The way she made him feel.

And then he remembered. She was a liar, a manipulator. She cared only about winning.

Except she'd just announced to 80,000 people that she'd lost. And she'd told him in no uncertain terms that only promoting EA International could get her in front of a camera. Obviously she'd found another motivator, but what?

A cameraman followed her into the suite, lens on Dax. He couldn't even muster a fake grin, let alone his "camera" smile, not when Elise had effectively pinned him to a piece of cork after all. "What is this all about, Elise?"

"I told you. This is your shining moment. It's your chance to ruin me. Go ahead." She nodded to the stadium, where this nightmare was playing out on the screen.

Thousands of eyes were riveted to the drama unfolding and it needed to be over. Now.

He opened his mouth. And closed it. Not only was he pinned to a cork, on display for everyone to examine, she was daring him to lie in public.

He wasn't a liar.

So he didn't lie.

"My soul mate doesn't exist."

Something sharp and wounded glinted in the depths of her eyes.

"Tell them I didn't match you to the love of your life," she suggested clearly, as if the stadium deserved to hear every word regardless of what was going on inside her. "That I'm a fraud and my match software doesn't work."

Obviously, this was not going to end until he gave her what she was asking for.

"True love doesn't exist for me and your match process is flawed," he growled as his pulse spiked and sweat broke out across the back of his heated neck, though both statements were true. "Is that what you wanted me to say?"

It was done. He'd set out to ruin her and now everyone in the stadium, as well as those watching at home, heard him say it. His comments would be broadcast far and wide on social media, he had no doubt.

His stomach churned. The victory was more hollow than his insides.

All at once, he realized why. He'd called off the wager and meant it. But only because he refused to lose and calling it off was the only way to ensure that would never happen.

He and Elise were put together with remarkable similarity. Was he really going to blame her because she didn't like to lose either?

Leo might have had a small point about Elise bringing her A game.

Too bad the wager was the only real thing they'd ever had between them.

Vulnerability in her expression, she stared at him without blinking. "Is that all? There's nothing more you have to say?"

"I'm done."

Wasn't what he'd already said enough? His heart felt as if it were being squeezed from its mooring through a straw. Did she not realize how painful this was?

She crossed the suite, closing the few yards between

them, barging right into his personal space. Finger extended, she pointed right at the area of his torso that hurt the worst.

"You need to tell them the *whole* truth. You not only admitted love does happen to others, you started to believe in it for yourself. In the possibility of soul mates," she said. "Because I matched you with the perfect woman. And you fell in love with her, didn't you?"

He groaned. She'd seen right through his carefully worded statements. Right through him. The curtain didn't exist to her.

He crossed his arms over the ache in his chest. "It would be unfair to say either of us won when in reality, we both lost."

Tenderness and grief welled in her eyes. "Yes. We both lost something precious due to my lack of trust in you. But not because you were untrustworthy. Because I couldn't trust myself, couldn't trust that I was the right person to change your mind about true love. I was convinced you'd end our relationship after a couple of weeks and when I fell in love with you, I—"

"You're in love with me?" Something fluttered in his chest as he searched her face.

All her deepest emotions spilled from her gaze, spreading across her expression, winding through his heart.

It was true.

His pulse spiked and he fought it. What did that really change? Nothing.

"I'm afraid so," she said solemnly. "Nothing but the truth from here on out. I thought love conquered all. But without trust, someone can be perfect for you and still screw it up."

She was talking to him. About him. She knew he'd let his own issues cloud their relationship, just as she had. He'd let his fears about turning out like his parents taint his life, never giving anyone a chance to betray his trust.

He'd let anger blind him to the truth.

This had never been about winning the wager, for either of them.

"How do you know if you can trust someone forever? That's a long time."

"Fear of the unknown is a particular expertise of mine," she allowed with a small smile. "I like to know what's going to happen, that I can depend on someone. Especially when he promises something so big as to love me for the rest of my life. That's scary. What if he changes his mind? What if—"

"I'm not going to change my mind."

The instant it was out of his mouth, he realized what she'd gotten him to concede. And the significance of it.

"And by the way, same goes," he said. "How do I know you're not going to change yours?"

How had he not seen they were alike even in this? Neither of them trusted easily, yet he'd crucified her over her inability, while tucking his own lack of trust away like a favored treasure. She hadn't been trying to bring him to his knees. Just trying to navigate something unexpected and making mistakes in the process.

"Let's take it day by day. As long as you're in this relationship fully today, that's the only guarantee I need. I love you." She nodded to the stadium. "I'm not afraid to stand up in front of all these people and tell you how I feel. Are you?"

It was a challenge. A public challenge. If he said he loved her, it would be the equivalent of admitting she'd won. Of admitting she'd done everything she said she would in the interview.

"What are you trying to accomplish here?" he asked.

"I believe this is more commonly known as me calling you on your crap."

Against his will, the corners of his lips turned up. "Is that so?"

Only Elise knew exactly how to do that. Because she got him in a way no one else ever could.

She nodded. "But I had to wade through my own first. When my algorithm matched me with you, it wasn't wrong. But I was. I'm sorry I didn't tell you I was your match. I wasn't ready to trust you. I am now."

And she'd proved it by declaring her flaws to the world on the big screen, publicly. The one place she said she'd go only for her business. But she'd done it for him because *he* was her motivator. Because she loved him.

Somehow, that made it easier to confess his own sins.

"I…messed up, too. I wasn't about to stick around and find out I couldn't trust you to stay, so I didn't. I'm sorry I didn't give you that chance."

The exact accusation he'd flung at her. His relationship philosophy might as well be Do Unto Others Before They Do Unto You. That ended today. If he loved Elise and knew beyond a doubt he wasn't going to change his mind, he wasn't broken. Just incomplete.

His soul needed a mate to be whole.

Her smile belied the sudden tears falling onto her cheeks. "You didn't meet your soul mate because your soul mate wasn't ready to meet you. But I am ready now." She held out her hand as if they'd just been introduced for the first time. "My name is Shannon Elise Arundel, but you can call me Elise."

He didn't hesitate but immediately grasped her fingers and yanked her into a kiss. As his mouth met hers and fused, his heart opened up and out spilled the purest form of happiness.

He'd found his soul mate, and it turned out he didn't want a woman who didn't care what was behind his curtain. He wanted this woman, who'd invited herself backstage and taken up residence in the exact spot where she belonged.

She'd been one step ahead of him the entire time. She

was the only woman alive who could outthink, outsmart and out-love him.

Lifting his head slightly, he murmured against her lips, "I love you too. And for the record, I'd rather call you mine."

An "aww" went up from the spectators and without taking his attention off the woman in his arms, Dax reached out to cover the lens with his palm. Some things weren't meant to be televised.

Epilogue

Elise's first Super Bowl party was in full swing and surprisingly, she'd loved every minute of it. It had been her idea and Dax let her plan the whole thing. And he didn't mind that she spent more time in the kitchen with Dannie and a host of female guests cooing over baby talk now that Dannie was in her second trimester.

"Hon," Dax called from the living room. "I think you'd better come see this."

Immediately, Elise set down her wine and moved to comply. The other women snickered but that didn't slow her down.

"What?" she called over her shoulder. "If any of you had a gorgeous man like that in your bed every night, you'd jump when he said jump, too."

She sailed out of the kitchen to join Dax on the couch in front of the sixty-five-inch LED TV that now dominated her—their—living room. It was the only thing Dax had requested they keep from his loft when he moved in with her at Christmas.

How could she say no? They hardly ever watched it anyway. Neither football nor science fiction movies held a candle to doing everything together—going to the grocery store, dinner and sometimes even to work with each other. It was heaven on earth and it could not possibly get any better.

"I like what I see so far," she told him as her gaze lit on his beautiful face.

Dax grinned and took her hand, nodding at the TV. "You can look at me anytime. That's what you should be focusing on."

The game had cut to a commercial break. A Coca-Cola polar bear faded away as one commercial ended and another began. A familiar logo materialized on the screen. *Her* logo. EA International's, to be precise.

"What did you do?" she sputtered around a startled laugh.

"I owed you the match fee. Watch," Dax advised her and she did, fingers to her numb lips.

A montage of clips from her confessional at the Cowboys game flashed, interspersed with snippets of former clients espousing her praises in five-second sound bites. The whole commercial was cleverly edited to allow Elise's speech about true love to play out in real time in the form of happy couples. Then the last scene snapped into focus and it was Dax.

"EA International specializes in soul mates," the digital version of Dax said sincerely, his charisma so crisp and dazzling on the sixty-five-inch screen she nearly wept. "That's where I found mine. Elise, I love you. Will you marry me?"

Her pulse stopped, but her brain kept going, echoing with the sound of Dax's smooth voice.

The screen faded to a car commercial and the house full of people went dead silent as Dax dropped to his knees in front of her, his expression earnest. "I'm sorry, but I can't call you Ms. Arundel any longer."

And then he winked, setting her heart in motion again as she laughed through the tears that had sprung up after all. "You can call me Mrs. Wakefield. I insist."

Applause broke out and Elise was gratified to feel absolutely no heat in her cheeks. Dax lived in the spotlight, and she'd deal with it gladly because she wanted to stand next to him for the rest of her life.

The crowd shifted their attention to other things, leaving Dax and Elise blessedly alone. Or at least as alone as they could be with thirty people in the house.

Without a lot of fanfare, Dax pulled a box out of his pocket and produced a beautiful, shiny diamond ring, eclipsed only by the wattage of his smile. "I'm assuming that's a yes."

She nodded, shaking loose a couple of the tears. "Though I'm intrigued to find out what you'd planned as a backup to that commercial if I said no."

How could he come up with anything more effective than *that?* He'd declared his love for her, asked her to marry him and endorsed her business in the most inarguable way possible. He was brilliant and all hers.

It was better than a fairy tale. Better than Cinderella because he saw *her*, the real her, underneath. No makeover, no fancy dresses. If she gained a few pounds, he wouldn't care.

"No backup," he said smugly and slipped the ring on her finger, which fit precisely right, of course. Dax Wakefield never missed a trick. "I knew you'd say yes since I proposed during the Super Bowl. You know, because it's less predictable than Valentine's Day."

Her heart caught on an erratic, crazy beat. He remembered what she'd said on that park bench a season ago. That alone made him her perfect match. The rest was icing on the cake.

"I thought being with you couldn't get any better. How like you to prove me wrong," she teased and then sobered, taking his jaw between both of hands. His ring winked back at her from its place on her third finger, perfect and right. "Don't stop, even if I tell you to, okay?"